MOST WONDERFUL

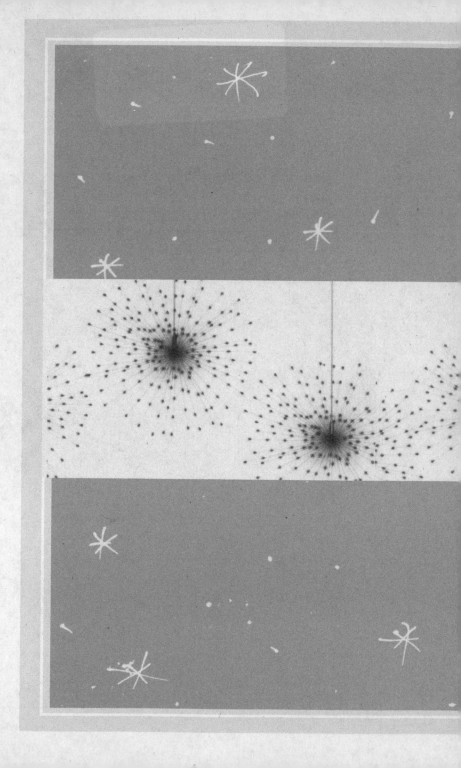

MOST WONDERFUL

GEORGIA CLARK

THE DIAL PRESS

New York

A Dial Press Trade Paperback Original

Copyright © 2024 by Georgia Clark

Dial Delights Extras copyright © 2024
by Penguin Random House LLC

All rights reserved.

Published in the United States by The Dial Press,
an imprint of Random House, a division of
Penguin Random House LLC, New York.

THE DIAL PRESS is a registered trademark,
and the colophon is a trademark of
Penguin Random House LLC.

DIAL DELIGHTS and colophon are trademarks
of Penguin Random House LLC.

LIBRARY OF CONGRESS CATALOGING-IN-PUBLICATION DATA
NAMES: Clark, Georgia, author.
TITLE: Most wonderful / Georgia Clark.
DESCRIPTION: New York: The Dial Press, 2024.
IDENTIFIERS: LCCN 2024000833 (print) |
LCCN 2024000834 (ebook) |
ISBN 9780593729083 (trade paperback; acid-free paper) |
ISBN 9780593729090 (ebook)
SUBJECTS: LCGFT: Christmas fiction. | Novels.
CLASSIFICATION: LCC PS3603.L3636 M67 2024 (print) |
LCC PS3603.L3636 (ebook) | DDC 813/.6—dc23/eng/20240119
LC record available at https://lccn.loc.gov/2024000833
LC ebook record available at https://lccn.loc.gov/2024000834

Printed in the United States of America on acid-free paper

randomhousebooks.com

2 4 6 8 9 7 5 3 1

Art from Adobestock

Book design by Barbara M. Bachman

For those who
create, seek, or champion
queer joy

Contents

MOST WONDERFUL

PART ONE

Christmas,
obviously, is
ruined.

1.

Twenty-four days till Christmas

*

OR LIZ BELVEDERE, THE BEST THING ABOUT THE HOLIDAYS wasn't the season's whimsy or wonder or the chance to indulge in a heavy pour of eggnog or thick cut of peppermint fudge. It was the chance to work. Crossing everything off her endless to-do list by Christmas morning was truly the greatest gift Liz could give herself. A festive inbox zero promised the same sort of delight most people felt from catching a snowflake on the tip of their tongue or having some other snowy, swoony moment. Liz had never had a snowy, swoony moment in her life and didn't have time to be prancing around with her mouth open in a snowstorm. It was December first, and she was very, very far from experiencing her unique brand of holiday magic. And so, despite driving past the tinseled palm trees and holiday window displays lining the streets of West Hollywood, she was not thinking about eggnog or fudge or Christmas at all. Liz Belvedere had other problems.

The cavernous parking garage was nearly empty when Liz pulled her Subaru into her dedicated space. Most people had somewhere else they'd rather be at 8:00 A.M. on a weekend. Liz, as always, was at work.

The bank of television screens in the lobby were all off, making the typically showy entrance feel like an empty theater stage. Liz flashed her ID at the security guard. "Morning, Carlos."

"Ms. Belvedere." He shook his head, beginning their standard riff. "It's Sunday. Don't you have any hobbies?"

"I tried origami," Liz offered. "Turned out it was just a lot of paperwork."

He chuckled, waving her through.

Because it was the weekend, Liz was in high-waisted jeans and an airy lilac cardigan over a vintage David Bowie tee. Comfortable but not so casual she would be embarrassed running into any of the executives. Who all knew her name, for two reasons.

The first, of course, was bloodline: Liz was the eldest daughter of Barbara "Babs" Belvedere, the entertainment icon who'd navigated the choppy waters of show business for five decades.

The second, and, Liz hoped, more important: she was the showrunner of *Sweet*, a funny, racy teen melodrama that was currently the number three show on the popular streaming service she'd partnered with to make it. Being the showrunner meant she'd written the pilot, sold the show, and led the overall creative vision. This included being the key point of contact between an experienced, talented crew and the slightly terrifying, slightly annoying execs. It was a dream job, and one she'd been working toward ever since she moved to L.A. a decade ago.

A dream job that'd be in jeopardy if she didn't come up with a strong concept for a second season. An overarching idea that proved the first season—and, by extension, Liz herself—wasn't a one-hit wonder. Hence, work on a Sunday.

No one was in the corridors as she headed for her elevator bank, no one in the elevator when it opened directly into *Sweet*'s production office on the fourth floor. Liz flipped on the lights, illuminating the colorful, organized chaos. Reception, and beyond it, the open-plan bullpen and senior staff offices. Liz craned her neck, calling, "Hello?"

No one. Just as she'd hoped.

Liz made herself a strong black coffee in the kitchen, then headed to her office, where color-coordinated folders and alphabetized binders filled the neat shelves. Everything in its place, a Virgo's wet dream.

Slipping into her leather office chair, Liz opened her laptop to the work-in-progress pitch doc. For the past two weeks, this was the only thing she'd been working on. Everyone she crossed paths with eagerly asked the same question: How was the second season going?

Great, she'd reply, assuring everyone from the head of Programming to her very invested dry cleaner, who'd already watched the first season twice, that *It's coming along!*

But it wasn't coming along. The pitch doc remained unchanged. As blank as a field of fresh snow.

It wasn't technically writer's block. More like an inability to prioritize the writing. And that was because Liz's brain was a theater playing only one clip.

Sweet had sold into half of Europe, prompting a European press tour Liz had returned from two weeks ago. Eight different cities, each with full days of interviews and shoots and events hyping the show. The moment endlessly looping in Liz's broken brain had occurred on the tour's last night, outside a wooden hotel door in Rome.

And the person in her arms? The person gazing back at her with puffy lips and hungry eyes? The person she'd kissed as if the planet were about to explode?

The star of *Sweet*. Her leading lady. Violet Grace.

Liz's lips tingled with a sense memory of softness. Heat. Giving in. Letting go. Her heart swooned like a lovestruck teenager mooning over a photo of a crush.

A crush. Only when you had one did you realize how accurate the term was. Liz felt crushed—wonderfully, terrifyingly, completely *crushed*—by Violet Alice Grace.

Who she should *not* be thinking about that way.

"Focus!" Liz hissed, mortified to find herself flushing. Having feelings for her star didn't just make her a pathetic Hollywood cliché. It was a surefire path to heartbreak, and Liz had already experienced an unfair share of that in her thirty-seven years on this planet.

Her personal life, such as it was, was not important. What was important was work. She needed to come up with a strong concept for season two *as soon as possible*. Their production office for *Sweet* felt homey, but it was temporary— they had the office space only because *Sweet* was one of the streamer's top shows. If Liz didn't nail a pitch for the next season, all of this would disappear. Everyone was counting on her.

Crunching a few of the tamari roasted almonds she kept in her top drawer, Liz refocused on her laptop, determined that today would be the day she'd forget about kissing Violet and get some freaking work done.

She stared with purpose at the blinking cursor. The rhythmic black line silently tapped like a heartbeat.

Like a pulse point.

Like the way a body can throb.

On the far side of the office, the elevator doors dinged.

The high-pitched sound struck Liz in the chest, reverberating into her limbs.

Someone stepped out.

Footsteps sounded from up the hall, and every one of Liz's nerve endings stood at attention. Even though they hadn't spoken since they'd all flown back from Rome, there was a chance it could be *her*. Violet had often come by the office if Liz was there, and Liz was always there. Even though Liz had been avoiding her, suddenly Liz *wanted* Violet to walk in. She anticipated the rush of their eyes meeting, the two-week self-imposed silence collapsing like a flimsy bridge. Liz fiddled with her bangs, praying she didn't have almond shards stuck in her teeth, wishing she had time for a swipe of tinted lip balm.

The footsteps got louder. Liz held her breath.

Cat stuck her head around Liz's doorway. "Of course you're here."

Liz tried not to look disappointed, or worse, guilty. No one could ever find out what had happened, including the show's best and too-observant publicist. "Hey," Liz said. "Haven't seen you since we got back."

Catherine "Cat" Hunter had been with them for the European junket. The senior publicist had wrangled the press, style team, and four twentysomething cast members. Who, of course, included Violet.

"I was in New York for a thing." Juggling her phone, leather tote, and extra-large takeout coffee, Cat took the seat on the other side of Liz's desk. Even on a Sunday, Cat was put together in a black jumpsuit and crisp white sneakers. Her signature lick of eyeliner gave her face a feline quality. "Creepy being in here on a weekend, right?" Cat said in her slightly scratchy smoker's drawl. "Just us and the ghosts of shows of Christmas past."

As if Liz needed reminding of what might happen if she didn't come up with a solid idea.

"Speaking of shows that *aren't* going to be canceled," Cat went on, "tell me about the second season pitch. *Dying* to hear."

"Soon. I promise." Liz closed her computer. "Anyway, what is Hollywood's hottest publicist doing at work on a weekend?"

"Oh, a million things, as usual. Just picked these up." A thud as Cat dropped a dozen glossy proofs on Liz's desk. "Can't wait to hear what Vi thinks!"

The proofs were the cover of next month's *Elle*, featuring Violet. Cat had worked hard for the actor's first major national cover. Violet smoldered, a vampy Hitchcock blonde sultry in dark red Dior. Vi would love this picture: its sensual moodiness, its gothic beauty. In elegant font, the cover line read *Fall in Love with Violet Grace.*

Liz's breath caught in her throat.

Cat took it as wonder. "*Right?*" She scooped up the proofs. "I heard she asked her agent about being an EP on the next season."

Liz blinked hard. Executive producer? Had she heard that right? "Sorry, what?"

"Isn't that great?" Cat said. "It shows she's committed, and her name will help with, well, everything."

Violet wanted to be an EP on *Sweet*'s second season? It was good news, but it'd mean even more time together. Liz could still remember what Violet tasted like when they'd kissed. Red wine and gelato. It was an effort to keep her expression even. "Of course she'll be a great EP. She's smart and has great story instinct."

Cat stood up, shouldering her tote. "You can discuss it all with her on Friday."

"Friday?"

Cat looked as if Liz had just asked if she'd ever heard of TikTok. "The party."

The streamer's annual holiday party, with a guest list topping a thousand. Including Violet. Acting normal around her in public, in front of everyone they worked with, was out of the question. "I can't," Liz blurted. The idea arrived without prologue. "I'm leaving. Tonight. For my mom's."

Cat looked thrown. "To . . . the Catskills? *Belvedere Inn?*" The name was spoken as if in lights.

The publicist had probably seen the *Architectural Digest* shoot that respectfully salivated over the six-bedroom estate belonging to Liz's mother.

"Yeah, I'm going up early to work on the pitch." Liz could pack a bag, take a red-eye to New York. She could be there by this time tomorrow.

"You're going *now?*" Cat gaped after her. "What about the party?"

"If I don't nail this pitch, I won't be invited to any more parties." Liz stuffed her laptop back into her bag and stood up. "I need some time away to focus. Then I'll dream up something incredible and we can do it all again next year. Promise." She was already halfway out the door. "Sorry! Merry Christmas!"

"Okay, bye?" Cat called after her, sounding confused.

Liz hustled to the elevator. Retreating to her mother's house certainly wasn't a perfect plan—one of the reasons she'd been working so hard for the past decade was to step out of the shadow of her formidable famous parent.

On the other hand, her mom lived in the quiet, snowy Catskills, where no one knew she and Violet Grace had kissed and it'd high-key been the best twenty-two seconds of her life.

The elevator doors dinged open. Stepping inside, Liz hit the down button then accidentally locked eyes with the life-sized promo cutout of Violet that was propped up by the water cooler, and stared at it helplessly until the elevator doors finally shut.

2.

"WHAT'S GAY ABOUT CHRISTMAS?"

The cute comedy nerd whom Birdie had been trading flirty little glances with for the past ten minutes double-took at Birdie's opening line. "Ex-squeeze me?"

Birdie took the chance to scooch closer. They were hanging out at a semi-famous West Village comedy club where Birdie was about to perform. Birdie and her new friend were watching from stools at the back bar, behind the rows of New Yorkers and tourists, whose collective attention was focused on the comedian onstage.

"What's gay about Christmas?" Birdie repeated. "Besides all the singing and drinking and tacky decorations?" She gestured with her beer at the comic who'd just started a bit about going home for the holidays. "I'm up soon. Need some good punch lines."

"Ah." Comedy Nerd nodded, tucking a lock of pencil-straight black hair behind an ear loaded with piercings. Between that, her Chuck Taylors and her beaded choker, definite I-kissed-a-girl-and-I-might-do-it-again vibes. "Gay happy meetings?"

"Bingo." Birdie nodded. "Good one. Also, isn't there something majorly queer about a holiday centered around a chick who gives birth without a dude?"

Comedy Nerd laughed. Her eyes were bright as she stuck out her hand. "I'm Amy, by the way."

"Birdie."

"I know." Amy's cheeks flushed the color of her lips. Her features were precise and pretty, like a particularly hot fox. "I've seen you before. You were dressed the same."

Amy's gaze skimmed Birdie's Oscar the Grouch T-shirt (*I Got 99 Problems but a Grouch Ain't One!*), baggy blue jeans, and dirty blond hair shoved under a backward baseball cap. Despite being thirty-three, Birdie regularly rolled out of her apartment dressed like a teenage boy.

"You did this bit about buying a case of wine," Amy recalled. "And how you got signed up to the company's aggressive email marketing campaign . . ." She looked expectantly at Birdie.

Birdie remembered. "And how those emails are like a one-night stand who won't go away."

"Yeah, like, *I'm done with you, get out of here, stop embarrassing yourself!*" Amy finished, breathless.

Birdie perked up. Amy chose to bring up a joke about clingy one-night stands in this moment? Potentially, the beginning of some sexual chaos.

"I'm thinking of doing something about clichéd holiday rom-coms," Birdie said.

Amy nodded, her smile willing. "Hit me."

Birdie cleared her throat, improvising. "In *Chestnuts Roasting on an Open Fire*, a high-strung big-city career woman who loves texting spills her peppermint mocha latte over the humble, beanie-wearing owner of a Christmas tree farm, while home for the holidays in a New England town. We know Christmas Tree Guy is the romantic lead because he has one of the universally acknowledged hot names of River, Bentley, or Chase. She has perfect hair, but he has perfect forearms."

Amy giggled.

Birdie kept her voice low enough to not distract from the comedian onstage, eyes trained on her own audience. "River/ Bentley/Chase turns out to be a volunteer firefighter who delivers healthy meals to homebound seniors with hearts of gold. He's also renovating an old house for his future family to live in. He doesn't have an Amazon account, and he builds everything from scratch, even toilet paper."

Amy laughed louder, one finger twirling a lock of her hair.

Riffing like this was easy and fun. Birdie relaxed further, switching her baseball cap to the side without breaking stride.

"Will High-Strung Career Woman look up from her phone long enough to realize River/Bentley/Chase's eyes are the exact same green as the Christmas trees he sells? Spoiler alert: she will!"

Amy cackled so loudly, a couple in the back row shot them warning glances. She edged closer. "More."

One of Birdie's all-time favorite words. She was in the zone. "Coming this Christmas, *All the Way Home I'll Be Warm* tells the story of Lucy, a super-pretty NYU grad student, who informs her meddling-but-lovable family that she finally has a boyfriend. She does not have a boyfriend, which is weird because she is so pretty! She pays fellow student-slash-archnemesis Bruno, also hot, to pose as her boo. At their first family dinner, they give contradictory answers about how they met, and Lucy's nephew asks Bruno if he has amnesia and why they never hold hands. So cute! So quirky!" Birdie paused for effect. "There is only one bed, and it's covered with her great-great-great-grandmother's fertility quilt."

Amy snort-laughed. "Of course it is."

Some people found meaning on the top of a mountain or in the pew of a church. This darkened comedy club, this entertained fan, this was Birdie's church. She moved to let someone order at the bar without slowing her roll. "Lucy and Bruno realize A, they don't hate each other and B, they want to bone." Birdie kept her eyes locked on Amy's. "When they decorate Christmas cookies, Bruno opens up to Lucy about a tragic bald eagle attack during a ski vacation that killed his entire family, which is very sad. Then they kiss, which is very hot, but no tongue because they're in her parents' house. Bruno gives all the money Lucy pays him to a children's charity that prevents bald-eagle-related skiing accidents. That helps Lucy realize what true love actually is, and it starts snowing. The end."

"I swear, I've seen that film!" Amy wiped away a tear of laughter, cheeks flushed. "Wow, you're funny. I *really* loved your special."

Birdie's post-joke high wavered. "Thanks, dude."

"Are you going to do another?"

At the time, Birdie ate up every morsel of praise about her first, and only, hour-long Netflix special, *Birdie in the Hand, Birdie in the Bush.* (Kate McKinnon famously tweeted it was "fucktastic.") But now, three years later, being proud of her *old* special was starting to feel a bit pathetic. Birdie finished her beer. "Trying. Keep getting distracted."

"By what?"

Birdie signaled the bartender, ordered a whiskey, then let her gaze land back on Amy. "Beautiful women."

Amy's expression was at the crossroads of incredulous and flattered. "Wow, what a line."

"It's not a line," Birdie said honestly. "It's my lot in life."

The bartender slid the whiskey across the bar.

Birdie took a grateful sip, the liquor dulling her professional insecurity. Other comedians used their specials to swan dive into acting or screenwriting or sold-out national tours. That momentum, that buildup of energy—Birdie never got there. Instead, she was still asking for one-off spots at local clubs. She tipped her glass to Amy. "Want one? On me." Birdie had spent her last drink ticket on that whiskey, and was pretty near broke, but that's what credit cards were for, right?

Something daring flashed in Amy's gaze. She leaned in and put her mouth right by Birdie's ear. "Want me to show you what's gay about Christmas, Birdie Belvedere?"

This tête-à-tête was back on track. Birdie grinned. "More than Santa loves the unpaid labor of elves."

And that's how Birdie ended up not finessing her material as she intended, but in the graffiti-covered bathroom, being pushed against the hand dryers, kissing like Christmas depended on it.

There were many things Birdie Belvedere was not good at: being on time, tidying up, wearing clothes without pizza stains. But she was good at making people laugh, and she was very good at making out. Especially this kind of make-out: all hot breath and desperate hands.

Birdie allowed herself to be backed into an empty stall, Amy locking the door behind them.

Amy's fingers paused on the top button of Birdie's jeans. "Can I?"

Even though one part of Birdie's brain warned her this might not be the best time, the larger, hornier, beer-soaked part nodded enthusiastically. "Hell yeah."

Amy slid her fingers inside Birdie's underwear, pressing up.

Birdie gasped, then groaned. "Holy mother of *mistletoe.*"

Amy's tongue was back in Birdie's mouth. The pleasure radiating through Birdie's body was exactly why she considered plans to be loose suggestions. Going with the flow was way more fun. As Amy tugged her jeans lower for a better angle, Birdie panted, eyes squeezed shut, anticipating the delicious rush about to come.

"Birdie?" a voice called from outside the bathroom.

Birdie's eyes flew open.

"Birdie?" the woman tried again, the sound of the bar briefly flooding into the bathroom as she stepped inside. "You in here?"

Mouthing *sorry* to Amy, Birdie called back, "Yup. Just a sec."

This was not the first time Birdie Belvedere had been caught with her pants down. There was high school summer camp with Tracey Jenkins-Jones, whose breath always smelled like Doritos. Britney Liu, at a sleepover party while everyone else was watching *Candyman.* Michelle Paris, in a hotel suite bathroom, until her boyfriend walked in.

Birdie wriggled her jeans back over her hips. Unlocking the door, she tried not to look guilty as she came face-to-face with her no-nonsense manager, Issa Mitchell.

Issa folded her arms, assessing Birdie head to toe.

"Issa, hey!" Birdie began brightly, adjusting her baseball cap. "Sorry, just using the can . . ."

Amy slipped out from behind her, waggling sticky fingers in farewell.

". . . with a friend?" Birdie ended, cringing. "Anyway, I didn't know you were coming tonight. What a rad surprise."

Issa's eyebrows narrowed in disapproval. "I came to see your set. Which you just missed. Didn't you hear them calling your name?"

"What?" Birdie gaped at Issa. "No!" She hustled for the bathroom door and back into the club.

Marin, a comic who definitely wasn't on the lineup, was onstage, starting a set. People were already laughing.

She'd missed it. Birdie had been looking forward to this hard-to-get slot all week and she'd missed it.

"That's three strikes, Birdie." Issa was beside her, counting off her fingers in a low voice. "You missed that improv podcast last month, and you were so hungover at your Just for Laughs audition, you may as well have missed it."

Birdie puffed a breath, hiding her shame with a flippant response. "I'm a hot mess; that's my brand! Give the people what they want."

"It's not what I want. I'm sorry, but I can't rep you anymore." And with that, Birdie's manager headed for the club's exit.

"Wait a sec!" Birdie followed Issa up a flight of stairs clogged with people waiting to get in, taking the steps two at a time. "Issa!" Birdie called. "C'mon, wait!"

Outside, West Third Street was busy with holiday shoppers and honking yellow taxis. The first snow of the season was starting to fall, dusting the piled black garbage bags with white.

"Issa, please!" Birdie bounded after her, shivering in her T-shirt. "I lost track of time. I was workshopping my set with . . ." In her panic, Birdie could not remember her hookup's name.

Issa called over her shoulder, "Your fly is undone."

Birdie cursed, zipped up, and hurried to get in Issa's path.

"Gimme another chance. I'm good! C'mon, you know I'm good!"

"I do know you're good—that's what makes this so hard." Issa tightened her coat around herself. "You're wasting your talent. You swore you'd be performing a new hour by the end of the year. Well, it's December first. Have you even started working on it?"

If only it was as easy to *do* things as it was to *say* them. Yes, Birdie had said she wanted to work on a new show. But the doing of that was proving harder than anticipated. "It's been a tough year," she said. "The world is a dumpster fire. I haven't been able to focus."

"But you are able to focus on drinking. You are able to focus on your very active personal life." Issa's face screwed into an expression Birdie had grown familiar with— somewhere between bewilderment, affection, and disap- proval. Snow dusted the top of her voluminous Afro. "You're like a hot, gay frat boy who never wants to grow up."

It wasn't not true. "I know that's meant to be an insult, but thank you?"

Issa didn't chuckle as Birdie had hoped. Instead, she shook her head in frustration. "There are more comedians in this city than cabs and bodega cats. You need to take yourself and your career way more seriously."

What Birdie needed was to make people laugh. Make them feel good and hopeful in the face of the relentless ter- ribleness that was, well, life. A manager was someone in the trenches with her, who believed in her potential. Someone to help her stay accountable and stick to her commitments. Someone who could help her take herself and her career way more seriously.

"What about four strikes?" Birdie tried. "Or five?"

Issa smiled, but it was closer to pity than amusement. "Happy holidays, okay?"

One final nod, then Issa was off, striding down West Third Street, taking all Birdie's hopes and dreams with her.

The air left her lungs like a spent balloon.

Fired for missing a slot due to tipsy bathroom sex.

Her mother would find that amusing.

Her beloved big sister, Liz, would shake her head in concern, a line forming between her meticulously tweezed brows. *I just want you to be happy, Squeak.*

Her hopeless-romantic little brother, Rafi, would be worried about her heart.

At least she had people biologically compelled to love her.

So what was getting in the way? Why did she feel so blocked when it came to the idea of new material?

Birdie trudged back down the stairs, reentering the dimly lit comedy club and making her way to the back bar. Onstage, a spotlit Marin was getting big laughs. *Her* laughs.

The whiskey she'd abandoned ten minutes ago was nowhere in sight. The bartender gave her a bloodless nod. "Another?"

Desperate times. Even though she really couldn't afford it, Birdie felt grateful for the offer of booze. That understanding friend. That sympathetic confidant. "People claim I'm not reliable, but clearly, I am: Yes please."

He poured it neat. The first sip spread like sunshine in her belly, fuzzing out the edges.

"Hey." Amy was back. "Everything cool?"

"Not really. I missed my set," Birdie told her. "Will you console me?"

Or, more accurately, distract her from her epic screwup, in the same way the glass in her hand was already doing.

Amy grinned, edging close enough to hook a finger around Birdie's belt loop. Skin on skin: yeah, Birdie could use a little more of that. "With pleasure."

3.

RAFI BELVEDERE LAID TWO UGLY CHRISTMAS SWEATERS on his bed, side by side. The first was bright red, embroidered with Snoop Dogg in a Santa hat and the words *'Twas the Nizzle Before Chrismizzle*. The second was emerald green and featured a gingerbread man with a broken arm and the phrase *Oh Snap!*

The choice of which to wear to tonight's office holiday party was much more than merely sartorial. Because Rafi would be wearing one of these two cheerfully hideous Christmas sweaters when he got *engaged*.

In classic Rafi Belvedere fashion, he'd made this decision yesterday.

Rafi had been dating senior software engineer Sunita Jackson for just over six months. Their friendship had evolved from platonic to romantic during the office's first summer Friday drinks on the back patio of a local Irish bar. One by one, their co-workers peeled off, until Rafi and Sunita were the last ones standing. *Should we do another?* he'd asked, ready to pay for their fourth round.

Sunita had arched a brow, smile wicked. *Or you can just do me.*

They'd tumbled into a taxi, into bed, and that was that. Their relationship had been under wraps for the first month or so, but after getting busted kissing in the supply closet, they'd quietly informed HR. There were no more supply closet make-outs, but it was general knowledge that Rafi and Sunita were dating.

Sunita was confident and outgoing and *fun*. Her love language was unprompted gifts, and her thrilled screams at the House of Horrors company offsite on Halloween were the stuff of legend. Work had brought them together, so to Rafi, proposing at their holiday party sounded like the height of romance. Tonight would be Sunita's all-time biggest and best surprise.

He just had to decide what to wear.

Snapping pictures of both sweaters, Rafi texted them to his longtime best friend—and personal fashion consultant— Ash Campbell.

RAFI: Fashion emergency! Chrismizzle or Oh Snap?
My office holiday party has an Ugly Sweater theme.

It was about six in Philadelphia, which made it 11:00 P.M. in London. Ash, a night owl, would still be up.

While he waited for a reply, Rafi did a quick tidy of the apartment so his fiancée wouldn't have to step over his dirty socks later that night. (*Fiancée!* The word made him feel like a just-exploded firework.) Luckily his roommate was out of town for the weekend—Rafi piled all of Phil's gaming equipment back into his bedroom.

He was all set: the Prosecco they'd had on their first official date? Check. Homemade chocolate-covered strawberries? Check. Ring still in the ring box? Rafi flipped open the velvet box for the one millionth time. As a community manager for a nonprofit, Rafi was paid more in karma than cash. But when he'd spotted the locally produced, conflict-free soli-

taire, something about it just *felt right*. The swipe of his credit
card had filled him with hope. His future was quite literally
in his hands. The diamond that glinted back at him reminded
Rafi that this was all as real as the stone was.

His phone dinged.

Ash had sent a meme of Miranda Priestly from *The Devil
Wears Prada*. Haughty Meryl, sitting behind her desk, looking devastatingly unimpressed, saying, *You have no style or
sense of fashion.*

Rafi chuckled. Ash and Rafi messaged pretty much daily
ever since they'd moved away from their shared hometown
of Woodstock, a small artsy town in upstate New York,
where Rafi's mother, Babs, still lived. The two went to different colleges. Before he eventually landed in Philly, Rafi had
gone to Georgetown, drawn to nonprofits and the idea that
politics might be noble (turned out, it wasn't). Ash got into
NYU, pursuing interests in writing, fashion, and the idea
that Brooklyn boys might be hot (turned out, they were).

Ash followed the GIF with a text. JK, these bad boys
cross the line from ironic to iconic. Big yes to both.

Rafi snorted in amusement, thumbing a response. Right,
but which one says Husband Material . . .

He frowned, deleting it. Tried again.

RAFI: Which gets your final rose? One of these icons
will witness my engagement!

Nope, didn't feel right, either. This wasn't the kind of
thing you announced to your best friend since age fourteen
over text.

Rafi called Ash. A surge of spidery anxiety caught him

unawares. Ash would be surprised, sure. He wasn't spontaneous like Rafi, preferring a measured approach to big decisions. And Ash wasn't a romantic. Since high school, Rafi
had been with four girlfriends and one boyfriend while Ash
dated only casually. Ash had never been in love, never talked
about marriage or commitment.

Still, Ash would think the proposal was a good idea, right?

Just as Rafi started to regret calling, Ash sent it to voicemail, followed by a text.

> ASH: Sorry man, at a jazz club. If I pick up, I'll be side-
> eyed to death.

Rafi let out a breath of relief. They'd discuss this *after* he
was engaged. Rafi pictured his future best man huddled in
the corner of an East London jazz bar, perhaps with a coterie
of cool, classy queers, drinking red wine out of balloon
glasses. Probably wearing some sort of fitted cashmere
sweater, his dark blond hair swept under a classic knit beanie.
Soon after he moved, Ash had landed the prestigious position of style editor for *London Man*, a respected men's life-
style website and quarterly magazine. Now Ash inhabited
the life of an urbane gay man in the way he never quite had
in the States.

Ash texted again: Gingerbread boi. The green is better for
your skin tone.

Rafi grinned. He yanked the winning sweater over his
head, examining his outfit in the bathroom mirror. Ash was
right: the emerald green did look flattering against his light
brown skin. Rafi scrubbed a hand through his thick, loose
curls, hoping for sexy-messy, not just messy-messy. All in all,

a possibly cute young man gazed back at him, big brown eyes brimming with hope.

Husband. The word had weight. Enough to eclipse that nagging, imprecise sense of his real life not yet kicking into gear.

RAFI: Thanks dude. Miss you.
ASH: Have fun. Miss you too.

THE HOLIDAY PARTY WAS being held in the back room of a dive bar in South Philly. Rafi threaded through the already tipsy crowd, greeting his friends, scanning for Sunita.

He found her laughing with the other engineers over a plate of pimento cheese dip.

"Hey, stud." She greeted him with a quick kiss on the cheek. "Cute sweater."

"Thanks." He blushed, silently thanking Ash for the suggestion. "You look unfairly sexy."

His girlfriend tossed her head back to laugh. Her confidence was like her features: bold and unapologetic. Her thick black hair was swept into a lustrous high ponytail; her front teeth were charmingly crooked. Sunita's sweater was, technically, ugly—a reindeer in sunglasses, holiday lights tangled around its antlers—but she was wearing it tight over an extremely effective push-up bra, along with a leather miniskirt, sheer stockings, and six-inch heels that made her taller than him. He didn't recognize the stilettos and felt a burst of excitement for the familiarity they'd soon share. He had the rest of his life to learn everything about this woman, down to her shoes.

"Come on." Sunita looped her arm in his. "Let's get you drunk."

Rafi had strategically offered to emcee the night. His sister Birdie was far more gifted in the public speaking arena, but given his mom was Hollywood legend Babs Belvedere, he'd picked up enough to pull off a decent hosting job.

It took forever to get through the founder's overly earnest sentiments, then there were some prizes for Office Clown, Caffeine Fiend, and Meeting Addict. With every passing minute, Rafi's nerves quickened from a jog to a trot to a full-on sprint. Finally, the formalities were finished. The DJ started Ariana Grande's "Santa Tell Me," and chatter rose in anticipation of a balls-to-the-wall dance party.

Rafi cleared his throat. "I just have one more order of business. Can we cut the music?"

The room fell suddenly, strangely, silent.

He peered into the sea of faces. "Can I ask Sunita to join me?"

The crowd shuffled, looking for her. Sunita made her way through to climb the two steps onto the stage with a wry smile. "Don't tell me I've won Office Boozehound," she joked, eliciting a wave of laughter.

"Yup." Rafi nodded. "The prize is a lifetime supply of seltzer."

"Kill me!" Sunita groaned, to more chuckles.

"But seriously," Rafi said. "You all know Ms. Sunita Jackson. She's your co-worker. Your friend. Creator of Margarita Mondays."

A smattering of applause. Everyone liked Margarita Mondays.

"And," Rafi continued, "to my endless amazement and sometimes confusion, my girlfriend."

A few loose-lipped hoots and hollers.

Sunita's smile slipped, but only for a second. "Dude." Her tone stayed light. "No need to get mushy."

Rafi gave her an *I got this* smile and went on. "We all do this work because we care about people. We care about their happiness. We care about their futures. It's not just about access to clean drinking water in a world where that isn't a given. It's about access to a full and satisfying life. And when I think about what that life looks like for myself, it couldn't be more clear. It means being with Sunita—"

"Raf!" She gave his arm a friendly punch.

"—for the rest of my life."

The words hovered in the air, unable to land. Rafi's heart was pounding so loudly he could barely hear the excited murmurs of his co-workers. There was an air of wonderful unreality to this moment, the feeling of magic happening to him, around him, right now.

Sunita let out a confused laugh. "Ummm . . . okay?"

Rafi slid his hand into his back pocket.

A woman in the audience gasped.

"Rafi." Sunita's tone sharpened. "What are you doing?"

He pulled out the ring box and got down on one knee. He wanted to remember every second. The tight stretch of his jeans over his skin. The whoops and whistles from the crowd. The way Sunita's jaw had fallen all the way open, her dark eyes like saucers, her entire attention poured onto him.

The best surprise. Ever.

He flipped the ring box open. "Sunita Jackson. Will you marry me?"

Sunita had both hands over her mouth, her blood-red nails pressing into her cheeks. Ordinarily she loved attention. But right now she looked almost scared. His girlfriend dropped her hands and took a step forward. "Rafi." Her voice was low. "Is this a joke?"

Rafi shook his head, as much to say no as to eradicate the sense that this wasn't playing out the way he'd hoped.

Sunita darted a look at the crowd, then back at Rafi. Her eyes flickered between his. Left, right, left, right.

Rafi's knee started to hurt. He was sweating. The stage lights bounced off the diamond, making him wince.

"Raf, for chrissakes, get up," Sunita hissed. "Get. Up."

THIRTY SECONDS LATER, they were facing off in the front room of the bar, which was empty but for a handful of patrons watching ice hockey on TV.

Sunita's eyebrows were halfway up her forehead. "What the hell, Rafi?" She looked equal parts mad and scandalized. *"We've never even talked about marriage.* And then you go and—in front of everyone we work with?"

The first time Rafi visited his mother on a film shoot as a boy, he'd been confused by the set. The family kitchen wasn't real, just painted plywood. That same feeling of uncovered illusion disoriented him now. "But—you said you loved me."

Sunita's eyes were so wide he could see the entire shape of her irises. "When did I say that?"

"Like—when—at the end of every call!"

Something clicked in Sunita's gaze. *"Love ya?* That's how I say goodbye to everyone! I say it to my UPS guy! Love ya!"

"But—but you kept talking about getting your grandmother's dress refitted."

Sunita gaped at him. "A *cocktail* dress. Not a *wedding* dress."

The possibility that Rafi had done something extremely

misguided and deeply inappropriate made him lose his center of gravity. He grabbed a nearby table for support. "So, you don't love me?"

Sunita made a desperate noise. "Yeah, sure. Like I love— I don't know—cheeseburgers and puppies. I'm only twenty-eight! You're twenty-*nine*. This is casual."

"Is it?" This was news to Rafi.

"Of course it is! We're not meant to be together *forever*."

Rafi's heartbeat boomed in his ears. "Oh."

"I never wanted to hurt you." Sunita puffed out a breath. "It sucks we have to end things like this."

Rafi struggled to maintain decorum, but he was close to full-blown panic. "Why are things ending?"

Sunita squinted, one hand on her hip. "So you'd be fine not getting married and going back to dating?"

"Yes?" His brain decided now would be a great time to replay being down on one knee as Sunita's jaw dropped in what he now recognized as horror. *In front of everyone they worked with.*

"Oh, Raf." Sunita rubbed his arms like a consoling friend. "You'll find your person. And we can be buds, I promise. I won't make it weird or anything." Sunita adjusted her skirt. "I'm sorry. Merry Christmas."

Then she was gone. Back into the party full of his co-workers who'd all just witnessed his indecent proposal.

Reality wobbled. It was too late to call Ash. Too late to do anything. Wild emotion sloshed in his body, a sickening tumble of confusion and shame and regret. His heart felt like it'd been stomped on by a rogue herd of reindeer.

He'd gotten it so, so wrong. *Again.*

4.

Twenty-three days till Christmas

*I*T WAS LATE ON MONDAY MORNING WHEN BIRDIE CLAWED her way to consciousness, battling a hangover the size of New York's trash problem. Next to her, Amy slept, her black hair spilling over a slightly grubby pillowcase. Dust motes floated in the bruised-yellow light seeping through the window. Birdie's Brooklyn studio looked as it always did: recently burgled. Overdue bills crowded her fridge, and she definitely needed to do laundry. Keeping a place clean and tidy was more her sister's speed. Birdie really wanted to pull the covers back over her head so her problems would give up looking for her and find someone else to bother. But alas. She wasn't responsible for just herself. From his position at the end of her bed, her fat black-and-white tabby aimed his one good eye at her and yowled, sounding like a car engine slowly conking out.

Amy stirred, blinking blearily as she focused on Birdie, who saluted as cheerfully as she could. "Greetings and salutations."

Amy yawned, rubbing mascara-smeared eyes. "Oh my god, my head."

Birdie handed her a glass of water from the bedside table. "It's an excellent head."

"Speaking of excellent head . . ." Amy finished the glass. "Last night was—wow. Award-winning."

"It's nice to be nominated, but it's even nicer to win." Birdie addressed an invisible camera.

Amy giggled, then stretched with a groan. Her gaze roved over the signed posters of Birdie's heroes (Steve Martin, Hannah Gadsby, Wanda Sykes) before landing on an old photograph taped to the wall beside the bed.

In it, Birdie, her older sister, Liz, and her younger brother, Rafi, all in black tie, flanked their mom, Babs, on a red carpet. Babs's pile of coiffed strawberry-blond hair and trademark twinkle in her bright blue eyes were, evidently, recognizable.

"*Wow.*" Amy leaned closer to the picture. "I can't believe your mom is *Babs Belvedere.*"

Birdie didn't respond, feeling the familiar suspicion that she was getting attention because of her mother, not her own appeal. Publicists and reviewers always underlined the Babs Belvedere association. It was a blessing in that it opened (some) doors and secured (some) meetings, but a curse in that Birdie was never considered as funny, charming, and quick-witted as her very famous parent. Because Babs was, well, Babs. Starting with the fact her three children were born to three different fathers. *What can I say?* Babs had joked a thousand times. *Variety is the spice of life. And honey, I've always liked it spicy.*

Amy looked from the photo of the glammed-up Belvederes to the dingy kitchenette and mismatched chairs. Birdie could see the question hovering on her lips. Some version of *Why do you live like this?*

Because Birdie was fiercely devoted to an independent creative career and had never accepted money from either parent, despite their respective offerings. She didn't deny her mother's wealth meant she'd always have a safety net. But, unlike some New York nepo babies who didn't feel embarrassed using a credit card whose statement they'd never see, Birdie had paid her own way since moving out as a teenager. A decision that usually felt noble and great. Until recently. Being broke in your twenties was a rite of passage. In your thirties? Less cool.

"Hungry?" Birdie kicked her thoughts and the covers aside. "I need to feed my cat. Sadly, not a euphemism."

Amy elected for a shower first. "Then maybe we can get some brunch? I have the day off."

Brunch cost money. And was dangerously close to girlfriend territory. "Sorry, I have some stuff to do today." She did not. "But I can make you my famous Sunday eggs? Even though it's Monday."

Amy pouted, nodding. "Deal."

While Amy showered, Birdie shook some dry food into Mr. Paws's bowl and unearthed a cast-iron skillet so old it remembered dial-up internet. She doused it in olive oil then hunted around the swampy inside of her fridge for eggs. Victory! A cardboard six-pack hid behind a stack of takeout. A six-pack . . . that contained only empty eggshells (ugh, why was she like this?). She was out of bacon, and the bag of day-old bagels she'd purchased for a buck last week were as hard as Dwayne "the Rock" Johnson.

Okay, coffee for breakfast. Coffee was the most important meal of the day, after all. Except *she was also out of coffee.* Now she'd have to fork out for a breakfast she couldn't afford or send her lover off with nothing more than a handshake, and that just seemed rude.

How did everyone manage their lives with such seeming ease? It befuddled Birdie that she was expected to be excellent in her chosen profession *and* possess skills in money management *and* home organization *and* healthy eating *and* one million other things. These were the people who'd be smiling smugly from the onslaught of squeaky-clean holiday cards that'd soon be coming her way. High school friends and former comics who gave it all up for life in the suburbs with kitchens full of coffee and bacon and eggs. Birdie sank down at her tiny kitchen table, unexpected tears blurring her vision. Christmas was coming, but the endless twinkly festivity felt like a cruel joke. How the hell were things supposed to be joyful and jolly and bright? God, she just wanted a sign. A sign that the holidays could be—and it felt so ridiculous to wish for this—magic.

Birdie's buzzer sounded.

She stared at it in surprise. Had the universe obeyed her wish and served up Cara Delevingne in an elf costume?

The buzzer sounded again. A woman's voice crackled over the intercom. "Squeak! It's me, let me in. I'm freezing my tits off!"

Better than Cara Delevingne. Because one minute later, Birdie's favorite person in the entire world was standing on her doorstep with a black roller suitcase and a smile.

"Liz Fizz!" Birdie gasped, flying into her arms with such force, her sister laughed, stumbling.

"Hi, Squeak." Liz hugged her tightly, then pulled back to examine Birdie's face. "Is everything okay?"

Weeping over an empty egg carton? Who was she, Rafi?

"Of course! I am hunky *and* dory, together at last." Birdie nudged her embarrassing emotions off a cliff, focusing on her sister. "What are you doing in New York? I thought you weren't coming back till right before Christmas."

"Change of plans." Her tall, neatly presented older sister held up a paper bag. "I bought coffee and breakfast sandwiches. Have you eaten?"

Birdie fist-pumped. "Holy guacamole, I love you."

Liz stepped inside. "I love you, too."

"I was talking to the sandwich."

Liz chuckled and hung up her coat. Where Birdie was messy, Liz colored inside the lines with flattering neutral tones. But beneath her big sister's unassuming exterior beat the heart of an insanely talented writer and ambitious boss-bitch showrunner who'd spent the year crushing it in L.A. Liz's unexpected presence was like sinking in front of a crackling fire on a cold and blustery night.

Birdie cut her breakfast sandwich in two, offering half to Amy after she came out of the shower. Liz, who had very little experience with casual sex, was the most flustered out of them all.

Amy accepted the sandwich to go. "Nice to meet you, Liz. Maybe I'll see you again?"

Liz blushed. "Sure. I mean, maybe? I live in L.A., so . . ." She trailed off, staring helplessly at Birdie.

"You'll have to excuse my sex-starved sister," Birdie said, snorting laughter as Liz whacked her arm.

"See you around." Amy directed a kiss at Birdie's mouth.

Birdie swerved her head so the kiss landed on her cheek. "Happy holidays, lady. You're the best."

Liz watched Amy leave in fearful bemusement. "Don't you find one-night stands *so awkward*?" she asked Birdie, unwrapping her sandwich. The smell of melting cheese and crispy bacon filled the small kitchen. "Both going your separate ways like you just shared a cab instead of a bed?"

Birdie shrugged. She'd never had a long-term relationship. Wasn't in her DNA. "So, Liz Fizz: What brings you to town?"

As they ate, Liz explained she had to figure out the second season of her show, as soon as humanly possible. "But I can't focus in L.A."

"Why not?"

Her sister glitched for a microsecond. "Too many holiday parties. I'm heading up early to Mom's to work from there. And I was hoping," she wheedled, "my very favorite sister in the whole world might come with me."

"Now?" It was December second. Birdie usually wouldn't head up for another couple weeks.

Liz nodded, hopeful. "Do you have any shows booked? Any auditions?"

Birdie cringed. The effort it'd take to land a new manager—inviting them to sets she had yet to book, to see new material she had yet to write—loomed like a specter who cared about professional development. "Not exactly. Is Ma home right now?"

"She's in Connecticut till tomorrow—something about an audition. Whaddya say?"

Birdie took another bite, examining her somehow-put-together-after-a-red-eye older sister. This was all out of character. Liz Belvedere was as spontaneous as linear time. She'd never had trouble "focusing" before—Liz could put on headphones and work through a raging house party, which, sadly, Birdie had witnessed more than once. Liz had been distant much of the year, which Birdie understood as a side effect of living her greatest professional dream. But was something else going on? Birdie narrowed her eyes. "Why are you really here?"

Liz demurred, tucking her curtain bangs behind her ears. A nervous habit. "I told you: work. Please? It won't be any fun if you're not there. You're Mom's favorite."

"We both know Raf is the favorite."

"You love Christmas," Liz reminded her. "You're a sucker for Santa hats."

"A fan girl for festivities," Birdie agreed, finishing her sandwich. "A nerd for nativity."

Their mom's place was huge and clean and well stocked. Plus, the Catskills was not crawling with her many exes . . . managers or otherwise. It wasn't running *away* from her problems. It was running *toward* temporary reprieve from them.

"Okey dokey, Mrs. Claus," Birdie announced, "I'm in. Saddle up the sleigh." Then, as if it'd just occurred to her, "You know Dasher, right? And Dancer? You've definitely met Prancer and Vixen."

"Pack." Liz pointed to Birdie's closet, smiling.

"Comet? Cupid?" Birdie called over her shoulder. "Tell me you know my boys Donner and Blitzen!"

HALF AN HOUR LATER, Birdie stepped onto the cold Brooklyn street shouldering a backpack, two tote bags of dirty laundry, and Mr. Paws's elaborate cat carrier. In her neon-orange puffer, Snoopy Christmas sweater, and rainbow-print scarf, Birdie was a spot of color against the flat gray of the sky. Her sunglasses were oversized and deliberately ridiculous: chunky eighties frames that looked like sci-fi ski goggles.

Liz examined her phone. "I figure we Uber to the nearest Enterprise and rent a car."

"Rent a car? Why would we rent a car?"

"No." Liz's expression was a mix of surprise and dismay. "Don't tell me . . ."

"We have a perfectly serviceable car right here," Birdie said, gesturing down the street. "We have Ray."

Ray was an early-nineties station wagon so antique it had wood paneling and a cassette player. Yes, it was a gas-guzzler and a beast to park, but it was cool and kitsch and Birdie never wanted to give Ray up.

A familiar-looking orange parking ticket was tucked under the windshield wiper. Birdie stuffed it in her pocket—a problem for later—and patted the hood proudly. "Hop in."

Her sister looked openly horrified. "It's not a car—it's a sight gag!"

"It's the Millennium Falcon of its generation," Birdie corrected, placing her cat carrier and luggage in the back seat.

Liz climbed into the passenger side gingerly. "When was the last time you changed your oil?"

"No one needs to change. Everyone's perfect as they are." Birdie slid into the driver's seat, revving the ancient motor to life. "Bring on Christmas in the Catskills, baby!"

5.

*D*RIVING OUT OF THE CITY WAS EXTREMELY STRESSFUL, and not just because Ray was a terrifying vehicular dinosaur. Because of: *"Violet!"* Birdie flung a finger at an old billboard for *Sweet*, then started screeching like an excited chimpanzee.

Extraordinarily difficult to evict someone living rent-free in your head while whizzing by two thirty-foot photographs of them. As the source material described, two sets of blue-green eyes, the color of the ocean. Two manes of "sun-streaked blond." Two bodies boasting "peaches and cream skin" and "perfect size six figures," the first female measurements Liz had ever internalized.

Sweet was a loose adaptation of *Sweet Valley High*, a sudsy teen book series from the 1980s. As in the original paperbacks, the show centered around identical twins with polar opposite personalities and rigorously dictated versions of 1980s American beauty. As depicted on the billboard now in Ray's rearview mirror, Violet Grace portrayed both rebellious Jessica Wakefield (Dionysian smirk, lip piercing, eighties leather jacket with the collar popped) and bookish Elizabeth Wakefield (razor-sharp bangs, librarian glasses, Peter Pan collar with apple embroidery). The tagline: Twin Flames. The character of Jessica Wakefield was pansexual, funny, and totally outrageous. Her twin sister, Elizabeth, was bright, ambitious, and a square. As Liz had explained many times, Jessica was id, and Elizabeth was superego. *Sweet*'s characters were teenagers but the actors playing them were all young adults.

"Oof," Birdie groaned, glancing back at the billboard. "Violet is *sexy.*"

Liz lobbed her an annoyed look. "Birdie!"

Her little sister appeared genuinely confused. "Am I not supposed to think she's sexy?"

No. That's exactly what she was meant to think. Violet was now the fantasy of thousands—a reality Liz helped create. Which was as weird as it was disorienting. Liz tried not to let her sister see how ruffled she was. "Eyes on the road, Squeak."

THE SISTERS ARRIVED AT their mother's manor at sunset, rolling up the long driveway that kept the house hidden from the street. Babs had purchased an ugly pile of bricks and spiders for peanuts fifteen years ago. Now the fondly nicknamed Belvedere Inn was whitewashed and majestic, aglow in the final rays of the setting sun.

It actually was an old inn, a B&B built in the 1920s that flourished through the Catskills' heyday of the forties through the sixties, until the late owner's coke problem ran it into the ground. After being abandoned for years, it was eventually marketed as a *renovator's dream!* At five thousand square feet, the bones were solid, but when Babs first laid eyes on it, every window was broken, tiles tumbling off the roof at the suggestion of a breeze. A family of raccoons had enacted squatters' rights on the second floor.

Babs took one look and declared, *I'm home!*, ready to trade noisy New York for peaceful country living. Rafi was the only child who moved with her: Liz was already in college and Birdie was eager to strike out on her own.

Over the years, Babs painstakingly transformed the ugly old inn. With every significant payday came another residential milestone: a new roof, a new kitchen, central air. An ad campaign for a minor airline funded careful restoration of the greenhouse, a hundred-year-old glass-and-iron building filled with ferns and orchids. When Babs booked *Palace People*, the TV show that kicked off her second significant comeback, she put in a pool and hot tub.

Birdie parked in the covered garage. A small mountain of cards and presents crowded the *Come the Fuck In* doormat, including a seasonal arrangement from Flower Power, Honey!, Babs's favorite florist in the city. Their mom's assistant must be traveling with her, Liz figured as, balancing an armful of packages, she punched in the code for the cherry-red front door.

It opened into a marbled foyer with a long entrance table and one too many mirrors. A staircase curved up to the four guest bedrooms on the second floor. To the right was a formal living room and a dining room, used for entertaining. Babs's master suite and bath dominated the northwestern corner of the first floor, overlooking the back patio and pool. Next to it was a large guest bedroom that'd been Rafi's room when he was a boy.

Even though the Inn was fully renovated, it still held its original charm. The aesthetic was farmhouse-meets-Hollywood: modern, but not the clean, all-white kind. Eclectic was a better description. Eccentric and colorful, a nod to Babs's travels and interests. Hand-carved puppets from Thailand were mounted alongside contemporary photography of Parisian street scenes. Funky Moroccan rugs lay over rustic Spanish tiles. The bathrooms were wrapped in vibrant wallpaper featuring flamingos or exotic flowers. When dinner was served, it was on mismatched plates: some fine china, some chipped vintage unearthed in a secondhand shop.

Their mother was bold and had no time for prudishness, evidenced by the very first thing visitors laid eyes on: an oversized, artfully shot nude. Of Babs herself.

Liz balked at the artwork, photographed when her mother was disturbingly young and supple. "Nothing like coming eye to eye with your mother's areola."

"Lookin' good, Ma." Birdie gave the portrait a thumbs-up before heading upstairs with the cat carrier.

Each of the four bedrooms on the second floor paid homage to a Hollywood great. One was already occupied. Liz couldn't get a read on the chunky sneakers, Japanese snacks, and obscure music magazines scattered around the Josephine Baker suite. When their mother returned tomorrow, they'd presumably meet whoever was staying in the bedroom wrapped floor to ceiling in banana-themed wallpaper.

Liz selected Audrey Hepburn—feminine, with accents in Tiffany blue. Her choice was defined by practicality; it was at the far end of the corridor and thus the quietest. Birdie chose Humphrey Bogart, all masculine leather, with a replica of the Maltese Falcon statue and, fittingly, a full wet bar.

Liz unpacked, putting away clothes and toiletries and setting her bedside table with necessities—sleep mask, melatonin, and earplugs for Birdie's after-parties. Then Liz made her way downstairs, ready to snack and chill after a long travel day.

Rounding the bottom of the staircase, she headed toward

the kitchen, past framed family photos featuring unfortunate haircuts, and a fertility statue from a lesser-known comedy Babs shot in Bali.

Babs had ripped out multiple walls to create a light, bright kitchen, whose many windows overlooked an evergreen hedge and wintered backyard. Burnished brass cookware hung on hooks above a commercial range that easily fit the Christmas ham each year. The turquoise tiles above the backsplash and the gold faucets and cabinet pulls gave the space Babs's signature luxe touch. Most meals were eaten around the long marble-top kitchen island, lit overhead by hand-blown vintage glass pendants.

The kitchen opened into an equally large family room. An enormous L-shaped sectional scattered with colorful throw pillows faced the original stone fireplace. Mohair knee rugs were folded in wicker baskets alongside potted houseplants (only the kinds that were easy to keep alive). The overflowing bookcases held everything from Jane Austen to new releases, plus Babs's three biographies (*Babs Belvedere: A Life Lived in Color; She Did It Her Way; Babs: The Woman Upstairs*). An armchair had been shifted to make room for the Christmas tree, not yet there.

Liz poked around the walk-in pantry for a quick and easy dinner. "How about mac and cheese?"

"Or I can pick us up something in town. The wine cellar's locked, and this"—the sole bottle of Cabernet Birdie had found—"won't even get us through happy hour."

"But it's thirty minutes into town!" Liz exclaimed. "And you've been driving for three hours." Birdie's devotion to drinking bordered on religious. "Let's just skip wine tonight."

"Skip wine?" Birdie made it sound like Liz had suggested they skip Christmas. "Not really an option for me."

Liz raised a deliberate brow, hoping that'd help her sister replay her slightly worrying words. "It's not an option for you not to drink?"

"I need something else," Birdie said, "to get me through this semi-charmed kind of life." She tossed Liz a tin of needlessly expensive cat food. "Give this to Mr. Paws in half an hour. *Don't* put it in the fridge, it *has* to be room temperature."

Liz rolled her eyes. "You realize you treat that cat better than you treat yourself."

"Mr. Paws is the only man I could ever love." Birdie twirled her car keys, already on her way out. "Seriously, no fridge, or I'll be hearing about it for months in therapy."

"Please don't tell me your cat is in therapy when you refuse to go!" Liz called after her.

The only answer was the slam of the front door. Moments later, Ray's engine coughed to life, wheezing up the drive until the sound faded and the house fell quiet.

For a long moment, Liz looked around the large, empty kitchen. It was dark outside, even though it was only five. She should get a head start on sorting the mail. Her mother would appreciate it, or probably even expect it. That was how things went around here. Birdie and Rafi often devolved when returning to Belvedere Inn, regressing into their childhood selves. Not Liz, and she was never quite sure if that was because she was too comfortable being the responsible eldest, or because it was too uncomfortable not to be.

But Liz didn't start on the mail. This was the first relaxed, private moment she'd had since she landed in New

York, and so, Liz tapped open her text thread with Violet. Scrolled to the top, past hundreds of messages, time traveling back to February.

> LIZ: Hi, it's Liz. Looking forward to this afternoon—
> what can I bring?
> VIOLET: Something to go with Sancerre?

Their first one-on-one hang, at Violet's Airbnb, the garden apartment up the road from Liz's bungalow in the hipster neighborhood of Los Feliz. They'd just shot the pilot. Violet had proven to be a versatile, fearless actor who attacked the complex performance required to play identical twins who appeared in multiple scenes together. In Violet's hands, Liz's screenplay, already polished to perfection, became luminescent.

Liz had rung Violet's doorbell at three o'clock on a Sunday afternoon, armed with Castelvetrano olives and the good bread from the good bakery. Violet's backyard was pocket-sized, wind chimes tinkling from the branches of an orange tree. They'd sat underneath it until the moon rose, talking about books and film and music. Their childhoods, their nicknames. Violet was thoughtful, intuitive, and clever. It was pre-crush, pre-feelings. On that mild winter evening, Liz simply felt that she'd finally met a kindred spirit.

Liz scrolled past more messages, landing months later.

> VIOLET: Yo
> LIZ: Yo
> VIOLET: Yooooo
> LIZ: Yooooo

LIZ: What's up?

VIOLET: Nothing, just wanted to say yo.

Sent at a table read when they were waiting on a cast member stuck in traffic. Liz had snort-laughed into her iced coffee and Violet had smirked, pleased.

Liz continued scrolling until she got to August.

VIOLET: This weather 😵 I'm melting like a popsicle.
Any tips on surviving L.A. summer?

LIZ: Gazpacho baths.

VIOLET: Cold . . . baths?

LIZ: Bingo.

VIOLET: 🏠 In other news, the loungers
arrived. The stripes look tres chic 😎

LIZ: That's how we're surviving the summer, babe!

Violet's cute new house in the Hollywood Hills had a gleaming blue pool; Liz had helped pick out the loungers after considerable debate over stripes versus solids.

Another swipe of her thumb brought Liz to their last exchange, sent on the final afternoon of the press junket.

LIZ: LOL. Your fans are . . . a lot.

VIOLET: Strangers are fun!

LIZ: Strangers are fun. 😊
Coming to the dinner tonight?

VIOLET: Come by my room and we'll go together?

Liz had indeed gone to pick up Violet from her room on that warm afternoon, setting into motion the plot twist she hadn't seen coming, and yet maybe had been hoping for all along.

Liz pocketed her phone. Blowing out a breath, she refocused on the task at hand. She wasn't the one who recklessly made out with people she worked with. She was the one who sorted the mail.

To treat herself, Liz cut a big piece of the traditional British Christmas cake her mom's favorite hair stylist sent every year. Sinking her teeth into the brandy-soaked fruitcake slathered with marzipan icing, she was reminded of the pleasures of the season. Liz started sorting everything into piles.

Bills. Local flyers. The first dispatch of holiday cards, sent from a former co-star, Babs's pickleball instructor, and—

Liz froze as if someone had just hit pause on a remote. His name was there, *right there*, before the return address on Long Island. The Hegartys. What the hell?

Liz had just taken a bite of Christmas cake that she now couldn't swallow, letting it fall gracelessly from her mouth to the plate. She shouldn't open the card, yet it was already happening, one shaking finger tearing the heavy envelope's lip.

Liz inhaled a sharp breath. There he was. A smile edging into a smirk, one arm around Melissa, his wellness influencer wife whose personality was her Peloton. It was a punch to the heart to see she was pregnant. Again. Lined up in front of them were their three (three!) towheaded children, nightmare nesting dolls in matching pajamas.

Liz's clutch on the card tightened. Melissa was pregnant *again*? What was she, made of eggs?

Well, he was always going to father a brood, wasn't he?

Noah Hegarty. Her college sweetheart. Her ex-husband. Of course he was still sending Babs a holiday card. He'd always been a bit too enamored with his famous mother-in-law.

Liz hadn't seen a recent picture in years. The fact that Noah had aged reminded Liz she had too. Would this have been her life? Days divided by school drop-offs and pickups, heavy pours with neighbors and proximity friends, dissecting it all afterward in a bed with a tufted headboard? Liz imagined her face superimposed on Melissa's, the weight of Noah's arm on her shoulders, the children's hair not blond but dark brown like her own. Wrongness twisted inside her, slithering snakelike. A horror-show supercut burst into her mind—the exhausting, escalating fights with the man she no longer recognized. Having to tell her family, her friends, a thousand institutions: *It's over.* The unbearable silence of the Clinton Hill apartment after he left, the home that transformed from a place of hope into an interactive scrapbook of painful memories. Seeing a sentimental ad for home insurance and crying. Hearing any song with the word *miss* in the title and crying. Thinking about their honeymoon in Paris/their inside joke about dog parks/an overly zealous purchase of a newborn onesie and crying. The way her life became a cruel trick mirror. The way she lost everything.

After months of stasis post-breakup, Liz had fled New York for L.A., throwing herself into work and never telling anyone the impetus behind her life pivot. Not even Violet knew the full story.

Liz tossed the card on the kitchen island, distraught at the memories it'd churned up. Mending her pulverized heart had felt like trying to fix a can of crushed tomatoes. In her darkest moments, she wondered if she'd done such a bad job that it wouldn't work the same ever again.

This was why she couldn't think about Vi as anything

other than a co-worker. A co-worker Liz had one minor slipup with because they were in Rome and the entire city was a sexy booby trap. It happened, but it wouldn't happen again. Tomorrow she'd send a text—no, an *email*, with Cat cc'd—congratulating Violet on her *Elle* cover, rebuilding a rock-solid professional boundary between herself and her lead actor. A boundary that'd keep her heart safe and her sanity intact.

For now, she'd do what her mother had obviously been doing for years and bury Noah's card in the recycling, never to be discussed or thought of again.

Forget the cake. Birdie was right; it was definitely time for a big glass of wine.

6.

$\mathcal{B}$IRDIE WAS WHISTLING WHEN SHE LEFT THE WINE STORE, a spring in her step despite the evening chill. The staff inside had greeted her by name *and* she was able to put six bottles of the good stuff on her mother's account. Things were looking up! The insurmountable problems of this morning now seemed entirely surmountable.

The busy crunchy-granola town was centered around a few main streets lined with quirky boutiques, cozy cafes, and chichi general stores, most with hand-painted signs. It wasn't technically *home*—her mother and Rafi had moved up after Birdie was already living in Brooklyn to pursue a career in comedy and kissing. But considering she'd been visiting several times a year since then, being in Woodstock felt like wearing a favorite sweatshirt, with exactly zero ex-managers or former one-night stands to kill the vibe.

Birdie was putting the wine in Ray's back seat when a gathering across the street caught her eye. Woodstock Art, one of the local galleries, looked like it was hosting a party or an opening. The sign out front declared FREE MULLED WINE!

Birdie loved community events and spontaneous plans and, most of all, free wine. After all, it was Christmas! Not for another twenty-three days, but Birdie would absolutely be using this excuse to do just about anything for the rest of the month.

Inside, many of the attendees were older, close to her

mom's age—women with "fun" earrings, men with leather bolos who looked lightly stoned. There'd famously been an influx of Brooklynites moving upstate for whom art and wine were obviously a draw. Much of the crowd wouldn't look out of place at a Bushwick poetry slam. Ironic stick-and-poke tats? Check. Flawless ombré locs? Check. Gender-nonconforming progressives who were passionate about composting? Sweet bébé Jesus, *check*.

"It's the simplicity for me," Birdie overheard Flawless Ombré Locs say to the person next to them. "The negative space, the austere aesthetic. Jacob's a master of what's un-said."

"Mmm," agreed the friend. "Yes, *exactly*."

Birdie sipped her mulled wine, which was delicious, as she examined the paintings. Thick black strokes on raw canvas. The kind of thing a billionaire might have hanging in a loft the size of Delaware. Was it any good? Birdie had no idea. She liked art but would never pretend to "get it" any more than she understood state taxes or NFTs.

Her phone pinged. Liz, texting her a picture of their mother's vintage-sexy 1983 *Playboy* cover in the downstairs guest bathroom. Terrifying. Birdie thumbed a reply—Hello doctor? I need to remove both my eyes.

A droll female voice sounded next to her. "The art's on the walls, you know."

Birdie huffed a laugh and looked up. The chatter and movement around her seemed to fade away.

It wasn't just that the woman standing next to her was beautiful: tall and long-limbed in a white men's button-down belted as a dress and thigh-high cream boots that looked in-credibly hot against her brown skin. And it wasn't just that she was clearly a badass, with her gold septum piercing and her shaved head that was somehow the most elegant haircut of everyone in the gallery. This person glowed, like a house decked out with non-tacky Christmas lights.

"Hi." Birdie pocketed her phone. "It's me. I'm the problem, it's me."

Sexy Head's lips twitched with cautious amusement. "Someone said you're a comedian. I guess they were right?"

Sexy Head had been *asking about her*? A Christmukkah miracle! Birdie turned on the full Belvedere charm. "I'm Birdie, and I am a comedian, sadly. I'd describe my personality as a mix of narcissism and crippling self-doubt, but I am fun at parties. I'm very into *The Great British Baking Show*, my cat, and breakfast. Wow, you really have a way of getting people to open up."

Sexy Head rewarded all this with a half smile. Her eyes were licked with liner in a way Birdie was incapable of executing but always appreciated. "Favorite breakfast food?" the woman asked.

"Bacon."

"Perfectly cooked or burnt to a crisp?"

"Ah, trick question. Burnt to a crisp *is* perfectly cooked."

Like it was a secret: "Bacon is also my favorite breakfast food."

"Should we start a podcast?" Birdie phrased her question like it was obvious they must.

Sexy Head laughed, a real laugh, and the sound was like a glitter gun going off in Birdie's heart. "Sure," she said. "Humorous self-care or grisly murder-of-the-week?"

"Let's mash it up," Birdie riffed. "*Massage Oil and Massacres. Death and a Long, Hot Bath.*"

Every laugh was a good one. But amusing this attractive stranger felt better than any laugh Birdie had gotten in months.

Sexy Head nodded at the paintings and lowered her voice. "So. What do you think of the art?" She phrased it as if she found all of this a bit pretentious and definitely not worth whatever insane price tag Jacob was charging.

Birdie told the truth. "I don't get art."

"Oh c'mon." Sexy Head nudged Birdie's ribs. "What's your first impression?"

Birdie was nothing if not a master of reading the room. Obviously, this divine being who radiated a self-realization Birdie would never achieve wanted her to snark on the art. Bond over being snobby contrarians. Something Birdie was 100 percent capable of. She edged closer, speaking as co-conspirators. "Let's not kid ourselves. Art is a scam."

Sexy Head's eyes widened, scandalized. "What sort of scam?"

"The kind where anyone can slap some paint on a canvas and charge a million bucks for it. It's giving Theranos, it's giving Ponzi! Art is actually the greatest con of all."

"At this point—" Sexy Head started.

"A rich man's racket, a sexy swindle," Birdie went on, gesturing at the bold brushstrokes of the painting in front of them. "My *cat* could pull this off." She scanned the crowd. "Jacob is probably some douche in a beret who thinks that—"

The woman cut her off, speaking rapid-fire. "At this point I should tell you that this is my show."

Record scratch. Birdie froze, mouth hanging open. "Wait, what?"

"Jecka Jacob." Sexy Head indicated some words stenciled on the far wall.

IT'S NOT BLACK & WHITE BY JECKA JACOB.

The wooden floorboards beneath Birdie's feet seemed to warp. She only half heard someone in a floating dress offer a *Hey, Jecka, great stuff.*

Birdie's mouth was dry, her mind tripping over the insane things she'd just said. *Art is a scam. A rich man's racket. Jacob is probably some douche in a beret.* "I didn't know. I didn't mean that. I said all that to impress you."

Jecka looked incredulous. "You told me your cat could 'pull this off' to *impress* me?"

OH FUCK. All caps, neon bright. Birdie shook her head so frantically it threatened to pop off. "I didn't mean that! I was just trying to be funny!" Nothing mattered except Jecka understanding she'd been kidding. "I love your paintings. My cat could never get on your level."

"For a comedian, I think your material could use some work." Jecka's face was stuck somewhere between amazement and disbelief. "I'm getting a drink. It was very . . . weird to meet you."

"No, wait!" Birdie lurched forward.

It happened in slow motion. The mulled wine still in Birdie's grip arced up and out of her plastic cup. The graceful crimson wave sailed through the air before hitting the canvas they'd been standing in front of. The tossed wine seeped into the canvas, running in rivulets toward the floor. Jecka's black-and-white painting now featured a third color.

The gallery became pin-drop silent. Not hushed. Not briefly muted. Violently still.

Birdie didn't need to look around to know everyone was staring at her with the horror she was feeling one hundred-fold. There had been nightmare silences before. Onstage, after the audience had turned against her for any number of reasons (too confident, not confident enough, too vulgar, too coy). The silence every time her deadbeat director dad stood her up, let her down, made her feel like an inconvenience. But this silence was different. This silence was worse. A bad joke was one thing. Destroying someone's artwork was unforgivable. It was immoral.

Birdie was panting, her gaze ricocheting from the cup to the canvas to the artist, the cup, the canvas, the artist.

Jecka looked on the brink of hysterical tears. Or the swift and effective firing of an artillery of expletives. Then her expression relaxed. Jecka started clapping. Cheering, like her team had just scored the winning goal.

"Congratulations, Birdie," Jecka announced to the entire gallery. "You just bought the first painting."

Birdie's gaze landed on the informational placard next to the artwork. The price tag of her accidental new purchase? Eleven thousand dollars.

7.

*

 IFTY-TWO MINUTES LATER, BIRDIE WAS BACK HOME WITH
Liz at Belvedere Inn, tucked into the enormous squishy sectional in the family room, steaming bowls of mac and cheese
balanced in their laps. A fire crackled in the stone hearth opposite them, filling the room with warmth and a hint of
woodsmoke. Over the speakers, Ella Fitzgerald crooned
"Baby, It's Cold Outside" in her silvery, sultry voice.

In between forkfuls of cheesy noodles, Birdie recounted
Winegate to her sister. The floaty-freaky panic of the gallery
was starting to dissipate, but Birdie was still struggling to
understand the cost, which she'd only been able to cover by
maxing out all three of her credit cards. "Is it legal to charge
that much for a painting?"

"I don't understand." Liz blinked in slow motion, chewing
a noodle. "Why did you tell her that her art was a scam?"

"Because I didn't know she was the artist!" Birdie exclaimed, hating herself. "I was shooting my mouth off, trying
to be 'funny,' when instead I was exposing myself as a total
loser who has no business co-existing with cool artists with
shaved heads!" She rubbed at her chest, trying to alleviate
the pain in her heart. "Feeling this bad is giving me major
Stanley flashbacks."

Stanley Green, Birdie's biological father, Babs's second
husband, wasn't about to win any Father of the Year awards.

Not only because he was dead. Stanley's emotional negligence had always cut Birdie the deepest.

"Where is it?" Liz asked. "The painting."

"She's dropping it off sometime this week." Birdie let out a groan. "How am I going to make this right *and* scrounge together eleven grand?"

Liz slurped some wine. "How much do you usually make at a show?"

"Fifty bucks. Or just drink tickets."

"I think I've figured out the flaw in your business plan, Squeakie," Liz said, giggling.

Her sister sounded tipsy. Birdie peered at her. "How many glasses of wine have you had, Liz Fizz?"

"Two," Liz replied, indignant, before frowning, unsure. "Maybe three."

Birdie's smile was fond. "You are such a lightweight. Okay, what gives?"

"What d'you mean?"

"I mean, you're toastier than a freaking Pop-Tart and you only drink alone when something's wrong. What is it?"

Liz covered her face. "Nothing."

Birdie put their bowls aside, prying her sister's fingers away and hazarding her best guess. "Is this about your writer's block?"

Her big sister's voice came out the size of a single macaroni. "Sort of?"

Remembering the way Liz had glitched at seeing the *Sweet* billboard on the ride up, Birdie guessed again, "Is this about . . . Violet?"

At the sound of her name, Liz bit her lip until it turned white, looking away. Liz Belvedere didn't just keep her cards close to her chest. They were vacuum-sealed in a locked box, inside a vault, inside Fort Knox. Birdie only found out Liz had dated a woman a few years ago *after it ended*.

Birdie understood that this situation—whatever it was—was delicate. Top of a crème brûlée delicate. Tiny tap: "Do you have a crush on Violet?"

"I can't tell you," Liz whispered.

"You can tell me anything." Birdie patted her sister's thigh. "We have sister-sister confidentiality, and that will stand up in a court of law, maybe."

A tight, shuddery breath and then: "I—*we* . . . crossed a line."

"You hooked up with Violet?" Birdie couldn't keep the surprise—and, frankly, admiration—out of her voice. "I didn't know she was a lady of the labia."

"She dated girls in Portland, before she moved to L.A. It's not a secret, it's on the internet." Her sister was vibrating with queer drama—Dickinson, Colette. "We've become sort of . . . close."

"Ladies who lunch?" Birdie guessed. "Or ladies who text each other every hour and wear each other's denim overalls—that 'sort of close'?"

Liz blew out a breath. "The latter."

"The classic obsessive friendship." Birdie nodded in understanding. "How I've bed many a lover."

Liz's expression was tortured. "It was the last day of the press junket, in Rome. We were alone, at the hotel, and somehow . . ."

Birdie leaned forward. "Somehow?"

"Somehow, we . . . kissed."

Birdie inhaled theatrically, shoving her sister's shoulder. "Mamma *mia*! You *necked*?!"

"Just once. One kiss." Her sister's eyes went dreamy, lost

in the memory before snapping back to reality. "I haven't spoken to her since." Liz's skin had paled, but her eyes burned with intensity. "I don't know what to do."

If this was how a crush was supposed to feel, Birdie definitely felt like she was doing them wrong. "And that's all that's happened? *One* kiss? You haven't taken V.G. to pound town? Thrown your hot dog down her hallway?"

Liz's eyes went wide. "No! Of course not!"

"Why not?"

"It's not professional." Liz flapped her hands around, looking like she was literally grasping at straws. "I have to set a good example."

"For who?"

"Just . . . everyone!"

Ah, Liz. Forever the perfect student even when school was long done. This "professional" argument was as flimsy as a spring break bikini, and Birdie wasn't buying it. "Isn't getting down with a stone-cold fox in Italy setting the *best* example?"

Liz let out a frustrated breath. She ducked her eyes to the carpet. "Vi's twenty-seven. Ten years younger than me."

At this, Birdie actually laughed. "Um, Ellen and Portia," she said. "Olivia Wilde and Harry Styles, never forget. Also, pretty sure if you were a straight guy in Hollywood, you wouldn't legally be allowed to date anyone *less* than a decade younger than you. A ten-year difference, at your age, definitely isn't a thing." Birdie had met Violet at a group dinner when visiting Liz in L.A. this past summer. Violet and Liz had seemed close—inside jokes, a subtle codependence—but Birdie's gaydar had not been activated. Maybe Violet was as skilled as Liz at hiding her feelings. "Wait—do you actually want to *date* Violet?"

"It doesn't matter what I want!"

Birdie had long maintained that "type A" stood for "type anal" (not the fun kind), but this was a new level of ludicrous. "Riddle me this, Batgirl: Have you porked anyone at work before?"

Liz looked offended. "No."

"If it didn't work out, would you treat Violet like shit? Get her written off the show, generally be a massive dick?"

"Birds." Liz made a disgusted face. "Of course not. But—"

"But nothing!" Birdie took her sister's hands, making her voice as earnest as possible. "Since you bounced to L.A., you've been crushing this TV stuff. And from the sound of it, you *really* like this chick, hashtag Roman-Holiday, hashtag Italy-is-for-lovers. You can have both! What am I missing here?" Birdie pushed. "Not to sound too woo-woo, but why are you getting in the way of your own happiness, blah blah blah chakras?"

Her sister refused to meet Birdie's eye.

"Liz?" Birdie prompted softly. "What are you not telling me?"

Liz let out a long, broken sigh. "It's too much. The idea of being hurt again. After everything with . . . Noah."

Okay, Liz was definitely drunk, because she *never* brought up her ex-husband. Of course Liz was nervous to date again—her divorce era had been extremely painful to witness, let alone live through, especially for someone who craved stability and routine. Birdie's heart squished like a lemon in a lemon squeezer. "I hear you," she said, gentling her voice. "Noah the Fuckface can suck my dick forever. I know I'm not the pinup girl for romance or good decisions, but I think trying something with Violet is worth the risk if you're, y'know . . ."

Liz stared back blankly.

It seemed so obvious. Her big sister was never this worked up. ". . . if you're in love," Birdie finished.

Liz spluttered into a strangled coughing fit, face blooming Christmas-cracker red. "In love? *In love?* She hasn't spoken to me for two weeks!"

"I thought you hadn't spoken to her."

"I don't know!" Liz flung up her hands. "You saw how long it took me to get over Noah. *So* much therapy, *so* much work. And I'm happy now, finally! I can't throw it all away to become a footnote in Vi's life! I need to protect my own happiness, and so it's. Not. Happening."

There was a noise. From inside the house, maybe the foyer. A muffled *thunk*.

The sisters whipped their heads toward the front door. Liz's voice was low. "What was that?"

Birdie didn't reply, her senses sharpening. The only sound was the ticking second hand of the retro black-and-white Kit-Cat Clock hanging in the far corner. "Hello?" Birdie called.

The nothing they heard now sounded ominous.

Liz kept her voice quiet. "Did you lock the front door?"

Birdie couldn't remember; she'd been so distracted by the gallery drama. Sweet bébé Jesus: What if one of her mother's insane fans had wandered in again, an occurrence Babs was far too forgiving of? Or a raccoon? Those things could get vicious.

Birdie slipped off the sofa, extracting an iron poker from the set of tools by the fireplace.

"What are you going to do with that?" Liz whispered.

Birdie sliced the poker through the air, narrowly avoiding knocking over a vase. "What are *you* going to do with *that*?"

Liz mimed stabbing someone with the fork in her hand.

"Perfect," Birdie whispered back. "Saved by the world's tiniest pitchfork."

They crept through the kitchen, toward the foyer, ready for a horror-movie jump scare. The front door was open.

Birdie rushed into the foyer with a "Gahhh!"

Someone spun around and yelled in fright.

Liz yelled. Birdie yelled. They were all yelling until Birdie recognized the man with the mop of dark curls and light purple hoodie. "*Rafi?*"

He pulled an earbud from his ear, spilling Adele's "Someone Like You." He gaped at Birdie, then at Liz. "What the hell are you doing here?"

They gaped back. Rafi's big brown eyes were wet and wild. A five o'clock shadow stubbled his boyish face.

"What the hell are *you* doing here?" Birdie parroted back. "Why do you look like the downfall of society?"

"Why aren't you in Philly?" Liz followed up.

Rafi wiped his nose with the sleeve of his hoodie, his expression stunned. "I just detonated my entire life."

8.

IN RETROSPECT, RAFI REALIZED, IT WAS OBVIOUS.

When Sunita said she didn't want to label their relationship, Rafi thought she was modern and progressive: a warrior against gender norms and patriarchal bullshit. But now he understood the whole thing was as casual as a summer Friday. He'd mistaken a grab bag of good emotions—pleasure, attraction, respect—for true love. And it hadn't been the first time.

"This is like what happened with Jia." Rafi jammed the palms of his hands into his eye sockets, wishing he could unsee the memory of getting a spontaneous tattoo of the word *Hope* with his college girlfriend. A week later, Jia had broken up with him. *Hope* still sprang eternal on Rafi's left butt cheek. "And Axel." Rafi's first and only boyfriend, an emotionally unavailable German musician with preternaturally beautiful hair whom Rafi fell hard for two summers ago.

"Ah yes," Birdie recalled. The siblings were settled back on the family room sectional. "Your Eurotrash moment. Whatever happened to axman Axel?"

"Axman Axel broke up with me before moving back to Germany," Rafi reminded her. "I flew to Berlin, where he broke up with me *again*. I was so sure we'd get back together I hadn't bought a ticket home. I had to crash at his loft while I figured it out. *For a week.*"

Birdie let out a whistle, speaking in a German accent. "Das is way harsh."

"Did you go into work today?" Liz said from the other side of the sofa, cradling a very full glass of wine. "Was it excruciating?"

"I called in sick." Rafi slumped farther into the couch. "My manager said I could do the next few weeks virtually. So I bid farewell to the last scraps of my dignity and fled."

"Oh, Raf." Liz reached over to squeeze his leg. "Baby boy."

Being the baby of the family was a role Rafi typically leaned in to. But right now, the word, and its implicit condescension, irritated him. Jesus, he was almost *thirty*.

He couldn't relax, still shimmering with anxiety, and regret, and, frankly, astonishment. Why had he *proposed*? How could something that felt so right turn out to be so wrong?

"I feel like an idiot," Rafi admitted, breaking off some ginger milk chocolate from a block Birdie offered. "I obviously don't get how love works at all."

"Well, you know how getting dumped works," Birdie drawled. "You're an expert in that. You could teach a course."

"Birdie," Liz chided, folding back a smile.

"No, she's right." Rafi couldn't even summon outrage at his sister's needling. "Christmas, obviously, is ruined."

"Hear, hear." Birdie raised her glass in solidarity. "Christmas is the takeout container left in the fridge so long it's become sentient. Christmas is the moment you realize you sat in fresh gum. Christmas is the bad reboot no one asked for, with none of the original cast, and it's not getting a theatrical release, it's going straight to Crackle."

"Crackle?" Liz winced. "Brutal."

Rafi managed a smile. Despite them giving him shit, he

was grateful his sisters had also come up early to Belvedere Inn. Even though they were all technically half-siblings, they'd grown up together. The half was never considered.

Liz nudged Rafi with a socked foot. "We'll get Christmas back on track for you."

But how would he get his life back on track? A log in the fire shifted, sending up a spray of sparks. Bright as the diamond ring he would have to return.

Rafi let his head fall back against the couch cushions. "How did I misread it so badly? This is, like, Four-Seasons-Total-Landscaping-press-conference bad."

Birdie high-fived him for the deep cut. "You've always wanted to get hitched. You've been talking about settling down since college, which is actually not normal." His sister recrossed her legs on the sofa. "I'm sorry about Sunita, I liked her. Unexpected upside: she lent me fifty bucks, which I might not have to pay back."

Liz gave Rafi a horrified smile, which he barely managed to return. It was true he'd always wanted to get married. But was Birdie right? Was it normal to have such a single-minded focus on settling down?

"Once you're ready to get past all this," Birdie went on, "you'll see there are plenty more crustaceans at the seafood buffet."

"No." Rafi felt certain. "I am off love for the next . . . I don't know, but definitely for the holidays. Maybe all next year. I need to stop falling for people so quickly, and start seeing things *clearly*. No love for me."

"Me too." Birdie broke off another piece of chocolate. "Why do I keep doing things that confirm everyone's worst suspicions of me? I'm like Amy Winehouse circa 2010."

"I'm off love too," Liz announced in a too-loud voice. "I need to focus on work. *Writing*, not . . . anything else. No love for me."

Birdie snapped her fingers. "Black Hearts Club!" Then, seeing her siblings' stares, she said, "This year's club. *Obviously.*"

Every year, the siblings invented a new club name over the holidays, themed to whatever serious or stupid thing was front of mind. It'd started when they were kids. A producer on one of Babs's films had made them all T-shirts for the When's Lunch? Club, inspired by their singular devotion to that question when on set. In recent years, there'd been the More Negronis Club, the No More Negronis Club, the Our Mother Is Totally Fucking Nuts Club. "Club meetings" took place in the wine cellar on the basement level and were just an excuse to drink wine and talk about whatever was *really* going on.

"Black Hearts Club." Liz already had her phone out, changing their group text name from last year's inside joke: Justice for Mrs. Claus Club. "Done."

EVENTUALLY, THE BLACK HEARTS CLUB dispersed to their bedrooms. Uncharacteristically quiet, the house felt like an unpopulated luxury hotel—its own kind of holiday miracle.

Babs had redesigned Rafi's bedroom in a Swiss chalet style after he moved out. The ceiling was crossed with raw wood beams. Red plaid blankets were folded on the backs of two deep-seated leather club chairs. The supremely comfortable chairs faced the unlit fireplace, original stone from the Inn's first life, just like in the family room. Royalty checks from Babs's biographies had funded her upgrade of Rafi's childhood bed to a plush king, fitted with soft jersey sheets and a down comforter.

Rafi put his suitcase in the corner, taking in every inch of his old bedroom. Everything was exactly the same as the last time he was here. Ordinarily, the consistency was comforting. Now the familiarity gave him the uneasy sense of being trapped and never-changing. Doomed to keep repeating the same mistakes.

He ran a fingertip over the framed photographs on the mantel.

Rafi and his sisters lying on their bellies in Central Park, sunburned and grinning.

Graduation day at Georgetown, Rafi laughing, maybe even handsome, in a cap and gown.

He and Ash, arms slung around each other on a beach in Mexico, barely twenty-one. Ash's hair was an overgrown mess, his cheap glasses slipping down chubby cheeks.

And on the far end of the mantel, the faded color photograph of a young Indian man leaning against a motorbike, arms crossed, face in profile. Nikhil Daruwala had been younger than Rafi was now when he'd worked as a stuntman on *The War of My Heart*. The mid-nineties war epic ultimately won Babs an Oscar, pulling her out of a mid-career slump. The story centered around a plucky American reporter (Babs) who falls for a noble Indian general, set against the backdrop of India's independence from British rule. Babs had snuck beautiful, cocksure Nikhil into her hotel room only a handful of times during location shooting in Mumbai. Despite being on the pill, she got pregnant. Nikhil, who still lived with his parents, was horrified at the news. He quickly signed the paperwork awarding Babs full custody. He kept apologizing, saying he was too young to become a father—he was only twenty-two. His parents could never find out.

Babs told the world she'd decided to get pregnant a third time, and, since she was single (twice-divorced by now), a friend had donated the sperm—a friend whose privacy would be protected. And it was. Babs never told anyone the truth outside her inner circle.

His father's identity was never a secret to Rafi or his sisters. Babs had repeated the whole story from such a young age it felt like something he always knew. The way he felt about it, however, changed over time.

Babs took the task of raising a half-Indian son extremely seriously. The entire family celebrated Diwali, made home-made curries, and got season passes for South Asian film festivals. Rafi's early memories were positive—the difference between him and his sisters felt like a good thing; he was special. But as he got older, his identity started to feel more complex. Difference wasn't always a good thing, even in New York City. He was teased. Then bullied. Most of his classmates in his Soho middle school didn't look like him, and most had fathers—his sisters certainly did. Rafi felt suspended between two worlds—his white mother and sisters in New York City, and his Indian side—never fully embraced by either.

The desire to connect with his biological father, to understand who he really was, erupted in his mid-teens. His family would never understand him—he barely understood himself, and that was *their* fault, specifically his mother's. All of the cooking and film festivals and observance of Indian holidays seemed like a gross approximation of a true connection to culture, a tone-deaf colonialist charade that meant absolutely nothing. He began feeling a persistent, anxious responsibility to fully embrace his Indian identity, but he didn't know how, or even what that really meant. A difficult year as a nineteen-year-old prompted a much-anticipated visit to Mumbai to finally meet Nikhil in person.

The whole family and Ash traveled with him for support. Rafi was preparing for a transcendental moment that would finally click his identity into place. He couldn't sleep for a week leading up to it, imagining good tears, bad tears, something explosive, something that would change *everything*. But when Nikhil sat opposite him in the restaurant of Rafi's hotel on that humid morning in June, Rafi's racing heart started to slow. His biological father was nervous but kind, and made an effort to be interested. But he was clearly out of his depth. They didn't have a lot in common. Nikhil had never married, so there were no half-siblings to meet, and the photos of his nieces and nephews didn't stir much in Rafi's chest. They were all strangers. The whole thing was oddly underwhelming.

The trip did deepen Rafi's relationship with Nikhil—they began talking every year on Rafi's birthday in January and exchanged the occasional letter. But Rafi stopped feeling a need to "be more Indian": his experience as an Indian American boy growing up in a white family, without a father, was valid in its own right. Then, in college, when Rafi realized he liked boys as well as girls, he became focused on an entirely different journey of self-discovery, finding community with other queer people of color. Now, at twenty-nine, he felt comfortable inhabiting both his biraciality and his bisexuality. What he didn't feel comfortable with was this feeling that his life hadn't yet begun, and he didn't know how to get it started—like Birdie said, he seemed to know only how to get dumped.

Rafi washed up and got into bed, trying to relax. His sisters had helped, but there was only one person who could give the emotional support he needed.

He tapped open his phone and FaceTimed Ash. A pleasurable crunch of anticipation squeezed Rafi's midriff.

And then there, on the small screen, was Asher Sebastian Campbell. No bad haircut, no cheap glasses—Ash had Lasik after he moved to the UK. But his eyes were the same. A warm, butterscotch brown. "Raf?" Ash croaked. "What time is it?"

"Oh shit, sorry," Rafi said, checking the clock. It was 1:00 A.M. Which made it 6:00 A.M. in London. "Should I call back?"

"S'okay." Ash yawned, glancing offscreen. "What—did you just get home from your Christmas party? How was it?"

"No, that was two nights ago, and it was very bad." Here goes nothing. "I asked Sunita to marry me in front of everyone we work with but she said no and then she dumped me."

"*What?*" Ash floundered upright so fast he lost his balance and promptly fell out of bed.

"Ash?" The screen was dark, the phone tangled in sheets.

There was some muffled cursing and then another voice, male with a British accent, asking what the bloody hell was going on.

Great: he'd woken not only Ash, but whomever he'd brought home. Vaguely humiliating that while Rafi had been driving the three and a half hours to the Catskills while tearfully listening to Adele, Ash had been getting his dick sucked by some cryptocurrency journalist who was into Proust, or whatever. Ash's cool new life made Rafi seesaw between being absolutely thrilled for *London Man*'s style editor and desperately missing the boy he used to roam the woods with.

A minute later, Ash was pulling on a T-shirt and sinking

to the floor of his flat's small bathroom, listening to Rafi re-count the whole excruciating scene. "So there I am, asking Sunita for her hand in marriage, and she's looking at me like I'm holding a gun to her head."

"Oh no." Ash was half cringing, half laughing. "Oh, Raf."

Rafi dropped his head into his hand. "I'm never going to trust my stupid heart again."

"Hey, your heart is not stupid." Ash's voice was deep and soothing in the way of a good radio host. "Nothing about you is stupid. You're emotional and imaginative and an optimist. You're thriving!" He frowned, puckering his full lips. "Well, maybe you're not thriving right now."

"I'm definitely not thriving right now!" Rafi almost had the urge to laugh. If only he could Command-Z undo the last forty-eight hours. "I don't know how I misread everything. Why I even did it in the first place. I . . . I wanted it so badly, but *it* wasn't marriage to Sunita."

"What was it, then?"

"I don't know." He couldn't articulate this disorienting longing and itchy dissatisfaction he was suddenly feeling. Or, had been feeling for a while and was only acknowledging now. "I just want my real life to start. Even though I know this *is* my real life. I have a job, an apartment, friends. This is it. But it doesn't feel totally right. Maybe this isn't where I'm meant to be. Maybe this isn't what I'm meant to be doing."

Ash's face crumpled in empathy. "I wish I could give you a hug right now."

"I need one. I've just been dumped! Again!" Rafi snuggled farther into the sheets, gaze not straying from Ash-in-miniature on his phone. "How is it you've never once been in this position? Getting your heart squashed like a cockroach?"

Ash considered the question. He tended to do that:

thoughtfully process anything that fell out of Rafi's mouth. "I guess I keep it simple."

"How?"

"I have boundaries. I keep a balance."

"I literally have zero idea how to do that."

It was painfully ironic that Rafi wanted a partner and couldn't find one, while ambivalent Ash always had some guy on the periphery. Ash had gotten a fair amount of play before leaving the States, but London Ash appeared to be, as Birdie once tastelessly put it, *freestyling through a swimming pool of cock.*

Ash let his head rest against the Turkish hand towel hanging behind him, his broad shoulders relaxing. "Oh, Raf Attack." His pet name since childhood. "What are we going to do with you?"

"Nothing. I'll survive." Rafi didn't want the pity party to go all night. Or all morning. "What about you? Do you want to go back to bed or tell me about who's in it?"

Ash laughed, pushing a hand through his hair. Unlike Rafi's looping curls, Ash's dark gold hair had only the slightest wave to it. "No one special. But I do have some work fuckery I need your emotionally intelligent take on."

The conversation shifted onto Ash's difficult new editor in chief. Ash was better at his job as a thinking man's fashion writer than he was at workplace politics, and so they spent a few minutes brainstorming how to respond to his boss's mood swings. Rafi's natural empathy made him able to see both sides of the story, and his customer service experience made him good at expressing those ideas with sensitivity. He offered to write up some suggestions and send them through in the morning.

"Thanks man." Ash smiled at him.

"Anytime. Wish you were here." He sat up, hopeful. "Any chance you're coming home for the holidays?"

Ash hesitated. "I was going to stay here."

"Again?" Rafi said. "But—"

A deep voice cut in from the other side of the bathroom door. "Hey mate. Got any coffee?"

Ash glanced away from the screen. "Yeah, there's a French press on the counter."

Envy spread like an inkblot in Rafi's stomach. How badly he wanted to be making that French press and having this conversation in person, not three and a half thousand miles apart.

Ash refocused on their FaceTime. "Sorry. What was I saying?"

"You have to come back sometime. You're not still getting settled; it's been two years. I miss you. My family misses you." Rafi hesitated. "And there are other, um, things you could do?"

Ash stiffened, his eyes flashing hotly to the screen. "What things?"

Things like visiting your dad's grave? were the words Rafi didn't say. Ash's father, Willie Campbell, had died of a heart attack five months after Ash moved overseas. They had not been close, the relationship had always been difficult, but everyone was surprised when Ash didn't come back for the funeral. The only people gathered around Willie's gravestone on that blustery day were a local chaplain, a few of Willie's drinking buddies, plus Rafi, Babs, and Birdie. Ash never even asked about it. It was the one thing they just didn't talk about.

Rafi was not about to rip open that hornet's nest now. He'd made enough mistakes for one week.

"Just our holiday traditions," he pivoted. "Scrabble and snowball fights. Buying a tree. Our double feature." *Die Hard* and *Gremlins*, the best alt-Christmas movies of all time, watched back-to-back each year.

Ash promised he'd think about it, but he sounded non-committal. They said their goodbyes, then the room went quiet. It felt so much emptier without Ash in it.

Deep in his gut, Rafi feared that Ash would never come back. That slowly, in a way imperceptible to the human eye, he was fading away, until one day he'd be gone for good, his memory relegated to photos above the mantel, sun-faded images of a boy Rafi used to know. The disturbing idea only increased the disorienting wrongness of the last forty-eight hours.

It was cold in the bedroom. Rafi switched off the bedside light, burrowing deep under his covers. Hopefully, when he woke up, things would be calmer.

9.

Twenty-two days till Christmas

✳

THE NEXT MORNING, LIZ WAS ATTEMPTING TO WORK IN HER bedroom when a scream ripped through the Inn. Ordinarily, a bloodcurdling yell would be cause for alarm. But in the Belvedere household, it was just Tuesday.

"Are all my children home at once?"

They came home every year, and Liz'd already told her mother that she and Birdie were heading up early. But Babs Belvedere liked to make an entrance.

Liz and her siblings emerged from their respective bedrooms, responding to the maternal foghorn.

In the downstairs foyer, reflected by three different mirrors, Babs stood, arms outstretched to receive them, while her three fluffy Pomeranians, Huey, Dewey, and Louie, yapped with excitement. Their mother's short, trim stature was contained in a robin's-egg-blue jumpsuit. Her strawberry-blond hair was styled in soft, short curls, and she was wearing a full face of makeup. Distressingly put together for 9:00 A.M.

Liz stepped around the dogs to give the six-armed family clump a hug. "Hi, Mom. Welcome home."

"My *kids*." Babs breathed them in. "My *loves*. I've said it before and I'll say it again—"

"Here we go." Liz grimaced.

"—you were worth the seventy hours of labor." The oft-repeated tally for all three. Over their rising protests, Babs continued, "You ripped up my pelvic floor like unlicensed contractors and turned my vagina into the size of a wedding tent, but I have no regrets."

"Ma!" Birdie shouted, untangling herself and heading for the kitchen. "We're pre-coffee!"

Babs cupped Rafi's chin with a jeweled hand, giving him the tender smile reserved for her youngest. "Why'd you come up so early, hon?" Then, taking in the dark circles and glum expression: "Baby boy, what's wrong?"

He scowled, jamming his fists into his pajama bottom pockets. "Sunita dumped me."

Babs gasped. "No! I never liked her! When? Why?"

"Tell you later," he mumbled, trailing after Birdie.

Babs looked to Liz, her performativity mellowing into concern. "Was it bad?"

"Let's just say it made Big standing Carrie up at their library wedding look like a fun excuse to get dressed up." They were both devotees of the franchise. "So, what were you doing in Connecticut?"

Babs's eyes drifted to a mirror and she patted her hair. "Well, if you lot are here early, we should probably call Siouxsie."

Siouxsie was the local chef who'd catered dinners for the family since Babs moved to the area. Food was a focus of the Belvedere holiday season.

"I already have." Liz did not miss that her mother avoided

her question. "She can't start till tomorrow night, so I put in a grocery order that'll be here by lunch." Liz had been up for hours. Indicating the eye-catching arrangement on a side table, she went on. "The flowers are from Henry and Gorman—I've already sent a thank-you card. Laundry's done, guest bathrooms are clean, and the thermostat is set to sixty-eight."

"My Liz." Babs gave Liz an approving nod, leaning forward for a hug. "I can always count on you."

Liz hugged her mother back. They didn't have an overly affectionate relationship, but whenever Liz took on responsibilities, Babs rewarded her with the praise and affection that still had the power to light Liz up.

They broke apart. Babs reached for something leaning against the entrance table. A shiny black cane with an elegant, etched gold handle. A very expensive-looking *cane*.

"Rolled my ankle." Babs answered Liz's unasked question. "Promo shoot for season five had me in six-inch stilettos and down I went."

Shock pitched into Liz's chest. "What were they doing putting you in *stilettos* at your age?"

Babs shrugged airily. "You've seen the show. Crystal *treadmills* in stilettos."

Four years ago, Babs had been cast as scheming matriarch Crystal Palace in the pitch-black ensemble comedy *Palace People*. The show was a fast-paced satire centered around a dysfunctional family of corrupt New York real estate moguls. The cast was stacked: Babs's three terrible stepchildren were played by John Early, Phoebe Robinson, and Florence Pugh. Crystal's devastating put-downs were the stuff of viral memes. When Babs won an Emmy for Outstanding Lead

Actress in a Comedy Series last year, she resolidified her place in the cultural conversation.

Babs dismissed Liz's look of concern with a flick of her hand. "I'm fine. Jin-soo's looking after me. My new assistant."

"Jin-soo?" Liz frowned. "What happened to Kameron with a K?" Their mother's apparently former assistant was an older, charismatic gay man who loved the sun, his Corgis, and dairy.

"He took the dogs to Florida to open a frozen yogurt shop," Babs replied.

Liz followed her mother into the kitchen, where Babs took a seat at the island, selecting a blueberry muffin from a plate of pastries Liz had defrosted. "Jin-soo is amazing! *Very* multitalented."

"Let me guess." Birdie commandeered a second muffin. "As well as being your assistant, Jin-soo's a . . . cranial reader. No—TikTok dance instructor."

"Massage therapist." Rafi spoke without looking up from his phone.

"Bodyguard-slash-breakdancer." Liz scooped up Huey, the fluffiest Pom, recalling their mother's previous "multitalented" employees. "Hair colorist who's permanently stoned. Stalker claiming to be a professional driver."

Babs looked over her glasses in disapproval. "Physical therapist and health coach."

"And there we have it." Birdie took a bite of the muffin, then made a face. "This is drier than a lesbian in a locker room. A male locker room. That joke needs work."

"Also," Babs went on, voice swelling with pride, "she's binary. Her pronouns are they/them."

The sisters exchanged an amused glance.

"You might mean Jin-soo's *nonbinary?*" Liz's question was gentle.

"And *their* pronouns are they/them?" Birdie suggested.

"Exactly!" Babs took a bite of muffin. "I don't even know I need something until *they* hand it to me."

Liz put Huey down, feeling a little dusty from all the wine last night. "What I need," she said, "is—"

Before she could say *coffee*, a steaming cup of it materialized in front of her, offered by a serious-looking young person with an asymmetrical black bob, the ends tinted lime green. Oversized round glasses covered half their face. They looked like someone who had extremely cool pop culture interests you'd never heard of.

"Oh," Liz said in pleased surprise. "Thank you . . ."

"Jin-soo Chung." Jin-soo handed Birdie the butter dish. "My friends call me Fun Chung."

Birdie took the dish in amazement. "That's exactly what this dry lesbian muffin needs! Butter makes it better: Jin-soo for prez!"

Liz shook Jin-soo's hand, noting their firm, confident grip. "How bad is my mother's ankle, Jin-soo?"

They spoke in a wry deadpan. "She'll live."

"On a scale of one to ten, it's minus seven!" Babs exclaimed. "The biggest problem is rethinking my shoe collection."

Liz knew a sprained ankle was relatively minor. But their mother was sixty-nine. Her body would take longer to heal. Liz resolved to have a proper check-in with Jin-soo when Babs was out of earshot.

Jin-soo looked to Babs, who shrugged, shaking her

head—no immediate needs. Jin-soo nodded. "Then I'm going to finish unpacking."

Babs called after them. "Don't forget—"

"—to unpack, clean, and store the kimonos," Jin-soo finished.

"See?" Babs said to Liz as Jin-soo left the kitchen. "They're *very* good."

Birdie spoke through a mouthful of buttered muffin. "Hey guys, is this joke any good? For the platform formerly known as Twitter." She read off her phone. "'The Twelve Days of Christmas' needs rethinking. Five golden rings do not make up for giving me a bunch of useless birds."

Babs honked a laugh. "Brilliant! There's my funny girl!"

Birdie preened, pleased. "Posted." She dropped her phone on the counter, stretching. "My work is done for the day."

Liz lifted a brow. "That's it?"

"I'm on holiday," Birdie huffed. "I'm here to relax."

"What about looking for a new manager?" Liz pressed— Birdie had filled her in on the drive up. "Or working on a new show?"

"Manager?" Babs frowned at Birdie. "What happened to Issa?"

Birdie shot Liz a *thanks so much* look. "Issa . . . is no more. We weren't a fit."

Babs made an apologetic face. "Sorry to hear that. Well, keep your sense of humor about it all. That's what'll get you through."

"I will, Ma." Birdie gave her a grateful smile. "Thanks."

Liz couldn't resist pushing the point. "A few hours of work might also get you through."

"Don't badger your sister." Babs flicked through the *New*

York Times entertainment section. "She's a *comedian.*" Said in the way one might refer to an exotic animal on the brink of extinction.

Liz resisted the urge to roll her eyes. "Well, I'm here to work. See you all later."

"Before you run off." Babs removed her glasses, expression sweetening. "Would you mind helping me with a tiny phone problem?"

Inwardly, Liz groaned. The claimed size of her mother's IT dilemmas were usually diametrically opposed to how much time they took to solve. "How tiny?"

"It says my cloud is full. I'm out of storage? But I'm not sure what my password is . . ."

Liz sighed. Her morning would almost certainly devolve into hours of tech support. "Can't Birdie help? Or Raf?"

Babs looked mildly offended. "Your brother's heartbroken! Again! And this isn't Birdie's forte."

As if on cue, Birdie popped a bottle of Champagne. "Merry Christmas! Who wants Mer-mosas?"

In the adjacent family room, Rafi lay prostrate on the couch, staring at the ceiling with doomed eyes. His words were quiet, only for himself. "Why? Just . . . why?"

"What about Jin-soo?" Liz said, trying not to sound irritated.

"They're unpacking! The kimonos cannot be rushed. Please, sweetheart. It'll give us a chance to catch up. I want to hear all about your show."

Tempting: Liz did want to gush about *Sweet* and all she'd accomplished. Babs had been supportive, but Liz got the impression her mother didn't really get the fast-paced pilot (*it's certainly very "hip"* had been her review), and she seemed a little too surprised the show got green-lit with Liz as showrunner. Birdie was the creative, funny one in the family—Liz suspected her mother thought she was more suited to a glorified administrative role, a quiet helper, behind the scenes.

What Liz really wanted to do right now was work. "Sure, Mom," she said instead. "Whatever you need."

10.

AFTER DEALING WITH FOUR CUSTOMER SERVICE AGENTS over three hours on the phone, two lost passwords, one trip into town to buy a new external hard drive, and a partridge in a freaking pear tree, Liz finally solved all her mother's tech issues and was able to escape outside with her laptop.

The fresh air was bracing, her breath leaving her lungs in white puffs. Tiny icicles clung to the juniper bushes, sparkling in the afternoon sunlight. Liz hurried around the side of the house, through the small, wintered orchard, toward the Barn.

In decades past, the Barn had been an actual barn. When Babs bought the house, it sat unused, full of creepy-crawlies in the woodpiles, until Babs booked the part of wacky lawyer Dolores Ding in the network sitcom *Kangaroo Court*, and the Barn was fully renovated.

Liz switched on the heat and the lights, illuminating polished wood floorboards, thick, sturdy beams, and rows of arched windows. The ground floor was empty except for some yoga mats—Liz and Birdie had taught Rafi how to do a downward dog in here, many years ago. A circular metal staircase wound up to the carpeted second floor and balcony that overlooked the main space. Toward the back, the Barn widened. There was a desk and two comfy beanbags facing the huge semicircular window of the Barn's rear, which looked onto trees and greenery. The kitchenette in the corner had a microwave and kettle. A bookshelf housed an array of screenwriting books. Babs had been convinced she'd write a screenplay here—*the light is inspiring!*—a dream that lasted as long as it took for the kettle to boil.

Liz was grateful to be able to work in a beautiful space like this. She'd spent years in airless writers' rooms or on sets. After moving to L.A. as a freshly heartbroken divorcée, she didn't just want the challenge of brutal production schedules—she needed it. Hollywood rewarded tunnel vision. Liz worked hard. Networked strategically. Never missed a deadline and relentlessly improved her craft. And now she ran a successful show on the most powerful streaming service in the world. To keep doing that, she just needed to crack this goddamn pitch. And stop thinking about Violet. And what Violet was doing right now.

Liz had left L.A. in such a hurry she'd forgotten to pack her tamari almonds, the ones she could find only at a mom-and-pop grocery store on her block. As she settled into a beanbag, she told herself it didn't matter, but not having part of her writing ritual felt like a bad omen. Since her routine was all off anyway, Liz figured a *very quick* check of Insta wouldn't hurt. But when she tapped the app open, Liz saw she'd been tagged in some shares of Violet's just-released *Elle* cover. Gothic Vi in Dior the color of blood. Lips parted. Eyes low-lidded.

Liz's heart gulped, fanning itself.

And that led Liz to spend her precious time in the least productive, most ridiculous way imaginable: combing through the last two weeks of posts on the account whose bio read: I play twins on @SweetTV. At a party, you'll find me napping.

Of the many actors Liz had worked with, Violet was the

most private. She also had the biggest public profile. In a matter of months, she'd gone from three hundred followers to thirty thousand to three hundred thousand to more than a *million*. Liz knew the self Violet presented to the world via her social media was 5 percent of who she was. Even so, Liz's focus sharpened as she started to scroll, attuned to the fresh breadcrumbs in the mysterious path that was Violet Grace.

A pretty but unrevealing skin-care selfie from her partnership with Maybelline, which paid the same as her first-season salary for *Sweet*. Even understated, her beauty was Grecian; natural and lush.

A spare photograph of Violet's shadow against her bedroom wall, the caption promoting a nonprofit that offered low-cost therapy. Violet was open about having a therapist. It was one of the reasons why Liz initially felt confident Violet could manage the pressure and visibility *Sweet* would bring her way.

Liz recognized the third picture. She'd taken it herself, on the Charles Bridge in Prague. Violet and the three other actors from the junket, grinning. Xiao Zhaolin, who played bad boy Bruce Patman; Cashmere Crowe, the TikTok star who portrayed Jessica Wakefield's number one frenemy, Lila Fowler; and Diego Carbon, the former Disney star who played Jessica and Elizabeth's mutual love interest, hunky Todd Wilkins. Egotistical Diego tended to date underfed models. *Not my type*, Violet had said once, which reassured Liz more than she wanted to admit.

Liz's breath quickened when she scrolled to the three black-and-white shots. A photo shoot by someone's pool, a full style team tagged. Violet in seamed thigh-high stockings, a high-cut bodysuit with puffy satin sleeves, and a long pair of slinky gloves, her body an exercise in fluid curves. She met the viewer's gaze with a sizzling sidelong glance. The caption: welcome to my ego death. 💀

In the next, Vi stood tall in the same outfit, ass cheeks pressed against a clear glass balcony. Head thrown back, neck exposed, legs spread. The caption: who's got the windex?

The third was a portrait. Violet holding her breast through a bikini top, squeezing gently, hair poufy, gaze distant and dismissive. came to crush your dreams 🏃‍♀️

Desire awoke in Liz like someone being shaken awake from a nap. Beautiful Violet, gently squeezing her own breast. Vi's nipple brushing the inside of her own palm. Liz had thought too many times about what that might feel like. The roundness of Vi's ass, pressing against the clear balcony. The sass in her gaze, looking directly at Liz. It was all such a turn-on, Liz could practically feel her own pupils dilating.

It was one thing to find another human attractive. It was another to be served up insanely hot photographs of them. *After* you'd kissed. Photos one million other people were seeing, too. Photos not just for her at all.

Frustrated, Liz hoisted her arm and threw her phone across the room. It bounced against the wall, landing on the carpet. Liz immediately stood to retrieve it, embarrassed by her outburst and very glad no one saw. She plopped back down on the beanbag and turned her phone *off*. She had to stop thinking about Violet.

Liz had to stop thinking about how the bridge of her nose crinkled when Violet grinned, extra happy.

She had to stop thinking about how she'd tilt her head and bite her lip when she was especially focused on set.

She had to stop thinking about how she'd looked that fateful night in Italy.

But it felt so fucking good to remember every last detail.

It had been early evening. They were at the hotel in Rome, in Violet's suite. The sun was setting, the light the color of Aperol spritz. Violet was getting ready for their last group dinner, putting on a pair of delicate gold hoops. They were done with press commitments: they were alone. Liz recalled chattering about something geeky—regional viewing numbers? A half smile twitched Violet's mouth.

Liz had paused, noticing Violet's amusement. *What?*

You're cute when you're nerdy.

Violet had never called Liz cute before. Not in such a playful, almost seductive way.

Vi was in a white cotton dress. Her hair was pinned back in a loose bun. A strand had come loose. Liz moved to tuck it back. She was close enough to smell Violet's spicy-sweet shampoo—rose and black pepper. Close enough to feel the warmth of her skin. In the show, she wore Mediterranean-green contacts, but Violet's actual eyes were the color of storm clouds: bruised purple-gray with lightning streaks of gold. They'd been intimate before—they watched movies with their feet in each other's laps, they hugged hello and goodbye. But this closeness was different. Liz felt a strange, nervous heat as she finished tucking the soft lock of blond back into Violet's bun. The inside of Liz's arm brushed Violet's cheek.

Violet caught her wrist. Circled it with her thumb and forefinger. Violet pressed it to her lips. Her plump, warm lips. A pulse of energy had kicked up Liz's arm. Violet didn't look away. Her eyes were as authoritative as the moon. Her lips were still on Liz's wrist. Her soft mouth, on Liz's skin.

Their train jumped the tracks. They were going somewhere new.

And then, they weren't. Their publicist, Cat, had bustled into the room, asking if they were ready to go. Vi switched instantly into pleasant, professional mode. The whole thing lasted three, maybe four seconds.

Their big, noisy group left for dinner at a rustic trattoria wrapped in little white lights. But something had shifted between them. Liz couldn't meet Vi's eyes without blushing. Violet was paying attention only to Liz. This was a rewrite Liz wasn't aware of. A scene she hadn't approved.

Afterward, everyone wanted to go out. But Violet had curled her fingers around Liz's arm. *Let's go home.*

Liz went with Violet because Liz would've followed Violet anywhere.

They meandered along Rome's charming cobblestone streets. The air was silky on their bare arms, and the night felt ample and ripe. Violet tipped her face to the moon, admiring the sky. She'd had only one glass of wine. Liz had had a few more. All she could think about was Violet's lips on her wrist. Had that really happened? Was something going to happen now?

The hotel was beautiful, ancient, all stone walls and cascading plants, wending around a circular internal courtyard. Outside Violet's door, they paused. Moonlight washed Vi's face silver-white.

Liz said good night.

Yes, Violet had said. *Good night.*

They hugged. It was different. They didn't separate. Liz's hands dropped down the curve of Violet's back, lingering on her hips. Violet's arms stayed looped around Liz's neck as she pulled back slowly. Her gaze dropped to Liz's mouth. Liz's chest was rising and falling, the faintest scent of red wine on her breath. They were back on that train, destination unknown. Liz knew she should step away. Pretend her body wasn't coursing with golden heat. Pretend everything hadn't been leading to this.

Violet cupped the back of Liz's head, and then there was no distance between them. Their lips touched. Something finite inside Liz dissolved.

The first few seconds were giddy, dreamlike, an experiment of mouths colliding, opening wide. Liz wasn't in her body; she was fifty places outside it. What was happening? Were they really doing this?

They'd broken apart, staring at each other, wide-eyed in the dark. Liz had grasped for something to say—*guess we've had too much wine*. Before she could, Violet was on her. This kiss was deeper. Deliberate. Violet kissed Liz like she was afraid someone was going to take her away before she was done. Liz sensed the animal in her, flexing its claws.

Vi backed Liz against the hotel room door, crowding close. Her hunger switched Liz on like a light, her nipples becoming stiff peaks inside her bra. Abandoning all restraint, Liz kissed Violet back, finally giving in to her own desperate need.

So, Violet had panted, still pressed close, *you do want to kiss me*. Her eyes were lit with mischief, and something else— vindication. *I've been wondering*.

Liz half groaned, half laughed, drunk with the feeling of this girl in her arms, the taste of her, the feel of her skin. *Of course I want to kiss you*. The truth was a drug. Liz wanted to get as high as she could.

For how long?

Just—always.

Violet laughed and tugged them back together, kissing

Liz in a way no one else ever had. Single-minded focus undershot with something huge and mystic, as hard to pin down as music. Desire exploded in Liz's body like illegal fireworks. And for just one moment, everything was perfect. This felt *right*.

Then, the sound of too-loud voices ricocheted up the stone staircase: tourists, returning from dinner.

Panicked, Liz broke the kiss, putting a foot of air between them before Violet even opened her eyes.

The tourists passed, a chatty American family with adult kids. The youngest, maybe seventeen, looked twice at Violet. A glance and then a stare. Maybe because she was beautiful, or maybe because he recognized her.

Liz's heart boomed in her ears like a bass drum. What was she doing? Kissing her lead actress? On a work trip?

The tourists disappeared. Violet floated forward. Liz stopped her. *Wait. What are we doing?*

Violet's voice was teasing, her fingers curling around Liz's collar. *I think this is called kissing.*

But I'm—and you're—

Yeah. Violet spoke like it was a no-brainer. *Hot.*

But Liz was Vi's showrunner. The person who cast her, who wrote three of the ten episodes. That seemed to bear some sort of responsibility to resist temptation, be noble, be *good*. And the last time she'd felt this happy with another person, he'd taken her heart and blown it up. She'd barely survived.

Liz backed up. *I can't.*

You can, Violet had whispered, unlocking the carved wooden door.

But warmth had been replaced by fear. *I'm sorry. I can't.*

She'd stepped away. Run away. And the next day they flew home to Los Angeles as if nothing had happened, and they hadn't spoken since.

The piercing screech of the kettle jerked Liz back to the present. She was in the Barn in the Catskills, not outside a hotel room in Italy. She wasn't supposed to be replaying her kiss with Violet—again—she was supposed to be working. If she didn't, her dream job would slip through her fingers and this dream girl—dream *actress*, Liz corrected herself—would be cast in something else, disappearing from Liz's life. Liz Belvedere was the responsible one, and the responsible one didn't cultivate a crush on someone she couldn't have.

Liz made herself a coffee and resumed her position on the beanbag, exhaling slowly. Inhaling a lungful of air. Exhaling again.

In. Out.

In. Out.

Inside Liz's head, the scene rewound and started again. A hotel room. Light the color of Aperol spritz. *You're cute when you're nerdy.*

11.

Twenty-one days till Christmas

＊

THE NEXT DAY, BIRDIE TUCKED HERSELF INTO THE FAMILY room's squishy sectional in a comfortable cow-print onesie, armed with a hot toddy and half a chocolate yule log, ready to spend the afternoon with *The Great British Baking Show: Holidays*. But she couldn't sink into the mindless enjoyment of festive treats baked by quirky Brits.

She wanted to apologize to Jecka Jacob but didn't know the right way how.

Birdie muted the TV and called out to Jin-soo, who was preparing Babs's daily green tea smoothie in the kitchen, "How do you issue an apology? Like, if my mom said something really offensive?"

Jin-soo replied in their slightly deadpan voice, "Like the time she tweeted 'Why is West Virginia so depressing?'"

"Ouch." Birdie forked some chocolate log into her mouth. "Exactly."

"Apologize. But not an I'm-sorry-you-feel-this-way non-apology," Jin-soo said, adding a spoonful of green powder into the blender. "An actual apology takes full accountability."

Birdie nodded. Full accountability. Right. "What were you doing before this?" Birdie was curious. "Stuff on the assistant side? Or more in the health world?"

Jin-soo looked directly at Birdie, unblinking. "I was a children's birthday party clown." They switched on the blender.

Birdie couldn't tell if Jin-soo was kidding. Did clowning pay well? Birdie still had no idea how she was going to come up with $11,000 to pay off her credit cards.

On the silent television, an ambitious gingerbread house was spectacularly collapsing. What an apt metaphor for her so-called life. Her hope of performing a new show by the end of the year was definitely not going to happen at this point, but she wanted to make some progress. But how? All Birdie could imagine was a blank page, taunting her. A paralyzing sort of fear twisted into her throat and around her heart. It wasn't anger or sadness or regret or shame, but an unnamed combination of the four. It all seemed impossible to tackle. So, Birdie had a better idea: take a nap instead.

HOURS LATER, BIRDIE WAS awoken by her mother's three Pomeranians yapping excitedly and Rafi calling for her. "Birds! You have a guest!"

Bleary-eyed, she followed the commotion to the foyer, where Huey, Dewey, and Louie were lick-attacking Jecka Jacob.

"Hey, hi!" Birdie waved, instantly wide awake and slightly embarrassed to be caught in her cow-print onesie. "How udderly great to see you again."

The dogs trotted off. Jecka circled her fingertip at the house in general. "This wasn't what I was expecting."

No doubt she was imagining something closer to Birdie's

Brooklyn hovel, not a manse full of familial erotica. "This is my mom's place. Home for the holidays."

Jecka nodded at Babs's enormous seminude portrait. "Your mom really likes Babs Belvedere."

"My mom is Babs Belvedere."

"Oh." Jecka's entire face lifted—she found the association impressive, and, thankfully, she didn't already know. "Okay." Jecka flicked Birdie another glance, this one softer, curious, perhaps joining the dots between Birdie's face and her mother's.

In turn, Birdie drank in Jecka. She seemed like the sort of person who subscribed to *The New Yorker*, who knew how to make an old-fashioned, who was good at standing up for herself. Her boyfriend jeans and oversized sweater looked both casual and classy. The bone structure, the septum ring, the aura of being an actual artist—it was all giving off-duty Zoë Kravitz. Clearly, Jecka Jacob was so far out of Birdie's league, she was playing a different sport.

Jecka indicated the wrapped artwork. "Where do you want this?"

The busiest areas of the house were the kitchen and family room. Birdie led Jecka in the opposite direction, to the formal living room. White lounges, antique side tables, stiff settees. A gleaming white Steinway sat in one corner. Above it hung an energetic painting of a jazz quartet, mid-show. "What a fantastic piece," Jecka said with approval. "I can practically hear the music."

"Mom's something of a collector." Birdie had never noticed the artwork. She gestured to a long white sofa. "You can put yours here."

Jecka peeled off the brown paper wrapping and propped up the painting.

Black brushstrokes on white. And right in the center, like a Cabernet Rorschach, Birdie's gash of red wine.

Seeing it brought back a rush of embarrassment and, more powerfully, regret. Birdie looked Jecka square in the eye. "I really am sorry. I take full responsibility for my actions. I'm obviously a ridiculous person"—the cow-print onesie—"but I'm not a mean one. I really was trying to flirt with you, as truly pathetic as that sounds."

Jecka didn't move her head, but a tiny smile ran across her lips. She let out a breath. "You didn't know it was my show."

"I did not."

"You thought it was what I wanted to hear."

Birdie nodded. "I did."

Jecka considered Birdie as if she were raw material the artist wasn't sure what to do with. Then she shrugged, softening a little. "Okay. You bought the painting. We're cool."

Relief winged through every cell of Birdie's body. "Thanks dude." Absolution never tasted so sweet. "Seriously: thank you."

"Hello." Babs appeared at the other end of the room. She was dressed in a pink velour tracksuit and was using her cane.

"Hey, Ma." Birdie felt Jecka stiffen next to her.

Babs glanced at the painting, then back at Jecka. She offered her trademark bright smile. "Are you a friend of my daughter's?"

"Not exactly," said Jecka, at the same time Birdie said, "Yes."

"Jecka's an artist," Birdie amended. "With a show in town. I just bought one of her paintings."

Babs's penciled-in eyebrows hiked up. "Reeeeally?" She drew the word out, sensing there was more to this story. "Is this the painting you bought?"

Birdie nodded.

"And you made this painting?" Babs asked Jecka.

Jecka nodded, obedient, even nervous. "Yes, Ms. Belvedere."

"Oh please, call me Babs." Babs turned her attention to the painting, slipping on the glasses that hung from her neck on a beaded chain. A minute passed as she looked from one angle. Then another. And another. "Well, I love it," she announced. "Sophisticated but not pretentious, simple but not easy." Babs Belvedere, instant authority on this painting. She moved closer, leaning in to examine the brushwork. "Earthy but not—" She paused. "Why do I smell red wine?"

Birdie winced. "Because this was a—"

"—collaboration," Jecka jumped in. "Between Birdie and me."

Birdie was going to say *mistake* or *accident.*

"How much did you pay for your *collaboration*?" Babs asked her daughter.

Birdie swallowed hard. "Eleven thousand dollars."

Babs let out a puff of disbelief. Even at the height of Birdie's career, that kind of spending was unprecedented. Her mother's expression settled into grim understanding, with just the faintest look of reprimand directed at her middle child. "I see. Well. I've been meaning to buy more art from local artists. I know you're going to fight me on this Birdie, but I'm going to *insist* I buy this extraordinary painting from you. When you want it back, you can buy it back off me."

"What?" Birdie squeaked. "No, you can't, how dare you."

"Oh, if you want it for your own collection, I won't stand in your way."

If Birdie wasn't so embarrassingly desperate, she would've laughed. "My collection is, um, complete. If you insist, Ma, then you . . . insist."

Babs leveled Birdie with a final look of reproach. Not that she needed any help feeling ashamed, Jecka having now witnessed both her financial struggles and being bailed out by her mom. At thirty-three. Sexy.

Babs sidled up to Jecka. "What's your name again, sweetheart?"

"Jecka," she replied. "Jecka Jacob."

Jin-soo appeared so suddenly, everyone startled. "Don't call women you don't know *sweetheart*," they said to Babs.

"What should I call them?" Babs asked.

Jin-soo pushed their glasses up their nose. "Use their first name."

"*Jecka*." Babs turned back to twinkle at her. "Your work tells me you have a great eye and excellent taste. Maybe you can help me find some new pieces?"

Jecka looked wary. "What do you mean?"

Babs waved a hand, nonchalant. "Get a sense of my taste and then point me in the right direction. If you're interested, send me your fee and we'll make a time to chat."

This was standard Babs behavior: Birdie's mother was a seeker, a collector of people and things. "It's a legit offer," Birdie assured Jecka.

Babs waved goodbye, heading toward the kitchen. "Be fun to have you in the mix, Jecka Jacob!"

"Also," Jin-soo said, addressing Birdie, "a pot of mulled wine will be ready in a few minutes."

Birdie gave Jecka a rueful smile. "Yikes."

Jecka almost smiled back.

THE SUN HAD ALREADY sunk behind the tree line, the cloudless dusk a wintry blue. Birdie hopped from foot to foot, arms wrapped around herself for warmth as Jecka unlocked her car, a shiny black Land Rover she clearly took good care of. The pristine vehicle looked far more at home in front of grand Belvedere Inn than rusty old Ray.

Birdie's breath puffed white in the crisp air. "Think you'll take the gig?"

"Not sure." Jecka held Birdie's gaze for a beat longer than necessary. As if really trying to see her.

Something passed between them. A flicker of something delicate. Light as a snowflake. It was no more than a flash, but Birdie felt it down to her toes.

Birdie looked away first.

Jecka got in her car, reversing, before pausing and rolling down the window. "If I don't see you again," she said, "Merry Christmas, Birdie Belvedere."

This woman was obviously too cool and together to be dragged into Birdie's messy life. But deep in Birdie's dumb heart throbbed a desperate desire to see her again.

"Merry Christmas, Jecka Jacob." Birdie waved, smiling, a timid swell of hope inside her cresting, then receding, as the car disappeared from view.

12.

Twenty days till Christmas

*

THE NEXT MORNING, LIZ WAS UP EARLY TO COOK BREAKFAST for everyone and get a jump start on the day. By the time Babs, then Jin-soo, wandered into the kitchen, hair rumpled, looking for coffee, Liz was dusting icing sugar over a towering stack of lemon-ricotta pancakes, a test run of the specialty she always made on Christmas morning.

Babs forked airy pancake into her mouth, moaning in approval. "Orgasmic." She cut her maple syrup pour short after catching Jin-soo's disapproving frown. Addressing Liz, she said, "Working on your pitch today?"

Liz nodded, finishing her last bite. It was imperative to get out early before being roped in to squeezing her mother's blackheads or reorganizing the attic.

"Writing is harder than people think," Babs mused, flipping through a copy of *Deadline*.

Was that a compliment or a warning? Best to sidestep. "How was the audition?"

"Audition?" Babs looked over her glasses. "Darling, I'm offer only."

"I know," Liz said. "But I thought you said you were at an audition in Connecticut?"

"Oh." Babs lost interest, turning back to her magazine. "Not an audition. An appointment."

"For what?" Liz asked.

The lines around her mother's mouth pursed, almost imperceptibly, as she chewed. "For myself."

Babs had denied having plastic surgery for years until the cultural tide turned and it became acceptably feminist. Liz didn't probe. Everyone was entitled to their boundaries.

THE SUNLIT BARN was cozy and quiet as a church. Liz sank into a beanbag, promising herself she was checking social media only for professional reasons—casting updates, showbiz news, general writing inspo.

Violet had posted. Yesterday. Black text on a white background.

> *My heart is a swollen plum*
> *You plucked it from my tree*
> *And squeezed*
> *Juice ran down your wrist*
> *Past the place I first kissed*
> *And bled onto this cold earth.*

Liz knew Violet dabbled in poetry, but to Liz's knowledge she'd never posted anything publicly. It took several surreal moments for the words to sink in. Then Liz's heart reared up and took off at a gallop.

Past the place I first kissed.

Liz was back in the suite with billowing curtains, the light the color of Aperol spritz, Violet's lips warm on her wrist. The poem had to be about her, right? *Right?*

Liz read it again. And again. And again.

When she looked up from her phone, the sun was low in the west. Violet's poem had swallowed her entire day. Liz groaned, speaking aloud to the empty Barn. "I am in dire need of a Christmas miracle."

Her phone lit up. Violet, cosmically connecting? No. An incoming call from Cat. *Sweet*'s publicist did not qualify as a Christmas miracle. Dutifully, Liz answered. "Catherine."

"Elizabeth! What's our favorite writer up to?"

Memorizing poems from Instagram. Liz grimaced before making her tone peppy. "Hard at work!"

"Then our timing is perfect: Violet will be arriving tomorrow afternoon."

"Arriving where?" Liz asked, confused.

"To you. Or wherever you've agreed to work from."

Liz floundered, trying to sit up straight in the unstable beanbag. "Sorry, what are you talking about?"

A micro-pause. "Hasn't anyone been in touch?"

Liz switched the phone from one ear to the other, almost dropping it. "No."

Cat let out an annoyed breath, but when she spoke it was breezy. "Then I'm thrilled to be the bearer of *good* news. Everyone here is very excited about Violet being an EP on the second season, and this is something executive producers do. Brainstorm. Develop. You said yourself that Vi has great story instinct."

"I did?" Liz's heart started throbbing in her chest.

"Yes! She's in New York for a press event and I mentioned you were up at your mom's. We thought it'd be great for her to sync up with you and help bring the pitch into the home-stretch!" Cat was all positivity. "I just forwarded you her hotel confirmation."

Under no circumstances could the source of Liz's writer's block be hand-delivered to her. That'd be like presenting an open bar to a recovering alcoholic. "But I'm used to writing solo. And it's so last-minute! Is this actually a good use of everyone's time?"

A slight pause. When Cat spoke, her voice was more direct. "Liz, I'm confused. Aren't you and Violet friends? What's the issue?"

On one hand, Liz truly believed she worked better on her own—in life and in work. Time with Violet could lead to heartbreak. But another worry also loomed large: she had zero ideas for season two. Liz hadn't considered that Violet could help, but now that Cat had brought it up, it made sense. Despite her desire to make progress, all Liz had actually done these past few days was relive Italy. Avoidance wasn't working anyway.

"Liz?" Cat said.

"Of course we're friends." Liz willed herself to sound normal. "I just feel bad making Violet come all the way upstate. This is just . . . *so* . . . great!"

LIZ DIDN'T REMEMBER ENDING the call. She returned to the main house in a daze.

"Greetings and salutations, Liz Fizz." Birdie swanned down the stairs, wearing a fuzzy robe embroidered with *Squandered Youth.* "How'd your day o' work go, m'lady?"

Liz let out a tense breath. "I need to call a meeting of the Black Hearts Club. Right. Fucking. Now."

Five minutes later, the siblings gathered in the downstairs wine cellar. The low-ceilinged, stone-walled room housed a hundred or so bottles on wooden racks and in squat black fridges. Liz closed the thick glass door behind them as Birdie uncorked a bottle of red and splashed them each a glass.

Liz took a fortifying sip before addressing her expectant brother and sister. "The streamer is sending Violet here to work with me on the pitch."

Birdie whistled. "Plot twist! When?"

"Tomorrow. I'm totally stuck, and everyone thinks maybe Violet will . . ."

"Oh, Liz Fizz. I don't think Violet's going to unstick you." Birdie gave her an understanding smile. "She's going to make you very, very sticky."

"Birdie!" Liz aimed a kick at her sister.

"You walked right into it!" Birdie was laughing. "C'mon, that was a gimme."

"Violet's the lead actress of your show, right?" Rafi hopped onto a stool in the cellar's corner, putting his wine on the ledge that extended from one of the racks.

Birdie nodded, grinning. "Yeah, Vi's dope. Remember I told you I partied with a hot blonde from Liz's show when I was in L.A.?" Birdie prompted her brother. "Vi's a keeper. Aaaand Lizzie just macked with her in Roma." Birdie started bopping. "*Spinderella, cut it up one time.*"

Rafi gasped, staring at Liz. "You two hooked up?"

"She kissed my wrist," Liz confessed. "And my mouth. And wrote a poem that I think is about all that and posted it online."

Rafi's jaw loosened in shock. "*What?*"

Birdie's face flashed through a carousel of shock, confusion, and crazed delight. "And that is the moment I ceased to exist. Please, donations instead of cards." Her voice rose in fervor as she advanced on Liz. "Wrist kiss? You never said anything about wrist kiss!"

"Shh, Birdie, calm down." Liz ducked away, embarrassed that one tiny part of her was actually enjoying this. "It was just one wrist."

"Just one wrist?" Birdie shouted, working herself into frothy hysteria. "*Just one wrist!*"

"There's no freaking reception, I can't read the poem." Rafi pawed uselessly at his phone.

"My heart is a swollen plum," Liz recited from memory. "You plucked it from my tree, and squeezed. Juice ran down your wrist, past the place I first kissed, and bled onto this cold earth."

By the way her siblings were looking at her, Liz could tell that this was not her most sane moment.

"Who are you and where are you hiding Liz Belvedere?" Rafi asked.

Birdie started a slow clap. "Oh, you have snapped. Bye-bye, Lizzie. Nice knowing you."

Liz sank to the floor, wine in hand. "I did read it approximately one thousand times today. I'm doomed."

"Let's say it was a poem about you," Rafi posited, joining her on the floor, pushing up the sleeves of his purple hoodie. "A public declaration of love. You into that?"

The truth? Liz Belvedere couldn't think of anything more romantic. The idea of someone declaring their feelings for her to the world made her feel fifteen and giddy. This highly embarrassing fact had come out in the writer's room—they'd written two very different prom-posals into *Sweet*—and was now general knowledge in the insular world of the show. A world that included Violet.

Liz was blushing. "Everyone likes public declarations."

Birdie flung a finger at Rafi. "Not Sunita!"

Their brother winced and took a sip. "Thank you for re-surfacing my greatest humiliation."

"Sorry, bro." Birdie made a guilty face before joining them on the wooden floorboards and squeezing Liz's knee. "Look, I know you're trying to Scotchgard your sweet baby heart, and I obvy get why—we both know what you've been through."

Rafi nodded in sympathy, and some of the tension in Liz's stomach ebbed. As painful as her past was, it helped that her siblings could acknowledge how bad it'd been.

Birdie went on. "But at least you've got some intel on how Violet's feeling about everything. That's good, right?"

Liz frowned. "You mean the poem? It might be about someone else. It might be about no one."

"I mean her *coming here!*" Birdie gestured with her glass, wine spilling over the rim. "If you've had your tongue in someone's mouth and you don't want to do it again, you *don't* volunteer to go see them with some flimsy work excuse!"

The double negatives tripped Liz up. "So, you're say-ing . . ."

"I'm saying she wants another serving from Lizzie's kitchen!" Birdie exclaimed. "With *all* the trimmings and *all* the sides. And yes, she would like to take a look at the dessert menu, thank you *very* much."

Rafi laughed.

Liz's skin warmed a thousand more degrees. "Is it weird I can't imagine her being attracted to me? At all?"

Birdie's reply was breezy. "Yes, you have very poor sexual self-esteem. Have her come 'brainstorm' and see if, y'know . . ."

"I *don't* know," said Liz. "I'm terrified to know."

Birdie was on her feet, swinging her dressing gown cord and strutting like Jessica Rabbit. "See if she's putting out the vibe."

Liz raised her eyebrows as high as they could go. "The *vibe?*"

"The vibe." Birdie nodded, jutting a hip and batting her lashes.

"Violet will not be putting out a vibe." Liz was certain.

"Christmas comes but once a year," Birdie intoned in a ye olde storyteller's voice. "As does my sister, Liz." She grinned. "Maybe Vi will change that."

"Birdie!" Liz whacked her giggling sister as their mother's voice floated down from the first floor: "Kids! Dinner!"

"SIOUXSIE!" BIRDIE BELLOWED, standing at the foot of the dining room table. "You have *officially* outdone yourself."

Siouxsie beamed. Their local chef always went all out with the first meal of the season. Her long hair, which had silvered over the years, was plaited into two French braids, and she always wore jumpsuits in the kitchen, rolled up at the sleeves to display tattooed forearms.

The chef announced the meal as they took their seats. "Cauliflower gratin with a Gruyère and Parmesan cheese sauce, topped with toasted breadcrumbs; pan-seared asparagus with crispy garlic; steamed vegetables with parsley-lemon tahini; and Julia Child's recipe for Beef Bourguignon, simmered for three hours with pearl onions and mushrooms."

Everyone applauded, which Siouxsie waved off modestly, leaving them to it.

Babs addressed Liz from across the table. "How did it go today, sweetheart?"

Liz cut into her beef, avoiding her siblings' eyes. "Less productive than I'd hoped."

Babs gestured at Birdie. "Get your sister to help!"

Liz and Birdie exchanged a glance. Wordlessly, Liz told Birdie not to mention Violet. "Help . . . how?" Liz hedged.

"*Hire her*, as a writer, or a consultant! She needs a job, and *you* need ideas!"

Liz's stomach flipped. There it was: proof her mother believed Liz's creative voice just wasn't good enough.

"Liz Fizz doesn't need to hire me." Birdie speared a pearl onion. "I'm happy to kick ideas around for gratis, or grass, if you're carrying."

Liz's smile was tight. "Appreciate the offer, Birds, but I'm close to cracking it on my own."

"There's no shame in asking for help," Babs insisted. "It's a complicated path you're on, Lizzie—the life of a creative is very unstable. We all have our strengths, and our weaknesses."

Liz couldn't help it. "What do you think my weaknesses are?"

"Your *strengths* are that you're always prepared, always organized," Babs replied. "But creativity can't be contained. It's not a rule-follower. Your sister is living proof of that."

Liz bit the inside of her cheek.

But Birdie wasn't holding back. "Ma, she *created* the show! It was in *New York* magazine's approval matrix! Lowbrow brilliant—goals for life!"

"Lighten up!" Babs waved a forkful of beef. "It was just an idea. Something to help you too."

Rafi broke in. "How about charades tonight? Mom, you're on my team."

The conversation moved on. Liz told herself her mother was only trying to help and it really didn't matter who she thought was the most creative and talented . . . even if it was obviously Birdie.

THE BELVEDERES ALWAYS PLAYED "three-tiered charades." First, everyone wrote half a dozen answers on bits of paper—celebrities, expressions, objects—which were put into a bowl. In the first round, players could say anything to get their teammates to guess the answer, except the answer itself. In the second round, they could say only one word. In the third, they had to act out the answer, generally in a frantic, expressive mime.

Birdie, Liz, and Jin-soo formed one team (Team Festivus), with Babs and Rafi on the other (The Pregnant Virgins).

Birdie was first up. She pulled the first scrap of paper from the bowl. "Nonunionized seasonal workplace!"

Liz could read her sister's humor like a map. "Santa's workshop!"

"Yes!" Birdie pulled out the next answer. "We leave these out for Santie Claus!"

"Milk and cookies?" guessed Jin-soo.

"More my speed." Birdie mimed swirling a glass.

"*Rum* and cookies," Liz guessed correctly.

Next one: "I'm small with a bum leg and Cockney?"

"Tiny Tim!"

When all the answers had been correctly guessed, the first round was done. Babs usually dominated in the second round—one-word clues—but tonight she was off, forgetting what'd already been established in the first round. She was getting older, everyone was, but Liz had never noticed it so starkly in her formidable mother.

It was Liz's turn. She grabbed her first crumpled answer from the bowl: *All I Want for Christmas Is You*. Liz thrust a finger at her sister, the perfect one-word clue bursting out of her. "Palms!"

Palms was an underground karaoke bar in Los Feliz that Liz had taken Birdie to the last time she visited. It was a quintessential L.A. night, starting with grilled-shrimp-and-chipotle-cream tacos in the cute backyard of Liz's favorite Mexican joint. At Palms they scored a booth and did shots (shots!). Birdie performed a surprisingly pretty rendition of "Stay" by Lisa Loeb, then Liz brought it home with "All I Want for Christmas Is You," even though it was a hot summer evening. The whole bar ended up on their feet singing along.

Palms wasn't just a great clue. It was a memory of one of their greatest nights, ever.

"Palms!" Birdie shouted back. "Palms?"

"Palms!" Liz repeated, waiting for Birdie's eyes to light up. *"Palms!"*

But her sister's face remained stuck on a look of unmet expectation.

With a cold jolt, Liz's memory clicked into place.

It wasn't Birdie with whom she'd had a perfect Palms night. It was Violet.

"Palms?" Birdie said again, now thoroughly flummoxed.

As Liz stood in the middle of the family room, mute and

helpless and feeling like an idiot, she had the disorienting thought she would always be like this: alone and misunderstood. She knew it was just charades, but this was a familiar sensation. Rafi made people feel. Birdie made them laugh. And she was alone, too proud and self-sufficient to be loved in the way that, deep down, she desperately wanted to be. In this moment, she missed Violet more than ever.

Liz stared at the carpet with the horrific realization that she might cry.

"'All I Want for Christmas . . .'" came a voice from behind her. "'. . . Is You.'"

"Yes!" Liz gasped as if coming up for air, spinning around.

Violet Grace was standing ten feet away. Looking right at her.

Oxygen stopped entering Liz's body. She was engulfed in flames. She was plunged into ice. She couldn't move.

For a moment, the room froze in tableau, all eyes on the blonde with the duffel bag slung over one shoulder. Then Birdie jumped to her feet. "Violet, hey! Good to see you again!"

The tableau relaxed into movement, everyone getting up, offering wine and to hang up their guest's coat. But not Liz. Liz still hadn't exhaled, her entire body pulsing hard like one giant heartbeat.

Violet Grace was here.

13.

✳

AN HOUR LATER, VIOLET HAD BEEN FED AND GIVEN A TOUR
of Belvedere Inn by an energized Birdie and a slightly star-
struck Rafi, Liz wordlessly trailing behind them. Liz's heart
was blaring like an alarm. *Violet. Is. Early. Violet. Is. Here.*

Cat had booked Violet into the Woodstock Way Hotel: a
collection of log cabins and studios overlooking a small waterfall, just off the main street. The artsy, boutique rooms
were the nicest ones in town, but Birdie insisted Violet at
least stay the night—the Marilyn Monroe suite was the small-
est on the second floor, but it was already made up. "And
right across the hall from Liz Fizz," Birdie added, gesturing
for Violet to go check it out.

Was that a good idea? Liz stared at Birdie, panicked.

Birdie nodded in Violet's direction and mouthed back,
Vibe.

Oh boy. Liz sucked in a breath and followed Violet in.

The bedroom had a hushed, simple beauty. Violet's bag
sat on the canopy bed. Her back was to Liz as she stood admiring the four framed photographs on the far wall. In them,
an auburn-haired Marilyn Monroe lounged on a beach in
1940s swimwear, laughing in a way that looked natural, un-
posed.

Violet was a different woman from the one Liz had first
met at an audition back in January. That Violet was raw talent. Emotional and strong but shy and inexperienced. This

Violet was more polished, more luxe: her dyed honey-blond hair was swept into an elegant braid, something a stylist taught her. Her luggage was monogrammed, and her jeans were expensive, hugging an ass she worked for with a personal trainer. Her sweater was the color of muted winter sunshine and looked soft. Touchable.

Not that she should be thinking about Violet's ass or how touchable her clothes were. Liz cleared her throat.

Violet looked back over her shoulder and smiled. "I love these. She looks happy."

Liz grasped for a response. Typically, she informed houseguests her mother purchased the photographs at an auction, but her friendship with Violet had been forged outside Babs's shadow. That felt important to maintain.

It used to be so easy to talk to Vi. Why did it feel like the first read-through of an unfamiliar script?

After it became apparent Liz wasn't going to respond, Violet wandered to the bookshelf, walking a finger over the books' leather spines. Camus, Proust, Beckett. "Gang's all here."

Liz regained the power of speech. "Some of her favorite authors. Marilyn was actually a big reader."

Violet looked impressed. "Don't judge a blonde by her cover."

It took Liz a second too long to parse the wordplay. "Exactly! Sorry, I'm just . . ."

"Surprised I'm here," Violet finished. Her gaze was steady, reasonable. "I hope it's okay I came early."

"Of course." How much eye contact was too much? This much? "I'm grateful for the help."

"I hope I can. Help, I mean. I've been doing some reading to prepare." She indicated a book on the nightstand. *Save the*

Cat!, a screenwriting how-to. "But I'll take your lead. I'm here to learn."

Charmed, Liz picked up the book, which was already filled with multicolored stickies and notes in the margin. "I didn't realize you were interested in this. Writing, producing."

"I didn't, either. But I am." Violet's smile flickered—she was nervous, Liz realized, trying her best to put on a brave face. "I'm more of a reader than a writer, but I'd like to try."

"Amazing. Cat booked you a good hotel, but you're welcome to stay as long as you like."

Violet glanced around the perfectly appointed room. "I wouldn't want to intrude, but I'm a little bit in love with this room."

Somehow, this was happening. Violet was here. Sleeping in the bedroom across the hall. Her rose-and-black-pepper shampoo perfumed the air, a little sweet, a little spicy. God, Liz had missed that smell.

Violet smiled at Liz. Liz gazed back. The moment lengthened. The air between them thrummed, like a just-plucked bass line still quivering in the room.

Violet was still just *looking* at her, her purple-gray eyes the color of moon rocks, arteried with gold. "So . . . what's up with you?"

The question was light, but Liz understood the subtext: *Why haven't we spoken? What's going on?* Liz's neck flushed. "Well, I've been stressed about the show," she began. "The second season, this pitch. That's all I've had time to think about." Her words sounded more defensive than she intended.

"So, the fact we made out in Rome," Violet spoke casually,

as if it barely mattered. "Have you had time to think about that? Or am I the only one who remembers that we kissed?"

Every inch of Liz's skin went red-hot. She'd thought they'd never acknowledge the kiss, an assumption that now seemed incredibly naive. If only she could be as relaxed as Birdie around her many lovers. Instead she was a glitchy robot, a total square.

"I remember," Liz murmured. "Low-key tattooed on my brain for all time." She met Violet's gaze with caution. "But I think it's best if we keep things professional."

"Why?"

Liz wasn't prepared for her stance to be questioned. "Because it could ruin things."

"What could ruin things?"

Liz's heartbeat was a jackhammer level of subtle. "Breaking up, I guess."

Violet's brows flicked down, either amused or thrown. "Breaking up . . . from a relationship?"

Liz was officially out of her depth and sinking fast. Violet sounded surprised Liz brought up a relationship, and fair enough—they'd kissed *once*. One time. Liz was the only one worried about a future fictional breakup, and that was *so* embarrassing and further proof Liz wasn't equipped for any of this. "I think we should just be friends." She sounded like a bad actor. "Don't you?"

Violet lifted one shoulder in a half shrug. "I want what you want." She sounded like a good actor. "I want to be on the same page."

"Great." And even though a friendship was more than Liz felt she could hope for at this point, she still felt a jab of disappointment. Anger at her own stupid hypocrisy welled up before she forced it away. They'd work together to figure out this idea, then Violet would fly home to L.A., and they'd never bring up the kiss again. "Glad that's sorted."

"I brought you something." Violet unzipped her duffel bag. "Figured we couldn't have a writing session without these." She pulled out a giant bag of Liz's favorite tamari roasted almonds. The ones sold only in Liz's neighborhood.

Liz gasped in delight.

Maybe this really would work.

Sitting in the velvet love seat by the window, Liz steered the conversation into casual territory while Vi unpacked clothes and toiletries, puttering around. Soon, the pretense at casual stopped feeling like an effort and started feeling closer to something familiar: an ease. They were both giggling as Liz described Birdie's Winegate, and Liz thought, *See? Maybe we really can be friends.*

Until Violet unpacked her *Teenage Mutant Ninja Turtles* T-shirt.

The vintage one, gray and soft. The cartoon picture of the four turtles was so faded, it was almost indiscernible. Vi wore it with sweats: her "cozy clothes." The material had stretch. It molded to her breasts like a second skin. She'd worn it for the first time during a movie night (*Irma Vep*, the original), months into their friendship. The sight was so unexpectedly sexy, Liz had blushed. The recurring fantasy that Violet was about to lean over and kiss her tended to happen when Vi was wearing that shirt.

Liz lost her train of thought. "I . . . I just thought we could . . ." Nope. Nothing. "Sorry, I forgot what I was talking about."

Violet's attention dropped to the shirt in her hands before

returning to Liz, curious. "You were wondering if your mom had a printer."

"Right. We'll need to print stuff out." Liz got her phone out, relieved for the distraction. "If Mom doesn't have one, I think there's a print shop in town."

"I could go tomorrow. I rented a car."

Liz looked up. "Or I can give you a—"

Violet was holding a white lacy thong. The sort of thing sold at high-end lingerie stores decorated with velvet drapes. The sort of thing Liz secretly found unbearably, almost painfully, sexy. First the shirt, now this? Liz stared a second too long at the underwear before wrenching her gaze to Violet's look of total innocence.

"—a, um, lift." Liz's face started to flame again. "In Rafi's car. Birdie's is—a disaster."

"That'd be great." But Violet wasn't putting the underwear away like Liz needed her to. "What do you think of this?"

Dear god. She was talking about the thong. "Mm?"

Violet held it up. A delicate scrap of lace the color of fresh snow. So pretty. So easy to slip off. The idea made Liz feel giddy.

"Some company sent them to me." Her tone was so blasé Liz couldn't tell if she was being tortured on purpose. "I can't tell if they're too much."

Her mind was held hostage by the image of Violet in the *Turtles* T-shirt. And the underwear. The white of the lace against her bare skin. The fullness of her breasts underneath the old shirt. Her nipples, sensitive and erect, ready to be touched. What might've been waiting for her in Violet's hotel room in Rome.

Thick waves of heat pulsed between Liz's legs. She pressed them closed, hoping Violet couldn't tell how flustered she was. Liz looked back at her phone, mortified. "It's, um, nice."

"You think?" Violet's tone was noncommittal.

"Of course. It's really . . ." What word was most innocuous? Cute? Sweet? ". . . fetching."

"Fetching?" Vi let out a delighted laugh. "Then I guess I'll keep it. Must have *fetching* undies."

Liz wished for sudden and immediate death. She looked up only when she heard the dresser drawer close.

"Okay, all done," Vi announced. "Should we see what the others are up to?"

Liz followed Violet into the second-floor hallway. The distant laughter of the group echoed up from downstairs. "Go ahead. Just gonna freshen up."

"But you already look so *fetching*." Violet grinned back, heading for the staircase.

Liz crossed the hall into her room, locking the Audrey Hepburn suite. Alone, she let her head fall back against the door, trying to catch her breath. Her heart felt like a car yard inflatable. Her blood was gasoline: flammable.

I am in so. Much. Trouble.

14.

Nineteen days till Christmas

✳

RAFI'S WEEK OF VIRTUAL WORK WAS EXCRUCIATING. Conducted mostly in bed, each minute felt like an hour, capped off by one of the assistants accidentally Slacking the entire team with *I know, I feel sooooo sorry for him! #shesaidno.*

He logged off early, closing his laptop with a drawn-out sigh. It was Friday afternoon, but Rafi was unable to muster any enthusiasm for the weekend. Just more time to quietly question his entire existence.

The sun was setting, a burning lip of red visible in the west. The family room was empty—it was a little too early for the happy hour Birdie enthusiastically hosted each evening. He flopped onto the sofa, needing the kind of reality TV that puts your brain in a box and hurls it off a cliff. Opening the drawer in the coffee table for the remote, Rafi noticed a deck of cards, designed in minimal black-and-white. Bold block letters on the front read THE BIG QUESTIONS, and underneath, in smaller font, YOU ALREADY HAVE THE ANSWERS. Well, he was in need of some answers, wasn't he? Flipping it over, he read the instructions. *Shuffle before every pull. Reflect.*

What the heck. He tipped the cards out. The backs were

illustrated in a trippy visual illusion: a monochrome maze impossible to solve. Rafi turned the top card over. On a white background, a question in black font: *What is your dream house?*

Rafi perked up. He could waste an hour thinking about something like a dream house. To follow the rules, he started to shuffle, letting his mind wander, ready to receive divine inspiration. He pulled a card and read its question.

What do you want?

Rafi blinked. What did he want? Just . . . in general? Not as in . . . for dinner? In his career? He flipped the card over. No addendums, no clues. Nothing but the same enormous question, which was still there when he turned it back over. *What do you want?*

Rafi tossed the card aside with a huff. Some game. There was nothing fun about it!

His sisters had always known what they wanted. Even if their desires changed—like how Liz first worked in publishing before switching to TV—they were both motivated to keep working, keep trying, even in the face of rejection. Rafi didn't share that urge. He'd never been interested in going into entertainment, maybe for that reason, or maybe because it didn't feel like there was room in the family for another showbiz darling.

He'd always been motivated by the idea of giving back and helping others. Community manager for a clean-water nonprofit had sounded like a dream job but turned out to mostly be answering testy customer support complaints, a grind he endured by dating someone fun at work. Philly was a nice enough city, but it wasn't his forever home. It was a temporary solution to New York being too expensive. It was

MOST WONDERFUL • *121*

almost a shock to realize that he'd been living in Pennsylvania for three and a half years.

This couldn't be it. This life, his life, it couldn't be all there was. Because if it was? Rafi pitched forward on the sofa, his heart rate spiraling. Because if it was, he'd made some serious mistakes. He hadn't gotten the right degree, dated the right people, made the right choices. He wasn't fulfilled, his work was mindless, he wasn't building a life with anyone. He was newly single, still living with a roommate, years away from marriage, even further from kids. Did he even want the white picket fence fantasy, or was that just another illusion? He was twenty-nine, a third of the way through his life, and what did he have to show for it?

"Oh shit." The curse left his mouth as a gasp. "I'm fucked."

"Who's fucked?" Birdie strolled into the family room.

"No one." He gathered up the cards, shoving the deck back into the drawer. "What's up?"

Birdie dangled her car keys. "Feel like enabling my procrastination?"

He'd never said yes faster.

HIS SISTER DROVE THEM into town, where they spent a cozy hour nursing hot toddies at Tinker Street Tavern. As they sat side by side on stools at the bar, Birdie regaled Rafi with tales of her most cringeworthy sexual misadventures and Rafi let himself be entertained, avoiding his thoughts for as long as he could. About fifty-seven minutes.

"Birds?" Rafi shifted to face his sister directly. "What do you want?"

"Like, for Christmas?" Birdie brightened.

"No, I mean, in general."

"Oh." Her face fell before quickly reanimating. "It's a cold and rainy night. Someone knocks at my door." Birdie rapped on the bar for emphasis. "It's Margot Robbie! Thoroughly drenched and begging to be let in. I stand aside, noticing as I do that her nipples are clearly visible through her—"

"Cut." Rafi rolled his eyes. "I'm serious. What do you want in life? Big picture?"

Birdie frowned, considering the question. A longish pause. "I keep coming back to Margot Robbie's tits . . ."

"Birdie!"

"I don't know!" She laughed, draining her hot toddy. "Just, do comedy. Make a bit more money. Get my shit together. Why, what do you want?"

That was exactly what he needed to figure out.

BIRDIE TOOK THE LONG way home, claiming the "scenic" way would cheer him up, even though it was pitch-black and starting to snow. By the time they rolled down the driveway to Belvedere Inn, it was past dinner.

"Aren't you starving?" he asked his always ravenous sister.

Birdie parked the car. "We have a surprise for you."

They walked up the front steps, which were already dusted with snowflakes. "If it's the dogs' tuxedo outfits, Mom's already shown me."

Birdie punched in the door code, antsy with excitement. "It's not the dogs."

"Okay . . ." Rafi followed Birdie through the foyer, toward the kitchen.

The entire house—Liz, Violet, Jin-soo, and his mother—were hovering around the kitchen island, faces lit with expectant grins.

Rafi frowned at them. "What's going on?"

Birdie spun him around so he was facing the adjacent family room. "Ta-da!"

In the middle of the family room stood a young man wearing dark-wash jeans and an expensive-looking navy sweater. His hair was the color of dark honey, wavy on top, short on the sides, freshly cut. Gold stubble shaded a square jaw.

Rafi's eyes widened as he sucked in a stunned, delighted breath. "No *way*!"

It was Ash. His best friend in the entire world, a boy he'd known since they were both fourteen. He almost didn't recognize him. Not only because Rafi wasn't expecting him, but because—

"Dude." Birdie clapped Ash on the shoulder. "You got hot in London."

Rafi's mind was spinning. He couldn't stop smiling. "What the hell are you doing here? How did this happen?" He almost tripped over his feet pitching forward to hug Ash.

"Raf Attack." Ash wrapped his arms around Rafi.

His skin smelled the same, musky and sweet, but a new deodorant or cologne was layered over it—a delicious mix of citrus and bergamot and something like blown-out birthday candles. His body felt different. Stronger. More muscular. Rafi squeezed the hidden new strength in surprise. "Jesus, what's all this?"

Ash chuckled in a self-effacing way. "I started swimming." He squeezed Rafi's shoulder, friendly and brimming with good feeling. "So good to see you, man."

"The *best*," Rafi echoed, but he was still getting his head around it all. The surprise. The new body he hadn't registered on FaceTime; the unfamiliar, sophisticated scent.

"The category is cheekbones!" Birdie yelled, and the family descended, proffering their honorary son a glass of merlot, a plate of shepherd's pie.

Ash had been part of the family since he and Rafi had met on the first day of high school. Birdie and Liz had attended elementary, middle, and high school in New York City, after the family moved back from L.A. when the girls were little. Rafi had gone to elementary and middle school in Soho like they had, but unlike his sisters, he'd finished school upstate, being the only child to move with his mother to Belvedere Inn. Rafi could still remember the neatly pressed, if clearly secondhand, shirt Ash was wearing on their first day. Now nothing about him was secondhand.

From the chatter whirling around them both, Rafi realized everyone was in on the surprise but him. Which was so thoughtful and generous . . . but was it because they were worried about him? His family hadn't shipped Ash back to help pick up the pieces, had they?

No. That was ridiculous. Ash was here because this was where he belonged.

EVERYONE WAS KEEN TO stay up, but Rafi knew even night owl Ash must be jet-lagged. At the first hint of a yawn, Rafi hauled him up from the sofa. "I'm calling it on London Man's behalf."

In the foyer, Ash retrieved a hard-shell suitcase from the hall closet, glancing up the staircase to the Inn's second floor. "Which room is mine? Marilyn? Audrey?"

"Actually," Rafi informed him, "all the suites are taken. You'll have to bunk with me."

Ash blinked. "Oh." His eyebrows dipped. "Okay."

The boys had shared a bed dozens of times—on trips, while camping, at sleepovers. But as kids, not grown men. Ash looked as if Rafi had just announced they'd be showering together. Obviously sharing a bed was something you jettisoned when approaching thirty. "I'll sleep on the sofa," Rafi amended. "You take my room."

"No, it's fine—"

"I really don't mind!"

"Raf, shut the hell up." Ash grinned, nudging him. "I've missed sleeping with someone who snores like a swamp monster."

"Fuck off!" Rafi grinned back, relieved.

The bedroom was toasty. Ash surveyed the plaid blankets and club chairs, his gaze snagging only briefly on the bed. "Wow. It's all exactly the same."

Rafi remembered thinking the same thing. He sat crosslegged on the bed to watch Ash unpack. "I can't believe you're here and not there. I've missed you. More than I realized, I think."

"How are you?" Ash examined Rafi in concern. "How are you feeling?"

There was an odd moment of disorientation, as if the proposal disaster had happened to someone else. It was almost an effort to recall Sunita's broad smile and easy laugh, and the subsequent stab of sadness and regret. "It's definitely made work harder. And I'll never wear an ugly Christmas sweater again." There was much more to say—especially everything he'd been thinking about this afternoon—but Ash was tired; this wasn't the right time.

Rafi got into bed while Ash showered and changed into pajama bottoms. Peeling back the comforter, Ash slid in, relaxing all six feet two inches of him into the soft mattress. "God, that feels good."

"Thank you for coming so far," Rafi said. "I already feel better."

Ash grinned back, and it felt like the old days. "You're welcome."

"What made you decide to do it?" Rafi asked, remembering Ash's reticence in their last FaceTime.

Ash rolled to his side, propping his head up with one hand. "Your sisters are very persuasive. But I came because you needed me."

Rafi smiled, pulling the comforter closer. "Can I ask why you haven't come back until now?"

Ash let out a slow breath. His words sounded very carefully chosen. "I've been in New York and a part of your family for my entire life. I think I just needed to . . . experience something else. Strike out on my own to see who I could become, and what was possible when there was no safety net. When I let go of certain . . . ideas."

Rafi wanted to hear more: How had Ash gotten in touch with what he wanted, what was his life in London like, what did the future hold? For now, Rafi just punched his now very solid arm. "I'm so fucking proud of you, man. You spread your wings and you soared. London looks good on you."

"It feels good," Ash said. "But being back here . . . it's strange."

"How so?"

Ash frowned, settling on his back, gaze lifting to the ceiling. "My life in the States started to feel like a memory, or a story I read once. And now that I'm back, in this room, I'm reminded it's not. That it's been existing this whole time, concurrently. Like a multiverse, or whatever. And everything in it feels just as real as when I left."

They were quiet for a minute. Rafi assumed Ash was too tired to keep chatting. But then Ash faced Rafi again, his expression slightly pained. He opened his mouth, closed it, opened it again. "Look, I know you think I should've come back for Dad's funeral."

Rafi couldn't deny it. "Why didn't you?"

"Because I'd just moved! Just got the job! There were so many logistics, and flights were expensive, and . . ." Ash ran out of steam, kneading the skin between his eyes. "And obviously that's not the reason why." He let out a tight sigh. "My dad was a dick. He barely tolerated me—you know that better than anyone."

Ash's mom died when he was a toddler. Ash's father was the only living family he'd had left. They couldn't have been less alike. Willie was prone to conspiracy theories and extremely fixed ideas about gender and sexuality. He was the reason Ash had all but grown up at Belvedere Inn. Ash didn't come out to his dad until he'd left for college. Rafi didn't think Ash should've gone to the funeral for Willie. He felt Ash should've gone for himself: his own healing, his own journey. But clearly, Ash didn't agree.

"It's not my place to pass judgment," Rafi said softly, "and I never will. I just felt if I was in your shoes, I'd want the closure. But it's your decision, and I one thousand percent support you. In this, and everything, always."

"Thanks, Raf." Ash examined him. "Can I ask you something?"

"Of course."

"Did you love Sunita—really *love* her?"

Rafi had been expecting a question about what the funeral had been like. Where the grave actually was. "I did love her," he said. "In the way I love cheeseburgers and puppies." Even though they'd been his ex's words, they sadly summed things up. "Maybe I don't know what real love is."

"Don't be silly." Ash fought a yawn. "Of course you know what real love is."

Rafi switched off the bedside light, wondering if that was true.

Outside his window, fat snowflakes continued to fall. He imagined them blanketing the house in flawless white, cocooning the seven bodies inside, warm in their beds. Rafi fell asleep picturing snow filling the surrounding meadows, a whisper of sleigh bells ribboning through the silent woods beyond.

PART TWO

It's not the holidays without a holiday fling!

15.

Eighteen days till Christmas

*

BIRDIE THREW HERSELF INTO HER ANNUAL HOLIDAY traditions: Wearing reindeer antlers wrapped in blinking holiday lights while running errands in town. Bellowing "And to all a good night!" before going to bed each evening. Doing shots of spiked apple cider every time there was a moment of old-school sexism in *Love Actually*, which was pretty much the entire film. But this year, Birdie's Christmas traditions weren't bringing her the same joy they usually did.

"Am I outgrowing *Love Actually*?" Birdie let her head fall back against the wine racks. It was happy hour, and the Black Hearts Club was in session. "Is that *physically* possible?"

"No." Liz was certain. "No one ever outgrows *Love Actually*. I'll be on my deathbed, unable to recognize you two, but still telling the hospice nurse, *To me, you are perfect.*"

"Want to pull a card?" Rafi extracted a black-and-white deck from his back pocket. "Big Questions. I tried it and they're sort of . . . insightful."

"Pass." Birdie refilled her wineglass. "I've been insight-free since 1991."

"You're a comedian," Liz said, shaking her head no when

Birdie offered a top-off. "Your entire career is insights. And I thought you were driving us to go pick up a tree? Maybe you should take it easy on the wine."

"Career?" Birdie scoffed, splashing Cabernet into Rafi's glass. "You're the only one in this wine cellar with a career."

Rafi let out an insulted cough. "So my nine-to-five is, what, an elaborate hobby involving a lot of time on Slack?"

"You don't like your job." Birdie dismissed this with a wave. "You've been complaining about it all week."

"That may be true," Rafi replied. "But I'm the only one who can dis my career, Birdie."

Rafi usually dismantled boundaries rather than set them. Birdie was so thrown, her reply was atypically sincere. "Sometimes I think everything that's happened in my 'career' has been because of Ma or Stanley, somehow." Even though Stanley had been far from a perfect father, his career as a director of popular nineties rom-coms had given him professional clout right up until the day he died. Birdie went on, "Like, people cutting me breaks to get in my parents' good books."

"I hear that," Liz said. "I think I made it a lot harder on myself not using Mom's name. I kind of want her to acknowledge that. Or just acknowledge the show and what I did." She leaned forward. "Did I tell you guys that the night *Sweet* premiered, she called asking if I could brainstorm talking points for some interview? I'm literally at my own launch party, telling her which of her charitable foundations to mention. What's wrong with me?"

"What's wrong with her?" Rafi exclaimed. "I swear she thinks I'm still ten years old. Last night I was making a hot water bottle for bed and she *insisted* she pour the water for me. Like, she was horrified I was doing it myself. I'm twenty-nine! I can make up my own hot water bottle!"

"I can't believe you still use a hot water bottle." Birdie peered at him. "Are you a lost time traveler from the 1800s?"

Liz and Birdie dissolved into giggles before Liz checked the time. "We should get going. Is Ash coming?"

"Yup. Just finishing up some work," Rafi said, as they all got to their feet. "How about Violet?"

"She's discovered Mom's screenwriting books in the Barn," Liz said. "She wants to keep reading. She's taking this all so seriously."

"Admit it," Birdie said, as they all filed out. "That turns you on."

BIRDIE, LIZ, RAFI, AND ASH piled into Ray and drove into town to the high-pitched strains of *Christmas with The Chipmunks*, an album Birdie proudly owned on tape. All four of them sang in unison, *"We can hardly stand the wait; please, Christmas, don't be late."*

The station wagon was a smudge of merriment and light zooming through the silent, winter-crisp night.

THERE WAS ONLY ONE Christmas tree stand in Woodstock, set up near Fox & Fawn, a wood-paneled bar where Birdie had sometimes performed stand-up. She got a parking spot out front, the street freshly plowed after last night's dump. Birdie peered through the bar's frosted windows. Sydney, a local comic who hosted and booked a weekly show, was on the small back stage, microphone in hand. Laughter spilled from under the front door, closed against the cold. Birdie felt a twinge of longing, followed by a wallop of frustration; she should be up there, workshopping a new show.

The group dispersed among the rows of pine trees lined up for sale. Birdie hummed along to "Jingle Bell Rock," which was playing over the speakers, as her eye snagged on someone across the street. Christ in a crackerjack: it was Jecka Jacob. Approaching the Christmas tree stall at the other end, a good distance from where Birdie was standing.

Acting on pure instinct, Birdie started hustling through the rows of pines to get closer to the entrance where Jecka was heading, aiming to be inspecting a tree at the exact moment Jecka entered. But it'd been a minute (years) between treadmills, and so when Jecka arrived, Birdie was out of breath and puffing.

"Birdie?" Jecka pulled up short in alarm. "Are you okay?"

It probably looked like she was having a heart attack. "Me?" Birdie affected confusion, even as she continued to pant. "I'm just—overwhelmed. By the trees. Aren't they—beautiful?"

Jecka glanced at where Birdie had come from, narrowing her eyes. "Does this happen every time you see a tree? Or just Christmas trees?"

"Just Christmas trees. I'm very—festive."

The corner of Jecka's mouth ticked up.

"Haven't seen you around," Birdie said, regaining her breath. "I take it you passed on the job offer with my mom?"

Jecka looked mildly surprised. "I took it. We had a call yesterday."

"What?" Birdie almost shouted, before regaining her composure. "Sorry, it's just—no one told me."

"And why would we need to tell you?"

"You wouldn't." Birdie was already preparing the berating she'd give Babs for keeping her out of the loop. "How was the call?"

Jecka let out a wry half laugh, beginning to stroll through the forest-green pine trees. "Well, I'm not actually a curator, but I can already tell this is going to be a learning journey. Your mother's taste seems . . . eclectic."

Birdie trotted alongside Jecka. "That's a very generous interpretation."

Jecka chuckled. Birdie spotted Rafi and Ash up ahead and subtly rerouted her and Jecka's stroll so as not to cross paths with them.

"So, what else is going on?" Birdie continued. "Breaking hearts? Or heads? I'm a lover and a fighter myself."

"Actually, I just picked these up from the printers." Jecka pulled a stack of leaflets from the pocket of her wool trench. "I designed them myself."

Birdie accepted a colorful printed flyer. "A map?"

Jecka nodded, thumbing through the hundred-odd stack. "Of local artists who open their studios to the public on Sundays."

Birdie examined the neat map of the town and surrounding woodland, dotted with a dozen studios and little illustrations of their noted specialty: ceramics, portrait photography, landscape art. "This is dope."

"Thanks." Jecka shrugged. "I think it'll help. Anyway, how's the comedy going? Hopefully you haven't destroyed any more works of art for the sake of entertainment."

The shock and excitement of Jecka remembering that she was a stand-up was dulled by Birdie's realization that she had nothing to show for herself as cool or community-minded as Jecka's awesome artists map. Birdie's dumb brain urged her to share something, anything. "I'm, uh, trying to think of some new material. Just don't ask me to tell you a joke."

Jecka arched a brow. Her smile was cheeky. "Tell me a joke."

Birdie cleared her throat. "Girl walks into a bar, asks the bartender for a double entendre." She wiggled her eyebrows. "He gave it to her."

Jecka snorted, seeming surprised that she did. "You actually are pretty funny."

"Are we just stating facts? Okay. You're intriguing."

"Intriguing?"

"Yes." Birdie nodded. "You intrigue me."

"I intrigue you."

"The word *intrigue* is starting to sound weird," Birdie said.

"The word *intrigue is* starting to sound weird."

Birdie gestured over to the Fox & Fawn. "Should we get a couple of double entendres and discuss?"

Jecka's expression stayed bemused, her lips pressed together. "Maybe I'll see you around." She reached down to select one of the smaller trees.

"That's your guy?" Birdie had assumed Jecka would choose a full-sized tree.

"What can I say? I'm a sucker for the underdog." Jecka flashed Birdie her most promising smile to date and headed off to pay.

Warmth floated into Birdie's chest, making her feel like a hot-air balloon.

Liz edged through a row of trees, looking scandalized. Evidently, her sister had been spying. "Was that *the* Jecka? Oh, you look *smitten*."

Birdie wiped the grin from her face. "I'm not smitten. *No one* is smitten."

"Should I call a wedding planner?"

"Shut up." Birdie was mortified. "I'm not marriage material."

"Yes, you are," her sister said, too seriously. "Of course you are. You're kind and funny and touchingly devoted to the world's worst cat. Anyone would be lucky to marry you."

It was so far-fetched, Birdie almost felt angry, even as she kept her tone light. "Babes, I'm the one they sleep with *before* they meet their husband."

"But the look on your face just now!" Liz pressed. "You obviously—"

"Looks like the boys found a tree," Birdie interrupted, determined to end this ridiculous conversation. If anything happened with Jecka Jacob, it'd be just like all her other hookups: exceedingly casual.

As far as Birdie was concerned, that wasn't just the responsible thing to do. It was the only option available to her.

BACK HOME, IT TOOK all four of them to carry the enormous tree into the family room and get it situated in its traditional spot. Then Siouxsie announced dinner, a hearty minestrone soup served with piles of pillowy Parmesan and hot buttered toast, followed by a warm apple cobbler with French vanilla ice cream.

After finishing with the dishes, the others wanted to play cards, but Birdie elected for an early night and quality time with Mr. Paws. She was halfway upstairs to her room when her mom called from the foyer. Behind Babs, Jin-soo was carrying an oversized cardboard box, a dozen rolled posters sticking out of the top.

"All this talk about buying new art reminded me you need to do something with all this." Babs waved at the box.

"With all what?"

"Posters, scripts, photos—I don't know." Babs shrugged in mild irritation. "Your father kept everything."

Jin-soo handed Birdie the box. The weight sank heavy in her arms. Film reels, press clippings, old magazine covers featuring her parents—gross. *Stanley Green: King of rom-com finds love with rising star Babs Belvedere!*

Birdie's throat went tight and prickly: a paternal allergic reaction. "I don't want any of his crap."

"Then throw it out." Babs shrugged, leaning on her cane, sounding both practical and empathetic. "Or sell it. It's been sitting in the basement for three years. He did leave it to you."

"Would've preferred if he left me a house." Birdie aimed for dry, but it came out bitter. They both knew Stanley's new family were the ones his will had favored. There had been a small lump of cash, which Birdie donated to a children's charity to avoid the shitty feeling she'd get spending it herself. Given her current financial situation, maybe that was just another mistake.

"Well, me too, sweetheart, but your father was, to put it delicately, a selfish shitbox." Babs patted Birdie's shoulder with a smile. "Keep your sense of humor about it. Turn one of the film reels into a cat toy."

The smile Birdie tried to muster dodged her first and second attempts. "Maybe."

Her arms already ached as she about-faced up the stairs,

trudging to her room. She dumped the box on her bed with an exhale, distraught at getting shoved down memory lane.

Stanley Green. Director. Sports car collector. Selfish shit-box father.

He'd first met Babs when seeing her in a quirky off-Broadway production of *Pickles & Hargraves and the Curse of the Tanzanian Glimmerfish*, a comic murder mystery centered around a talking mouse detective. Babs was recently divorced from her first husband, Liz's father: Pete Miller, a New Jersey tradesman. Pete hadn't approved of Babs's acting ambition—they'd parted ways after Liz's first birthday. Babs was in her early thirties, juggling motherhood and clawing her way up the New York theater scene. Just as she began to wonder if she'd made a terrible mistake, her big break arrived.

In the snap of a clapboard, Babs was not only in cinemas nationwide in Stanley's smash romantic comedy *The Upstairs Girl*, but walking down the aisle with Stanley into marriage number two, already pregnant with Birdie. True to her identity as an independent broad, Babs insisted on keeping her new, post-divorce surname—Belvedere—and giving it to baby Birdie. Stanley moved them all to Los Angeles, where Babs was in demand as a first-rate comic actress who could also sort of sing. She starred in a few more hits and a few more flops, appearing on talk shows, in magazines, at awards nights . . . but the marriage was rocky. Stanley was rich, respected, and a rogue with an eye that didn't so much wander as shamelessly swagger. Their booze-fueled fights were legendary, but Babs stayed with him, right up to the day Stanley left her for another of his bright-eyed ingenues. Ten years Babs's junior.

Birdie was four when they split and thus remembered little of this, piecing it together from her mom's memoirs and interviews. Her own memories kicked in postdivorce, when she'd visit her father in L.A. And they ended three years ago, when, just after midnight on an otherwise ordinary Tuesday, Stanley's orange Lamborghini sailed off a hairpin turn on Mulholland Drive, killing him instantly. His blood alcohol level, 0.31 percent, aka flammable, made the front page of the *Los Angeles Times*.

That clipping was decidedly not in this grim Pandora's box currently getting dust on Birdie's duvet. She yanked open the closet, pushing the box and its hurtful souvenirs into the far corner, piling some extra pillows on top to keep the bad juju at bay.

16.

Seventeen days till
Christmas

*L*IKE MOST WOMEN, LIZ WAS A SKILLED CHAMELEON, ABLE to seamlessly transition between being entertaining, helpful, chill, sympathetic, or whatever else a situation called for. They weren't behavioral shifts that usually resided close to her consciousness, but now Liz was overly aware of playing a new role: the perfect host. Attentive and friendly, the first to offer Violet a drink, or check that she had enough bedding. But living under the same roof made Liz feel lightheaded and slippery. When they did the dishes together yesterday morning, she'd almost dropped a plate. Twice. Violet had touched her arm with a sudsy hand. "You okay?"

Violet's fingers were warm and wet. Liz imagined pulling Violet into a bubble bath. Kissing her, as water flowed over the sides of the tub. The bubble of her daydream popped when Liz caught Birdie's eye. Her sister was grinning, mouthing, *Vibe, vibe, vibe!*

Violet hadn't mentioned checking into the hotel Cat had booked—she was still sleeping in the suite across the hall from Liz. She and Liz worked separately during the days, rereading the first season's scripts and making notes. Today,

Sunday, was their first official brainstorm. Liz felt hopeful, but Violet seemed edgy. When they'd parted ways last night, Liz made some reference to tomorrow being *the big day*. Violet had winced, her face collapsing into worry, murmuring something about Liz lowering her expectations.

Annoyingly, Friday's snowstorm knocked out the heat in the Barn, making the space unusable until it could be fixed. They'd have to work from the main house. Liz didn't want to work from a bedroom—far too intimate—and assumed they'd have no trouble finding a quiet corner. But this morning the house seemed overly full.

"Having everyone around will make both of us nervous," Liz confessed to Birdie. The sisters were huddled by the Christmas tree. The enormous undressed pine almost tickled the family room's ceiling. Liz kept her voice low so as not to be heard by her mother, Jin-soo, Ash, or Rafi, who were all in the kitchen making breakfast. "There's no privacy."

As if on cue, Rafi wandered over, peeling a banana. "What are you guys doing?"

"Having a private conversation," Liz informed him.

"About what?" He took a bite of a banana. "Violet, and how it's full lesbian period drama between you two?"

Even though Violet wasn't yet downstairs, Liz felt a slap of panic. "No, it's not!"

"Yes, it is," Birdie said patiently. "You're starring in a modern-day remake of *Carol*. Are you missing a glove?" Then, to their brother: "We're talking about periods. Lizzie has a superheavy flow, and I'm trying the Diva Cup, which is like a tiny cocktail of my menstrual lining—"

"Ew, Birdie!" He gave them a horrified look, backing away.

There was no privacy. Birdie cocked her head. "What about a hike?"

Liz gestured outside. It was drizzling. The forecast predicted rain all day.

Birdie chewed her bottom lip, her blue eyes bouncing to the kitchen, the tree, then back to Liz. She grinned. "I may have a solution."

Oh no. Not another Birdie solution. When they were teenagers, Birdie's "solution" to the problem of Liz being tongue-tied around boys involved an earpiece and relayed flirting. The earpiece crossed wires with a nearby Chinese restaurant, resulting in Liz attempting to order moo shu chicken off her confused date. Liz groaned. "Don't get involved."

"I got you, sis!" Birdie was off, stage-whispering over one shoulder. "Need to make a call!"

Liz hoped she wouldn't regret opening up to her sister. She settled into an armchair, angled to give her a clear view into the kitchen, and poked around her laptop, waiting for Violet. It was 9:15 A.M. They'd said they'd meet at 9 A.M.

Everyone gobbled up breakfast before dispersing to various corners of the house. Only Babs was at the kitchen island when Violet padded in a few minutes later, wearing a light pink hoodie, her blond hair plaited into a braid. In her arms were her laptop, a notebook, and a pile of season one scripts and craft books.

Liz waved, wanting to project ease and confidence and not—as she truly felt—like her stomach was full of tiny lizards. "Morning! Ready for today?"

"Yep." Vi dumped everything on the kitchen counter. "I'll just make a tea. Any takers?"

Liz gestured to her already full mug of coffee.

Babs nodded. "Brew me up, buttercup."

Violet found a box of loose-leaf tea. Fumbling it, the entire box spilled onto the kitchen counter. She let out a sharp exhale. "*Shit.*"

Liz rose to help, but Babs was closer, already scooping up the mess. She eyed Violet. "Everything okay?"

She'd always been especially attuned to fellow performers.

"Oh, it's our first writing session today." Violet shot Liz a slightly helpless smile. "Little nervous."

"When I was your age they didn't let actresses anywhere near the scripts," Babs said, dumping a handful of leaves into a teapot.

"Honestly not much has changed." Violet filled a kettle with water. "It was my idea, and I really had to fight for it. Swimsuit shoot? No problem. Something that uses my brain? Suddenly, it's an issue."

This was news to Liz.

"Good for you for advocating for yourself." Her mother settled back on a stool, zeroing in on the woman switching on the burner. "So. Where are you from, Violet Grace?"

"Portland."

"Nice city."

"I only lived there until I was eleven. My parents died in a car accident, and then I lived with my grandfather."

Babs straightened in shock. "My god, you poor thing. Where did he live?"

Violet explained to Babs what she'd told Liz during one of their first hangouts—that she'd spent her teenage years in the Oregon Coast Range, deep in the backcountry. Wet, misty mountains of old-growth forest: western red cedar and Douglas fir. Miles from the closest neighbor.

"Gave me a certain strength of character," Violet told Babs. "An acting teacher once told me it deepened my well."

It was true: Violet could draw upon an emotional depth most performers her age could only fake. It was one of the reasons *Sweet* had been so successful. Once the writers grasped the extent of Violet's range, the show evolved into darker, richer territory.

Liz listened as Violet described how her parents' death ended her childhood. From it, a new dream emerged. "Being a performer," Violet told Babs. "Being someone else. Somewhere else."

Babs nodded. "I lost my family, too. My first husband, Liz's dad, didn't approve of my career. Neither did my father. But I have no regrets over my choice." Her gaze became soft. "There's something extraordinary about the way it lets you step into different shoes. See the world through someone else's eyes. It's like . . ."

"Magic," Violet finished.

"Exactly."

They exchanged a smile.

Bittersweetness bloomed in Liz's chest. Violet had opened up to Babs in the way she used to with Liz. Despite the fact that they were, ostensibly, friends, their ease and intimacy hadn't returned. In its place was either an effortful attempt at professionalism or intrusive thoughts about kissing in bubble baths.

"Ma!" Birdie rocketed back in. "Great news! Jecka wants to host us all on an art crawl!"

With the enthusiasm of a game show host, Birdie explained that their mom's new art advisor could accompany the family on a drive to local studios. She proudly displayed a hand-illustrated map Jecka had designed, of artists' spaces that were open to the public on Sundays.

"You could buy some art," Birdie said to Babs. "Or just

window-shop. It'd be a great way to meet local makers. The boys are in, and so is Jin-soo. Go get your raincoat!" she ordered, ushering their delighted mother in the direction of her suite. Babs loved a spontaneous plan, especially if it was all organized for her.

"Art crawl?" Birdie asked Liz and Violet.

Liz fought a smile. "I can't, unfortunately . . ."

Birdie slapped her forehead, affecting confusion. "Today's your big brainstorm, I *totally* forgot." She sauntered into the family room so only Liz could see the wink Birdie gave her. "Guess you'll have the whole house to yourself *all day*."

"You're officially my favorite sister," Liz murmured, giving her a hug.

"It's win-win," Birdie whispered. "Maybe Jecka won't think I'm such a hot mess."

"I thought that was your entire brand," Liz teased her.

Birdie stuck out her tongue, then spun to address Violet, still at the kitchen island. "Sorry you'll miss it, Amazing Grace. Violet Crumble. Grace Face. We don't have a nickname for you yet, do we?"

Violet rested her chin on her hand. "Prefer if it wasn't Grace Face."

"Grace Face it is!" Birdie gave a thumbs-up. "Have a great day. If your poem is anything to go by, the words will flow like sweet, sweet honey."

"Poem?" Violet's look of confusion clicked into embarrassment. Her shoulders slumped. "Oh. The one on Insta. Yeah, I deleted that."

Birdie frowned. "Why?"

"Obviously you didn't read the comments." Violet's tone was edged. "People had a lot of opinions. *Actresses trying to be smart is like seeing a dog walk on its hind legs. Funny, but very wrong.* That sort of thing."

A surge of protective anger balled Liz's hands into fists. She hadn't read the comments, either—she'd forgotten how painful the tsunami of attention Violet now received could be.

Birdie shrugged. "Whatever; it was dope, people are dicks. Come out from behind your avatar, brah! Wait! I should take a picture of you guys." Birdie's phone was in her hand. "You can post about your first writing sesh and stick it to the haters."

"Oh no." Violet flinched, as if Birdie had just swung a punch. "Please don't. I can't handle a thousand people in my DMs telling me I'm dumb or fat or that I should just stick to being a pretty face they want to fuck."

"Whoa." Birdie pocketed the phone. "My bad."

"Let's keep Vi offline," Liz said, getting to her feet. "We need to focus on work today."

Violet gave Liz a grateful smile. Babs reentered the kitchen in a cherry-red raincoat, her waterproof Chelsea boots squeaking on the tiles as she used the cane for balance. Was it Liz's imagination or did her limp seem worse than yesterday?

"You're not coming, Lizzie?" Babs asked. "Then could you do me a tiny favor and print out the addresses for my holiday cards and get them in the mail?"

Liz stiffened. This "tiny favor" would take more than an hour. "Mom, I can't—"

"You need to find the sticker paper," Babs spoke over her, "and the stamps. And make sure you—"

"Mom, I can't." Liz made her voice firm. "I have a work-day planned with Vi. That's why she came all this way."

Babs scoffed. "It'll only take a minute!"

Liz was ready to acquiesce; it was easier than arguing, and it would get her mother out the door quicker. But then she glanced at Violet, whose presence reminded Liz she wasn't protecting just her own time. She was also protecting Violet's.

Liz steeled herself, feeling more nervous than a grown woman should. "No."

Babs looked taken aback. ". . . No?"

It was a complete sentence. "No."

Her mother narrowed her eyes, mouth turning thin. People rarely said no to Babs. Liz never did.

"Raf and I will do it." Birdie leaped in. "When we get back."

Liz shot her sister a grateful look. That was a first.

Babs looked from Liz to Birdie then back to Liz, before shrugging. "Fine." She raised her voice, the tense moment already in the past. "Someone get my checkbook and all three of my Pomeranians!" Babs zipped up her raincoat with a flourish. "Let's go buy some art."

The house rolled out. As the sound of the two car engines dwindled to nothing, Belvedere Inn fell silent. The only noise was the soft patter of rain against the old glass windows.

They set up at the kitchen island, laptops and notebooks open, a bowl of roasted almonds within reach. Liz explained they had to deliver what everyone liked about the first season without repeating all the same ideas. "Up the stakes while staying true to what we've established." Liz checked her notes. "Introduce additional characters, without taking the spotlight off fan favorites. In general, be awesome. Er. Awesomer."

Liz knew that on paper, *Sweet* sounded like empty calories, no substance. The books were fast food for preteens, and a twenty-first-century remake risked being all winks. But Liz had grown up on witty, self-aware teen shows: *Veronica Mars*, *Freaks and Geeks*, *The O.C.* She envisioned something that was extravagant and playful. Carefully plotted, smartly paced, and emotionally grounded. Something with a generous eye for its three-dimensional characters. Sexy, sure, but ultimately romantic, in surprising ways.

The original book series blended typical teen stuff (sexy young love) with the truly insane melodrama of the series' later spin-offs. The first season of *Sweet* careened through *Sweet Valley High* canon, with story arcs that focused on juicy secrets, forbidden romance, and the unraveling of the seemingly perfect facade of Sweet Valley. Jess joined a cult called Good Friends, the charismatic leader of which she had culty sex with before he was exposed as a shady fraud; Elizabeth was almost killed by a murderous doppelgänger—"The Third Twin"—while simultaneously investigating the story for *The Oracle*, the school's internal TV channel; the twins were nannies for the royal family, wherein Liz fell in love with a prince, and Jess, a jewel thief. The emotional arc of the first season focused on the love triangle between the Wakefield twins and their love interest, Todd Wilkins.

For the highly anticipated second season, it was Liz's aim to once again strike a balance between the ridiculous and the sublime: the truly batshit and the surprisingly smart and tender. "I need to open a new world, take the show into new territory. It has to be a big swing, I think, because the first season was so . . ."

"Good?" Violet guessed.

"I was going to say nuts," Liz said.

"Oh. Sure."

Shifting on their stools, they exchanged another shaky smile.

"Do you have any ideas?" Liz asked.

"I do. I was trying to think of something that'd"—Violet flipped through her notes—"generate a lot of story and emotionality, as well as provide opportunity for escalating tension and meaningful character development." She took a deep breath. "What if one of the twins got pregnant and had a baby?"

Instantly, Liz knew that wouldn't work. It wasn't canon: established and accepted as true in the fictional world of Sweet Valley. Neither twin had ever gotten pregnant. It might work in season six or seven, but it was too early to introduce the unsexy problem of being a teen mom into their sexy, extravagant world.

But Liz wanted to be a good brainstorm partner, which meant supporting Violet's suggestions. She typed it down. "A baby. That's interesting. Maybe Jessica—it'd be the most challenging for our bad girl. Not sure how much microdosing she can do in a mother's group."

"Yeah, she might not be a great mom right now." Violet frowned, as if mentally playing the concept out in more detail. "On second thought, that's a dumb idea."

"This is a brainstorm; all ideas are good ideas." But Liz was relieved to add a question mark next to it.

They met each other's eyes, then bounced their gazes away. Radio silence; dead air.

Vi cocked her head to the side and bit her lip, the look she always got when she was focusing hard. "Maybe—" she started, then stopped. "Nothing."

"How about—" Liz started, before realizing she had: "Nothing."

"Maybe . . ." Violet wiped her hands on her sweats. "Maybe . . ." She let out a frustrated, embarrassed breath. "Maybe I'm not very good at this. God, why didn't I just stay in my lane?"

"Vi. Hey. We just started. And your lane is whatever the hell you want it to be. Let's throw around some ideas for Jessica's second season arc—the big-picture journey our pansexual queen will go on."

But the conversation didn't flow. Violet was closed, second-guessing herself, growing more and more anxious as the minutes crawled by. Finally, she pushed back from the island, chair legs screeching against the tiles. Her face was as stormy as the rain clouds outside. "I'm not feeling great. I need a minute."

"Oh, sure." Liz's concern deepened. "Can I get you anything?"

But Violet was already walking away.

17.

*

AT LUNCHTIME, LIZ BROUGHT UP A TRAY OF SOUP AND
buttered toast to Violet's room. Her soft knock went unanswered. Hours later, the food still sat untouched in the hallway. As time ticked by, Liz grew increasingly worried. She
should've led with more ideas—she'd been trying to give Vi
space to speak, but she saw now that was the wrong strategy.
The impostor syndrome Liz valiantly tried to ignore reminded her it was highly doubtful she was qualified for any
of this and who the hell did she think she was? With her
family still on the art crawl, Belvedere Inn was oddly quiet.
Liz tried not to ruminate on the fact that the one day they
had it all to themselves was a wash.

In the late afternoon, Liz lit a fire and decided to start
decorating the tree—something productive to distract from
the failed workday.

Each decoration was wrapped in old newspaper, a mix of
priceless and pedestrian. A handblown glass ball that'd belonged to Babs's grandmother. Santa hoisting a beer. An
angel edged in real gold. A reindeer made from popsicle
sticks. She'd just unwrapped a neat black-glitter star on a
wood slice when she heard footfalls.

Violet entered the family room, eyes soft and regretful.
She was still in her pink hoodie and sweats, but her braid was
mussed, hairs falling out of the plait. "I am so sorry—"

"It's fine!" Liz practically yelled, dropping the decoration in a fluster. "This is all my fault, I never should've—"

"Liz." Violet interrupted what was sure to be a long, self-punishing rant. "Let's sit."

They took a seat on the squishy sectional, the fire crackling quietly opposite them.

Violet took a deep breath. "I know that what people say about me on the internet shouldn't matter. But it does. It affects me, makes me question my self-worth, my ability. My voice. Working with you, on these ideas, is something I really want to do. To help you, and the show, because I really care about it. But this morning my fear got the better of me, and I'm sorry."

"Vi, it's okay," Liz said. "Really. I can only imagine how hard being in the fishbowl is. I'd forgotten how much everything you say and do gets picked apart. It's not natural, especially for someone as private as you are."

"I am private," Violet said. "But I do have things to say."

"Like what?"

"Like . . . well, I want to talk more openly about being queer, but I get the impression the higher-ups think that'd be a bad idea because I'd lose fans. Or because I'm not actually dating someone, everyone would be like, *Prove it!*"

Liz chuckled, feeling a tickle of pleasure at Vi referencing liking women.

"Or they'd be way worse," Vi went on with a shudder. "The comments can be vicious."

Liz sobered, nodding.

Violet sat up straighter, her voice sounding more urgent. "Sometimes I feel stuck between having a really big voice and not having one at all. Like—I have a platform, people pay attention, and I'm so grateful for everything that means. But I haven't figured out how I want to use that privilege. Cat keeps saying I should be free to express myself, but at the same time, she kinda keeps warning me against it."

"I think you should say what you want to say," Liz offered. "And if that loses you fans, who the fuck cares? Your truth, and being able to express it, is way more important than how many followers you have, and if Cat has a problem with that, I have a problem with her. And when it comes to the comments . . ." Liz let out an annoyed sigh. "Not everyone has permission to affect your emotions. You can choose who you listen to, whose approval means something. Just because someone wants to hurt you doesn't mean they get to."

Violet looked doubtful. "That's easier said than done."

Liz smiled sympathetically. "I know."

Violet let out a breath. "I'm still figuring it all out. What I want to keep private. What I want to tell the world. Even just what I want to tell my friends. There are things about me hardly anyone knows. Sometimes that feels safe, and sometimes that feels hard."

What did Violet keep hidden? Liz tried to stay focused. "You can always tell me anything, if that feels right. Just never forget you're a wonderful, talented actor and so many people believe in you, including me. I will always have your back, and I will always fight for you. If you want. If I've earned that."

A smile bloomed across Violet's mouth. They were sitting so close, Liz could see the baby hairs at her hairline. The unbearable way her top lip was slightly fuller than the bottom. Violet's voice was soft. "Can I give you a hug?"

Liz's heart filled with helium. "Of course."

Violet shifted close enough to circle her arms around Liz's neck, softening their bodies together. Liz inhaled the familiar scent of rose-and-black-pepper shampoo. The smell sent a flush up Liz's body. Violet's chest pressed into her own.

When she was with her ex-husband, Liz had focused on making herself desirable. But when it came to women, her instinct was to desire. And desiring Violet was as easy as breathing.

Liz pulled back first. Vi's cheeks were pink. She smiled at Liz, pupils dilated. "You always know the right thing to say."

Liz smiled back. "Just doling out some Christmas magic."

Violet rolled her eyes, impish. "Ugh."

In an effort to calm her heart rate, Liz got to her feet, focusing on the decorations. "Want to help hang a few?"

"Sure." Violet gazed up at the pine. "We never had a Christmas tree—my grandfather and me. We weren't that into the holidays."

Liz affected horror. "Sacrilege. Santa sacrilege!"

They both laughed. Real laughs, the kind that make you feel like you're lit up from inside. It wasn't that Liz's joke was so hilarious, more that they both seemed more relaxed around each other. Connected. A mellow, solid feeling settled into Liz's bones. Hope, perhaps. Happiness. This was how it used to be.

Violet picked up the black-glitter star Liz had dropped. So perfect it could've been store-bought. "This is cute."

"That's one of mine. Craft project from middle school. Everyone else's was a mess."

Violet made a sound of charmed delight. "It's adorable. I bet you were such a cute kid."

Liz shrugged, hiding a pleased smile. Birdie and Rafi were the cute kids. "The rest of the class did gold or red stars."

Violet ran a finger over the black glitter. "A rebel from way back."

Liz almost laughed. "I think you're the only person who has ever called me rebellious."

"You're the showrunner of a show that featured pegging."

Liz recalled the comic-sexy scene with a chuckle (Jessica Wakefield wearing a strap-on and declaring herself—what was it? Pirate Peg?).

Maybe she could be a rebel. Maybe she already was.

"So," Violet said. "Should we try again?"

Excitement fizzed into Liz's chest. Take one hadn't worked, but there was always take two. "If you want."

"I do." Violet smiled. "Let's talk about our show."

And how different the conversation felt now: not like a test they might fail, but a door to walk through if only to see what lay beyond.

Liz thought aloud. "I was thinking I could generate the B-plot melodrama between the parents. That's just an endless war for control of the PTA and all their shady business shit."

Violet grabbed the bowl of almonds from the kitchen island and brought it back to the coffee table, sinking into the sofa. "And they're all screwing."

"Exactly: sexy musical chairs."

Violet snorted, crunching a mouthful of nuts.

"But we still need some big, overarching idea. Something wild. Something . . ." Liz looked to Violet for help.

Violet crossed her legs, wiping off her hands. "What are your favorite second seasons of television?"

Liz had considered this question before, but worried

about being influenced by other creators' ideas. Now, with Vi asking it in such a straightforward way, her brain started whirring, surfacing everything she loved about TV: The way a great show could break your heart, then put the pieces back together in a way you never expected. The way you could feel so close to the characters that they felt like friends. The comfort and pleasure it offered, the connection being part of a show's community could bring. "*Parks and Rec* leveled up with a more generous tone, more emotion, better use of the ensemble," Liz thought aloud. "*The Sopranos* humanized Tony, and the new characters dished out all those amazing plot twists. Season two of *Buffy*'s my all-time fave—so clever, genuinely hysterical, but also emotionally devastating. 'Halloween,' 'School Hard,' 'Becoming.'" Liz named the classic episodes with ease. "The world-building was incredible."

Violet hugged her knees to her chest. "I had such a crush on Willow."

"Checks out." Liz nodded. "I was more into Faith." It felt like the old days, chatting on Liz's sofa or Vi's pool loungers. "Y'know, Jessica, our Jessica, dated a vampire."

Violet looked intrigued. "Really?"

Liz had skimmed most of the original *Sweet Valley High* paperbacks while writing the pilot. "*Tall, Dark, and Deadly, Dance of Death*, and something like *The Killer's Kiss*. No: *Kiss of a Killer*." Liz recalled the plot revolving around a mysterious new student whom Jessica was into, and a bunch of creepy bite-mark-related deaths. At the end, Vampire Boy turned into a bird—yes, a bird—and flew away. "Vampires are canon in Sweet Valley."

Violet's pretty face lifted with surprise. "Vampires are canon?"

Liz nodded. "Vampires are canon." Something clunked in

Liz's brain, like a heavy trunk falling open. "Vampires," she repeated. "Are. Canon."

They could introduce a supernatural element. One with a rich and fascinating lore. One that offered the potential for danger and secrets. Sexiness and surprise. Liz's breath clipped. The tips of her fingers started tingling. This was either the best idea or the craziest. In the world of *Sweet*, that was a good thing.

Liz stared at Violet, wide-eyed. "We could do a vampire season."

Violet nodded, slow, then quicker. "I like vampires."

"I *love* vampires." Liz began coursing with something electric, otherworldly. "*Buffy*, obviously. *True Blood, The Lost Boys, Interview with the Vampire. Twilight!*"

"*Let the Right One In*," Vi supplied. "That one with David Bowie—*Hunger?*"

"*The Hunger.*" What if Jessica dated a vampire? Became a vampire? What were vampires like in Sweet Valley? Ideas were raining down faster than Liz could catch them. Her brain sparked and popped like a live wire. She knew this feeling. Inspiration. Imagination. An *idea*.

Over the next few hours, Liz and Violet brainstormed. Liz typed so fast every second word was misspelled, but that didn't matter because *this was something*. Liz knew it as clearly as recognizing her own face. Some ideas were silly (the twins become vampires and start robbing blood banks?), some were impossible (the show flashes a thousand years into the future!), but *this was progress*.

"I can totally see Jessica being like"—Violet slipped into character—"*there's something about the undead that gives me life.*"

Liz snickered, typing it down. "That's perfect."

"And Elizabeth would be like, *I know this sounds a little cuckoo Cocoa Puffs, but would being a vampire help me get better grades?*"

Liz laughed. It was like being kids let loose at a carnival, jumping on every ride, trying every piece of junk food, giddy with the thrill of being alive. No: being *together.* Liz had had breakthroughs before, but never one this important, and never with another person.

By the time they came up for air, it was early evening. The fire was low in the hearth, the bowl of almonds empty. Liz let her head fall back against the sofa, her fingers numb from typing. They found each other's eyes. In the space between them, mischief and mayhem and maybe even a miracle. Liz let out a satisfied groan. "God, that was *productive.*"

"Is that your biggest turn-on?" Violet teased.

"Maybe."

Violet's smile was affectionate. "You're such a dork."

"Never said I wasn't." It was the happiest Liz had felt since arriving. The room was toasty, work had been done, and Violet was here. "Great work today, partner."

Violet smiled back, her doe eyes catching the firelight. "Thanks for being so understanding. You're a really good friend." She squeezed Liz's forearm, letting her hand linger.

The sensation flooded Liz's veins like melted milk chocolate.

The moment lengthened. Neither of them looked away.

Liz's heart was thumping so hard she could practically hear it. No, she *could* hear something. From outside, a rumble. A car. The others. "They're back."

Disappointment flitted over Violet's face, echoing Liz's feelings. Vi drew her hand back. "Pick this up again tomorrow?"

"Count on it."

Liz told herself to go put the kettle on—surely, the rain-soaked art lovers would all want a hot cup of tea.

But she didn't want to leave the comfort of the couch and the woman next to her. Rebelliously, Liz stayed right where she was.

18.

Sixteen days till Christmas

*

HAVING ASH BACK WAS A FESTIVE FEVER DREAM RAFI never wanted to end. They'd spent the weekend doing what they'd always done in December: Playing boisterous games of Scrabble in front of a crackling fire. Going for snowy romps in the backwoods that inevitably descended into snowball fights. The art crawl on Sunday would be a new tradition, Rafi decided, given how cool it'd been to visit all the local art studios. They agreed it reminded them of trips to the Guggenheim or the Met as kids—Babs used to drive both boys down to see a new exhibition, then they'd all get ice cream in Central Park.

At dinner on Sunday evening, Ash had regaled the family with stories about all the quirks of London life: the Tube, the black cabs, the fact that no one owned an umbrella even though it rained every day. Rafi fell asleep that night feeling light and happy. Maybe all his anxieties were already resolving themselves, thanks to Ash and the comforts of home.

But as soon as Rafi awoke on Monday morning, he knew he was wrong. Dread pounced, knocking the breath out of him. When he opened his laptop at 9:00 A.M., his entire body recoiled. The vague dissatisfaction he'd identified last week grew with every keystroke as he answered the same mind-numbing questions and complaints.

How do I postpone my recurring donation for next month?

Then I need to change credit cards but the website doesn't let me?!

Then Your organization SUCKS!!! How do I cancel my fucking donations?

The nonprofit was technically doing a good thing, but the work, Rafi was realizing, was a grind. It was like dating Sunita had been a veil, and now that veil was lifted. He definitely did not want his manager's job, so where was this leading? Nowhere.

At lunch, Ash was energized, recounting an interview he'd conducted with a young designer who made upcycled jewelry out of household waste. Through his work for *London Man*, Ash was carving out a beat that explored fashion through the environmental and social issues he cared about. Rafi hung on to every word, desperate to absorb his best friend's enthusiasm. But somehow, Ash's good mood made the dreary afternoon even worse. In the weekly all-hands meeting, the grid of faces staring back from his screen made him want to dissociate, in the same way he would when facing a wall of photographers on a red carpet with his mother, an invasive experience he'd never enjoyed.

By the end of the day, Rafi didn't just dislike his job. He hated it, and himself, for ending up in this situation. He couldn't just quit: he had a lease and car payment and expenses. But the idea of getting back on the hamster wheel of his life after Christmas made him want to throw his laptop out the window, get in his car, and just *drive*.

———

DINNER WAS PAINFUL. Babs and Birdie held court, and while Rafi tried to enjoy the hijinks, he couldn't manage more than a few bites and one-word answers. As soon as the dishes were done, he caught Ash's eye. Without needing to exchange a word, they peeled off in tandem, heading for Rafi's bedroom.

"Are you okay?" Ash asked, as Rafi shut his door.

"I've entered the Ninth Circle of Hell in Dante's *Inferno*." Rafi collapsed into one of the leather club chairs facing the fire, which he'd lit earlier.

"That bad, huh?" Ash fished an expensive-looking bottle of whiskey from his suitcase. "I was saving this for a rainy day."

"Crack it open, man." Rafi sighed. "It's pouring."

Ash found two rocks glasses and splashed them each a finger, handing one to Rafi as he sank into the other club chair. "Is it Sunita?"

Rafi puffed a humorless laugh. "God, I almost wish that was it." He swallowed a mouthful of whiskey, fortifying himself to share the bitter truth. "I think I'm having a quarter-life crisis?"

Ash's eyes widened.

"I'm not happy. At work. In . . . life?" As Ash listened, Rafi tried to put into words everything that had crystalized for him ever since he pulled that damned card. Everything he'd quite possibly been in denial over prior to this week.

"Well, you can absolutely quit your job," Ash said. "Maybe not tomorrow—you'll need to get some savings together first, talk to some recruiters, or whatever. But if you're not happy, don't stay. Find something else."

"But I'm not like Birdie and Liz, and you: I don't have a creative passion that drives me. I've never wanted to be a full-time artist, or founder, or mid-level marketing manager." Zookeeper? Kindergarten teacher? Pastry chef? Nothing he could think of set his soul on fire. "I can't think of a job that'd give my life meaning."

Ash's smile was fond. "Raf, that's completely normal. For some people, their identity and passion are tied up with their work. But plenty of people I know have a job they like well enough that funds the things they really enjoy doing. Like travel or spending time with family. A hobby. Not everyone needs to find meaning in work."

Maybe because he'd grown up in such a creative family, Rafi had never considered that he didn't need to be fulfilled by his work. That he could find his passion *outside* of work. That his passion and his work might be two completely different things.

"That actually makes me feel a bit better," he admitted, taking another sip. "Even if I still need to figure out what I want my life to be about, big picture." He swirled the whiskey in his glass. "I really wanted to get married, but I don't think my true desire was to marry Sunita, specifically. It was about . . . something else. Something I still haven't figured out."

A log in the fire shifted, the pieces of wood rearranging. "Well, what does marriage mean to you?" Ash asked. "What about it appeals?"

Now, that was a good question. Rafi inhaled several deep breaths, trying to push past discomfort. "I think what appeals about it is having a family. Of course, I already have a family," he added, "and you're part of it. But as a husband, with a spouse, a couple kids running around? In that little unit, I'd always . . . belong."

His breath hitched in his throat. Something in his chest cracked open.

Across from him, Ash's voice was soft. "That's something you've struggled with in the past."

Ash was right—he'd been there for all of it. Rafi had always struggled to truly, deeply, belong.

Was that why he'd proposed to Sunita? Why he'd always wanted to get married?

"Whoa." Rafi sat back in his chair, letting out a stunned breath. "I think I just had a breakthrough." He looked at his empty glass. "I think I need another drink."

Ash chuckled and rose to retrieve the bottle.

"You should pull a card!" Rafi felt like he'd been the focus for long enough. "You deserve a breakthrough too."

Ash refilled their glasses. "Don't know if I'm ready for one of those."

Ash's thirtieth birthday wasn't until April of next year. Even though it didn't seem to be a source of tension for him like it was for Rafi, Ash still deserved the chance for self-reflection. Rafi scooped up the deck from his bedside table. *"The Big Questions. You already have the answers,"* he read aloud from the black-and-white packaging, then handed the deck to Ash. "Shuffle, pull, reflect. It's easy, if you don't mind the potential side effect of a full-blown existential meltdown."

With a playfully wary expression, Ash started shuffling. They both leaned forward as Ash pulled a card, flipping it over so they could read it at the same time.

What simple things make you happy?

Rafi slapped Ash's knee. "Oh, that's an easy one!"

"What makes me happy? Hmm . . . ." Ash took a slow sip of whiskey, which was, Rafi noticed, the exact same mellow brown as his eyes. "Whiskey in front of a fire on a cold night.

'Cakewalk' by the Oscar Peterson Quartet. Ella Fitzgerald, Miles Davis, Sam Cooke." His eyes went a little starry, a smile on his lips. "Laughing so hard you feel like a kid. Finding the perfect cashmere sweater. Pasta, in general. You."

Ash smiled at Rafi and Rafi smiled back, feeling a surge of affection so powerful it almost made him woozy. How goddamn lucky he was to have a friend like this, one who'd known him for so long, through so many different phases, all the ups and downs. And how lucky he was to know Ash in the same way. The moment stretched, but neither looked away.

God, Ash was beautiful. His words. His heart. His *mouth*. Had his mouth always looked like that? So lush and soft, especially when contrasted with the hard line of his jaw. No wonder he was so in demand.

"What about . . ." Rafi arched a cheeky brow. "Boys?"

"Boys?"

"Boys," Rafi repeated. "Sex. You know—that thing that happens when a man and another man love each other very much . . ."

Ash chuckled, shifting in the club chair. "Right. Not sure how much love has to do with it."

Only now did Rafi realize he was a little drunk. He and Ash didn't usually go deep on sex because typically, Ash kept his sex life to himself. What did Rafi *really* want to know?

"Do you want to get married?" Rafi asked, realizing he didn't actually know. "Y'know—one day."

"One day?" Ash tipped his head to the side, scratching his cheek thoughtfully. "Maybe. If I meet the right guy."

"Really?" Rafi pitched forward with a grin. "Why? What about marriage appeals to you?"

Ash squirmed, a nervous chuckle bubbling out of him. "Fuck, I don't know. I don't think about it that much."

"I've got all night, bro."

Ash took a measured sip. "I guess, it's a nice idea. To commit to someone I love, who loves me. To know we'd be together through all the ups and downs. To wake up every morning with my best friend."

The world tilted, just one degree. For a weird, wobbly moment, it almost felt like Ash was talking about him.

"Well, I'm very, very available," Rafi joked. "My mom could walk us both up the aisle."

"Sorry, I didn't mean—" Color was rising in Ash's cheeks. "I mean, my best friend who isn't you."

Rafi clutched his heart, feigning pain, before reaching for the whiskey. "What about kids?"

"Raf." Ash groaned. "Can we talk about something else?"

Rafi topped them both up. "You'd be a great dad."

Ash's thick gold brows jumped up. "Based on what?"

"Based on you!" Rafi waved a hand in Ash's general direction.

Ash rubbed the back of his neck, wincing. "Never thought I'd be a very good dad. Y'know: 'cause mine was so shit." He narrowed his eyes. "Remember the time when he took off for a month? When I was like, what, fifteen?"

Rafi's heart felt like a dishrag being wrung out. Privately, Rafi had always wondered if Willie's emotional negligence was related to Ash's reticence to let someone in, long-term. Or maybe he just enjoyed casual sex and didn't need a relationship to be fulfilled. "I didn't even have a dad and I think I'll be okay at it," Rafi said. "I can definitely see you being a great dad."

"You can?" Ash sounded doubtful.

"I can."

Rafi pictured a park. A little boy on a swing. Ash, in the

same jeans and sweater he was wearing now, pushing the kid in a way that looked natural, easy. Fun, for both of them. The day was overcast, the sky a pearly gray. Smart white row houses faced the park—Rafi recognized it as London, cribbed from the movies; he'd never actually been. He imagined Ash and the little boy holding hands as they crossed the street, entering one of the gorgeous townhouses. Wooden floorboards, walls lined with art. A hallway that opened into an airy kitchen, where a man—Ash's husband—was at the stove making dinner: pasta, in general. The little boy ran to him— *Daddy, Daddy!* Smiling, the man turned to swing the boy into his arms as Ash leaned down to plant a kiss on his mouth.

The man was Rafi. Rafi, in an apron, holding a sauce-covered spoon. Rafi, kissing Ash, holding their son, in their London townhouse.

The fantasy screeched to a halt. Rafi landed back in his bedroom with a jarring thud. "Fuck."

"What?"

"Nothing." Jesus, it'd seemed so real. So . . . normal. He could practically feel Ash's mouth pressing into his own. The weight of that kid in his arms. The smell of the sauce lingered in his nose.

He was obviously much drunker than he thought he was. "No more whiskey for me." Rafi wobbled to his feet. "Woah." The room was spinning. Swiveling for the bathroom, he lost his balance, toppling headlong toward the fire.

"Raf!" Ash dashed forward to catch him. He grabbed both of Rafi's arms, steadying him with a strong grip.

On feeling Ash's hands on his bare skin, a jolt of electricity arced up Rafi's arms and across his entire back, where it stayed, fizzing under his skin. Rafi sucked in a gasp.

Okay, he was definitely *very* drunk. Way too much whiskey, way too much talk about marriage and best friends and sex. He opened his mouth to make an excuse, looking up to find Ash's gaze.

Ash was staring down at him. Concern and a strange sort of heat turned his eyes into molasses: golden-brown and sticky. The temperature in the room was suddenly triple digits. They were standing so close. Ash was still holding Rafi's arms with his warm, strong hands. He wasn't letting go. Time seemed to slow, then stop.

They were still. Just. Staring. Directly into each other's eyes.

Ash's gaze moved to Rafi's mouth.

A spike of heat plunged into Rafi's stomach. No: lower.

For one wild second, Rafi imagined Ash cupping the back of Rafi's neck, then dropping his head to slide his tongue into Rafi's willing mouth.

Ash. His *friend.*

"Sorry," Rafi blurted, breaking the embrace to back up. "I'm such a lightweight." His heart was floundering, blood hurricaning around his body. "Bedtime for me."

In less than a minute, he had the covers pulled up tight, facing away from Ash, feigning sleep.

Ash took his time showering, getting into bed to read for a while before switching off the light.

Rafi squeezed his eyes shut, willing sleep to come and erase the end of the night from the record, praying he didn't remember his ludicrous fantasy tomorrow.

But somehow, he already knew he'd never be able to forget it.

19.

Fifteen days till Christmas

⁕

THE NEXT MORNING, BIRDIE TOOK PITY ON HER VERY HUNGOVER brother and made him and Ash a double helping of Sunday Eggs. Her attention was on the clock: Jecka was coming by for a meeting with Babs to discuss the work they'd seen on the art crawl.

When the doorbell rang in the early afternoon, Birdie ensured she got to it first. "Jecka, hello. Come in." Birdie gestured in a way that was meant to be welcoming but made her feel like an English footman. "Welcome back to Belvedere Inn."

"Thanks." Jecka stepped inside, oversized black tote on one shoulder, looking both wary and amused. In her black leather pants and pale silky blouse, she looked like someone who knew how to pronounce *Viognier* and already had a will.

"Ma! Jecka's here!" Birdie hollered. Then, to Jecka, "She'll just be a sec." Birdie rocked on her heels, hands in her jeans' back pockets. Her hair was combed, and she'd double-checked her Moontower Comedy shirt was stain-free. "Thanks again for showing us around the other day. Ma loves her new sculpture."

The bronze sculpture Babs had purchased on Sunday was

now on display out front—everyone agreed it looked like a pair of breasts and therefore was fabulous. Their meander to half a dozen local art studios had been one of Birdie's favorite days all year.

"I'm pleased." Jecka glanced from Babs's seminude portrait back to Birdie. "Your family is very . . . fun."

"My family is nuttier than a fruitcake," Birdie corrected, earning herself a smile. "So, how's that pint-sized Christmas tree of yours working out?"

Before she could answer, Babs bustled in, already yammering on about wanting to see Jecka's portfolio and did Jecka want a coffee and what did she think of photorealism? Jecka pivoted away, focusing on her client as they both left the foyer.

"Bye." Birdie waved to no one before trudging back upstairs to the Humphrey Bogart suite, seeking solace in the arms of her cat. She'd just managed to wrangle him into sitting in her lap when someone rapped on her door. Startled, Mr. Paws bolted.

Jecka stood in the second-floor hallway.

Birdie glanced past her, confused. "That was quicker than heterosexual lovemaking."

Jecka's snort seemed like a decisive co-sign. "Your mom forgot she had a call." She stepped inside Birdie's bedroom. "Guess I've got fifteen minutes to kill."

Only now did Birdie notice the clothes and plates and empty glasses strewn around. Despite her being here for only a week, the room had somehow accumulated a year's worth of mess.

Her guest's gaze landed on a pair of boy-short underwear hanging on a side lamp. "I'm suspecting you're not the clean-house, clean-mind type."

"You suspect right." Birdie tossed the undies in the direction of the laundry pile. "My mind is absolutely filthy. There's a community-organized effort to clean it up next weekend. Still looking for a *lot* of volunteers."

Jecka laughed.

Birdie moved in front of a plate of half-eaten lasagna. "I'm guessing your . . . room? House? Apartment?"

"House," Jecka confirmed.

"—is neat as a pin. Remind me, what's the address? And the spare key is . . . ?"

Jecka shook her head, but from the uptick of her lips, Birdie could see she was amused.

From under the bed, Mr. Paws yowled.

"Oh," Jecka said, surprised. "You have a cat?"

"The world's most unfriendly feline," Birdie was quick to warn her. "Who hates everyone, especially people he . . . people he hasn't . . . um, *what*?"

Mr. Paws was moving *voluntarily* toward Jecka. Mr. Paws was rubbing himself against Jecka's leg. Mr. Paws was *purring*.

Jecka knelt down to give him a scratch under the chin. "Doesn't seem unfriendly to me."

"What—who—how?" Birdie grasped for words. "I feel like I just walked through a wardrobe of coats."

"Cats like me. We had them growing up."

"That cat doesn't like anyone! He doesn't even like *me*." Birdie felt like her heart might blow up. "I'm gonna need a picture."

"Of me and the cat?" Jecka asked.

"Mostly the cat."

Jecka watched on in bemusement as Birdie knelt to snap

the never-before-seen sight of her cat enjoying meeting a human being, until, with one final yowl, Mr. Paws sauntered off.

Jecka brushed off her hands, her attention shifting to one of Birdie's notebooks, splayed open on the floor. Birdie scooped it up before Jecka could read any of her so-called jokes.

"Didn't pick you for a journaler," Jecka offered lightly.

Birdie sank down to join Jecka on the carpet, explaining it was a notebook for jokes. "I'm trying to work on a new show," she said. "Or, trying to start to try, if you know what I mean. I'm a bit of a procrastinator."

"Secret perfectionist?" Jecka guessed.

Birdie shook her head.

"Afraid of failure?"

Birdie squirmed. "Can you be afraid of failure if you already are one?"

"You're not a failure," Jecka said, straight as an arrow. "I watched your comedy special. It's really good."

A swift kick of pleasure had Birdie sitting up, fighting a grin. "You did?"

Birdie's one-hour comedy special revolved around her dating life from the perspective of a young, queer, born-and-bred New Yorker, a "dirtbag femme" who'd hooked up on the L train "more than once." The point of the show was to speak honestly about same-sexiness in a world that still centered men in queer women's relationships—"neither of us is *the man;* that's sort of the whole point."

Plenty of people had seen her stuff; the show had been out for ages. But knowing that Jecka had watched the thing she was most proud of gave Birdie an outsized rush of joy.

"Thanks, dude." Birdie flicked through the notepad, wincing at the many empty pages. "That's what I wanna work on next. Another hour, like that. Even though that one came out a million years ago and everyone's probably forgotten all about me."

Jecka ignored the last comment. "Good first step. An achievable goal." Jecka leaned back against the edge of the bed, her gaze softening into curiosity. "I don't know much about comedy. What's your process?"

Birdie did not like talking about her process. In her experience, few artists did. It wasn't just deeply personal. Sometimes it sounded silly or embarrassingly DIY when spoken out loud. There was no handbook for process. But Jecka seemed interested and nonjudgmental, and she was a fellow artist, so Birdie tried to put it into words.

She explained that she used both her physical notebook and two separate folders in the Notes app on her phone: *Working On It* and *Solid Gold*. Her physical notebook was where it all started, the place she'd scribble new jokes and ideas—an observation about human behavior, a funny or weird thing that happened, a take on a TV show everyone was talking about. She'd test those ideas in a regular, lowstakes set at smaller clubs or open mics. If the new joke got a decent laugh, she'd type it up and move it into *Working On It*. That was the place for good jokes that could be further explored, extended, riffed on.

"Jokes are kind of like a . . . recipe," Birdie said. "There's a million ways you can tweak them, and sometimes it's the tiniest pinch of salt that changes everything. But only from actually performing them—cooking them for other people to eat—do you know what works."

Once she had a joke that reliably hit, she'd move it to *Solid Gold*. Those were jokes ready to become part of a polished tight five—a five-minute set with lots of big laughs. Birdie had a few tight fives—material she'd been doing for years.

Jecka nodded, completely engaged. "So how do you create a whole new show?"

That was the sticking point. Birdie tried not to squirm. "Hours—or shows, specials, whatever—usually have a big idea at their center: a key framing device, with smaller sections. Like, a buddy of mine toured a show about becoming a father. The first part was his life pre-kid, the middle was about him and his wife trying to get pregnant, and the last part was about actually being a dad. There were a lot of detours, but the big idea was fatherhood."

"Do you know what the big idea of your next show will be?" Jecka asked.

Birdie blew out her cheeks. "Nope."

"Okay," Jecka said, undeterred, "what's the first baby step in getting there?"

"Writing, I guess," Birdie replied. "Thinking. Listening back to recent sets to see what gets the biggest response."

"You record your sets?"

"Yeah, most comics do. Recordings are better than memory. Hate listening back to myself, though. I'm always like, *Jeez, I sound like that? How can anyone stand talking to me?*"

Jecka laughed. "I think everyone feels that way. I've been interviewed a few times, and the first time I watched myself was the last."

Birdie perked up. "What about you—what's your process? What are your goals? Present your soul to me on a silver platter, please."

A wry smile. "We'll get to me, don't worry. I'm more interested in stripping you of the title of Ms. Procrastination."

Birdie smiled innocently. "Or we could just strip down, together."

Jecka groaned at the bad joke, but were her cheeks turning red? "You're incorrigible." She checked the time. "Your mom'll be done soon. Why don't you spend the afternoon listening back to some of your sets?"

Birdie squirmed, feeling a weird nervous wiggle in her belly. "I guess I could do a few."

"It's only one o'clock." Jecka got to her feet. "Why don't you do, say, three hours' worth?"

"Three hours?" Birdie scrambled up. "I'm down to work, but that sounds like three hundred years."

Jecka tapped her fingers against her lips. "You could break it up with the Pomodoro Technique. That's what I do."

"The pomo-what-now technique?"

"Pomodoro. You work for twenty-five minutes, take a five-minute break, then start again. After three Pomodoros, you take a longer break, maybe twenty minutes, then start the whole cycle again."

That sounded a pinch more reasonable. "But what if it's a waste of time? What if my best days are behind me? What if a new season of *Baking Show* drops—"

"Birdie." Jecka's expression was filled with compassion and cool intent. "Want to know the secret to doing the work, even when you don't feel like it?"

Birdie cocked her head. "Tequila?"

"Doing the work. Even when you don't feel like it." Jecka gestured at Birdie's notebook. "Twenty-five minutes. Starting now."

And for the first time in a long time, Birdie Belvedere did exactly what she was told.

HOURS LATER, BIRDIE WAS floating in the outer space of her imagination when a knock at the door landed her back on earth.

Jecka stuck her head in. "You're still going?"

Birdie blinked in surprise. "Holy ravioli." She felt dazed but energized. Brimming with ideas. "I just did"—quick math—"*six* Pomodoros."

Jecka's eyebrows jumped up. "Congratulations. If I sound shocked, it's because I am."

Birdie flicked back through her notebook. Eight pages of ideas. Eight! A burst of bewildered pride popped her to her feet. "At first it was taking forever, but then, I just . . ."

"Got in the zone." Jecka leaned against the doorframe with a knowing smile. "It happens."

But it didn't usually happen to Birdie. Her words felt clumsy, even as she aimed for sincere. "Thanks Jecka. For the advice. And for pushing me. And watching my show." Birdie gazed at the woman in her doorway, feeling an almost embarrassing level of gratitude.

"My pleasure." Jecka let their eye contact linger a microsecond longer than strictly necessary before stepping back. "Anyway, I just wanted to say bye."

"Do you want to come to our holiday party?" Birdie said quickly. "It's this Saturday. Ma throws it every year—it's a jam."

Jecka narrowed her eyes, mock-serious. "Are you asking me on a date?"

Birdie affected disgust. "What is this, the nineties? Have we just seen *Reality Bites* in the theater? Is my cellphone the size of your head?"

"Ha, ha." Jecka turned away. "Your mom already invited me."

"So that's a yes?" Birdie called after Jecka, as the artist headed for the stairs. "Okay, cool. I'm playing it cool. This is me playing it cool!"

"You're not doing a very good job," Jecka called back.

"Thank you for the feedback!" Birdie called after her, as the front door closed.

20.

Fourteen days till Christmas

*

AFTER THE HEAT WAS FIXED, VIOLET AND LIZ WERE ABLE to start working in the Barn. They'd bought a whiteboard in town and cleared out the secondhand bookstore of all thirteen *Sweet Valley High* paperbacks, for added inspiration. Now, on an overcast Wednesday afternoon, Violet was at the whiteboard, marker poised, as they brainstormed what vampires represented in their story world, the broader theme the metaphor could help the season explore. Between them was a mess of snacks—star-shaped cookies, chocolate fudge, and, of course, tamari roasted almonds.

"Vampires always need sustenance, right?" Squished into one of the beanbags, Liz was thinking aloud. "Blood. Maybe that's a stand-in for greed? Money?"

Violet wrote *Greed? Money?* on the whiteboard, underneath the phrases they already had, *Disinformation* and *Lust for power* being just two. "Youth? Although, I guess most of the characters are teenagers."

Liz gestured for her to write it down anyway, reaching for an almond. "I think what I find so fascinating about vampires is how they can be both sexy and powerful, and yet, so tragic.

So doomed and so vulnerable. That dichotomy is interesting."

Violet nodded, head cocked a quarter-inch, teeth pressing into her bottom lip. "It reminds me of . . ." She paused, looking uncertain.

"Safe space," Liz reminded her. "What happens in the Barn, stays in the Barn."

"Okay. That dichotomy reminds me of being a woman. Especially one in the public eye."

Liz nodded, listening closely. "What do you mean?"

Violet plopped down on the other beanbag with a sigh. "Well, if I'm being brutally honest, some days I feel attractive and confident, and some days I'm obsessing over a comment thread about, like, my chin being too pointy. I'm too fat; no, I'm too thin. My dress doesn't fit; no, I don't wear enough dresses. If I'm too sexy, I'm not smart. If I'm too smart, I'm not sexy. If I stand up for myself, I'm a bitch. If I'm too accepting, I'm a pushover." She let out a frustrated laugh. "I'm not supposed to care what people think, but I also must care what people think. I'm not allowed to age, but because I'm young, I'm not respected. I'm finally making money, but I'm not allowed to talk about that because that's gauche. And all of that can make being a woman really hard. Some days it's hard to get out of bed."

Empathy and anger flooded Liz's veins. She tried to sit upright, but the beanbag's plastic beads squished, tipping her off-center. "I'm going to—do something!"

Violet folded back a smile. "It's okay, Lizzie. This isn't our take-down-the-patriarchy brainstorm."

"Send me a cal invite when that *is* happening."

"My point is," Violet went on, "maybe our vampire metaphor can be used to explore modern womanhood."

"*Yes.*" Insight struck Liz like lightning. "That's brilliant!"

Violet and Liz kept talking, the conversation big and juicy and honest and fun. They only stopped when it was dark outside, stars winking in the night sky through the large windows.

Liz closed her laptop with a gratified sigh. "Amazing work today, Vi. We're onto something."

"You think?" Violet gathered their empty cups and snack plates, heading to the kitchenette. "This is less scary than what I was expecting."

Liz followed, curious. "What were you expecting?"

"I don't know. That I would have to"—she laughed, a pretty, musical sound—"do some creative writing, then read it out to you."

"I would love to hear your creative writing. Fan fiction about *Alone*, right?" The lost-in-the-wilderness reality show was Vi's comfort watch.

Vi giggled, rinsing the cups. "Right—two survivalists meet-cute over skinning a porcupine."

Liz found the dish towel. "Why did you decide to do something that you thought was going to be scary?"

Violet met her gaze, unblinking. Her eyes were the color of mist, swirling endlessly. "Sometimes, it's good to do things that scare you."

The air between them charged, a sudden crackle, as the rest of the room faded away. A crush of heat welled in Liz's stomach. "Do you want to stay for the holiday party?" Her question came out three times louder than Liz intended.

They hadn't nailed down how long Violet would be staying. She'd arrived one week ago, but now that they had a solid concept, perhaps she was ready to head back to the West Coast, to some chic holiday plans Liz wasn't aware of.

Liz went on in a slightly nervous rush. "It's this Saturday. All my mom's friends who live in a one-hundred-mile radius come. Mom sings, Rafi and Ash rip up the dance floor, Birdie does something regrettable. It's . . . boisterous." Liz wasn't used to selling the boozy Belvedere bash, but the idea of Violet leaving was unbearable. "There's this really good dip."

Violet raised a slow eyebrow, like a cat arching its back. "Tell me more about the dip."

At the risk of sounding name-droppy: "It's Holland and Sarah Paulson's secret recipe. We've been trying to figure it out for years."

Violet nodded thoughtfully. "I do want to try that dip. I didn't bring a dress."

"I can get you a dress," Liz said, too quickly. "Or wear whatever you like. Wear sweatpants!"

Violet chuckled, gaze still on Liz. "I'll get a dress."

"So that's a yes?" Liz wanted to make sure.

"That's a hell yeah." Violet deepened her voice, turning goofy. "Ho, ho, ho. Jolly Christmas!"

Was more time with Violet something she should be avoiding? In this moment, Liz truly didn't care. "No one says Jolly Christmas."

"They don't?" Violet grinned so big her smile wrinkled the bridge of her nose. "Maybe they should start."

21.

Thirteen days till Christmas

✳

To Rafi's relief, things with Ash returned to normal over the next few days. No intense moments of eye contact or heart-stopping touching, no bizarre near-future fantasies involving London townhouses and kids on swings. The more time passed, the easier it was to think nothing had happened at all—he'd gotten too drunk, misinterpreted things. As Rafi reminded himself hourly, he'd radically misread the romantic situation with Sunita, resulting in a public shaming that blew up his life. The absolute last thing he'd ever do was jeopardize his friendship with Ash. The absolute *last thing*.

Now that Rafi had committed to quitting his job and beginning the search for meaning outside a nine-to-five, work had actually gotten a little easier. On Thursday afternoon, he closed his laptop at exactly 12:30 P.M., ready for one hour of lunch break freedom.

Ash was at the dining room table, typing into his own laptop, brow furrowed in concentration. On seeing Rafi, he smiled, pausing. "Hey."

"Hi." Rafi plopped into an empty chair, stomach grumbling. "Ready for lunch?"

Ash glanced at his screen. While he didn't have to be on London time, he did have to bust out seven or eight hours of work a day. It was impressive to see Ash in this senior position, working so hard. "Give me twenty minutes?"

"Perfect. I'll make us some lunch and then, do you want to start on some cookies?" Someone in the family always kicked off making a batch of the soft, iced gingerbread cookies they had every year. "The dough can chill this afternoon."

"Sounds great," Ash agreed. "How about sandwiches. PB and Js?"

The comfort food he'd been eating since he was five. Rafi frowned. "We can do better than that."

RAFI MADE THEM TWO towering turkey clubs, with plenty of mayo and extra crispy bacon, just the way Ash liked it. Then he hunted around the walk-in pantry for flour, brown sugar, baking powder, and spices. He hummed as he lined everything up, then smoothed open Babs's grandmother's recipe, smudged with years of baking mishaps.

Ash wandered in, rolling his neck. They sat at the kitchen island and made short work of the sandwiches, Ash moaning over how good his was. "The Brits have no idea what a proper turkey club is." He licked mayo off his thumb. "They probably think it's an old-boys network for birds."

Rafi chuckled, savoring another bite.

When they were done, Ash washed their plates while Rafi found two of Babs's aprons. The first read *I'm Baking, Bitch!*; the second, *Now Watch Me Whip* in curling font around an illustrated whisk.

Rafi tossed him the latter. "Suit up, Campbell."

Ash caught it deftly. "Yes, ma'am."

They started on the recipe they'd followed so many times, Rafi could practically recite it in his sleep. Whisk the dry ingredients, set aside. Beat the butter, sugar, and molasses until creamy. They chatted as they worked, an effortless back-and-forth, punctuated by jokes and laughter. The two men were back to being in perfect lockstep. When Rafi needed a tablespoon of grated fresh ginger, Ash had it ready. When Ash decided the dough was too sticky, Rafi was right there with a handful of flour.

They were such a good team. When he was ready to try dating again, this was what Rafi wanted—someone with whom things were simple and fun. He'd never had this sort of ease with Sunita. He wanted to be with someone who felt like an equal. Someone he could eat a messy sandwich with. Someone like Ash. Who *wasn't* Ash. *Obviously.*

They covered the dough in plastic wrap and put it in the fridge.

Ash double-took at Rafi, huffing a laugh. "Dude, you're covered in flour." He gestured at Rafi's cheek.

"Where?" Rafi swiped at his skin, feeling the soft powder smudge into his stubble. He hadn't shaved since his breakup, liking the way it made him feel and look older. His thick, dark whiskers were already longer than Ash's, who maintained a classic five-o'clock shadow.

"You're making it worse." Ash wet a dishrag.

"Story of my life."

Ash chortled, taking Rafi's jaw in one hand to carefully wipe off the flour. The act was surprisingly tender.

They'd always been affectionate with each other. When they hugged, it was a real embrace, not the quick, back-thumping impersonation of a hug. And yet, there was something about the way Ash was holding Rafi's jaw that felt newly intimate. They were standing so close, Rafi could feel the heat rolling off his body. Ash's eyes were focused, a brilliant tawny gold. Rafi's pulse picked up, alert and alarmed.

"All good." Ash tossed the dishrag into the sink.

"Thanks." Rafi rubbed at his chin, willing the tingly sensation simmering under his skin to dissipate.

BACK IN FRONT OF his computer that afternoon, Rafi went through the motions as his mind wandered, tiptoeing past a DO NOT ENTER sign and into: Was friendship the best basis for romance? He'd known many successful couples who started as friends. Or became great friends. That mutual respect, and enjoyment of each other, those shared values. His mother hadn't been friends with any of the men she'd fathered children with, and look how those relationships turned out.

But for chrissakes, *why was he even thinking about this?* There was a reason why he and Ash had never hooked up, not even as horny teenagers, because they were *friends* and *nothing more.* Maybe there really was something wrong with his brain. Nothing was going on! Even if *he* thought it was. Giving his head a hard shake, Rafi forced his attention back on his screen.

LATER THAT AFTERNOON, BIRDIE, Babs, and Jin-soo were hanging around the kitchen when Rafi and Ash finished up work for the day. Everyone helped roll out the chilled dough and cut it into shapes with cookie cutters, except Birdie, who always did hers freehand.

"Is that . . . a dog?" Rafi peered at the unidentifiable shape of dough next to the more standard stars and Christmas trees.

Birdie looked crestfallen. "It's Ma."

"That's a tail." Jin-soo pointed.

"It's her cane!" Birdie corrected.

"I see it," Babs claimed, squinting uncertainly.

Ash and Rafi traded an amused look. "Bad dog," Ash reprimanded, making Rafi giggle.

"Is that an angel, sweetheart?" Babs examined Rafi's handiwork, her tone turning syrupy. "It's *very* good."

In the past, Rafi had enjoyed being coddled by his mother. Now it embarrassed him. "I used a cookie cutter. A literal child could do it."

"Children!" Babs flung her hands in the air. "Which one of you will give me grandchildren first?"

Rafi and Birdie exchanged a look of alarm. His sister cleared her throat delicately. "Jin-soo?"

Before anyone had a chance to speak, Siouxsie bustled in with two bags of groceries. Right behind her were Violet and Liz coming in from their day of writing in the Barn. All at once, the evening was in full swing. Ash streamed elegant, earthy jazz as Rafi put the cookies in the oven—they'd ice them tomorrow, after they cooled. Birdie opened a bottle of wine, weaving around Liz and Violet, who were putting together a snack board of cheese and olives. Babs regaled Jin-soo with stories of Christmases past—the ones when the money was flowing and all the kids got top-of-the-line bikes. The ones when she was broke and all the kids got bottom-of-the-line used books. "I remember!" Birdie crowed. "Nothing says Merry Christmas like a dog-eared copy of *Flowers in the Attic*."

Liz almost spat out a mouthful of wine, glancing at Violet. "May I remind you this is a family-friendly event?"

"Hey—love the ones you're with." Birdie clapped Ash on the back with a smirk. "Right, bro?"

He raised a sardonic glass. He'd taken off his sweater and was now in just a T-shirt, which clung to his biceps for dear life. "Hear, hear."

Ash caught Rafi's eye and winked. Goddamnit if Rafi's heart didn't trip over its next beat.

AFTER DINNER, THE FAMILY dispersed. Babs wanted an early night, while Violet and Liz were heading back to the Barn to work, something Birdie claimed she was also doing. "I *work*," she said indignantly, off Rafi's look of surprise. "I work all the time. I'm working right now." Birdie tapped her temple. "Writing a joke about a little brother who'll never cut the cord."

He gave his sister a tight smile. "Fuck off."

"Aw." Birdie looked truly touched, sauntering out of the kitchen. "I love you, too."

Ash pushed a hand through his dark gold hair, looking like an ad for literally anything. "Double feature?"

The hairs on the back of Rafi's neck lifted like startled meerkats. "Tonight?" They usually did their back-to-back screening of *Gremlins* then *Die Hard* closer to Christmas Day. "We won't be blowing our load too early?"

He said it. He heard what he said. *What the hell is wrong with me?* Rafi maintained a neutral gaze, even as his cheeks flushed.

But Ash just grinned, unfazed. (Why would he be fazed?

Nothing was going on!) "Christmas can come early. It's up to you."

All Rafi had to do was act normal, and everything would be normal. "Let the best holiday B movies of all time begin."

BABS HAD RENOVATED THE basement-level home theater after landing a Japanese endorsement deal for caffeinated chewing gum. The dark, cozy space consisted of three tiers of seven-foot-long velvet couches, strewn with throw blankets and cushions, facing the enormous screen. The boys had first watched the so-bad-it's-good throwback double feature when they were fourteen, and had done so every year since, except the last two.

They sank into the front row sofa, a bowl of popcorn on the coffee table in front of them. Ash tossed Rafi a happy grin. "I missed this."

Rafi smiled back, punchy with anticipation. "Me too."

Gremlins was paused on the title credit, but Ash didn't hit play on the remote, instead twisting to face Rafi. "Y'know, our double feature was an important part of my 'journey.'"

"I'd totally forgotten about that." Rafi tried to remember exactly how it played out. "We were what . . . ? Fifteen? Sixteen?"

Ash smiled, nostalgia softening his face. "Fifteen. It was the second time we'd watched it, and you were pining over Becky Ryerson."

Becky Ryerson! Their high school's queen bee, as beautiful and cruel as her equally hot twin brother, Brett. Rafi had to laugh. "Wow, I had *such* a crush on Becky Ryerson."

"And you assumed I did, too," Ash said. "After that second

screening, we were sitting on this very couch"—he tapped the space between them—"and you were going on about Becky, asking me what was my favorite thing about her. And I told you I didn't have a favorite thing about Becky. I had a favorite thing . . . about Brett." Ash shook his head, seeming awestruck at his younger self's boldness. "I don't think you got what I meant, so we talked in circles for a bit and in the end, I just told you the truth. That I had a crush on him. It was the first time I'd ever come out to anyone. I was barely out to myself." Ash wiped his hands on his jeans, shaking his head with a smile. "Even just remembering it now, my heart is racing. I'd never been so nervous. I thought I was going to throw up. I had no idea what you'd say, and I was so scared you were going to tell your mom, kick me out, and I really, *really* didn't want that because my home was terrible and you were my lifeline. My best friend. My only friend."

And for a moment, Ash didn't look like the style editor for *London Man*. He looked like a closeted fifteen-year-old boy, vulnerable and alone. He went on. "I saw it sink in, saw the mic-drop moment on your face. What you said next probably saved my life."

Rafi's breath hitched in his throat. "What did I say? I can't remember exactly."

"You looked at me with this big smile on your face and said, 'Well, that's perfect! I'll marry Becky and you'll marry Brett!' You barely even blinked." Ash's eyes were glossy with tears, his entire face flushed. "God, it was such a huge moment for me. For the first time since I realized I liked guys, I saw a future where I might actually be okay. Right here. Exactly where I'm sitting now."

Rafi's throat was tight, his entire body flooding with

emotion. His love for this human had always been galactic, but in this moment, galaxies *plural* didn't describe the size.

He had to protect this friendship. For both their sakes.

Rafi looked Ash in the eye, committing to what he was about to say with a ferocity he'd never felt before. "I will always be your friend. I will *always* be there for you."

Ash's face was open, his eyes soft. "Love ya, Raf." Ash shifted closer and then, they were hugging. Holding this man in the dimly lit theater, Rafi was overly aware of Ash's hard, muscled body. The softness of his hair. The smell of his musky-sweet skin mixed with that delicious cologne: citrus and bergamot and blown-out birthday candles. The prickle of his stubble rubbed against Rafi's cheek and neck, a murmur of enjoyment reverberating deep in Ash's throat. Holding him, being held, was Rafi's new favorite feeling.

Ash pulled back, his strong hands sliding down Rafi's arms in a way that felt noticeably slower than usual. The intense expression on his face was unreadable. Deep gratitude? Unspoken affection? For a long, heated moment, they both gazed silently at each other.

"Ready?" Ash shifted back to face the screen, aiming the remote and hitting play.

Rafi had always loved the ridiculousness of the absurd nineties Christmas-set horror-comedy. But Rafi couldn't concentrate on Gizmo, or the microwave scene, or the film's allegory about the dangers of unchecked capitalism. Because less than a minute in, Ash reached forward for some popcorn, and when he sat back, his left leg was pressing into Rafi's right leg. And he didn't move away.

Rafi stopped breathing. Did they usually sit so close in the home theater that their legs were touching? There was plenty of room on the sofa; it wasn't a matter of a lack of space. It was quite possible they *did* sit this close, and he'd just never noticed. Every time Ash reached for another handful of popcorn, his leg rubbed against Rafi's, sending a rush of heat stampeding into his chest that came out as a choked gasp he pretended was a reaction to something happening onscreen. The entire universe—every planet, every star, every piece of space dust—had narrowed to the point in this basement home theater where two legs touched.

Sitting there in the dark, replaying everything that'd happened since Ash had arrived—the moment of tension on Monday night, his musings about friendship and love, Ash sitting so their bodies were pressed together—Rafi couldn't stop the impossible idea sneaking inside his head. And once it was there, the impossible idea was impossible to ignore.

Was he, or was Ash, or were they both . . . *putting out a vibe?*

22.

Twelve days till Christmas

THE NEXT DAY, RAFI CALLED A MEETING OF THE BLACK Hearts Club.

He was waiting in the wine cellar with a plate of freshly iced gingerbread cookies when his sisters rolled in. Liz was amped from another productive writing day with Violet, and Birdie was giving her shit about when they were going to hook up already. "How's it knowing you literally *could* throw a hot dog down her hallway," Birdie drawled, uncorking a bottle, "because you're sharing the *same* hallway? That's a joke about your rooms upstairs, not about the fact you both have vaginas."

Liz gave her a look, selecting a star-shaped cookie. "Not all of us hook up with our friends."

"Friends make the best lovers." Birdie poured the wine. "Until it all goes horribly wrong."

Rafi choked out a cough, reddening.

Birdie handed him a glass. "What's on your mind, little bro? Breakup blues?"

"Not exactly." He double-checked the cellar door was securely shut. "It's about Ash."

Birdie hopped up onto a stool, munching one of her free-form cookies. "Because of the glow-up? He ditched the frumpy frocks and ponytail and now you're jelly as hell because he's a ten and you're a seven?" She squinted at him. "A six."

Liz laughed, then covered it with a frown.

"Fuck you, and no," Rafi replied, trying to keep his voice reasonable. "Things between us have just been a little . . ." Heat crept up his neck. His pulse was picking up. "I'm definitely not sure, but I'm kind of thinking maybe I . . ." His hand tightened around his wineglass. "I know this sounds really weird, but it's possible . . ." Rafi ran out of words, hoping his sisters would catch on.

They stared back blankly.

Rafi had no choice but to spell it out. "Maybe I'm realizing Ash is . . . sort of . . . hot."

"Of course Ash is hot." Birdie finished her cookie, licking crumbs off her fingers. "That's seventy percent of his brand."

"Sixty percent," Liz argued. "He's a great editor. That series on the paradox of fashion and sustainability was really—"

"As in," Rafi cut in, "a *vibe*?"

Birdie blinked a few times, unsure. "As in a *vibe* vibe?"

"Between you and Ash?" Liz squinted uncertainly. "You're vibing . . . together?"

Rafi shrugged helplessly. "Maybe?"

Both sisters' mouths fell all the way open. In their eyes were stunned disbelief and a good pinch of horror.

"Wow." Liz arranged her face into a don't-freak-out-I'm-freaking-out expression. "Okay. Wow."

Birdie's voice was squeaky. "You and *Ash*?" She started shaking her head. "Uh-uh. No way!" She gagged. "That's like kissing your brother!"

"I don't have a brother, I only have two very annoying sisters." Rafi explained the moment of tension on Monday, when he'd almost fallen into the fire after a lot of whiskey, and how last night, they'd watched both movies with their legs *touching*.

"*Wow*," Liz said, exercising one of two words she now used exclusively. "Okay."

"Not sure whether to laugh or throw up," Birdie mused, before closing her eyes and grimacing. "Oh god. I'm imagining you kissing. I am scarred for life."

"Are you sure about this?" Liz stared at Rafi with should-we-call-a-therapist eyes. "You do have a history of reading things wrong. I mean . . . Sunita."

"I know!" Rafi exploded. "I'm not sure *at all*. I don't know if it's all in my head or if something's *happening*. I keep telling myself I'm totally deluded, but then he'll just sort of look at me and suddenly, I'm swooning. Over *Ash*."

Birdie was massaging her temples, eyes still closed. "Fuck me. I'm at you-have-a-time-share-together-in-Rhode-Island-and-you've-adopted-a-poodle-named-Barbra-Streisand. I am not okay."

"Well, are you attracted to him?" Liz sounded like she couldn't believe the words leaving her own mouth.

"I don't know!" Rafi gestured with his wineglass so emphatically some sloshed onto the floorboards. "I've never thought about him that way!" He replayed Ash getting changed in his bedroom: the hard shield of his stomach, the muscular curve of his butt. "I mean, obviously he's *attractive*," Rafi allowed.

Birdie cracked an eye. "Dude makes Greek gods look weak."

Rafi's pulse was spiraling. "But we're friends. Best friends. And best friends don't go there. Right?"

"No!" Liz exclaimed. "Never!"

Birdie raised both palms. "To play devil's advocate, two words: Bert. Ernie." She shrugged. "They made it work."

Rafi was too wound up to laugh. "Well, what do I do? Do I say something . . . ?"

Both sisters spoke as one. "*No.*"

Liz shook her head, eyes the size of basketballs. "Take some time. A *lot* more time. If you still feel this way down the road, maybe, *maybe*, it's a conversation."

"How far down the road?" Rafi asked.

Liz nibbled her cookie, considering. "A year or two?"

Rafi choked out a laugh. "Not exactly my style."

"Right, and the leap-before-you-look tactic has been working so well." Birdie clamped a hand on his shoulder. "How many of your co-workers were there when you proposed? All of them, right?"

"Fuck off," Rafi said, but she had a point. "So, I do nothing?"

"*Nothing*," Liz emphasized. "You can certainly feel your feelings, but if you're wrong, saying something will make things *really* awkward. Change things *permanently*. Raf, it's Christmas! Maybe all the mistletoe's messing with your head?"

These were all fair points. "Birdie?" Rafi turned to her.

"Making an ill-advised romantic move is certainly dumb." His sister swirled her wine like a connoisseur. "But might also be fun?"

"Birdie!" Liz was horrified. "*Please*," Liz begged Rafi, "for the love of Christmas—*don't* do anything rash."

"Or," Birdie countered, "do."

Liz and Birdie began bickering. Rafi tuned them out.

Liz was right: this wasn't worth risking their friendship over, especially as there was a very good chance Rafi was completely wrong. He'd heed his oldest sister's warning and continue *quietly* and *slowly* feeling things out. He could manage that. Couldn't he?

23.

Eleven days till Christmas

*L*IZ SPENT SATURDAY MORNING PLACING ELECTRIC TEA lights on every windowsill and shelf of Belvedere Inn, confirming and printing the final RSVP list for the hired help doing check-ins, then solving the last-minute drama of not having enough holiday-themed plastic cups by doing a quick run into town. When she returned, Babs was directing a local electrician to ensure her seminude portrait was appropriately lit, waving her cane at the red-faced man atop the ladder. "More light on the left nipple!"

"Are you sure you don't want to move it to your bedroom?" Liz asked. "The president of your network just RSVP'd."

"Richard?" Babs appeared unfazed. "He's an old friend. And Dickie's seen much more than a picture," she added with a wink.

Liz regretted bringing it up. It was already 3:00 P.M. Guests would be arriving in a few short hours. "Okay, I really need to shower and figure out what I'm wearing."

"Do you mind checking the caterers signed the NDA first?" Babs begged. "And handling the wine selection?"

Liz swallowed an irritated huff. "Can't Birdie do the wine? Raf handle the caterers?"

"You'll get it done better in half the time!" Babs exclaimed. "Those two never sent off my Christmas cards, y'know."

Liz recalled Birdie promising she'd handle the cards the morning of the art crawl. Of course her sister hadn't.

"No, no: *more light.*" Babs refocused on the electrician, gesturing again with her cane. "I want to see those nips from outer *space*—"

Her mother stumbled, pitching forward.

Liz shot her arms out, catching Babs before she fell. They staggered back against the wall, knocking a mirror askew.

"Careful!" Liz steadied them both in alarm.

Babs pushed herself away from Liz, flustered. "I'm fine." She glanced up at the startled electrician, who quickly went back to adjusting the lights.

How had her mother lost her balance? Shouldn't this so-called sprain have healed by now? It wasn't her imagination— her mother's limp *was* getting worse.

"Mom?" Liz addressed her mother directly. "What's really going on?"

Babs rubbed between her eyes and puffed a sigh. The confession was barely audible. "I was thrown off a horse."

"A *horse*?" Liz didn't mean to shout. The electrician looked down from the top of the ladder. The two women moved away from him, into a corner.

"Four legs, a tail, likes to whinny?" Babs clucked in annoyance. "I was visiting a friend with a stable. Some idiot hunter fired a gun and the thing bolted. Like being shot out of a cannon." Babs demonstrated with her hand: arcing through the air, then, *splat.*

"Oh, Jesus," Liz breathed in horror. "You could've died."

"My doctor was shocked it was just the ankle," Babs said. "But I'd done that silly Western, *A Cowgirl in Heels*, and I guess all the stunt training kicked back in. I fell the 'right' way." Babs met Liz's gaze. "I didn't want to tell you because I didn't want you to worry. And you don't need to worry. I'm fine."

Their mother had always been proud. Even vain. When her career was in a slump, she'd claim she was choosing to spend time with her kids. Liz recalled public events where lesser actresses wearing too similar an outfit were discreetly removed. Babs didn't simply manage her public image. She strong-armed it. Liz recalled the explanation her mother gave on the first day she arrived back at the Inn: *Rolled my ankle. Promo shoot for season five had me in six-inch stilettos and down I went.* Offered breezily, a perfect mix of contrition and carelessness. Such a consummate actress. Such a good liar. Had this horse thing really happened? What was the truth?

"No more lies," Liz told her. "Tonight, tell everyone what really happened."

"Fine," her mother huffed. "Black Beauty one, Babs zero."

"And next time, tell *me*." Liz shifted even closer, whispering. "Even if you don't tell Raf and Birds: Tell me the truth, okay?"

Babs made a show of sighing, then nodded, just once.

LIZ EXPECTED HER SIBLINGS to be as shocked as she was that their mother had lied to them. But Rafi had just discovered the suit he kept in his bedroom closet for this very occasion needed an express dry clean, and Birdie was focused on what to wear. Ordinarily her sister would show up in something silly (a reindeer costume, complete with four-foot antlers) or whatever was on her bedroom floor. This year was different.

"I want to make an effort," Birdie kept saying, rejecting everything Liz suggested. "I want to look *nice*."

"For Jecka," Liz guessed.

Birdie flopped onto her bed with a groan. "She's going to show up looking like the cover girl for *Fancy Pants Quarterly*, and I'm going to look like something catering keeps trying to push outside with a broom."

Liz hid a smile. "I've never seen you so worked up over a date."

"It's not a date." Birdie spoke into the pillow. "It's a hang. How's it going with Grace Face?"

Liz's amusement wavered. "Do you mean, like, the pitch?"

"No, I mean, like, your clits. Are you boning?"

Propriety and delight tackled each other in Liz's chest. "We are not 'boning.'"

"You should bone. She's not seeing anyone, right?"

"No!" Liz regretted sounding so alarmed. "As far as I know. She's always said she's too busy to date."

Birdie scoffed. "No one's ever actually too busy to date."

Liz wasn't getting into it. "What about this?" She held up a simple but classy little black dress.

"A dress?" Birdie gagged. "Have we met? I want to look nice, not like a bank teller at a funeral."

"This is what I was going to wear, so thanks for that."

They both giggled. Birdie held the dress up against herself, grimacing in the mirror above the Bogart bedroom's wet bar. "God, you're such a Kristy."

"Well, we can't all be Claudias."

"With a Stacey rising." Birdie tossed the dress onto the bed.

Liz picked it up, folding it neatly over one arm, like a total Kristy. "Why don't you ask Ash? Being stylish is his actual profession."

"Yes!" Birdie was off the bed, scrambling for the door. "Brilliant idea, thanks, Liz Fizz."

"Wait—should I wear the bank teller dress?" Liz called after her, but her sister was gone.

Liz decided against it. She needed something special this year.

She knew as soon as she found it, deep in her mother's studio-sized closet. An emerald-green floor-length gown with a slit up the left side. A V-neck halter, backless. Babs couldn't remember where she'd gotten it, or why she'd never gotten it tailored (Liz was a good six inches taller than her mother). The neckline was low, and the slit was high—more va-va-voom than Liz would typically wear, but hey, it was the holiday party. The gown fit like a glove, which reminded Liz that in the dresser drawer of her Audrey-themed room lay a pair of gloves. Black silk and elbow-length, à la *Breakfast at Tiffany's*. After twisting her hair into a decent chignon, and paired with one of her mom's gold necklaces . . .

"Wowie zowie." Birdie whistled as Liz came down the stairs to the foyer, hours later. "Don we now our gay apparel: You look *scorching*, Liz Fizz! Definitely a contender for *Fancy Pants Quarterly*. I'm officially renewing my subscription."

Liz caught sight of herself in a foyer mirror. An elegant, grown-ass woman stared back, hair styled, brows darkened, lips a bold mulberry red. So different from the women she'd been before: The shy, bookish, well-behaved teenager. The naive twentysomething, certain she'd live happily ever after with her college boyfriend. Now Liz was struck by the thought that if things hadn't happened the way they did, she wouldn't be here now. Stronger and wiser for what she went through.

Liz focused on her sister, moving her aside to let a waiter carrying a case of whiskey pass. "You look equally scorching, Birds."

Birdie turned in a circle with a satisfied smirk. Tapered suit pants, a white button-down undone to reveal a peek of black lace, and an oversized ruby-red suit jacket, pushed up at the sleeves. Her wavy blond hair wasn't shoved under a baseball cap, it was pulled back in an artfully messy high pony, freshly blown out. The whole effect was very queer-festive chic. "Took me, like, *two hours*," Birdie said. "The pants are Mom's, shirt's Raf's, and the jacket's Ash's. Dope, right?"

"Hey, look at us." Rafi joined his sisters, three glasses of Champagne threaded in his fingers. He was in his classic tux, bow tie crisp. The facial hair he'd been growing out all month aged up his boyish looks. "Black Hearts Club kids scrub up okay."

The siblings always circled up for a toast before the party. When they were kids, it was juice in plastic cups; as teens, watered-down wine; in their twenties, some awful mixed drink. Now it was Moët in a crystal flute. "Cheers Belvederes," Liz said, raising her glass.

"To us," Rafi said.

"May we all enjoy the reason for the season," Birdie intoned, clinking glasses. "Yuletide hooch."

Liz and Rafi took a sip. Birdie downed the flute.

"Slow down, Squeak," Liz said with a frown. "You don't want to be full Lohan by the time Jecka arrives."

"Let's make a deal." Birdie squeezed Liz's shoulder. "You don't police my drinking, and I won't police your unresolved sexual tension with Grace Face."

Liz's cheeks heated. She turned to Rafi. "Where's Ash?"

He nodded toward his room. "Getting ready."

"*Ooh la la.*" Birdie poked him in the side.

"Just be careful with the whole Ash thing," Liz warned. Her brother seemed to have enough self-awareness to understand his rose-colored romantic brain regularly misread things. But did he have enough self-control to keep these thoughts to himself? "Especially tonight," she added.

"Or not." Birdie grinned impishly, skipping toward the kitchen. "It's not the holidays without a holiday fling!"

Liz cringed, but Rafi was already off, and the dogs were prancing underfoot dressed in puppy tuxedoes, and basically, it was all starting.

Liz spun for the kitchen. Movement on the stairs caught her eye.

Violet.

Descending the staircase. In *that* dress. Pale cream and pretty, floaty as a daydream. Swarovski crystals cascaded down the bodice, enhancing the garment's delicate, ethereal beauty. Vi had worn it on the show for the episode when both sisters, Jessica and Elizabeth, accept their respective prom-posals—from Todd—and go to the dance in the same dress, accidentally. *That's my favorite thing you've ever worn,* Liz had said, when Vi first tried it on. *You look like a princess.*

Now, with her buttery blond hair ironed straight and a dusting of gold on her eyelids and shoulders, Violet once again resembled royalty as she crossed the marble foyer, a shy smile on her barely glossed lips.

"Vi," Liz breathed, trying not to gawk and certain she

was failing. "You look . . ." Exquisite, celestial, transcendent: none of these words came close. "Like a snow angel."

Violet chuckled, leaning close to press her lips to Liz's cheek.

Liz had only a second to register the hot, light sensation. To smell Violet's rose-and-black-pepper shampoo. The combination of Violet's sweet, spicy scent and the feeling of her lips on Liz's cheek made Liz feel as luminescent as the little white lights wrapping the staircase.

Vi pulled back to smudge out the gloss with her thumb, smiling. "I remember you liked this dress. I pulled some strings."

Liz was glad there was a no-phones rule at the party. A thousand pictures and opinions of this dress and the person wearing it wouldn't show up online. Liz could keep this private for her.

Violet took a step back to admire Liz's gown.

Liz waited, breathless for Violet's summation.

Violet met Liz's gaze. "Very fetching."

Liz laughed louder than she expected.

Violet smiled, her expression turning heartfelt. "You look *beautiful*, Lizzie."

Liz tried not to melt.

Outside, a car honked, pulling up. As always, Louis Armstrong's "Cool Yule," a jazzy holiday classic, was the first song to light up the house. *From Coney Island to the Sunset Strip; Somebody's gonna make a happy trip; Tonight, while the moon is bright.*

A waiter whisked by with a tray of flutes. He was extremely handsome and, distressingly, shirtless.

"My mother hires male underwear models to serve the drinks," Liz said, shaking her head. "She thinks it's funny."

They each plucked a glass and took a sip, holding each other's gaze.

"If you get overwhelmed," Liz said, "come find me."

Vi tilted her head to the side, still smiling that charming, self-conscious smile. The gold flecks in her eyes shone like tinsel. "I'd rather just stick with you. So we don't lose each other."

"You won't lose me, Vivi." The old nickname unearthed itself. Violet hadn't been Vivi since Europe.

Violet rested one hand on Liz's forearm. "Promise?"

All the pre-party noise and hubbub faded away. Liz wasn't aware of the barking dogs or the semi-naked waitstaff. It was just her and Violet. She'd only have to drop her mouth a few inches to feel it connect with Violet's lips. Liz's voice was barely a whisper. "Always."

The doorbell rang. The spell was broken. They shifted apart.

Birdie flung the front door open. It was Holland Taylor and Sarah Paulson—as always, the first to arrive. Birdie screamed in delight at the sight of the family friends. *"Did you bring the dip?!"*

"We brought the dip!" they cried, presenting a bowl to a general cheer.

Liz caught Violet's eye and they laughed. The Belvedere holiday party had officially begun.

24.

ARTYGOERS FILLED THE FORMAL LIVING ROOM, KITCHEN, and family room. Plenty of past and present co-stars were on the guest list, but many of Babs's inner circle were non-famous folk from way back. High school friends who traveled up from Jersey; moms she raised her kids with; boys from acting classes who went on to become life coaches or dentists. Babs was an extrovert, charged up by new ideas, so there was always a smattering of interesting people she'd met at dinner parties or fundraisers: a world-famous sex therapist, a brilliant new playwright, a climate scientist with a viral TED Talk.

Birdie drifted from group to group, her gaze twitching to the front door every time it opened. No sign of Jecka. Maybe she'd gotten in the zone in her studio. Maybe she'd decided Birdie Belvedere was bad news.

Birdie had just gotten another refill of the themed cocktail—Rudolph's Regret: a boozy muddle of gin, fresh berries, and rosemary—when someone started dinging a glass from the living room. It was time for Babs's speech.

Ash had helped style Babs in a high-necked glittery black dress, smoky-eye makeup, and all the diamonds. As always, her strawberry-blond hair was piled atop her head (extensions, definitely) to add a few inches to her five feet two.

Typically Birdie would jostle for a front row seat in order

to heckle, get in the mix. But tonight she stayed by the room's entrance, with a clear sight line to the front door.

"Thank you so much for coming from near and far to be with us tonight." Babs twinkled her trademark smile as she waited for the room's attention to settle on her.

For as long as Birdie could remember, her mother wasn't just comfortable in the spotlight. It was her home, more permanent and secure than any house could ever be.

"I've been throwing this party since before my kids were born—all of whom are helping me host tonight," Babs added, pausing to acknowledge Birdie and, across the room, Rafi and Liz, to light applause. "And as the years roll on, my appreciation for you all deepens. As do my wrinkles; Paul"—her plastic surgeon, in the corner with his third wife—"you and I will talk about that later," she quipped, eliciting a wave of laughter. "But seriously, folks, you being here makes an old broad happy. You show up for me, and I love you for it."

Babs could usually drink like a sailor, but her words were on the edge of slurring. *Seriously* was close to *sheriously*. Birdie caught Liz's quizzical eye. Her sister had noticed, too.

"So, these holidays, be kind to your loved ones," Babs went on. "Hold them close. Tell them how special they are. And have yourself a merry little Christmas."

A tinkle from the piano. One of Babs's oldest friends from her theater days played the opening chords of the classic holiday tune. The crowd applauded as Jin-soo handed a surprised-looking Babs a cordless microphone, like this was all happening spontaneously and Babs didn't perform at every single party she'd ever thrown.

Her mother broke into her rich mezzo-soprano, gesturing over the crowd at Birdie with a knowing smile. "*Make the Yuletide gay.*"

Birdie smiled back, shaking her head in amusement. Even half in the bag, their mother was a consummate ham.

Babs moved on to serenade Liz and Rafi, just as someone appeared by Birdie's side.

Jecka Jacob. In a short, one-shouldered shiny red dress. Birdie let her mouth fall open. "Hide your diamonds, hide your exes: How are you a real living person? You look like an eighties pop song come to life!"

Jecka grinned, striking a pose. "That's what I was going for."

Finally, Birdie could relax.

After listening to the end of Babs's performance, Birdie and Jecka joined in with the crowd cheering on Florence Pugh arm wrestling her pretty plus-one, then sampled the famous Taylor-Paulson dip alongside Babs's longtime hairdresser and Cher. Was the secret ingredient dill? Thyme? It remained a delicious mystery.

Jecka wanted to say hi to Babs. Birdie located her mom sitting on one of the living room's white sofas, the center of a crowd enraptured by her horse story who wanted to know how far she was thrown.

"Thirty, forty feet," Babs answered airily. "And as I was sailing through the air, unsure if I would live or die, do you know what went through my mind?"

"What?" a guest asked, and everyone leaned in.

Babs playacted deep thought. "I have no idea where I parked the car."

The small crowd broke into laughter. Birdie stepped in. "Ma, look who's here."

Babs looked up, taking in Jecka, her hostess smile intact. "Who?"

"Jecka," Birdie said. "Jecka Jacob. Your new art advisor?"

"Oh, Jecka!" Babs said, convincingly enough. "Of course!"

Had she forgotten who Jecka was? Birdie couldn't tell.

Birdie and Jecka continued to mingle. In the crowded foyer, Birdie bumped into one of her invites, Sydney, the booker for Fox & Fawn. Birdie introduced Jecka and talked shop for a minute: the local stand-up scene, who was killing it, who hadn't been around. When Birdie mentioned she'd begun work on a new hour, Sydney offered for her to test it out: the late-night slot on the 28th was open. Two weeks' time.

"Ah, no way I'll be ready three days after Christmas," Birdie told Sydney. Her future failure was momentarily sobering.

"How long does it usually take you to write a show?" Jecka asked, after Sydney headed for the bar.

Birdie shrugged, raising her voice to be heard over the blistering Christmas pop that'd replaced the jolly holiday jazz. "The last one came together pretty quickly, but that was a million years ago."

Martin Short zoomed past on a child's tricycle followed by Jin-soo on a skateboard holding all three dogs. Somewhere, a glass smashed. *Opa!*

The furniture in the formal lounge was being pushed back to make room for a dance floor. Ordinarily this was Birdie's cue to start dancing on the piano and handing out shots. But all she wanted to do was hang out with Jecka. She cupped her hand to speak in Jecka's ear. "Wanna go somewhere—"

"—quieter?" Jecka finished. "Yup."

Birdie knew the perfect place.

25.

THE SOUNDS OF THE PARTY WERE ALMOST ENTIRELY MUTED in the wine cellar, save for the reverberating bass beat and occasional squeal. Birdie explained this was where she and her siblings hung out—or hid—whenever they were all home, and invited Jecka to choose a bottle. After surveying the shelves, she selected a 1990 Penfolds Grange Shiraz. Australian, expensive, delicious.

"A woman with excellent taste." Birdie plunged a corkscrew into the cork in a way that struck her as vaguely sexual.

Jecka slipped off spiked ankle boots and sank down to sit, crossing her long legs in front of her, the hem of her dress riding up to reveal smooth, muscular thighs.

Birdie pulled out the cork with Arthurian grace.

"You're good at that." Jecka gestured for the corkscrew, twisting off the cork and pocketing Excalibur.

"Lots of practice." Birdie poured them each a glass, handed one to Jecka, and held her own aloft. "A toast!"

Jecka tipped her head to the side. "Really?"

"I'm a Belvedere, I always make a toast." Birdie summoned her most earnest self. "To forgiveness, and art, and your art, in particular, and how fucking cool it is, and to our painting, which is my favorite painting of all time. A toast to Christmas, and parties, and Christmas parties, and . . . to . . . us?" The last words were offered tentatively.

"To us." Jecka tapped their glasses together with a *plink*. "Please be quiet now so we can enjoy the wine."

Birdie sipped, savored, and swallowed, speaking the flavors as they bloomed on her tongue. "Black Forest cake. Wild strawberries. Ooh, plum."

"Coffee." Jecka's eyes were closed, pleasure softening her face, her mouth turning almost sulky. "Licorice?"

"Definitely licorice."

"Amazing finish." Jecka opened her eyes and looked directly at Birdie, gaze sizzling. "Can't wait to see how it opens up."

Birdie's heart did a double take. She willed herself not to start glowing like Rudolph's goddamn nose. "So, I got a ton of work done this week using the Pomo-doro-moro technique."

"I think it's just Pomodoro." Jecka smiled in amusement. "But that's great. Did you decide what you want your new show to be about?"

"Only just finished listening back to all my sets." Birdie frowned, thinking. "I want to come up with something new. Something . . . meaty."

"Just keep doing the work." Jecka rolled the glass's stem in her fingers, seeming to consider her next words before speaking again. "Hey, is your mom okay? I thought maybe she didn't recognize me."

Birdie felt more relieved than uneasy that someone else noticed. "I was wondering that too." She summarized her mom's initial lie, then the truth about being bucked off a horse. "She's getting older. Which is sort of scary."

"My dad fell off a ladder a few years ago, cleaning out the gutters. It is scary seeing your parents get hurt. But Dad's a doctor—he usually takes pretty good care of himself."

Birdie settled back against the racks of wine. "What kind of doctor?"

"Obstetrician. At Mass General. The most senior Black physician on staff."

"Wow. That's so impressive. What's he like?"

"Single-minded. A perfectionist. Very dedicated." Jecka focused on Birdie. Her gaze had obvious strength, a smooth, strong topside, but it reminded Birdie of glass—forged in fire, resilient and clear, but strike it in the right place and the whole thing might shatter. "Of course I love my parents and I know they love me. I'm just not what they expected."

"Because you're more creative?" Birdie guessed.

"Not at first. I was actually a science kid. I wanted to be a doctor, just like my dad. And that's what I almost became. Before I fell in love with art and gave it all up. Moved here, to paint."

"Wowsers." Birdie tried to piece together the timeline. "So, when did you drop out of the Doogie Howser track?"

"A year into my residency—I was twenty-seven. I'm thirty now." Jecka explained how she'd started messing around with art for stress relief, just on weekends. Then weeknights. Then instead of studying. "I liked medicine. But I *loved* painting. It turned my entire world inside out. I liked being a beginner. There was freedom in it. I realized I could make anything. Be anyone."

Birdie could relate. A microphone and an empty stage were just as magical.

Jecka went on. "In the end, I had to choose between pleasing my family and pleasing myself. I chose myself. It wasn't easy—Dad made me feel pretty guilty. But I just couldn't live one more day not meeting my own eye in the mirror each morning. I wanted to be someone I admired."

The sentiment held unexpected weight. Birdie couldn't say that she admired herself, but wow, she really, really wanted to. How did one feel such a thing? What changes would she have to make that it was even a possibility? "That's so rad," Birdie said. "How have your parents handled it?"

"They still haven't come to my show, if that's any indication," Jecka said. "They think I've become some sort of anarchic queer deviant determined to sabotage my own success. Which is a shame, because I think Dad would like my work. I think he needs to have a bit more fun. Me too. Maybe that's why . . . maybe that's why I'm here." Jecka met Birdie's eyes with a tentative smile.

Birdie smiled back, letting the story settle, like the sediment in the bottom of her wineglass.

"Tell me about *your* dad." Jecka recrossed her legs, eyes narrowing in playful curiosity. "I read your Wikipedia page. Stanley, right?"

Birdie chuckled, flattered Jecka had looked her up. "I don't remember my parents being together; they divorced when I was little." She'd visit him in L.A., Birdie explained, go on spontaneous adventures. "Just get in the car and drive. He'd do these silly voices that always cracked me up. Dad didn't care about rules—he was always talking some maître d' or studio exec into whatever he wanted. He got so many parking tickets." Birdie recalled the way her dad would pluck them from the windshield, stuff them into his pocket. "I still get way too many."

Jecka smiled, listening.

"But the older I got, the more I realized Dad's spontaneity wasn't a quirky personality trait—he never planned anything around my visits. The silly voices weren't his goofy side—he was just drunk. I realized other dads didn't forget their kids' birthdays or where they went to school."

Jecka winced in sympathy. "He remarried, right?"

To the actress he left Babs for. "They stayed together, had a couple kids." The obnoxious half brothers who thought she was weird. "Even then, he slept around. His adultery was the worst-kept secret in town." Her truth was flowing, unedited, unchecked. "He's probably why I've never had a real relationship. Can't stand the idea I'd hurt anyone as much as he did—"

Birdie cut herself off, inhaling sharply. What the hell? She'd never admitted that to anyone. She'd barely admitted it to herself.

Jecka was listening closely. "You're afraid you'll hurt someone?" she reiterated. "Like your father hurt you?"

Birdie rubbed her sweaty palms on her pants, already feeling the vulnerability hangover. "Um, I don't know."

Jecka kept her voice soft. "When did he die?"

"Three years ago."

"Same year your special came out?" Jecka sounded surprised.

"The month I filmed it."

The taping fell on Birdie's thirtieth birthday. Ordinarily, she didn't invite her famous parents to her performances, but the special was an exception. Despite their differences, she wanted her father to be there for the most important night of her life. He promised he would.

Birdie executed her show flawlessly. Only at the end did her gaze snag on the empty front row seat. A wallop of pain undercut the joy of her standing ovation. Stanley hadn't come. He never even apologized. Three weeks later, he was dead.

"That's all so traumatic." Jecka shook her head in disbelief, eyes glued to Birdie. "How did you process all that?"

"What do you mean?"

"How did it feel to have that happen?"

"I mean, it destroyed me, sort of." Birdie wasn't used to investigating her feelings so intensely. The tentative pleasure at sharing herself with Jecka was being replaced by spiky emotion. "But I also don't want it to destroy me because my dad is a dick—*was* a dick—and thinking about him is a total waste of time." She felt herself getting heated, starting to ramble. "Sometimes I still find myself hoping he'll show up on my doorstep wanting to take me out for drinks. I have to remind myself that we weren't close. He didn't choose me. No one ever does."

The words hung in the air, too honest, too vulnerable, too much.

Jecka's next words were gentle. "Birdie, have you ever seen a therapist?"

Birdie blinked, taken aback. "Not really." The urge to run arrived without warning. How long had they been down here? "Um, how did we get into all this? It's the Christmas party!" Birdie scrambled to her feet, half wishing she could take everything back. "We're missing stuff. I need to see who else Flo is arm wrestling."

"Oh . . . okay." Following Birdie's lead, Jecka got to her feet. But as Birdie beelined for the door, Jecka put a hand on her arm. "Can I just say one thing?"

Birdie braced herself, even as she responded with swagger. "If it's about how good I look, I know."

Jecka's expression stayed compassionate, unwavering. "Your dad died three years ago, and from what I've gathered, that's when things stalled for you. From what you just shared, it doesn't really sound like you've processed his death. Made peace with it. Maybe that's why you're stuck."

Birdie stared back, not even bothering to mask her open alarm at this unexpected diagnosis. It took a long moment to stutter a reply. "Um. M-Maybe."

"It seems like your role in your family is the funny one— the comic relief." Jecka didn't break eye contact. "You're not expected to ever take things too seriously. But everyone needs to take their own life seriously. You deserve that."

Birdie's heart bashed in her chest. No one had ever said anything like this to her.

"I hope it's okay I said all that." Jecka squeezed Birdie's arm, her fingers warm, gaze kind. "I care about you."

Birdie's mouth opened in surprise. "You do?"

"Yes." Spoken with a half smile. "Maybe, if you stop flirting with me so much, you'll see that."

Upstairs, the party had reached the dancing-on-the-tables stage. Jecka said that was her cue to leave. They hugged goodbye on the Inn's front step, and Jecka promised they'd speak soon. But instead of heading into the festive fray, Birdie took their half-finished bottle of wine upstairs, slipping into her quiet bedroom and locking the door.

Her father's box was where she'd left it, underneath a pile of pillows. After a long moment of hesitation, and an even longer gulp of wine, Birdie took a deep breath and tugged the box out.

26.

*T*HE DANCE FLOOR WAS A NIGHTMARE. SLUMPED AGAINST the wall, Rafi couldn't tear his eyes away from the painful sight of Ash enthusiastically grinding with two ripped, shirtless underwear models like they were live streaming on Only-Fans. Now *that* was a vibe.

How had he ended up . . . here?

Oh, that's right. He'd ruined everything.

After his pre-party toast with his sisters, Rafi had gone to look for Ash in their bedroom, wanting to catch him before guests started to arrive. Ash was fiddling with his hair in the mirror above the mantel. On seeing Ash's outfit, Rafi stopped in his tracks. "*Dude.*"

Ash was wearing a tailored maroon velvet jacket. It fit him perfectly and looked both sharp and soft. Black dress pants hugged the curve of his butt. Add on a bow tie and smoking slippers, and Ash Campbell looked like a movie star ready for his own premiere.

Ash chuckled and cast an approving gaze over Rafi's party look, lingering on his face. "I really like the scruff."

Rafi's almost-beard. He scratched his chin self-consciously. "Don't know if I'll keep it."

"You should." Ash walked closer and skimmed his fingers down Rafi's unshaven cheek. Ash's gaze brushed Rafi's lips before meeting his eyes. His best friend's voice was hushed. "Looks cute."

Cute. The compliment fueled his growing state of nerves, a combination of bewildering excitement, sharp anxiety, and the disorienting sensation he was seeing things clearly for the very first time.

The entire day had felt more vibe than not. Their eye contact seemed loaded, longer than usual. The more Rafi thought about it, the more Ash seemed like the ultimate catch.

Yes, Rafi had resolved not to say anything, but that decision no longer seemed relevant. He didn't know what it meant or what would happen; all he knew was *this* was a *vibe.* More important, *this* felt *right.* Desire shoved self-control out of the driver's seat and grabbed the wheel.

Ash swiveled to face the mirror over the mantel, checking his hair one more time.

Rafi cleared his throat. "Have you ever thought about . . ."

Ash glanced over his shoulder, waiting for Rafi to finish.

"I'm just trying to figure out if something is . . ." Rafi tried to swallow. The air felt stiflingly hot. "Is there something . . . here?"

Ash's gold brows dipped in confusion. "Where?"

"*Here.*" Rafi tried to gesture between them. "With us."

Ash looked around the room, smiling in a slightly confused way. "Like . . . a ghost?" A look of understanding. "Did you watch *The X-Files* again? Raf, we've been through this. There's no real-life X-Files—"

"I'm not talking about *The X-Files!*" Rafi was sweating, almost trembling, and yet, he couldn't stop. What if this was their moment? Their chance? "Over the past few days, I think I've started seeing you in a . . . different light."

Baffled, Ash glanced reflexively at a lamp.

Rafi inhaled the deepest breath he'd ever taken. "I'm just

getting the sense that maybe there's something here. Chemistry, a *vibe*. Between you and me." The words were magic and terror and a dizzying, giddy high.

Ash's expression redefined the word *dumbfounded*.

Rafi couldn't stop talking. "Friends to lovers? Pretty sure that's a thing." His certainty that this was a good idea was waning terrifyingly quickly. "Just look at, um, Bert and Ernie."

"Bert and Ernie?" Ash stared at Rafi like he was dangerously unhinged. "The *muppets*?" He ran a bewildered hand through his hair. "Where is all this coming from?"

"The other night? Our double feature?" Rafi's heart was pounding so hard he thought he might pass out. "Our legs. Were touching."

Ash squinted, cocking his head, *trying to remember*. He wasn't pretending. He truly didn't know what Rafi was talking about.

The truth hit Rafi like a wrecking ball. It had all been in his head. All of it. He was back in Philly, on bended knee, in front of all his co-workers, the person standing across from him looking like a surprise recipient of electroshock therapy.

He'd done it again.

"Forget it. I'm obviously having some rebound-related meltdown." He cast around for something, anything, to walk this all back. In sheer desperation, Rafi made his voice jokey. "It's not the holidays without a holiday fling!"

The confusion and shock and wonder chasing one another around Ash's face condensed, instantly, into hurt. "A fling?" The words were quiet. "You think that you and I should have . . . a fling?"

"Yes? No." Tears were close. Rafi had completely lost control of the conversation. "Maybe?"

The laugh that left Ash's lips was ice-cold. "A fling." His voice was taut as piano wire. "We're not having a fling, Rafi. Not tonight. Not ever."

Ash moved past him, opening the bedroom door. Louis Armstrong's jazzy Christmas classic—*Have a yule that's cool!*—spilled in, along with the chatter and laughter of the first guests. Ash paused, taking a long breath. He shook his head, just once, and met Rafi's gaze. In his eyes: pain. "Enjoy the party," he said, and then he was gone.

THINGS WENT DOWNHILL FROM there. Guests clambered to tell Ash how much they'd missed him the past two years, how fantastic he looked. How was London? A fashion editor? So glamorous! But Ash didn't seem as interested in answering these questions as he was in flirting with every good-looking queer boy at Belvedere Inn, talking and laughing and beaming his light on everyone, while completely ignoring Rafi. Every smile, every touch, a knife in his heart. Yes, Rafi would do a deal with the devil to Eternal-Sunshine-of-the-Spotless-Mind their conversation in his bedroom, but Ash's behavior seemed designed to actively hurt or shame Rafi. Ash, whose greatest friendship betrayal had been streaming the final season of *Young Royals* without waiting for him. Was this Rafi's biggest betrayal of Ash? Stupidly misreading their interactions, or, worse, projecting his own pathetic rebound energy on his oldest friend?

EVENTUALLY, RAFI FLED THE sweaty dance floor for his bedroom, sinking into one of the leather club chairs. Disappointment and shame wound around his ribs, crushing him like a python. Why did he always have to be his own worst enemy?

The bedroom door opened.

Rafi tensed, readying himself to dismiss a random party-goer looking for a bathroom to puke in or a bed to screw in.

It was Ash. Shirt untucked, hair askew: the portrait of a man taking a breather from the best night of his life.

"No models in here, sorry," Rafi muttered, turning back to the fire.

Behind him, Rafi heard Ash shut the door and tentatively pad over to take a seat in the other club chair, spine as stiff as a cutting board.

Rafi wasn't one for the silent treatment. "Having fun out there?"

He hated how bitter his words sounded. If anyone should be angry here, it was Ash. Rafi had just single-handedly detonated their friendship.

Ash let out a pained breath. "It's not the holidays without a holiday fling, right?"

Inwardly, Rafi kicked himself. "That was something Birdie said and I just repeated it like a fucking moron parrot. Of course I don't want a fling with you, that's absolutely insane. I thought maybe something was changing."

The thumping bass of the dance floor was audible even with the door closed, but Ash's attention was only on Rafi. "For you?"

Rafi nodded. And then, because Ash was still here and because the tension was as thick as Christmas custard, Rafi dared to push. "You too?"

Ash let out a long, uneven breath. His cheeks were growing red. "Not exactly."

"Oh." Things weren't changing for Ash. "*Oh.*" So Rafi *had* read this all wrong.

People described the sting of rejection. It didn't sting. It was suffocating and heavy, like being buried alive. Death, right now, would be a relief. "Well, this is absolutely mortifying," Rafi mumbled.

But Ash didn't move. "What do you mean something's changing?"

Rafi took a deep breath, wanting this embarrassing inquisition to end while also feeling masochistically compelled to spill his guts. "I mean, maybe I'm seeing another way of being. One in which I'm . . . sort of . . . into you."

"It's been fifteen years, why now?" Ash asked, so quickly it seemed he'd been waiting to ask it all night.

But Rafi didn't have a good answer. "I don't know. I've been thinking about these big questions—where I am, what I want. And we're so close, and you'd finally come back from London, and things felt different. I thought maybe"—he forced himself to meet Ash's eye—"what I wanted was you."

Ash didn't respond for a good five seconds.

Then ten.

Twenty.

Rafi couldn't take it anymore. He was overcome with the need to escape. The room, the party, the country, his *life*. "Forget it." Rafi was on his feet, heading for the door. "If you care about me at all, forget about this entire night and I'll never—"

"*No.*" Ash grabbed Rafi's arm, spinning him back around. Before Rafi knew what was happening, Ash was kissing him.

Everything else dissolved and there was only this: Ash's lips, lush and warm, pressing urgently, breathlessly, into

Rafi's own. Ash's mouth. On Rafi's mouth. Not in a sloppy, drunken way. In an assured and powerful way. Rafi registered the sensation of lifting up, losing gravity. Of something untamed breaking free in his chest. And then, Ash pulled back.

As if waking from a dream, Rafi opened his eyes to see Ash anxiously scanning his face, checking for a reaction.

Rafi's brain wasn't able to process much more than: *That. Again.*

The instinct was so immediate, the newness so raw, the sound of his body so deafening, Rafi went nonverbal.

Ash was breathing hard, looking jacked with adrenaline. His eyes darted between Rafi's own. "Raf, I—"

Rafi grabbed the lapels of Ash's blazer and yanked Ash to him.

Relief and hunger surged onto Ash's face. Their lips crushed together. In a blur of movement, Ash had Rafi backed against the bedroom wall, one hand braced by his head, the other grabbing Rafi's shirt. His tongue pushed into Rafi's mouth.

This kiss was pure passion; it wasn't anything like the kisses Rafi had known before. They'd been gentle breezes. This was a hurricane, ripping up the earth, tossing brick walls with ease, exposing everything.

Ash came up for air, panting and windswept; he was in the storm, too.

Rafi couldn't breathe. Every cell in his body was rolling heat, smoking lava. He stared up at the man who'd just redefined everything he'd ever known. "Holy fucking Christ."

Ash ran his thumb gently over Rafi's lips. "Things aren't changing for me," he said, "because I've wanted to do that for fifteen years."

The words were such a shock, Rafi was barely able to register them. All he wanted was Ash's mouth on his, as hot and urgent as the pounding of his own heart. He pressed himself closer, stretching up on his toes, lifting his chin.

With a growl, Ash dropped his head and everything collided again: mouths, lips, tongues. This kiss was even wilder. An act of creation, the fucking big bang. Ash held Rafi's jaw with a hand that felt like the size of a bear paw, kissing him with such authority, Rafi's legs shook. The prickly sensation of Ash's stubble kept scraping against his cheek, and if he'd died before feeling this, had he even lived?

A groan of need that sounded a century old escaped Ash's throat. The sound reverberated into Rafi's mouth, and its desperation, its sheer need, made Rafi feel powerful. His mind was a mess, but his body knew what to do. Rafi grabbed a fistful of Ash's hair, a fistful of his blazer, yanking him closer. They staggered, mouths still connected as they knocked over a side table, crashing against the dresser, tripping over the carpet until it was Rafi who had Ash pinned against another wall.

Rafi pressed their hips together. Through the fabric of Ash's pants, Rafi could feel the distinctive shape of Ash's hardness, matching his own.

Rafi forgot who he was. They ground against each other, both hard as stones. The shock waves of pleasure were so acute and intense it felt like pain. Rafi was on the brink of losing control, everything rushing to an unmanageable point.

Ash pulled back, his lips swollen, panting for breath. "Wait, wait."

The words landed Rafi back in the room. His heart was

slamming against his ribs, gushing electric blood through his veins. The room was thumping with a bass line—oh god, *they were still at the holiday party.*

He and Ash. Had just made out.

No—he and Ash had just *invented making out.*

All he could do was stare at the man who was staring back at him, equally stupefied. Their suits were both wrecked, hair destroyed, lips puffy, eyes wild. Ash had scratch marks on one cheek (Jesus, had he done that?).

Ash touched his own mouth, blinking. Finally, he cleared his throat. "Well," he said, "that escalated quickly."

Rafi let out a stunned laugh, which almost became a sob. Not because he was sad. Because every emotion he'd ever felt was surging through his body in a frenzied river of pure feeling. It was the moment you flip on a light and everyone you've ever met screams, *Surprise!* Wonder, chaos, confusion, joy. He opened his mouth, but what was there to say? *Thanks for destroying me sexually for everyone else, forever?*

Disoriented, Ash ran a hand through his hair, making it stick up at the ends. "I didn't plan on . . ." He pointed back and forth between them.

"I didn't plan on . . ." Rafi imitated the gesture until they were both pointing back and forth at each other like a couple of lunatics. Each word felt like a dumb brick. Rafi's erection was the size of a Macy's Thanksgiving Day Parade float. "I didn't know," he said. "I don't know anything anymore." That, actually, felt accurate.

Something like a smile flung itself at Ash's mouth before he batted it away with bewilderment. "Did that actually just happen?" Ash seemed genuinely unsure. "Did we just . . ." He gulped, Adam's apple bouncing.

Rafi's blood was still singing, each nerve ending fizzy.

Without taking his eyes off Ash, Rafi nodded. "What happens now?" Rafi asked.

Ash's gaze dropped to Rafi's mouth. Yearning bloomed on his face before he scowled and shook it away. He, too, was still hard. "Look, obviously, I want to do that all night long. But I think we should slow down." His full lips pursed. His eyes were the color of molten lava. Ash raised a finger. "I'm . . ."

Rafi had zero idea what he was going to say: Going back to the party? Going to kiss you again anyway? A little teapot, short and stout?

". . . going to stay at a hotel," Ash finished.

"What?!"

Ash moved to retrieve a duffel bag, stuffing it with clothes. "We shouldn't sleep in the same bed."

Rafi was totally lost. "Why not?"

Ash cut his gaze at Rafi. As if the look transferred an image, Rafi pictured Ash hovering over him. Groaning. Gripping the sheets.

They shouldn't sleep in the same bed tonight because if they did, they would fuck.

Rafi broke into a sweat.

"I need some time." Ash zipped up the bag with shaking fingers. "To process. What just happened."

What just happened was they didn't so much cross a line as carpet-bomb that line out of existence. Rafi didn't know if leaving meant that Ash didn't want to do it again, or that he did. Rafi didn't truly know what he wanted, either. His legs gave way, and he sank onto the bed. "You don't need to go to a hotel. Just crash in the Barn. There are beanbags and blankets and a shower downstairs. For after all the yoga my mother doesn't do."

Ash shouldered the bag. "Okay." He crossed to the door, opening it. A Prince song strutted in. *I would die for you, yeah; Darlin', if you want me to.* Ash paused. Came back to where Rafi was still sitting on the bed, staring up at him. Ash took Rafi's chin in his thumb and forefinger. "Jesus," he murmured, almost to himself. "You're so fucking cute."

Cute. They were back to where all this started.

Still holding his chin, Ash lowered his mouth to Rafi's. Rafi closed his eyes. His best friend's lips were pillowy and warm. Not a kiss of feral passion. A kiss of care. His stubble grazed Rafi's own, a lovely scrape of rough whiskers and soft skin. They were kissing goodbye, as if that's what they'd always done. A soft groan reverberated up Ash's throat and into Rafi's mouth. Their tongues touched for no longer than the length of a breath.

And then it was over: Ash was pulling back, dropping his hand. The kiss couldn't have lasted more than five seconds. But in those five seconds, Rafi felt things he'd never felt before. New sensation, new emotion. Rafi kept his eyes closed, wanting to savor this glittery new feeling. The door shut, muting the party mayhem.

When Rafi opened his eyes, he was alone in his childhood bedroom. But nothing about it looked familiar, at all.

27.

＊

As the party started to wind down, Liz and Violet ended up together on a sofa. Liz was doing what she always did after alcohol loosened her tongue and armor: gushing. "It's not just that you're an *amazing* actress, Vivi." Liz was pure passion, adoration waterfalling out of her. "It's that you lead such a big life with such, like, *class*! You are *literally* a television franchise idol, and that means, y'know, navigating all this scrutiny, and doing photo shoots and events and interviews, as well as twelve-hour days on set?" The wonder of it was striking Liz anew. "And you didn't come from money or the industry or have any family support to help you figure it out. And that's all just so *impressive*. This week has been *so* fun and *so* productive, and this new season's going to be *fantastic* because you're also great at development! You're a great producer, too! I really admire you, like, *a lot*."

Violet's expression straddled sheepish and flattered. "I like Holiday Party Liz." She squeezed Liz's bare arm, and the sensation liquified Liz's spine. "You are equally badass. How many spec scripts did you write before you sold *Sweet*?"

"Seven," Liz admitted. Seven unsold pilots still buried in her laptop.

"Seven! You didn't let rejection stop you. It *fueled* you. You, Liz Belvedere, are a force," Violet declared. She leaned close, not even the length of a candy cane between their lips. "I admire you a lot, too."

Best. Holiday. Party. *Ever.*

When Violet excused herself to use the restroom, Babs took her place next to Liz.

"Mom!" Liz could hear the effects of the specialty cocktails in the pitch of her voice. "Did you have fun?"

"Of course." Babs's eye makeup had smudged but her gaze was sharp. "You and Violet seem cozy."

Liz blushed, secretly pleased her mom had noticed. "She's a great friend."

Babs looked like she didn't buy that for a second. "Oh, Lizzie. Can I give you some advice?"

"Of course!"

Babs's expression was tender as she took Liz's hand, folding their fingers together. "I don't think you should get together with Violet."

Reality teetered. Liz stared at her mother in disbelief. "Wh— Huh?"

"Sweetheart, you have a *hit show* on your hands. It's all everyone's talking about! An affair with your star is such a bad look. I know being top dog is exciting, but you *must* keep a level head about these things. That's who you are!"

Liz was flabbergasted. She'd been expecting a pep talk *in favor* of making a move. "But—I mean—plenty of couples meet at work. Look at you!"

"You want something like what I had with Stanley? Like Nikhil?" Babs let out a tired laugh. "Of course I don't regret having your brother and sister, but I wish I could've given them better fathers. Made better decisions." She squeezed Liz's hand hard. "Success is so elusive, so unpredictable, but you have it! Whatever you're feeling for Violet is *temporary.*"

Liz flinched, her hackles rising. "What if it's not?"

Babs dismissed this with a wave of her hand. "Honey, I lived it."

Liz had always assumed her brilliant, ballsy mother with her decades of experience in the industry knew best. But maybe she didn't. And she was pretty sure Birdie or Rafi would never be told not to follow *their* hearts. Was this really about Babs's concern for Liz? Or her inability to see Liz for who she had become and what she was capable of?

Liz kept her voice level. Respectful. But firm. "I'm not you, Mom."

LIZ COULDN'T FIND VIOLET downstairs amid the last of the party stragglers. Up on the second floor, Birdie's light was still on, but Liz didn't hear the typical after-party debauchery. Down the hall, Violet's light was also on, door closed. She must've turned in.

Liz stepped into a hot shower, washing away her carefully layered makeup and perfume. It was a relief to get into thick flannel pajamas. She was just about to peel back her covers when a soft knock sounded at her door. Liz padded in bare feet across the carpet to answer it.

Violet. Her snow angel was in pajama bottoms and her pink hoodie, hair wet and combed, face free of makeup.

She was the most beautiful person Liz had ever seen.

Nothing about this felt temporary.

"Advil." Violet held up a bottle. "For tomorrow."

"Thanks." Liz took it and their fingertips brushed, the sensation zipping up Liz's spine to her head, turning her brain hot and sparkly.

Violet lingered in the hallway.

If the conversation with her mother hadn't happened, Liz might've said good night and gone to bed. That was the responsible thing to do. But now responsibility seemed like behavior that benefited everyone else. Behavior motivated by fear and outdated ideas. What if she let her heart lead? Let her heart open?

Liz widened the door. "Wanna come in? We could watch a movie. Or—"

"Can we talk?" Violet sounded both nervous and determined.

Liz tossed the Advil on the bed. "Okay."

Violet came in and waited for Liz to shut the door. "Why do you think I'm here, Liz?"

Liz's pulse picked up. "So I don't get a hangover?"

"No, I mean, why do you think I'm staying with you and not at a hotel? Why do you think I haven't flown back yet?" Her indigo eyes caught the lamplight, a flicker of purple fire. "Why do you think I'm posting poetry on social media? Why do you think I haven't dated anyone else, all year?"

Liz was rooted to the carpet, unable to move, to think. The air between them seemed to shimmer. "Why?"

"Because," Violet said, "of you."

Liz felt like she was spilling out of her own edges, her heart too big for her chest, her blood too hot for her body.

Violet didn't break eye contact. Her words were soft and impassioned. "I want to be with you, Liz. I want to try this. You and me. I like you, and I trust you, and you make me laugh, and I think you're the coolest fucking person and I want to fuck your brains out. If you don't feel the same way, that's okay. I just need to be honest with you. On the same page. So there isn't any confusion."

Up until this moment, Liz had thought she'd experienced

every emotion a human could feel: the highest highs, the lowest lows. But the electric joy gushing into every cell in her body was new. As was the paralyzing fear in its wake.

Liz met Violet's gaze. "I have feelings for you, too. I think you know I do. I just don't want to be hurt again." Liz inhaled deeply, summoning the courage to speak honestly. "Remember how I told you I had a 'big breakup,' back when I lived in New York?"

Violet nodded.

"His name was Noah." Now or never. "Want the long or short version?"

"Director's cut," Violet said. "Extended version."

Liz lit a candle on the bedside table. They sat cross-legged on the bed facing each other, Liz with a pillow in her lap. She hadn't told anyone the full story since it first happened.

"We met my first week at college." The memory still felt fresh, as if she were back there, at NYU in early fall.

It was a slow-burn start. Unlike Rafi who was always besotted with someone, or Birdie who was always sleeping with someone, Liz was cautious. But Noah was persistent and uncomplicated. They became a singular identity. *Liz-and-Noah.*

Birdie called Noah a posh boy. He wore polo shirts; he sailed. He was the eldest of four, his family in finance. Liz assumed the Hegartys' wealth—their success—was one of the reasons why Babs approved.

"He proposed on Nantucket when we were twenty-five," Liz recalled. "We got married the next spring, here at the Inn."

"You were married?" The words seemed to fall out of Vi's lips before she could stop them.

Liz nodded. "Raf bawled, Birds hooked up with one of my

bridesmaids, and Mom gave a surprise performance of 'Dog Days Are Over.'"

Violet's eyes were still wide, reconfiguring her understanding of Liz to include this hidden chapter.

Liz went on. "I wanted kids, someday. Noah wanted four."

Violet let out a surprised puff. "Four?"

"I figured we'd start with one—eventually. We were both in publishing by then. I was an assistant editor; he was on the agent side. But I go off birth control and instantly, I'm pregnant."

Vi inhaled, her mouth falling open.

After the initial shock, the idea of motherhood had bloomed inside Liz, surprising her with its power, its heady, tender thrill. "It was like discovering another room in a house I'd lived in all my life," Liz remembered. She began fantasizing about her child, imagining a sweet, gummy smile and wide, curious eyes. They didn't know the sex, but secretly, Liz was certain it was female. Her heart was expanding. Her desire for this child was ravenous. "I was twenty-six, pregnant, married to the only person I'd ever loved, living in Brooklyn, working in publishing." Liz hugged the pillow. "It was the happiest I'd ever been."

The vision of that perfect life seemed to float before her, even now. Liz let out a harsh breath, blowing it away. "The nausea started one week later." One minute she was brushing her teeth, the next she was on her knees, throwing up. "Morning sickness, I assumed."

Liz threw up on the subway. Outside her office building. In the staff toilets. By the end of that first day, she'd thrown up nine times.

"I was sick a dozen times a day for four days straight. Anti-nausea medication didn't work. I ended up in the ER on a drip. Discharged with stronger anti-nausea meds. But everything kept getting worse."

She went back to the ER a second time. A third, now with her entire family surrounding her hospital bed.

"They were all there when I was diagnosed with hyper-emesis gravidarum." The term still felt familiar on her tongue. "Extreme, persistent nausea and vomiting while pregnant, the exact cause of which is still unknown."

"Oh, Liz." Violet reached forward to squeeze her knee. "I think I've heard of that. Didn't Kate Middleton have it?"

Liz nodded. "And obviously she had babies: some women can carry a pregnancy to term. But my doctor said I was the worst case he'd ever seen. *A ten out of ten*—his exact words."

As long as she was pregnant, every time she was pregnant, the illness would force her to reject all food and fluids.

"I was so weak, so out of it. Vomiting blood, my weight plummeting. I tried to hold on, as long as I could. A week later, I started to miscarry."

Tears shone in Violet's eyes. "Oh, Lizzie. I'm so sorry." She crawled forward across the bed to put her arms around Liz, wrapping her in a hug.

Liz let herself soften into the embrace, smelling Violet's shampoo, feeling the softness of her skin, before pulling back.

Now for the even harder bit.

"Noah was devastated, of course. He kept suggesting we try again—"

"Try again?" Violet frowned. "Wouldn't that have . . ."

". . . basically killed me. Yes. I kept delaying it until it all came to a head and I told him I couldn't. I physically couldn't. But he couldn't accept that."

"But you guys had options. Surrogacy?"

"Exactly, that's what I suggested. I donate an egg; he, his

sperm; someone else gives birth. But he just scoffed and said, *Can you imagine what my parents would say about that?*"

Violet made a disgusted face. "Are you serious?"

"He couldn't get on board with anything other than his wife birthing his children. I kept thinking he'd come around. But he didn't. Six months later, he asked me for a divorce."

"Oh, Liz. My god."

"I lost everything. I needed a change. That's why I moved to L.A. Started over in TV. Never really talked about it with anyone except my family." Liz met Violet's gaze. "Until now."

Liz had anticipated a painful conversation that would slice open old wounds, draw blood. But while they weren't easy memories, retelling them didn't hurt like she'd assumed. Instead, it felt like Violet had taken something heavy and hard from a bag Liz had forgotten she'd been carrying, lightening her load.

Liz tucked the pillow in her lap behind her back, relaxing into it. "That's why I've been resisting this, I think. All of that blew up my life and was just so hard and so painful. I didn't think I could go through it all again."

Violet nodded. For a long moment, they both sat there, letting everything settle. The candle on the bedside table burned even and steady.

"Have you heard of abandonment trauma?" Violet's question was gentle.

Liz was in therapy—she'd heard the term but couldn't place it. "Remind me?"

"When people who've been hurt self-sabotage to prevent a repeat of past pain."

The words were a key turning in a lock buried deep in her chest. Liz sucked in a breath. Her entire body rushed with the sensation of something loosening and breaking down.

People who've been hurt self-sabotage to prevent a repeat of past pain.

Maybe it wasn't just Violet who could hurt her. Maybe, in pushing Violet away, Liz was only hurting them both.

"I guess I'm not very experienced," Liz admitted, "in matters of the heart."

Violet's smile could melt an iceberg. "Well, you're in good company. I'm not very experienced in matters of the heart, either." She touched Liz's knee, her palm warm and reassuring. "Thank you. For sharing all of that with me."

"You're welcome. If you want to have your own lesbian confessional moment, feel free."

Violet chuckled, but her eyes were thinking. "Okay. Sure." Then, without further preamble: "I have depression."

Liz had been kidding. "Oh," she said, sitting up straighter.

"I've had it for years," Violet said. "I'm on medication, which works most of the time. But my brain chemistry is different from other people's."

Liz connected the dots. "The other day, in our first session. When you left."

Violet's expression was heartfelt and a little sad. "Yeah."

Liz remembered the way Violet seemed to shut down, close up. "What does it feel like? If you want to tell me."

"Like the world is a terrible place and there's no joy in anything. That deep down I'm a terrible person and I'll never be happy."

How badly Liz wanted to relieve Vi of this burden, even if she knew that she couldn't. "That sounds awful."

Violet nodded. "Hard days are hard. Sounds like we both know that."

The turtle had its shell, the shark had its teeth, the cat, its claws. But humans were so defenseless, just soft bodies and fragile hearts easily bruised. What a privilege it was to be invited into someone's painful places. To be trusted enough to be let in.

"When were you first diagnosed?" Liz asked.

Violet smiled, her shoulders relaxing. "How much do you want to know?"

"Director's cut," Liz said. "Extended version."

Outside it had started to snow. The night was a whirling, indistinct blur, but inside Liz's bedroom, things were finally becoming clear.

28.

Ten days till Christmas

*

THE NEXT MORNING, BIRDIE WOKE WITH LESS OF A HOLIDAY party hangover than usual. Rather than throwing back cocktails atop the piano, she'd spent the rest of the night going through her father's box. Her initial plan to spend a few minutes poking around had dissolved into hours of reminiscing, much of it painful. His Donald Duck voice that always made her laugh. His audacity. His talent. His stupid bow ties. Stanley was her *dad*, and even though she resented him, she also loved and missed him. As the party had raged below, Birdie felt it all.

Now, blinking awake in the milky morning light, she felt different, somehow. A little overwhelmed, but also curious. Open.

There was only one person Birdie wanted to talk to. Should she send a text? A thank-you for last night? Or would that be seen as flirting, something Jecka suggested she dial back?

Trying to decide, Birdie picked up her phone and saw that she had an unread message.

JECKA: Your mom said we could have the
day off her collection today. Are we hanging out?

Birdie's smile unspooled like a piece of red ribbon.

WHEN JECKA KNOCKED ON the front door a few hours later,
Birdie was ready. Shouldering a backpack full of surprises,
she led Jecka around the side of the Inn, to the thicket of
trees beyond.

"My mom told me never to go into the woods with strangers," Jecka joked, their boots squeaking through the snowy
path.

"I'm not a stranger!" Birdie lifted a tree branch for Jecka
to pass under, watching that her black beanie didn't snag.
"I'm pretty much your best friend."

Jecka belly-laughed, informing Birdie that her actual best
friend—a college roommate who now lived abroad—would
have something to say about that.

They rounded the last tree, arriving at their destination:
a small frozen pond at the bottom of her mother's property.
"Surprise!" Birdie extracted two pairs of skates and one set
of kneepads from her backpack.

"Ice-skating?" Jecka looked as alarmed as if Birdie had
pulled out two clown masks and a gun. "Never actually tried
it."

"Perfecto!" Birdie enthused. "Last night you were talking
about how much you liked being a beginner. So this'll be
fun!"

After a moment of hesitation, Jecka sat on the old wooden
bench overlooking the pond to begin lacing up her skates.
"Slapping paint on a canvas is one thing. Balancing on two

knives strapped to footwear on a sheet of frozen water is another."

Birdie giggled, already heading for the ice. The Belvederes had grown up ice-skating, first at the 30 Rock rink, then here. She skated the perimeter to double-check the safety—the pond had reliably frozen solid by this time of year for decades, but it didn't hurt to be extra sure—pulling up short with a spray of ice simply because it looked cool. "It's easy! I taught Rafi how to skate on this pond and now he's better than me. I can teach you."

Jecka started by clutching onto Birdie, reaching for her again and again. It felt great to teach someone a new skill: encourage them, help them get better. Jecka landed on her butt a few times, but she always got back up. Soon, she was skating in a wobbly but even sort of way, gliding with a thrilled, determined look on her face. "I'm doing it," she called. "I'm skating!"

"You're a regular Tonya Harding!" Birdie called back.

"Jeez, I hope not," Jecka muttered, concentrating on her balance.

Birdie shot past her, unable to resist another spin. Perhaps that was why she'd organized this: to display a side of herself Jecka hadn't seen, one that was competent and impressive.

"Show-off," Jecka teased, but her grin was approving. "I wanna try that!"

"No, no—" Birdie started, but it was too late. Jecka's attempt to pirouette landed her solidly back on the ice with a thud.

"Oooh," Jecka said with a wince. "That hurt my butt."

Birdie glided over and extended a hand. "Luckily, I brought some butt medicine."

Hot chocolate, still steaming in a thermos. They settled on the wooden bench to enjoy it.

Jecka nudged Birdie. "You surprised me today. I like being surprised."

Birdie high-fived herself, slapping her own palm. "I just need to impress hot, successful artists. Always have, always will."

Jecka's laugh was light. "I don't really think of myself as *hot*. Or *successful*."

"You're a stone-cold fox." Birdie swiveled to face her, their knees bumping. "And you have a solo show. In a proper gallery."

"In Woodstock. A hundred miles from New York City. If I want to make it in the art world, I need an offer from a bigger gallery, in Manhattan."

Jecka explained that a midsized Soho or Chelsea gallery was her coveted next step. Birdie asked if she'd had any interest so far.

"I did speak with one curator who said he wanted to see more of me in my paintings," Jecka recalled, nibbling a thumbnail. "That my current work is technically good, on a formal level, but to keep working toward something 'personal' or 'adventurous.'"

"Have you done that?" Birdie asked. "Personal, adventurous work?"

"Still thinking it through," she admitted.

Birdie pounced on this. "So, we're both figuring out new ideas!"

Jecka tipped the thermos to Birdie in a cheers. "I guess we are."

"What does being a successful artist mean to you?"

"Oh, wow." Jecka took a long pull from the thermos, her gaze lifting to the clouds overhead. "I have had some wins—getting the show at Woodstock Art being one of them. But then I get in my head over whether they're because I'm talented, or just a checkbox for diversity."

"That sucks." Birdie understood the need to feel celebrated purely because of ability.

"It does," Jecka agreed, passing Birdie the thermos. "It's hard to separate money from success. Capitalism equates profit with success, blah blah blah. If I sell X number of paintings or make Y amount of money, I'm a success."

Birdie nodded. A lot of the time, she felt that way, too.

"Reviews," Jecka went on. "Great reviews would mean I'm successful, right? But if I don't get them—or sell the work—that makes me question pieces I enjoyed making. Which feels really wrong." Jecka shifted to look directly at Birdie, the sides of their thighs pressed together. "I guess I try to think about success in terms of what I can control. How many hours I spend working. Paintings I produce, connections I make, proactively. Things I can realistically achieve on my own. Because otherwise, the goalposts keep moving."

"That's such a good mindset." Birdie cocked her head, thinking it all through. "So if you're doing that, which it sounds like you are, why don't you think of yourself as successful?"

Jecka blinked quickly a few times. "Um, I don't know." She laughed in a way Birdie hadn't heard before—embarrassed, even awkward. She toed the snow at her feet. "I guess I'm still figuring myself out, too."

"*Too?*" Birdie affected confusion before relenting with a smile. "Kidding."

"What about you?" Jecka's gaze was curious. "What does being a successful artist mean to you?"

Birdie took a slow sip. "Great question. That I'm mostly regretting bringing up."

Jecka laughed.

Birdie went on. "I mean, same: it used to be about crowd size. Laughs. Followers, likes, all that shit. But maybe it's not so much about the outcome, but the process. The trying." She spoke the words as they formed in her mind. "Maybe being a successful artist is just about waking up every morning and chipping away. Not giving up. Enjoying the things we make and do. Because success has to do with happiness, right? Or, that's what it should mean. Doing stand-up—the actual act of it—that makes me happy."

"So maybe, success is doing what you love," Jecka suggested. "Regardless of the outcome."

"Regardless of reception," Birdie thought aloud. "Regardless of how many people pay for it and what they think. Because we can never control that. And even though other people matter, maybe they sort of . . . don't."

"We decide if something is successful. If we are successful," Jecka summarized. "Not other people. Ooh, I like that. I like that a lot."

"The fact that I'm here with you, right now," Birdie said. "That feels like success to me."

Birdie had never had these kinds of conversations with crushes: honest and revealing. Real. She preferred to put on a show, probably another trait from her father, who needed to dazzle everyone, always. But dazzling by definition meant temporary blinding. Maybe if Birdie and her dad had been able to have more conversations like this, they would've seen each other more clearly. And if Birdie was less of a showman, her connections would be different. Deeper and more mean-ingful.

Maybe Jecka was right. Maybe she did need to take her own life more seriously.

Birdie inhaled a lungful of clean, cold air. "Last night, after you left? I opened my father's box."

Jecka arched a curious brow.

Birdie explained getting emotional over his old magazine clippings and shooting scripts. "I always assumed it was junk and that him leaving me all that stuff didn't mean anything. But maybe it was, like, a show of support. Artist to artist. Maybe he wanted us to have that connection?" Birdie fur-rowed her brows, trying to sift through her feelings. "I think I feel differently about him today. Less angry?" She consid-ered that. "No, I'm still angry. I don't know. Maybe my show could be about him?" She hadn't considered the idea before she spoke it aloud.

Jecka's eyes lit up. "That's interesting. It'd be meaty, like you said you wanted."

Birdie's head felt like it was opening, golden light pour-ing in. There were so many ways she could build a show around her dad. If she had the guts to do it. "Yeah. Yeah, it would be."

Birdie gazed at the woman sitting next to her. Her bird-bright eyes and soft lips. Her floppy black beanie, and Mona Lisa smile. Birdie had enjoyed many first kisses over the years. Dramatic and forged in fire, the messy first step of a tumultuous affair. But when she and Jecka leaned toward each other, it didn't feel desperate or dangerous. It was a kiss. A first kiss. As simple and sweet as the homemade hot choc-olate warming their hands.

They pulled back, smiling at each other, self-conscious

and amused. A thousand jokes ran through Birdie's head. *Yeah, I'm pretty sick at that* offered frat-boy style, or *My life coach told me I need to finish what I start, so we need to keep going until one of us is pregnant.* But sitting together in the cool, comfortable silence felt even more satisfying.

They could have this moment, just for them.

29.

RAFI DIDN'T FALL ASLEEP UNTIL WELL AFTER DAWN, AND not because of the banger beyond his bedroom walls.

Things aren't changing for me, because I've wanted to do that for fifteen years.

That being kisses that rewrote the very concept of kissing. *That* being douse Rafi's soul with sex-gasoline and set it on fire.

Ash had been attracted to him for the entirety of their friendship. Really? The idea was like the sun, too bright and too huge to look at directly. Rafi couldn't imagine himself as an object of unrequited affection. Typically, *he* was the one directing *his* boundless love at some slightly bewildered target. He knew that when those feelings weren't returned, it was one of the most painful things a human could endure.

Now, waking up alone the day after the party, Rafi wasn't sure if he could believe any of it. Ash had seen him at his best—on days of triumph and kindness and grace. But also at his worst—being childish or dumb or hopelessly naive. The idea that Ash harbored feelings for him through all of that didn't fit with what Rafi understood desire to be. Which made him feel stupid. But most of all, the last twelve hours just made him feel confused. Horny, and confused.

What did this mean for them? For their future? What happened now?

Was Rafi supposed to text? Or wait for Ash to text? His

thumbs hovered over his phone's keyboard, but all he could think about was Ash, spinning him around and kissing him with more intent, more need, than Rafi knew possible. The smell of his musky-sweet skin. The way he tasted. The rhythm they found after their initial stumbles. The kind of passion you feel only with the right person.

Ash was the right person. It felt like the end of a good mystery novel, when all the pieces click into place.

Or, Ash had been the right person only in that moment. A few cocktails deep, at the bacchanalian holiday party, after Rafi had spontaneously spilled his guts.

Maybe it was a one-off for Ash. One he was already regretting.

Rafi gave up on crafting a text, and that seemed ominous. If he couldn't manage the simplest form of communication, how the hell were they supposed to move forward?

THE ONLY PERSON IN the kitchen was Jin-soo, working on their laptop, typing a bit slower than usual.

It was early afternoon, and the house had mostly been returned to its pre-party state by the cleaners who'd already come and left. Only a few indications of last night's blowout remained: A black lacy thong hanging jauntily from the Christmas tree topper. A mysterious stain on the carpet in the family room. The faint scent of weed, mixed with something deliciously sweet.

"What smells so good?" Rafi said, by way of greeting.

Jin-soo pointed to the oven. "Pancakes, and bacon. Birdie cooked before she went out."

"Perfect." Rafi grabbed a plate. "Want some?"

"Sure." Jin-soo eyed him through their oversized glasses. "Hungover?"

Rafi nodded. "You?"

"Martin Short invented a cocktail in my honor. The Jin-soo Jingle." They shook their head like someone who'd seen far too much.

Rafi served them each a short stack with a side of crispy bacon. He slid Jin-soo's plate over. "You're going home for Christmas next week, right?" he asked. "What's it like with your family? The holidays, I mean."

"Not like this." Jin-soo twirled a hand to indicate the decorations, greeting cards, and enormous tree in the corner of the family room. "My mom gives me a hundred dollars to buy my own gift. I always get her the same face cream and my dad the same socks. We eat takeout in front of the TV from the one place in our neighborhood my dad thinks is better than my mom's cooking." Jin-soo tipped their head, as if picking through an odd assortment of memories. "One year carolers came to the neighborhood, so we switched the lights off and pretended we weren't home."

Rafi chuckled. "That is different. I guess we must seem a bit . . ." He searched for the word. Sappy?

"Nancy Meyers on acid? You do," Jin-soo deadpanned. "I've never met a family who hugs so much. It's weird. My mother's way of showing affection is force-feeding me, then criticizing my weight."

Rafi let out a soft laugh, but he could tell this was a tender subject.

Jin-soo picked at their pancake with nails bitten down to the quick. "And they've never gotten their head around the whole nonbinary thing."

"I'm sorry," Rafi said, awash with empathy. "That must be so hard."

"It's not the best. At least your mom makes an effort. Even if sometimes she gets it wrong." A faint smile. "When I first told her I was nonbinary, she asked me, in all seriousness, what I had against binders."

"No!" Rafi slapped his forehead.

The front door opened, Jecka's and Birdie's laughter announcing their return.

Rafi wasn't ready to face one of Birdie's joke-filled inquisitions, not with so much uncertainty churning inside him. He slipped off his stool. "Gonna bounce," he whispered, and hurried out the back.

OUTSIDE, HEAVY GRAY CLOUDS hung low and moody. Too cold to stay outside without a jacket, so Rafi headed down the cobblestone path to the greenhouse. The elegant glass building was just visible from the back patio, past the trees that surrounded the pool. Maybe he could find a little peace there.

Inside, a dozen orchids with delicate, spacey flowers had been freshly potted. The air smelled like green, growing things. Rafi wandered the aisles of leaves, letting his mind float into the past.

Ash dissecting a frog in tenth grade science because Rafi couldn't stomach it. Summers by the lake, rubbing each other's backs with sunscreen. Ash taking pictures of Rafi and his girlfriend at prom. Weekends in New York or D.C. or Philly, catching up over Thai takeout, talking until dawn. And all their texts and memes and FaceTimes, calls where they shared everything, and nothing was off the table.

Nothing except the most important thing of all.

Things aren't changing for me, because I've wanted to do that for fifteen years.

Someone opened the greenhouse door. "There you are." Ash sounded relieved.

Ordinarily, Rafi would spin around with a smile, a joke. But now he didn't know what to say.

Ash was in jeans and his navy Shakespeare & Company sweatshirt. The bags under his eyes suggested he hadn't slept at all. Still, he managed a cautious smile as he approached. "Raf Attack."

Instinctively, Rafi winced.

Ash noticed. "What?"

Raf Attack was his kid name, from a past that he wasn't sure existed in the same way. It was too complicated to put into words. "Nothing." Everything. "How are you?"

Ash looked thrown. Rubbing the back of his neck, he let out a short, confused laugh. "I'm okay. How are you?" he asked, each word tentative. "How are you feeling, about last night?"

A superstorm of emotion and memory raged inside Rafi. Ash pushing him against the bedroom wall, groaning into that epic kiss. The delicious scrape of his stubble, the hard heat in his pants.

The way Rafi couldn't craft a basic text this morning. The way he didn't know what to say now.

"I don't know," Rafi replied, honestly.

Air drained out of Ash, shrinking him to half his size. "Yeah. Sure. No, I expected— Once you sobered up . . ." He jammed his palms into his eyes. "Obviously I shouldn't have done anything, and now—" He let out a breath. "I should probably head back to London. We can talk after Christmas. We'll be okay, Raf—"

"London?" Panic shot through his system at the idea of Ash walking out, flying away. "Dude, I don't know how I'm feeling because . . . well, I just don't know what all that meant. I don't know what happens now." Rafi summoned his courage, ignoring his self-doubt. "Is it true you've had feelings for me? This whole time?"

Half of Rafi wanted Ash to confess it'd all been a Rudolph's Regret—fueled misunderstanding. But the other half, the braver, bolder half, wanted something different.

Ash shrugged, rocking back on his heels. "I had, like, a little crush. Wasn't a big deal."

"Oh." Rafi felt a crunch of disappointment even as he mimicked Ash's blasé nature. "Sure."

A moment passed. Then Ash raised his eyes to Rafi's sheepishly. "That's a lie. My crush wasn't little. Most of the time."

A bubble of conflicting emotions popped in Rafi's chest, sending him spinning in five different directions. Words started tumbling out of him. "Why didn't you say something, why didn't you do something?" How easily he could recall a thousand intimate moments—watching TV, getting coffee, making food. *Sleeping in the same bed.*

Ash met Rafi's incredulous gaze. "Because," he said slowly, "I'd rather be the friend you love than the ex you hate."

The logic was sound, if absolutely heartbreaking. "I hear that," Rafi said. "I feel that. No matter what happens, we *have* to stay friends. I cannot be the ex you hate, either."

"So, that's what you want?" Ash was listening closely. "To stay friends?"

Rafi considered it, his gaze arcing up. "It might be easier. Safer." His gaze landed back on Ash. His heart was doing some sort of Olympic-level bar routine. "But it's not what I want. I've started having . . . feelings for you. Feelings I've never had before. Feelings I can't unfeel." He frowned. "If that makes sense."

Ash nodded. His face was calm, but his cheeks were splotchy, his chest rising and falling fast. "So last night wasn't a 'rebound-related meltdown'? A 'holiday fling'?"

"No." Rafi took an urgent step forward. "*No.* Last night happened because . . ." He inhaled a lungful of air, summoning the truth. ". . . I'm attracted to you. Not just physically. I *like* you."

An amazed smile raced over Ash's lips. His cheeks were bright red. He had to clear his throat before he spoke. When he did, his words were soft. "I like you, too."

The surreality of all of this whirled around Rafi's head, unfiltered words falling out of his mouth. "But . . . but I'm not even your type!"

"What's my type?"

"You know." Rafi waved a hand, recalling the many, many boys he'd met or glimpsed in the background of their calls. "Underwear models and tattooed philosophy students."

Ash let out a laugh. His hands were in his pockets, and his eyes were glowing gold. "You're my type, Raf."

Those four words leveled Rafi. He clutched the edge of a wooden bench. Outside, a snowstorm had arrived. Fat flakes the size of rose petals drifted from the sky. Inside the greenhouse it was humid and warm, the green of the plants so alive against the slate-gray clouds.

"Can we start at the beginning?" Rafi needed to hear it. "The whole story. Everything you haven't told me."

"Everything?"

"*Everything.*"

"Okay." Ash inhaled a slow gulp of air, then finally started to speak. "At first, I didn't realize. When we first met, I just thought that's how friendship felt."

Halcyon days of adventuring in the woods and swimming in the Ashokan Reservoir. Laughing until they felt sick. Conquering each day like kings. A quote from *Stand by Me,* a shared favorite, summed up the feeling: *I never had any friends later on like the ones I had when I was twelve. Jesus, does anyone?*

"Back then, my feelings were something I co-existed with," Ash said. "They didn't upset me. They made me feel . . . normal." He paused, his gaze climbing up Rafi's body to land on his face. "That changed when we were sophomores. I realized that thinking about you constantly, wanting to spend every minute of every day with you: it wasn't platonic. For me, anyway." Ash's eyes pulsed with low, heavy heat. "I thought about kissing you. Touching you."

Only now could Rafi recall teenage Ash getting distracted, soft-eyed, in the middle of one of Rafi's stories. Blushing for no reason in the locker room.

"But you were my best friend." There was an edge of desperation in Ash's tone. "My family. I couldn't risk losing that. And for most of that time, you only dated girls. By the time you were seeing Axel . . ."

"You were in London," Rafi finished. It'd always bugged him why Ash seemed more ambivalent than thrilled that Rafi had a boyfriend.

Ash nodded. He pressed his lips together, seeming to come to an internal decision. "Why do you think I moved to London, Raf?"

"To spread your wings and soar without a safety net." Rafi recalled Ash's own answer, given a week ago.

"Yes," Ash said warily. "And. To get over you. The idea that we'd end up together."

Rafi's mind flashed to hugging Ash goodbye at JFK. *Why do you have to leave?* Rafi had asked when they finally broke apart. And Ash had given him a strange half smile, more sad than happy, that now Rafi finally understood. "I had no idea."

"I know. I figured it was safer that way." Ash raked a hand through his hair. "I didn't fully comprehend how much I'd missed you until I was back in your bedroom. I thought I might be over you, but . . . well . . ."

Rafi spoke without thinking. "Last night we attacked each other like carnivores at a meat buffet."

Ash blushed, chuckling softly. "Yeah. We kind of did, didn't we? I'm sorry about earlier in the night. I freaked out when you said that thing about a fling." He frowned, looking annoyed at himself. "I didn't do anything with any of those guys, obviously. I don't know why my knee-jerk reaction was to get so slutty."

"Because," Rafi replied in mock seriousness, "you are very hot."

Ash laughed. A teasing smile lifted his lips. "Flirt."

The word lit Rafi up. Flirting with women made Rafi feel tongue-tied. The idea of flirting with Ash made him feel like he'd just discovered his tongue for the first time.

It would take awhile to absorb everything Ash had just laid out. But the anxiety he'd been feeling all morning was gone. In its place was something different. Curiosity. Excitement. Hope.

Rafi nudged Ash. Ash nudged him back. Not how they used to touch each other as friends.

They couldn't change the past. But the future? That was yet to be written.

Rafi reached for Ash's hand. It was heavy and warm. Slowly, so slowly, Rafi spidered their fingers together. Laced and unlaced them, touching the back of Ash's hand with his thumb. Ash's thumb did the same, stroking his skin, sending showers of sparks up Rafi's spine. The greenhouse was quiet as both men stood staring at their interweaving fingers, mesmerized by exploration.

Ash's voice was low. "I really liked kissing you last night. Sorry if I was a bit, um, eager."

Rafi would never forget the way Ash had pushed him up against the bedroom wall, crushing their mouths together. The hottest experience of Rafi's life. "Please, kiss me like that again."

Ash paused, looking tempted before dropping their joined hands and shifting back. His words were careful and measured. "I don't want to rush anything. You just broke up with Sunita. You just *proposed* to Sunita."

"Who?" Rafi was joking but the meaning was real.

"You're really over her?"

"At the risk of sounding like a sociopath, I really am." Rafi gazed at the man whose face he could draw in his sleep, daring to tell him the terrifying, liberating truth. "You're the only one I want."

Ash let out a stunned, grateful breath. Tentatively, he raised one hand to Rafi's cheek. Ran his fingers through the soft hairs of Rafi's beard.

The movement filled Rafi's body with light. Instinctively, he tilted his mouth up.

Ash held Rafi's chin between thumb and forefinger. His gaze flickered around Rafi's face. Lingered on Rafi's lips, which were parted, breath coming quick. Ash's voice was a murmur. "Are you sure?"

Each of Rafi's internal organs liquified simultaneously. His answer was a pant. "Yes."

Ash leaned in closer. Close enough that Rafi could smell his breath: minty toothpaste and coffee. Rafi let his eyes drift shut.

Their lips touched.

Rafi had long held an egalitarian notion that kissing a man and kissing a woman was essentially the same—we're all just people, after all. But kissing a man was different. Being kissed by a man was different. Ash was taller than any boy he'd been with. Strong and dominant, but also soft and eager. Which made Rafi feel desired in a wonderful new way.

They sank into a kiss, luxuriant and slow and hungry. Rafi brushed his tongue against Ash's, the sensation hot and wet and *holy fuck*. In response, Ash's mouth opened wide. His best friend began kissing him with such single-minded focus, Rafi felt it down to his toes.

He felt it everywhere. Intoxicating strength flared up from his low belly, radiating into every cell. Rafi grabbed the back of Ash's head, a fistful of his hair, kissing him rougher, deeper. Stubble and muscle and heat.

A call sounded from the back of the house. Birdie, yelling into the snowstorm. "Raf? You out here? We need help salting the driveway!"

His sister's voice tipped Rafi back into the present. He broke away, backing up a step. "Yeah, here!" he called back shakily. "Just a sec!"

The back door banged shut in reply.

He swiveled to face Ash, feeling bashful and happy and insanely horny. "So, what's happening here? What are we doing?"

"Um, I don't know." Ash laughed, the unexpected smile bursting forth like sun through clouds. "I can't think straight."

"Amen to that."

Ash glanced in the direction of the Inn. "I think we should take things slow. Don't you?"

"First time for everything."

Ash slapped Rafi's butt. "I'm serious. I don't think we should tell your family."

Rafi imagined informing his sisters. Their hysteria and questions and warnings. He was definitely not ready for all that yet. "Right. So we're still just friends?"

"Just in front of the others. Until we get the chance to be alone and . . . talk. More." Ash's gaze dipped to Rafi's mouth.

A fist of heat clenched hard in Rafi's abdomen. "I can't wait to *talk* all night long."

Ash huffed a laugh, but his eyes were glazing, his hands sliding to cup Rafi's cheeks, his lips moving close.

Birdie's voice sounded again. "*Raf!*"

Rafi let out an annoyed groan. "*Coming!*" he called back.

Ash refocused, reluctantly dropping his hands and turning for the greenhouse door. "Let's go. Birdie sounds ready to—"

"C'mere." Rafi grabbed Ash's sweatshirt, tugging him back into one of the ferns. This kiss was different again. With Rafi at the wheel, it was more awkward, teeth bumping through their smiles, both guys stepping on each other's sneakers. It was quick, only a stolen moment, but in the too-short few seconds, Rafi felt everything. Desire, thick as the humidity. Lust, sharp as a knife. And something more tender and secret and true, written on Ash's breath as his lips broke away.

Oh, Rafi could definitely keep this a secret. Piece of *cake*.

30.

Nine days till Christmas

ON MONDAY MORNING, LIZ SUGGESTED SHE AND VIOLET go on a hike. "The pitch is close to finished," Liz pointed out. "I'll leave it for a few days, then do the final polish. Also," she added with newfound boldness, "I just want to. Life isn't only about work."

Violet's surprise took several beats to melt into a smile. "I couldn't agree more."

The day was vivid blue and crisp, the sky as clear as glass. The scent of pine needles and woodsmoke and snow braided on the breeze as they set off.

Continuing the free-flowing dialogue they'd started over the weekend, they discussed parenthood and how Liz's dreams had changed since her twenties. The social stigmas of mental illness and childless women. A deep dive into Violet's medication (Lexapro) and how she handled having depression in her professional life.

"Does being on set make it harder?" Liz recalled the early mornings and long nights, pained by the idea that her drive could've been making Violet's life difficult.

"Being on set can be hard for everyone, at times. But for

me, having a schedule makes it easier." Violet flicked Liz a smile. "Having people I can trust makes it easier, too."

"Can you keep letting me know? How I can help?"

"Of course." Violet squeezed Liz's arm with one gloved hand. "Thank you. I always thought telling a . . . friend, about my depression, might scare them off. But you're still here." She tipped her head to one side, smiling. "Being so sweet."

Liz had always believed she'd mapped out her own heart, understood its design. But new architecture was being revealed.

Violet went on. "I don't want you to think I just have one bad day every now and then. Depression is . . ." She puffed out her cheeks, searching for the words. "Trickier than that. It can rob me of everything—all hope, all joy, all belief in good things. It can kind of make me a bitch. That can be hard to be around. It's one of the reasons why I've never really dated a lot." She paused, assessing how these words were landing with Liz.

"You're right that I don't have experience being close to someone who I know has depression," Liz said. "But I want to know all of you. I like all of you. A lot."

"You don't really know all of me." Violet didn't sound defensive. It was stated as fact.

"You don't really know all of me either," Liz said. "How do we work on that?"

"We keep talking." Violet gestured at the path ahead of them. The snow was fresh, unbroken by footsteps. "We keep going."

Liz didn't know this part of the forest. They'd discover it at the same time.

Together, they walked deeper into the cold, peaceful woods.

———

THEY RETURNED TO BELVEDERE INN in the early afternoon, planning a decadent lunch to celebrate, well, everything. But Liz pulled up short when she saw Babs sitting at the kitchen island.

Liz had been quietly avoiding her mother, still annoyed at her shortsighted advice not to pursue Violet, a conversation she'd already confessed to Vi. The obedient, responsible side of Liz had no idea how to act around her mother after doing the exact opposite of what she'd suggested.

Babs also appeared caught out, not meeting Liz's eye as she gathered up her teacup and cane, saying something about a workout with Jin-soo.

Violet stepped between them, her smile defiantly cheerful. "Babs, would you join us for lunch?"

Both women shot Violet incredulous looks. "I'm sure you don't want me getting in the way," Babs murmured.

"Nonsense!" Clearly that's what Violet felt this mother-daughter standoff was. "I'll whip something up."

Violet did all the heavy lifting, which, Liz had to admit, was a pleasant role reversal from a typical lunch with her mother. In the dining room, Vi spread a floral tablecloth and set out the good china.

"Lunch with my girls!" Babs declared, as Violet presented steaming bowls of leftover French onion soup and a crusty baguette. "What could be better?"

Liz couldn't help but smile. Her mother had never been one to hold a grudge.

"I'd love to hear more about your background." Violet passed Babs a hunk of baguette. "Where did you grow up?"

Liz listened as her mom told the story of her early life:

Born in New Jersey as Barbara "Babs" O'Brien. A precocious child, headstrong teen. Married a local tradesman in her mid-twenties, Pete Miller. Liz's father.

"What was he like?" Violet asked.

"Tall." Babs popped a piece of baguette into her mouth. "Loyal. Hardworking. Reliable as the sun."

Violet slipped Liz a knowing smile. Liz had been relatively close with her dad before he passed five years ago from prostate cancer. At his funeral, they played Bruce Springsteen live albums and ate roast beef sandwiches.

"I started performing in local theater in my early twenties," Babs went on, "then at all these underground gay venues that were in New York at the time. Bathhouses. Big business—full shows, with piano, for hundreds of half-naked men." She twinkled at Violet. "Quite the scene."

It was here Babs had honed her onstage persona. A sassy, sharp-tongued broad who relied on charisma and cheek. Pretty but not beautiful, quick with a comeback or a long side-eye. Always on, larger than life, as flamboyant and cheeky as the audience for whom she belted out show tunes and jazz standards.

Liz regarded her mother with equal parts pride and affection. "You're an icon, Mom."

"As are you. Both of you." Babs's expression was thoughtful as it passed from Liz to Violet then back to Liz.

Babs spent the rest of the lunch waxing lyrical about her life as an actress—handsy producers and dismissive directors. The sexist media and their double standards. Some things had gotten better for female performers, some things much worse. "Your people are the ones who'll get you through," Babs advised Violet. "The ones you can trust: the good ones. You're lucky to be working with Liz."

"I know," Violet replied, smiling at Liz, who smiled back, unapologetically holding Vi's eye contact.

Again, Liz felt her mother watching them. Liz returned her gaze to Babs. "Tell us more, Mom."

And what was so pleasurable about all of this was not the chance for Babs to witness her and Violet's connection or the way Babs seemed more relaxed and open than she had all month. It was the use of the phrase *us*. Tell *us* more. *We* want to know. How badly Liz wanted to be an *us*.

It was time to make that desire more intentional.

LIZ WAITED UNTIL NO ONE else was around, finding a window later that afternoon. The light was lemon-pale and pretty, the entire house at peace.

Violet was reading alone in the family room. Liz approached, buoyed by nerves.

"Hi," Liz said.

"Hi," Violet replied, looking up from her book.

A pause. Liz fumbled for her next line, regretting not writing something in advance. The silence between them stretched.

"Well," Liz said. "Bye." She turned away and kept turning until she was facing Violet again, completing a full circle. "Date?"

"Excuse me?"

Liz's entire face scorched. "I'd like to take you on a date. Dinner. In town."

Violet positioned her bookmark, closing her novel. "A . . . date."

"Yes," Liz said.

"With you?"

Liz suspected she was being teased. "Yes. Dinner. With me. And maybe some candlelight."

Violet lifted a brow. "Sounds romantic."

"Yes. Unless you don't want romance. In which case, switch candlelight for fluorescents."

Violet fingered the pages of her book. "What girl doesn't like a little romance?"

"Confirming candlelight." Liz nodded, then winced.

"You're such a dork." Violet looked like she was trying not to laugh. "When?"

"Whenever you like."

Vi's eyes sparkled. "How about Friday night? If it's okay I stay till then."

"Literally never want you to leave." Liz's nerves were replaced by relief, shot through with excitement. "Friday it is."

"Well done," Vi whispered, giving Liz a thumbs-up.

"I'm out of practice," Liz confessed.

"Yes." Violet nodded sagely. "I could tell."

31.

Seven days till Christmas

∗

 IRDIE AND JECKA SAW EACH OTHER EVERY DAY—ON
Monday, browsing for books at The Golden Notebook, followed by lunch at the Garden Cafe. On Tuesday, Jecka came
to the Inn for dinner, leaving well after midnight. On
Wednesday afternoon, Birdie finally scored an invite to Jecka's home; Jecka was going to paint while Birdie worked on
her new show.

Birdie had suspected the artist's digs would be one thousand times nicer than her own disastrous Brooklyn abode.
She was right.

"Whoa," Birdie breathed, as Jecka let her in. "This is *sick*."

The two-story redbrick building was located just off the
main street in town. The entire bottom floor was raw space,
functioning as Jecka's studio. Half-finished canvases were
taped to the concrete walls, amid pots of paintbrushes and
palettes of paints. A record player sat in one corner, next to
an old orange armchair and a stack of art books. It smelled
vaguely of turpentine and incense.

"I live upstairs." Jecka gestured to a staircase. "But this is
where the magic happens."

Birdie liked the incongruity of the relaxed, unfiltered space with Jecka's cool, controlled exterior. Even in her baggy, paint-splattered overalls worn over a skimpy tank top, Jecka somehow still looked chic.

Birdie put on a Nina Simone record from those stacked by the player and settled into the armchair. For a few minutes, she watched Jecka mix up some paints and start slashing them onto a canvas, stepping back every now and then to consider the composition. Then Birdie flipped open her own notebook.

Her new idea, centered around an exploration of her dad, was taking shape almost of its own accord. Connections and themes and punch lines kept popping into her brain. Birdie had been working on it every day. Plenty of past hookups had seen her perform, but they never saw the effort that went into those seemingly off-the-cuff performances. Birdie liked that Jecka got to see this side of her—the side that took joke construction seriously, the side that wanted to dig into this difficult subject matter and unearth the gems buried in its dirt. It made her feel substantive. Like a real artist, not just comic relief.

Birdie hadn't stopped thinking about what Jecka had said in the wine cellar—that Birdie needed to take her own life seriously. This work felt like that. Instead of shrugging off her pain or making a joke about it, she was doing the opposite—looking at it even more closely. Seeing it differently, just as she was continuing to see Jecka in a new, more intimate light.

When the sun seeped away from the downstairs windows, Jecka put down her palette and stretched, head tipping back.

Birdie imagined tracing her tongue along Jecka's neck, kissing her collarbone, her mouth. The image stoked hot coals in her belly. She closed her notebook.

———

UPSTAIRS, THE LIVING QUARTERS were as clean and neat as the downstairs wasn't. Tall arched windows were set into an exposed brick wall. A fiddle-leaf fig that wasn't dead sat in one dust-free corner, near her fun-sized Christmas tree hung with tasteful silver baubles. The expensive-looking furniture was a palette of muted neutrals with a few carefully chosen pops of color: a bright orange cushion, a bold yellow jacket hanging on a hook.

Birdie placed the wine she'd brought on a dining room table the size of Alaska. The whole place was ten times the size of Birdie's crash pad. There was even *a laundry room.*

As Birdie explored, Jecka washed up, changing into snug denim shorts and a cropped sweatshirt that exposed a sliver of her taut brown skin.

Birdie smiled at the sight, pausing at the doorway to what had to be the bedroom. "And what do we have behind Door Number Five?" She twisted the knob, revealing a king bed with oatmeal linen sheets and pillows, straight from a Parachute Home catalog. Birdie gave Jecka a look of faux confusion. "What is this? Soft, elevated flooring?" She took a seat on the end of the bed, bouncing experimentally. "Springy. Comfortable. I'm just not sure of the *purpose* of such an item. Care to"—she cleared her throat—"enlighten me?"

Jecka rolled her eyes with a smile, coming to stand between Birdie's legs. "Maybe."

Birdie rose to her feet, wrapping her arms around Jecka's waist. Jecka's lips were warm. Birdie loved the way their mouths fit together. The way she didn't have to think about the rhythm of their breath and tongue. But Birdie was also eager to see how else they might fit together.

She let her fingers drift over Jecka's sweatshirt, brushing her breast.

Jecka let out a small sound of pleasure, her voice already a pant. "When was the last time you were tested?"

"Just before Thanksgiving." Birdie was pleased she remembered this. "But in the spirit of honesty, I did sleep with a couple different girls that weekend and haven't been tested since."

"A couple different girls," Jecka repeated. "In one weekend?"

She sounded more surprised than judgmental, but Birdie still winced. "I live to give? But right now I only want to give to you."

Jecka sat on the bed. "I've never had a one-night stand."

Birdie sank down next to her, stunned. "Never?"

Jecka shrugged and shook her head. "Serial monogamist. I've only slept with five people."

Birdie almost choked. "Are you joking?" Clearly, she wasn't. "Oh. Wow. Cool." Terrifying thought: "Do you want to hear my number?"

"Sounds like we don't have time for that math," Jecka said dryly. "Are you seeing anyone else right now?"

"No. I really dig you, Jecka. Just you."

Jecka smiled, tugging Birdie closer. "I really dig you, too."

Birdie pressed her lips to the curve of Jecka's neck, inhaling the smoky-sweet smell of her skin. "Awesome."

"But to be brutally honest—"

Birdie lifted her lips from Jecka's neck. "What a fun way to start a sentence."

"—I didn't think I'd start hanging out with someone so . . ." Jecka trailed off, eyes squinting.

"Feel like you're not going to say *mind-blowingly hot*," Birdie said.

"Unpredictable?" Jecka tried. "The last person I dated was a lawyer. Before that, a doctor."

The inference being that Birdie was very different from someone with a stable, lucrative profession. Hard to pretend that didn't sting.

"Right," Birdie said lightly. "Grown-ups with space-age vacuum cleaners and 401(k)s."

Jecka's eyes widened. "You don't have a 401(k)?"

Add it to the list of things to figure out. Birdie leaned across the duvet and Jecka allowed herself to be kissed. Once. Twice. Three times. "Oh, wow," she breathed. "You are troublingly good at that."

"Or maybe you just like kissing me." Birdie kissed her again, and again, shifting their bodies until Jecka was lying back on her mound of pillows. Birdie dropped kisses on her mouth, her neck, the elegant ridge of her collarbone, while Jecka let out sighs of pleasure.

Birdie moved her hand south, grasping the edge of Jecka's sweatshirt. Birdie enjoyed undressing any woman. But there was something particularly hot about removing clothing from this exquisite woman who was writhing with growing impatience underneath her. This was like unwrapping the world's best gift.

Birdie pulled the top over Jecka's head, tossing it aside. Jecka's full breasts were encased in a cream silk bra edged in black lace. The sight made Birdie's eyes feel like cartoon bombs exploding. Birdie was a breast man, always had been, always would be. She felt heavy with lust, eager to explore. To touch and play. Tongue Jecka's nipple, see if she liked that. Kiss and suck and stroke every inch of them. Birdie promised herself to take her time with these gorgeous tits. Slowly. Thoroughly. But not yet.

Birdie slid her fingers past the smooth flesh of Jecka's stomach. Over the top of her shorts. Cupping the denim between her legs with a quick, confident grasp, Birdie squeezed.

Jecka let out a cry, her eyes flying open.

"Here's what's going to happen, Jecka Jacob." Birdie spoke with quiet control. "I am going to take your shorts off. I am going to take your panties off. And I am going to make you come. Again and again and again. All. Fucking. Night."

"Oh Jesus," Jecka murmured, squirming.

"With my mouth," Birdie went on, rubbing her thumb up and down the seam of Jecka's shorts, watching the way it made Jecka moan. "With my hands. With whatever toys you've got stashed in that bedside drawer. And do you know what you're going to give me?"

"What?" Jecka panted.

Birdie took Jecka's earlobe in her mouth, biting gently, then speaking directly into the ear. "The benefit of the doubt."

Jecka's laugh became a groan as Birdie started circling her thumb with even more pressure. "Okay. Okay."

"Okay what?"

Jecka laughed then groaned, growing desperate, her control slipping. "Okay, I trust you! Just please, stop talking and fuck me."

With a flick of her wrist, Birdie unzipped Jecka's fly and did exactly that.

32.

Who knows how many days till Christmas

IME WAS IRRELEVANT. THE SEASON, HIS FAMILY, A NEW JOB, his future: nothing mattered except for this—kissing Ash. Being kissed by Ash. Every stolen moment was a pulse-pounding, thought-snatching, dizzying high.

In the wine cellar, Ash slipping in after Rafi volunteered to select the night's refreshments, his hand cradling the back of Rafi's neck while his tongue swirled inside Rafi's mouth, and Rafi felt like he might die.

In Rafi's car, on the way back from an afternoon run into town for firewood. Ash squeezed Rafi's thigh and seconds later, Rafi had pulled over and they'd pounced on each other, someone's elbow jamming the horn.

Rolling around on Rafi's bed, jeans intertwined, moving only because they'd found a better way to kiss, to touch, to play. Rafi had always enjoyed making out, but in recent years, the decadent hours-long make-outs of his youth had become a lost art. Now, because they were taking things slow, and because Rafi didn't want to rush any stage of this mind-blowing evolution of their relationship, he was discovering anew how totally hot just kissing could be. Kissing in a way that felt like falling. Sometimes slowly, as if through layers of thick cotton candy. Sometimes fast, a breath-stealing plunge that made his heart take off at a sprint.

And the fact that it was happening with Ash added to the sexy surreality. "I keep going to tell you about this superhot guy I'm hooking up with," Rafi murmured while they were wrapped around each other on the king bed. "And then I remember, it's you. You're the superhot guy."

Ash chuckled, his fingers winding into Rafi's hair. "I feel the same way. Like I've discovered hidden treasure. Pirate's booty." He squeezed Rafi's ass, and they both groaned.

There was only so long they could keep their clothes on.

ON THURSDAY MORNING, RAFI was in the walk-in pantry, searching for a missing pepper grinder, when he felt a strong hand at his waist, breath at his neck, then Ash spun him around, his mouth on Rafi's. For one, two, three gravity-defying seconds they were lost in each other, kissing as if Ash had just returned from war.

"Hi." Rafi panted. He ran his lips over the stubble on Ash's jaw, biting his neck. "What's up? Besides the obvious," he added, pressing their hips together to create agonizing friction.

Ash growled in pleasure, his gaze glazing over. "Slow down, cowboy, or I'll be on my knees in your mother's pantry."

The image almost had Rafi passing out. "And that would be a bad thing?"

Ash cocked a brow. "Maybe not."

Rafi inhaled sharply. Raising his hand, he ran a thumb over Ash's mouth, touching his plush, parted lips.

Ash took Rafi's thumb in his mouth. Without breaking eye contact, he sucked on it, moving it in and out. In and out. Licking and sucking, with the entire expanse of his experienced tongue.

Rafi couldn't speak. His vision blurred, his mouth going dry. The pressure between his legs was so intense, he had to back up before he lost control. "You'd better stop," he managed, "before these dry goods witness my final undoing." His heart was pounding, his need overcoming his ability to be pithy. "I can't wait much longer."

"We said we'd take things slow."

"Says the man giving my thumb a blow job." Rafi shook his head, impatience pushing him to the brink. "Fuck slow."

Someone from the kitchen called to ask if they'd found the pepper grinder. "Still looking," Ash called back, his gaze locked on Rafi. "Fine." His voice was a low scrape. "Tonight. Your room." Ash dropped his mouth to Rafi's ear. "I want to taste you, Raf."

Rafi's blood was scalding. "And I need to feel you. Inside me."

Surprise flickered over Ash's face. "You mean . . . ?"

Rafi nodded slowly, holding his gaze. "I mean."

From the kitchen: "What's taking so long?"

The pepper grinder appeared in Ash's hand like a magic trick. He glanced from it to Rafi's pants, crooking an eyebrow with a grin. Then he was striding out, announcing, "Found it!"

It took Rafi a solid thirty seconds to get his body under control, hobbling out after him.

—

LATER THAT AFTERNOON, BIRDIE cornered Rafi as he slunk out of his mother's study. "Hey Raf."

He tried to sidestep her. "Not now."

She wasn't having it. "I need to apologize. For saying all that dumb shit about making a move on Ash." Birdie let out a regretful sigh, sincerity in her bright blue eyes. "I was being contrarian, trying to get a rise out of you and Lizzie. Really immature. Obviously, you should never, ever screw things up with Mr. Campbell. You guys are better off as friends, right?" She peered at him expectantly.

Rafi's response got stuck in his throat. The sneaking around was fun, but a part of him was aware that none of this was real—permanent, a *thing*—until other people knew. Specifically, his family. Was that something Ash would ever be ready for?

Plus, there was a possibility that tonight wouldn't go as mind-blowingly great as he imagined. Hadn't that been the problem with Sunita? With all his exes? Rushing headlong into a life that didn't actually exist? "Obviously."

Birdie relaxed, rocking back on her heels. "Rad. Glad I didn't help mess things up. So, did either of you end up having a holiday fling?"

Rafi felt a snap of irritation at this particularly destructive phrase that he covered with a plastic smile. "Neither of us hooked up with anyone else." Actually, the truth.

"Cool." Birdie checked her phone. "I should get going. Sorry it took so long to say something—Jecka and I have been, y'know: making the beast with two backs."

"Ew."

"Horizontal folk dancing? Disappointing the wife? You get it: I'm heading over now." Birdie shouldered her tote, pointing to his hand. "What are those for?"

The tiny scissors he'd found in his mother's office that he definitely wasn't considering trimming his pubes with. "Oh, Ash and I are . . . vision-boarding tonight."

Birdie gave him a pitying look. "You realize you're more of a lesbian than I am, don't you?"

IN HIS BATHROOM, Rafi locked the door, putting the tiny scissors on the counter. Opening the cabinet under the sink, he looked past the spare toilet paper for a package he'd stashed two summers ago, when he'd invited Axel to visit, a trip his ex-boyfriend flaked on. Thankfully, it was all still there, in the paper pharmacy bag he'd bought it in.

Lube. Condoms. And a blue plastic douche. He held it up, examining the simple device thoughtfully. "Well, well, well. We meet again."

RAFI DIDN'T TASTE A single bite of the baked ziti and Greek salad that Siouxsie made for dinner. Instead, he and Ash kept catching each other's eye, legs pressing together under the table in a way that, unlike in their double feature, was extremely deliberate. The simmering heat in Ash's gaze, the tiny curve of his smile, made Rafi feel lightheaded and antsy.

He was the first one out of his chair when the meal was finished.

"Charades?" Liz suggested. "Or cards?"

"Can't. We're, uh . . . vision-boarding." Thank god it wasn't their turn for dishes. Ash was at his heels.

"Loving all this soul-searching you're doing this year . . ." Liz's voice was already faint, as the two men walked, then hustled, practically running, down the hallway, into Rafi's room.

They were laughing as they shut the door behind them. Ash slid his hand into Rafi's hair, fisting the roots. Pressing him against the closed door, Ash kissed him with a low groan. Rafi angled his mouth to deepen the kiss, his hands sliding down Ash's corded arms to circle his waist, pulling them closer. "I can't believe we haven't been doing this the whole time," Rafi panted. "Are we idiots?"

"Total idiots," Ash agreed.

Ash blasted jazz, overloud. Somehow, Rafi knew this was not for mood, but to drown out any noise.

Ash kept his gaze on Rafi as he unbuttoned his jeans and kicked out of them, revealing black Calvins. The boxer briefs were already straining. No two ways around it: Ash Campbell had a huge cock. Rafi had seen it many times, back when it was a source of schoolboy interest, not mouthwatering arousal. Now the sight of his bulging package jacked Rafi's heart rate double, triple time.

Grasping the edge of his T-shirt, Ash pulled it up over his head.

Rafi had seen Ash's body a thousand times. But he'd never really *seen* it. And he'd never gotten to touch it. His smooth golden skin. The light scruff of chest hair. Pecs the size of dinner plates, a stomach quilted with abs. Stepping forward, Rafi ran his fingers over Ash's muscles, wanting to feel every warm, firm inch of his body. "You're so beautiful," he whispered, dumbstruck. "I can't believe you're mine. My . . . friend," he corrected (ugh, why couldn't he think before he spoke?). "My, um . . ."

"Whatever you want me to be," Ash murmured with a smile.

He tugged Rafi's T-shirt off, chucking it aside. He let his gaze, then his hands, rove all over Rafi's body, fingers digging into his chest hair, tugging gently. A moan escaped his lips. "I've thought about this moment way too many times."

Rafi pressed their mouths together, speaking into the kiss. "The moment you realize exactly how hairy I am?"

"No. This one." Ash pulled back from Rafi, held his gaze, then dropped to his knees. In one quick motion, Ash undid the top button of Rafi's jeans. Rafi gasped, already throbbing. Then slowly, deliberately slowly, Ash unzipped the zipper.

Rafi's breath pole-vaulted into his throat. The edges of the room slid away. It took all his strength to stay upright.

Ash wiggled Rafi's jeans off then hooked his thumbs over the elastic band of his underwear. "Can I?"

"Not sure anything fun's gonna happen if they stay on."

Ash smirked, teasing. "Is that a yes?"

"It's a fuck yes," Rafi said, practically seeing double, "and why hasn't it already happened?"

Ash tugged Rafi's underwear down until he was able to step out of them, standing naked in the middle of his bedroom.

Ash stared at Rafi. All of him. At full attention.

"Oh. My. God." Ash rubbed his jaw. "I knew, but I didn't *know.*" He licked his lips, slowly. "Sit in the club chair."

"Not the bed?"

Ash shook his head. "The chair. Whenever I've imagined this—and I've imagined it a lot—you're in the chair."

Rafi sank into the club chair, the leather firm against his bare ass and thighs.

Kneeling between Rafi's legs, Ash leaned up for a kiss before moving his lips down Rafi's neck, kissing the center of his chest, a nipple, his stomach, the inside of his thigh.

Rafi was already panting, clutching the arms of the chair in anticipation, unable to tear his gaze from Ash. Rafi was so hard it almost hurt. He prayed to any listening deity that he'd remember this moment for the rest of his life. And that he wouldn't come in literally three seconds flat.

Ash caught Rafi's eye, flicking him a wicked smile. Then he lowered his mouth and Rafi's world blew up.

Turned out, no one else he'd ever been naked with before knew how to do this. It was a *journey*. A seven-wonders-of-the-world-flying-first-class-oh-wow-it's-a-waterbed *trip*. Rafi was swearing, groaning, grabbing at Ash's hair, tugging the soft, thick strands. His hips wanted to buck, but Ash kept them in place with a strong hand as his head bobbed, tongue working, lips sliding from base to tip, again and again and again. It was glorious and messy and insanely hot. Each stroke of his tongue, each moan vibrating from his throat, brought Rafi closer and closer until he was right on the edge.

"I'm close," Rafi gasped. "Fuck, *Ash*."

Ash came up for air, panting, lips puffy and slick. "Don't come yet."

Then Ash's mouth was on his, and they were kissing, hungrily, stickily, a deep, bruising kiss, and Rafi was beyond words, beyond thought, because the story of his life had just had all the pages ripped out and he was starting again. Here, from this point.

Rafi hauled them both toward the bed, staggering over carpet littered with their clothes until they were stretched out on the mattress, limbs intertwined, staring at each other with a new sort of wonder. Then they were making out again, rolling around, touching every inch of each other. Rafi reached for the lube.

Ash was on PrEP but Rafi wasn't, so Ash ripped open a condom and rolled it on. He positioned himself over Rafi so they were face-to-face, Rafi on his back, knees bent—*folded up like a lawn chair* was the way he'd once heard the position described.

"It's been a minute," Rafi whispered. "Go slow."

Ash nodded, hands braced carefully by Rafi's head. "I will." He lowered his mouth for a kiss. Touching his chest, Rafi could feel Ash's heartbeat, pounding in time with his own.

Slowly, without breaking eye contact, Ash rolled his hips forward, inch by inch. And it wasn't the hot, sweet stretch that made Rafi drop into this moment in a way he never had before. It wasn't the feeling of having a man inside him, deeper, then deeper still. It was this man. This boy. Someone he'd thought he'd done everything with.

Sex was usually a release, an escape. This was the opposite of an escape.

Their bodies adjusted to each other, and they began to find a rhythm. Ash's eyes were squeezed shut, as he focused on his thrusts. Rafi pulled Ash closer for a kiss. A deep, slow kiss. When they broke apart, Rafi caught Ash's gaze, holding it. Something like surprise flashed into Ash's eyes as he stared back, eyes open. As they continued to move together, Rafi held their eye contact. Neither looked away. Something huge and warm split open in Rafi's chest.

They were fucking, and it felt amazing: Ash knew exactly the right spot to hit. But there was something much bigger happening. Rafi was seeing Ash in a new way. Feeling him in

MOST WONDERFUL • 281

a new way. Feeling close to him in a new way. Their hands, laced together. Their exhales, in perfect sync. Rafi's heart was laid as bare as his body. He suddenly realized what *making love* actually was: it was this. This moment.

They were reaching a peak. Ash's thrusts were getting quicker, his eyes going dark, his face turning intense and desperate. Rafi was close, too. He never wanted it to end. The sex. These feelings. Any of it. Ever.

It hit him like a punch in the face. *Holy shit. I'm in love.*

"*Raf,*" Ash roared, coming hard. The sound of his name tearing from Ash's lips, a few strokes of his own hand, and Rafi was right there with him, white-hot pleasure surging, spilling, an epic release.

Ash collapsed on top of Rafi and lay there, panting.

The happiest moments of Rafi's life were mere footnotes to the feeling flowing through him. Nothing in his past compared to this wild, almost blinding joy.

Ash lifted his head. He looked equally dazed. His words were a stunned exhale. "Oh my god."

"My words exactly." Each of Rafi's nerve endings was still singing. He rubbed his face in a stupor. "Jesus, Ash. You could teach a MasterClass."

But Ash didn't smile back. He was staring at Rafi, breathless and so wide-eyed, he almost looked stricken.

Rafi touched his face. "What?"

Ash blinked, glancing away. "Nothing." He wriggled back carefully, heading to the bathroom to clean up.

Rafi lay there, his body still vibrating, his mind in pieces on the floor.

When Ash got back into bed, trouble still creased his brow.

Rafi snuggled close. "Are you okay?" he asked softly.

"Yes." Ash wrapped his arms around Rafi, holding him possessively.

But Rafi could tell something was up. "Hey." Rafi skimmed his fingers down Ash's jaw. "If this is going to work, we need to be honest with each other. Like we always have."

"You're right." Ash gazed at Rafi, something vast and wonderstruck blooming behind his eyes. "It's just . . . it's never been like that. That was different. Really different."

Rafi's heart fluttered. "Different how?"

"Well, I've never come that hard before. Ever." Ash ran his hands up and down Rafi's arms. "I really care about you. This isn't just about sex for me."

"Me neither."

"Right, but have you ever had casual sex? Like, sex without feelings."

"I'm sure I have." Rafi flicked through his memories. "At one point . . . ?" He couldn't actually pinpoint a single time, unless masturbation counted, and Rafi was pretty sure it did not.

"Well, I've never fucked someone I really care about." Ash's expression was intense and disarmingly sincere. "Certainly not as much as I care about you."

Extremely cute to see Ash so caught up in his feelings. "How does it feel? Being with someone you"—*don't say love*—"like?"

Ash traced the backs of his fingers over Rafi's cheekbones, his gaze pinning Rafi to the mattress. "Like I never want to let you go."

And Rafi couldn't even tease him for the earnestness overload because he was too busy melting like a dropped scoop of ice cream. The wonder of it all stole his breath. He tightened his arms around the man beside him, holding him as close as he could. "I know exactly how you feel."

LATER, AFTER THE REST of the house had been asleep for hours, Rafi and Ash lay in each other's arms, fingers swirling absentmindedly over each other's skin. Rafi didn't want the night to end. But his eyes were closing. Sleep was near.

"Raf?"

Ash's voice was so quiet, he almost missed it. He stirred against Ash's chest. "Mmm?"

"Never mind. It can wait."

"S'okay." Rafi fought a yawn, blinking up at him.

In the darkened room, Ash was a study in shadows. "I'm just . . . thinking about my dad." He glanced at the ceiling, then back at Rafi. "Maybe you were right. I should . . . y'know."

"Pay Willie a visit?" Rafi asked.

Ash nodded, just once. "Yeah."

Since Ash had arrived two weeks ago, Rafi had seen him looking happy, annoyed, exhausted, and energized. He'd seen him laugh and curse and lose control in a kiss. He'd seen him in his Christmas party finest, and stark naked, and in a *Now Watch Me Whip* apron. But Rafi hadn't yet seen this look. This Ash. Vulnerable and sad and a little out of his depth.

Rafi intertwined their fingers, squeezing his hand. "I think that's a really good idea."

Ash blew out a sigh, sinking into the sheets. His voice was barely audible. "I don't know if I can do it alone."

Rafi cradled Ash's cheek, meeting his gaze. "Then it's lucky you don't have to."

33.

Five days till Christmas

*

IT RAINED ALL DAY FRIDAY, HEAVY IN THE MORNING, THEN tapering off to a patter by early evening. Siouxsie's French braids were damp when she slipped off her Hunter boots in the foyer. "Thought I'd do tomato soup and grilled cheese," she told Liz, hefting two bags of groceries. "Perfect for a rainy night."

"For sure," Liz said. "Save me a taste? Vi and I are going out for dinner."

It was offered casually, but there was nothing casual about the high kicks her heart had been doing all day, or the outfit Liz had painstakingly decided on. The high-waisted black pants that made her ass look intentional, freshly polished heeled boots, her favorite green silk blouse, and the boss-bitch leather jacket she'd splurged on when *Sweet* got picked up.

Violet came downstairs in a tight black sweater and leather pants Liz hadn't seen before. Red lipstick she didn't usually wear. The whole effect was stylish. Sexy. *For me.* The realization sent a zing up Liz's spine, pinballing to three distinct points in her body.

The rain stopped right before they left. The air smelled washed clean. Liz borrowed her mom's Audi (hard pass on borrowing Ray), opening the passenger side door for Violet, which seemed to both baffle and please her date. Liz found the local indie radio station. "Underwater" by Tegan and Sara came on, jangly queer pop-rock. Liz turned it up.

I would go to jail with only boys, just to prove I was as tough as you.

It was different, this new space they were entering. Alive like adrenaline, brimming with promise and just a lick of danger. The road was empty, the landscape lunar. Liz had to remind herself not to speed.

THE FAMILY HAD BEEN coming to the Italian restaurant for years. It was upscale old-school: dark-wood paneling, vintage silver cutlery, tables set with tiny vases of wildflowers. And excellent food. The pink peppercorn mafaldini was famous in the tristate area.

The hostess led Liz and Violet through the main dining room. Liz watched for flares of recognition in the patrons' faces, but no one looked twice, engaged in their own pleasant evenings of carbonara and Chianti.

Upstairs, the table in their private dining room was set with a white linen tablecloth and, as requested, two tall candles, bathing the room in an elegant glow. Their server was polite and didn't hover, leaving them with menus and a dish of Liz's favorite marinated olives, on the house.

"So fancy," Violet said in approval once he was gone. "Thank you for organizing this. It's nice to have you all to myself."

Liz was pleased her instinct to book their own room had been correct. "My pleasure." She unfolded her napkin, daring to add, "Anything for a beautiful woman."

Violet shot back an impressed look.

They ordered a feast. Their wine came out first, followed by house-made focaccia with green garlic butter and a little gem salad. Next, grilled prawns with lemon, then clams with Calabrian chili and breadcrumbs. Finally, bowls of the pink peppercorn mafaldini coated in parmigiano for Violet, and the fettuccine with seared sausage and a tomato passata for Liz.

It felt like the old days, but different. Their legs brushed under the table and Liz didn't pull away. The fact that they were on a date, a real one, underscored everything with delicious tension, electric unknowingness. This script was still being written.

Their conversation flowed easily, starting light and bubbly before spilling into deeper crevices than it ever had before. Violet opened up about her parents' deaths, describing how no one sat next to her on the one-hour bus ride she took to her new school. "I think they all thought my tragedy was contagious." Violet speared a prawn contemplatively. "That I'd infect them with my grief. But I just wanted a friend."

"I was never the most popular kid either," Liz confessed. "Birdie had tons of friends. Rafi and Ash were—are—always together. I was the one tucked alone in a corner with a book."

"Same." Vi smiled, her gaze catching the candlelight. "Lucky we found each other."

"The luckiest," Liz said, smiling back, trying not to swoon. They split a tiramisu, plunging their spoons into the soft, sweet layers. Liz paid the check with a generous tip. On the way out, in the bathroom mirror, Liz wiped away a smudge of mascara. Excitement and nerves and hope blazed in her chest. She couldn't deny how much she liked the person she was in Vi's presence—a bolder, more playful, more lit-up version of Liz Belvedere. She couldn't deny the rush she felt when their eyes met. When they touched.

Dinner was over, but their date didn't have to be.

OUTSIDE IN THE PARKING LOT, Violet was leaning against the car, gaze tilted to the star-dusted sky. "So," she asked as Liz approached, "what do you want to do now?"

"We could get a nightcap," Liz said. "Or go back to the Inn. Or head somewhere a little more . . . private."

Violet's smile was dreamy. "That sounds perfect."

Liz drove Violet to the affectionately named Lover's Lake, a nearby reservoir. They parked in the empty lot and walked to the water's edge. In the summer evenings, it was busy with couples of all ages. But this late on a winter's evening, Liz knew they'd be alone.

"Oh, wow." Violet pointed. "Look at the moon."

It was almost full. Its bright light played on the shifting surface of the water, witchy. Liz considered the earth's biggest satellite. Could love, real and lasting love, be like the moon? Sometimes disappearing out of view, but always showing up again. Because in actuality, it hadn't gone anywhere.

Violet stepped close enough to tuck her hands into Liz's jacket pockets. "Hi."

The feeling of Violet being so close disappeared the night's chill. Liz circled her arms around Violet. "I've never wanted anything more," Liz whispered, "than how much I want to kiss you right now."

Violet's breath was sweet and hot. "Me too."

Liz closed her eyes, already knowing she would remember this kiss on her deathbed, the foreign yet familiar feeling of kissing a girl, this girl, her favorite girl in existence. Their lips touched and the rest of the world fell away. Violet's mouth was soft and insistent, coaxing Liz's lips open, one gloved hand on her cheek.

It was a crack of thunder and the touch of an eyelash. Sunday afternoon and Friday at 2:00 A.M. The first sip of wine and the last. Liz slid her hand to the back of Violet's neck, the skin warm under her ponytail and beanie. The point of existence was to kiss and be kissed.

In the arms of this woman on the banks of a quiet lake, Liz understood falling in love anew. But it wasn't Liz who was falling. Rather, her deepest fears and misconceptions were falling away, useless armor disappearing. As Violet's lips pressed into hers, again and again and again, Liz wasn't falling. She was finally being held.

34.

Four days till Christmas

WHEN BIRDIE CRACKED AN EYE OPEN LATE ON SATURDAY morning, the first thing she registered was light. Buckets of it drenching a bedroom that wasn't hers. It was the third night in a row she'd slept over at Jecka's. The third morning in a row she'd awoken to golden sunlight and Jecka Jacob. Birdie smiled dopily at her, awash in adoration. "Howdy."

Jecka smiled back, snuggling closer. "Hello."

Birdie rolled on top of her, trailing kisses up Jecka's jaw, landing on her mouth, once, twice, three times. "Do I have morning breath?"

Jecka kissed her back, holding her close. "You're good." She kissed Birdie again and again and again until they were both groaning. Jecka wriggled farther south, under the covers.

"Hang on." Birdie put a hand on her shoulder. "I can do you."

"You've done me the last two mornings." Jecka's grin was lazy. "Lie back and relax."

And if Birdie died right now, that might actually be okay. She *really* liked this person, and not just because Birdie was having the best orgasms of her life. Because for some out-landish reason, it felt like they might make a really good team. Long-term. Which wasn't something Birdie had thought about anyone ever before.

IT WAS EARLY AFTERNOON when they dragged themselves out of bed. Jecka didn't have to be at Woodstock Art as much now that her show was up and running—she could be more flexible with how she spent her days and when she worked on new pieces. Birdie started some Sunday-on-a-Saturday Eggs, while Jecka made a meticulously measured French press. "Oh, by the way." Birdie left her post at the stove to grab a printout from her tote. "I RSVP'd to that free art expo in Chelsea for us. The one you were telling me about."

"No way. The one in February?" Jecka scanned the confir-mation. "I tried to get tickets but they were all gone."

Only now did Birdie realize that February was *two months* away. It hadn't struck her as unusual to forward plan. Weird.

The doorbell rang.

"That's Liz Fizz. She said she might be running errands so I gave her your address in case she wanted to pop by. Watch the eggs?" Birdie called, hurrying down to the first floor and flinging the front door open with a lusty shout. "Good morn— Oh."

A Black man and a white woman stood on Jecka's door-step. Older and elegantly dressed. The resemblance to Jecka made it instantly clear who Birdie was meeting, dressed only in Jecka's Harvard T-shirt and boy-short underwear. "Shit, sorry." Birdie scuttled backward, grabbing two umbrellas from the stand by the door in an attempt to cover up.

"Dad." Jecka was on the stairs behind Birdie, looking stunned. "Mom. Wh-What are you doing here?"

"Visiting you," Jecka's mom replied. She looked to be in her sixties. Beautiful in a regal sort of way, like a stork.

"Hello, pet." Jecka's father was similarly stately, with fierce, unflinching eyes. Yet his step forward into the house was uncertain.

"Come in." Jecka double-took at Birdie's umbrellas, her tone hesitant. "We were just making eggs."

Jecka hugged her parents. Both embraces were quick and dry, the opposite of the affectionate bear hug Birdie always gave her own mother.

The trio looked at Birdie. Still holding the two umbrellas, she managed an awkward bow. "Greetings. I am Birdie. Friend of Jecka's."

Jecka looked very, very awake. "Birdie, these are my parents. Angela and Carl Jacob."

Angela and Carl Jacob traded a glance so loaded Birdie was surprised it didn't crash through the floorboards.

Upstairs, Birdie yanked on her jeans as Jecka's parents explained they'd booked a room at Woodstock Way Hotel so they could see Jecka's show before all driving back to Boston for Christmas, saving Jecka the cost of airfare.

"I'm so happy you're here," Jecka said to her parents, her expression still a little dazed. "Make yourselves at home," she added, subtly straightening the couch cushions.

"How do you two know each other?" Papa Jacob packed only one expression, and that was stern.

Jecka looked at Birdie. Birdie looked at Jecka. Birdie imagined clamping a hand on each parent's shoulder and telling god's honest truth, cribbed from every nineteenth-century-set lesbian movie: *She is my sun, my moon, my every star in the sky. I am hers: mind, body, and soul. We are* one.

"I'm doing some freelance work as Birdie's mother's art curator," Jecka explained. "Helping her buy some local pieces."

"Ma's quite the art lover," Birdie jumped in. "As am I. You guys ever see those Magic Eye things?" She mimed her mind being blown. "Now *that's* art."

Carl and Angela stared at her, confused.

"She's kidding," Jecka said, giving Birdie a look while fighting a smile.

"Hm." Jecka's mom removed a pair of slim leather gloves. The precision of her chestnut bob would impress a mathematician. "Well, if you're not too busy, Jecka, you can have dinner with us tonight," Angela said. "If we can get a booking," she added, with a touch of irritation. "I didn't realize how small the town is. I've tried three places already."

"What about that Japanese one?" Carl asked his wife.

"They practically laughed at me," Angela responded.

"It is the weekend before Christmas," Jecka tentatively pointed out.

"It is." Jecka's dad frowned as if this timing was a result of Jecka's own poor planning.

Birdie was overcome with a desire for the visit to go well. How awesome that her crush's parents had come to see her show, for the first time *ever*, which showed real acceptance of their daughter's new life path. She knew how much that meant to Jecka. Birdie wanted to help.

"What about we all have dinner? At my mom's?" Birdie glanced at Jecka. Her expression was surprised but didn't indicate this was an immediate no. "She lives outside town in this big ol' inn. It's a bit over the top." Birdie was typically tight-lipped over the family name, but she wanted to impress Angela and Carl. "My mom is Babs Belvedere."

"No way!" This, shockingly, was from Carl. "Babs Belvedere is your *mother*?"

Birdie nodded, sensing a fan. "Since the day I was born. Ma loves entertaining. She'd love to meet you both!"

Carl glanced at his wife, then back at Birdie. His demeanor had transformed from serious elder statesman to tongue-tied young man. "I have to admit, I'm a fan. Wow: Babs Belvedere. Can you believe that, honey?" he prompted his wife.

"She's a little ribald for my taste," Mrs. Jacob said.

"She's not as ribald in person," Jecka said. "Most of the time."

The three Jacobs ping-ponged looks among them. "I would love to meet her . . ." Dr. Carl said slowly.

"As long as we wouldn't be imposing . . ." Angela hedged.

"Not at all! It's sorted!" Birdie clapped Carl's shoulder, trying to drum up some excitement. "You can meet Ma, and my siblings, and our other guests." A perfect night started to form: Buckets of wine. The table groaning with Siouxsie's famous cauliflower gratin and Beef Bourguignon—the yummiest things they'd had this season. Babs telling stories about filming *The Upstairs Girl* while everyone was generous and good-natured. Birdie addressed Jecka's parents. "Why don't you check out Jecka's show then swing by at seven?"

IN JECKA'S BEDROOM, BIRDIE sent Liz a quick text telling her not to bother stopping by, then hurriedly packed her tote, readying to leave.

"Are you sure about all this?" Jecka whispered.

"It's going to be great," Birdie assured her. "I promise times a million billion." She went to kiss Jecka goodbye.

Jecka swayed back, darting a glance through the open doorway to her parents, who were examining one of Jecka's artworks in the main space. "Sorry. It's just . . . I am out to them. But they've never met a woman I'm dating or anything."

A woman I'm dating. Birdie was surprised by how much that phrasing did not terrify her. Before she could figure this out, Angela called, "Is something burning?"

Jecka and Birdie realized it at the same time. "The eggs!"

Now a smoking mess on the stove. Jecka switched off the burner just as a piercing smoke alarm started to wail.

That wasn't ominous. That wasn't ominous at all.

BIRDIE ZOOMED HOME, PLANNING festive cocktails and dinner party playlists. They'd keep the booze flowing and the conversation risqué but not absolutely filthy. A focus on Birdie's achievements would be ideal.

Birdie burst into the Inn midafternoon, shucking off layers, yelling for her mother. But the only person to appear was Liz, hurrying downstairs in a dressing gown, shushing her. "Mom's out. Jin-soo drove her to Manhattan for something."

"Manhattan?" The special guest star was hours away? "Damn it!" Okay. No worries. They'd still have a rollicking good time. Dinner was about the food first and foremost, right? Next step: commandeering Siouxsie.

Except Liz had given Siouxsie the night off.

"What?" Birdie gaped at her sister. "Why?"

"I didn't think Mom would be back in time for dinner. And you haven't been around. It seemed like a waste."

Birdie explained her plan to Liz, whipping out her phone. "We need to call her right now."

Liz looked apologetic. "I think she already got booked on a last-minute gig a few towns over."

Birdie let out a strangled cry. "What about Rafi and Ash?"

"I don't know where they are. Maybe Christmas shopping?"

"No!" Another chip in her perfect plan.

"Why don't you postpone?" Liz suggested.

That was an option. But Birdie wanted to prove to Jecka she could follow through on an idea. "I made such a fuss about it. Jecka's dad's a big fan."

"I can help with dinner," Liz offered. "Violet too."

Liz Belvedere and Violet Grace: yes, that was good. "Awesome! Where is Grace Face?"

"Taking a nap." Liz bit her lip. "In my room."

First Rafi crushing on Ash, now Liz and Grace Face? "Jesus, it's like a French boarding school around here."

"It's not like that," Liz protested. "I mean, it is, a bit."

"Okay, well, I have to cook dinner for the-best-sex-of-my-life's parents tonight, so we'll have to debrief later." Birdie grabbed a sweater and her coat, yanking open the front door. "I'll run into town, pick up what we need for Beef Bourguignon and cauliflower gratin!"

"You won't have time." Liz hurried after her. "Beef Bourguignon takes three hours."

"Does it? Then I'll figure out an express version! I'll be quick!"

But shopping wasn't quick.

It was four days until Christmas. It took forever to find a parking spot, then there was a line to get in.

Inside, the supermarket was packed with harried shoppers. Birdie threaded her way up and down the aisles, searching for the endless items the internet said she needed: pearl onions and beef and tomato paste and cheese.

By the time she made it back to Ray, it was 6:30 P.M. Which meant, of course, that Birdie pulled into the driveway of her mother's estate, still in her jeans and a ratty Christmas sweater embroidered with *It's the Most Wonderful Time for a Beer*, just as the three immaculately dressed Jacobs were ringing the doorbell.

"Hey guys!" Birdie called, hauling the bags of groceries from Ray's back seat. "Sorry—had some minor delays."

Liz opened the front door, looking—thank god—completely presentable. Her smile was a little too fixed. "Don't mind the dogs." Liz escorted the Jacobs around an excitable Huey, Dewey, and Louie, shooting Birdie a murderous *are-you-kidding-me* look.

"This is my sister, Liz." Birdie bustled past the trio of Jacobs, attempting to keep things upbeat. "The responsible Belvedere. Just kidding, I'm also responsible."

Angela took in Birdie's sweatshirt, then double-took at Babs's seminude portrait. "Oh my lord." No matter where you stood in the marbled foyer, their mother's nipple seemed to follow you. "That's . . . bold."

"That's Babs," Birdie said, desperate to dump the heavy bags and start on dinner.

"Sure is." Carl chuckled, looking left then right. "Will she be joining us?"

Birdie looked to Liz, praying she'd announce their mother was in the kitchen making everyone martinis.

"She's running an errand," Liz said.

Birdie didn't miss the look of confusion—and disappointment—on Carl's face.

Liz directed the three Jacobs to the formal lounge, where Violet was waiting to greet them with a snack board, bless her forever. Birdie got everyone situated, promising to return with wine. Liz was on her tail as the pair hustled into the kitchen, speaking in furious low whispers.

"Where have you been?" Liz asked. "What are you planning on doing with all this?" The groceries.

"Make dinner!" Birdie shot back, unpacking a bulb of garlic, a pint of ice cream, a tin of . . . tuna? The shop had gotten a bit hectic.

"But they're already here! Let's just order some pizzas."

"But they've already seen me with the groceries, they're expecting a home-cooked meal." Birdie sliced an onion, unwilling to concede defeat. "You and Violet talk to them and I'll throw something together. Please, Liz Fizz. *Please.*"

Her sister reluctantly agreed, leaving Birdie alone.

Right. Dinner for six in fifteen minutes or less. Being perpetually single and broke, Birdie had learned to cook for herself, at least a little. It was go-time. "You're Birdie Belvedere," she hyped herself. "Let's go. Let's go!"

TWENTY MINUTES LATER, DINNER was served in the formal dining room. The food, surprisingly, appeared edible. Birdie announced the meal as everyone took their seats. "Pan-fried beef with a garlicky gravy." She'd used all three frying pans to get them done on time. "Cauliflower and cheese." Not baked, just steamed and sprinkled with grated cheddar. "And a side of tuna, if anyone wants."

Jecka sliced the meat, chewing experimentally. "Actually, this is pretty tasty."

"Pass the tuna." Carl gestured for it. "Omega-three is good for your heart."

The six settled into the meal. Birdie exchanged a look of relief with Liz, then poured herself a huge glass of wine.

"So, Birdie," Angela addressed her. "What do you do?"

In some circumstances, Birdie's vocation was received as impressive. Unlikely this would be one of those times. "I'm a comedian. A stand-up."

Angela looked alarmed, as if Birdie had said working was against her religion and she'd never tried it personally. But Carl appeared more amenable, sawing into his beef. "Like your mother."

"Well, Ma never did much stand-up," Birdie explained. "She did cabaret, and theater, then film and TV."

"And you don't," Carl clarified.

It'd been awhile since this difference had been underlined. Birdie remembered she didn't like it. "Nope. Just the stand-up. Telling jokes."

"Birdie had a special." Jecka offered this eagerly. "*Birdie in the Hand . . .*" She trailed off.

Birdie could see her calculating whether the show name might be a little too *ribald*.

Fortunately, Violet stepped in, speaking confidently. ". . . *Birdie in the Bush*. I loved it."

"Oh." Angela pursed her lips.

"It was on Netflix," Birdie provided.

"Ooh." This seemed to resonate with Angela. "We have Netflix."

"Can't figure out how to turn off the subtitles," Carl said.

His gaze sidled to the room's entrance, as if searching for Babs.

"What was *Birdie in the Hand, Birdie in the Bush* about?" Angela asked, daring a nibble of the cauliflower.

"Oh, just my usual schtick." Birdie slurped some wine, tossing off the line she'd given a thousand times. "Sex, drugs, my train wreck of a love life."

Across the table, Liz's fork stilled in midair, her brown eyes widening.

Too late, Birdie realized how inappropriate that sounded. "I mean, a lot of it was exaggerated, obviously," she backtracked. "I sort of play a character onstage. A heightened version of who I am."

"And who is that?" Carl asked.

Mildly panicked, Birdie gulped more wine, aware the entire table was watching. What was she supposed to say? Hot mess? Lovable fuckup?

"A bon vivant," Liz jumped in. "A flâneur."

"A what?" Carl looked baffled.

"I'm actually working on a new show about my dad," Birdie raced on. Not even Liz knew this. "Jecka's been helping me."

"So now you're a comedian?" Angela addressed her daughter in a too-crisp tone. "As well as a painter?"

"No." Jecka's reply was controlled. "I'm just a sounding board." Jecka glanced at Carl. "Her father was Stanley Green, remember?"

"Oh, yes, you mentioned that." Carl tore his gaze from the room's entrance to Birdie, then, pointedly, to the wine in her hand. "I was sorry to hear about his passing."

"He was mostly a dick, but there are things to unpack."

The words were a bit thick on her tongue. Birdie was suddenly aware she was drinking a lot quicker than everyone else. But it was a dinner party, a slightly stressful one at that. "Maybe the character I play onstage will be different, this time." This was directed at Jecka. Because if things kept going this well, maybe the show would have a different lens than her usual sexcapades schtick.

But Jecka's expression was cool and unyielding. "Maybe."

There was a pause, during which Birdie regretted most of her past choices and a good deal of her future ones.

"So, Liz." Angela swiveled to her. "Tell us more about *Sweets*."

"It's just *Sweet*," Liz replied, nonplussed. "And actually, Violet and I might've just cracked season two."

The conversation moved on. As Liz began engaging the Jacobs, Birdie snuck another peek at Jecka, hoping to exchange an understanding smile. But Jecka wouldn't meet her gaze.

AN HOUR OR SO LATER, everyone was scraping clean bowls of peppermint stick ice cream. Birdie was enlivened by the evening. She felt generous and confident and naughty and *fun*. Her best self! Her very best!

Birdie was very drunk.

The dregs of their umpteenth bottle dribbled into her glass. "So!" Birdie clapped her hands. "Who's up for more wine?"

Jecka frowned. "It's getting late."

Angela shook her head. "I have to drive."

"Carl?" Birdie pushed.

Carl glanced at his wife. "I probably shouldn't . . ."

"C'mon." Birdie reached over to sock his arm. "I'm sure Ma'll be back any minute." Birdie pounded the table, rattling the silverware. "It's Christmas! Let's have a nightcap in the family room. The tree's tremendous this year!" Her words mashed together—*tresh tremendoush*.

"Birds, wait!" Liz called, but Birdie was already off, tumbling happily into the wine cellar to grab another bottle and a corkscrew.

When she bounded back up, everyone was milling in the kitchen. Not sitting in the adjacent family room.

Jecka had her coat on. "We might call it a night."

Birdie pulled out the cork. "Oops, it's already open. Papa Carl? You wanna wait up for Babs, don'tcha?"

Carl looked torn. "I suppose." Somewhat uncertainly, he held out a glass.

Elated, Birdie aimed for it. Misjudged the location. Poured wine directly onto the kitchen tiles, a mini-waterfall of Bordeaux.

There was a chorus of yelps as everyone edged back, away from the sudden stream of wine.

The spike of embarrassment Birdie felt was dulled by the effects of the booze sloshing in her stomach. "Shit, sorry!" She hastily put the bottle on the edge of the kitchen island, only landing it half on. As if in slow motion, the bottle toppled to the floor, hitting the tiles and smashing to pieces. The party shouted, collectively jerking back from the shooting shards of glass and explosion of red wine. "Whoops!" Birdie laughed, her drunken brain finding all this hilarious.

The room seemed to tilt, like a ship going under. Liz and Violet handed wet paper towels to the Jacobs to help them dab out their stains, cautioning them away from the glass. Her big sister's voice was steely. "Let's call it, Squeak."

"Was an accident." Birdie was slurring. "I'll get another."

"Don't." Jecka zipped up her coat, aiming her words at Birdie with cool finality. "The night is over."

35.

Three days till Christmas

✳

SUNDAY DAWNED COLD AND RAINY. THE SOMBER WEATHER seemed appropriate. The country cemetery where Willie was buried was located an hour away.

Rafi drove. Typically they'd chat or play music or a podcast, but today Ash was silent and on edge, rubbing his hands on his jeans as he stared out the window.

There were no other cars in the parking lot when Rafi pulled in. A murder of crows scattered when they slammed their doors, both men turning their collars up against the cool, misty rain.

"It's half a mile that way." Rafi pointed to a wintered rolling field, pockmarked with graves and scraggly trees.

Ash shoved his fists into his coat pockets, hunching against the weather. "Maybe this is a bad idea."

Rafi put a hand on Ash's arm, trying to find his gaze. "Just do what feels right."

Ash was silent for a long moment, glaring at the ground underfoot. Finally, he looked up. "Let's go."

The rain got heavier as they trudged along a dirt path. They took a left, and then a right, passed an oak, and then:

"There it is." Rafi pointed to a small, squat headstone, marked only with Willie's name, birthday, and deathday.

For a full minute, they stood in silence, staring at the grave, rain leaking under their coat collars.

Finally, Rafi looked over at Ash. "Do you want to say anything?"

"Like what?"

Rafi shrugged, shivering in the cold. "Whatever you like."

Ash squinted, shrugged, and cleared his throat. "Dad . . ."

Somewhere nearby, a crow called, a piteous, scratchy caw. "Ah-um . . ." Ash flicked Rafi a hesitant look.

Rafi made a *go on* motion.

Ash turned back to the grave. "Dad," he tried again. "Look, I'm sorry it came to this. I should've come earlier. I hope you get some good rest."

That seemed to be it. Short, but to the point. Rafi turned back in the direction they'd come, then paused. Ash hadn't moved. He was still staring at the grave.

"Do I?" he continued, almost to himself. "Wish you good rest? Is that something you'd wish for me? Something good?" He raked both hands through his hair, water dripping off the ends. "You didn't love me. You didn't even like me. But I was your kid. I was your kid, and you pushed me away." His voice was thick with tears, even as it rose. "It's taken me so fucking long to let anyone in because of you."

Rafi stayed quiet, not wanting to interrupt.

Ash took a few steps away, then wheeled around, addressing the grave. "Do you want to know what I felt when I found out you'd died? I felt relieved, Dad. *Relief.* That it was over. This. This relationship. The hardest one in my life. Finally done. God, that breaks my heart." His voice swelled, each word clear. "You broke my heart. Over and over and over again. But I'm done. I'm done." Ash's legs gave way. He sank down, knees in the mud, and began to sob. Clutching onto the headstone for support, Ash wept.

Rafi had never seen Ash cry like this. Gut-wrenching sobs. Tears filled his own eyes. The rain was pelting, and it was freezing, but Rafi would stand here for an eternity if that's what Ash needed.

Finally, Ash's body stopped heaving. Slowly, he got to his feet, and the expression on his face almost slit Rafi open. Such sadness and pain. Rafi wiped a smear of mud off Ash's cheek, then pressed their lips together. Despite the weather, their mouths were warm. He found Ash's gaze. "I'm proud of you."

Ash nodded. He looked about twelve years old. A little boy unloved by his parent. A little boy whom Rafi had always loved so deeply. In this moment, that love felt stronger than ever.

Ash reached down. He looped their fingers together until they were holding hands. His voice was barely audible above the drumming of the rain. "Let's go home."

LATER THAT AFTERNOON, RAFI lit a fire in his bedroom, finally in dry clothes, hot chocolates within reach. After the kindling caught, he settled on the carpet, leaning back against the club chair. When Ash came out of a long, hot shower, Rafi expected he'd sit next to him. Instead, Ash curled onto his side, putting his head in Rafi's lap. Rafi felt a rush of joy—they'd never sat like this. More firsts in a day full of them. Rafi stroked Ash's damp hair, relishing the solid weight of Ash's head on his thigh, and it felt so intimate. So close. Minutes passed as they watched the fire catch and crackle.

"I don't want to be that kind of father." Ash rolled onto his back, looking up at Rafi. "Distant. Cold. I don't want that."

Rafi got goosebumps. He recalled his daydream of Ash pushing a kid on a swing in the park. The dream that'd started everything. "You won't be. If you ever do it, I know you won't be." It was easy to speak with perfect honesty and faith.

Ash let out a happy murmur and shifted back to his side, facing the fire. Rafi stroked his arm, then slid his fingers up to massage the knots in his back. Ash made small exhales of pleasure, softening under Rafi's touch.

Only a few weeks ago, Rafi had realized his lifelong desire for marriage was related to a need to belong. He'd never felt more strongly that he *belonged*—was part of something, accepted, understood completely—than he did at this moment, with this man. They belonged here, together.

"Do you remember Career Day?" Ash asked.

Rafi let out a laugh. "I will never forget."

Parents were invited to explain their jobs to the eleventh-grade class. Willie had shown up, a few sheets to the wind, and proceeded to unleash a thirty-minute expletive-filled monologue that took aim at the government, vegetarians, the Illuminati, and coastal liberals. He did not mention what he did for work. At the time, Ash had been mortified, Rafi equally so. But now laughter rose in Rafi's throat. "He really let that class of sixteen-year-olds know what was up."

Ash sat up, hugging his knees to his chest and smiling for

the first time all day. "I thought poor Ms. Parker was going to pass out."

Rafi reached for their mugs of hot chocolate. He handed one to Ash, raising his own in salute. "To Willie. He was one of a kind."

Ash clinked his mug to Rafi's. "He certainly was."

They sipped the warm, sweet milk, their gazes only on each other.

Ash put his cup back on the coffee table and cleared his throat. "Thank you for today. I don't know if I could have done it without you."

Rafi reached for Ash's hand, pressing Ash's knuckles to his lips. "Just trying to show you we can weather any storm. Together." His tone was light, but he wasn't kidding.

Ash smiled, but his gaze stayed earnest. "So, you're serious?"

"About?"

"Us," Ash said simply.

Rafi didn't have to think about it. "Serious as a heart attack," he said, before catching himself. Joking about the cause of Willie's death the day they'd visited his grave? "Sorry. God. Why can't I think before I speak?"

"Because that's who you are." A fond smile lifted the corners of Ash's mouth. "You are impulsive and big-hearted and funny and so fucking cute."

Rafi wriggled closer, until their legs tangled. "And you are smart and thoughtful and talented and so fucking hot."

Ash chuckled. He looped his arms around Rafi, pulling him into his lap so they were snuggled together, facing each other. Without even trying, they fit together perfectly.

Ash lifted an eyebrow. "So, are we, like, boyfriends or . . . ?"

Rafi's eyes widened. "Just like that? You're ready—to be boyfriends?"

"I know it's fast," Ash admitted, "but I can't casually date someone I've known for fifteen years."

Boyfriends. The idea gushed into Rafi, filling him with joy. "Have you ever had a boyfriend?"

"Yeah. Lots of them." Ash frowned, considering. "But not . . . not like a *boyfriend* boyfriend."

"What's a *boyfriend* boyfriend?" Rafi was half teasing, half genuinely curious about Ash's definition.

"Someone I might—" Ash waved his hand.

Marry? Regularly fuck? Go to the bathroom in front of?

"Tell my friends about," Ash finished.

"Sweet." Rafi wound his fingers into Ash's hair. "Do you even have any friends apart from me?"

Ash grinned, poking him in the ribs. "Yes, actually. You'll meet them, they're great." He ran a hand through Rafi's curls. "Do you want to be my boyfriend?"

"I was going to suggest soulmates," Rafi told him, "but I can live with boyfriends."

Ash laughed. The first real laugh all day. "Compromise is an important part of every relationship," he murmured, tilting Rafi's chin up and drawing him closer until their lips touched.

36.

Two days till Christmas

THE EARLY DAYS OF LIZ'S SEX LIFE WITH NOAH WERE DEFINED less by desire and more by anxiety. Liz was overly conscious of her body, its unpredictable smells and sounds. She was paranoid about being too noisy. Her ex loved getting blow jobs but never showed much enthusiasm for returning the favor, so Liz stopped initiating. There were some early moments of passion, but sex quickly became routine. After Noah, Liz was in her thirties when it clicked that she didn't really enjoy sex with men. It was often a dissociative experience, focused around their pleasure, their needs. It didn't turn her on.

Violet turned her on. Every look, every touch, even the simple ones in passing. For so long, Liz had been fighting the way Violet made her feel, but now that she'd stopped, Liz was living in a single-minded sensory fog. A fog that made her want to touch and be touched. Give pleasure. Receive pleasure. This was lust, she realized, feeling both painfully naive and very excited. This feeling was lust. Alone in the shower, she'd only have to press between her legs for a second to summon hot waves of pleasure, at the thought of Violet doing just about anything.

They made out in the Barn's kitchenette. In the hot tub, under the stars. Behind the woodshed as snow fell like confetti. "Oh my gosh." Liz pulled back in amazement, gazing at the whirling white flakes. "This is a snowy, swoony moment. I'm having a snowy, swoony moment!"

Violet giggled, confused but not caring, and pulled her close. "Let's hang out tonight," she murmured, peeking up at Liz through lowered lashes. "In my room."

The sound of her murmur and the meaning behind it gave Liz full-body shudders.

THAT NIGHT, LIZ SHOWERED then slipped on her black silk dressing gown. Her pulse tapped an urgent beat at the thought of touching Violet in the way she hadn't yet. Discovering what Violet looked like when she lost all control.

Liz's underwear was already damp by the time she knocked softly on Violet's door, breathless with anticipation.

A lilting voice sounded from inside. "It's open."

Violet's bedroom was lamplit. A few candles flickered, filling the air with the scent of cherry and leather and plum. Violet stood in the middle of the room. Her head was cocked, blond hair loose around her shoulders. A teasing smile played on her bare lips. "Hi."

Violet was wearing her *Teenage Mutant Ninja Turtles* T-shirt and the white lace panties she'd taken such delight in unpacking the first day she arrived at Belvedere Inn.

Liz got woozy. Warm. Wet, as if her entire body had turned into honey. "Uh—oh—wow."

"So eloquent." Violet slinked forward.

Liz's heart was pounding. She'd never seduced anyone and certainly had never been seduced herself. She understood the wonderful helplessness of it. To be the target of someone you wanted, who also wanted you.

Violet pushed Liz back onto the velvet love seat by the window. Liz went willingly, legs collapsing underneath her. Finally, finally, she could stare at the shirt. The stretch of thin material over Violet's full, beautiful breasts. The outline of each nipple. The left one was under Michelangelo's smiling green face, the right at the tip of Donatello's staff.

Violet stood over her, pleased. "You like the shirt."

Liz tried to swallow, unsure what to do with her hands. "How can you tell?"

"You start blushing whenever I have it on."

Liz almost laughed, but she was too tongue-tied. Too turned on.

Violet dropped to straddle her, her bare thighs pressing against the silky fabric of Liz's dressing gown. Then Violet lowered her mouth and kissed her. It wasn't careful, sweet kissing. It was untamed and hungry. It was pedaling her bike as fast as she could as a kid, zooming downhill without a helmet. It was seeing the aurora borealis, beautiful dancing waves of ethereal green light. Realizing how full the world was of magic and wonder, if you just had the courage to seek it out.

Noises of need she couldn't control escaped Liz's throat. She dropped her hands to cup Violet's breasts, running her thumbs back and forth over the sensitive points of her nipples. Her breasts were as soft and heavy as summer fruit, unexpected August on this December night. Violet arched her back, urging Liz on. "That feels amazing," she panted. "Touch me, Lizzie. I want you to."

They rocked against each other, creating delicious friction. Liz felt the soft scratch of Vi's white lace thong rubbing against her aching center, again and again and again. Every time, a lightning bolt of heat. She was already so wet. Liz moaned. She dropped her hands to squeeze Vi's bare ass cheeks, kneading the curves of her flesh. "God, Vi. You're so fucking beautiful."

"I think you're fucking beautiful." Violet held Liz's face in her hands, thumbs on her cheekbones, and pressed their mouths together. Liz closed her eyes, lost in the ebb and flow of Violet's lips and skin and breath.

She could do this forever. Touch this woman forever. Smell her spicy-sweet smell forever. Then Violet pushed up against Liz, her thigh between Liz's legs, and Liz was rocketed back into her body and all its pent-up heat.

Violet pulled them up until they were standing. She tugged at the cord of Liz's dressing gown. It slipped off her shoulders, pooling at her feet. Liz stood in just her underwear. Violet let out a breath of pleased discovery. "You're a goddess."

And Liz didn't even think to bat the compliment away because Violet was kneeling on the love seat and taking one of Liz's nipples in her mouth.

Pleasure avalanched through Liz's body, a crash of heat. The feeling of Violet's tongue, warm and wet, sucking on her breast, centered everything Liz was feeling. It was so intense, Liz's knees almost buckled. She liked having her breasts touched, but comparing those past experiences to this was like comparing a child's drawing to a Klimt. Around and around went Violet's tongue, circling Liz's tight, hard nipples.

Liz's vision wavered, the room falling away. "Oh god," she heard herself gasping, over and over again. "Oh *god.*"

Vi pulled back. Her pupils were dilated, mouth damp. "Bed." Vi pointed at it. "Now."

A moment later, Liz was on the neatly made king bed, propping herself up on her elbows, her vision still spinning. The sheets smelled like Violet, intensifying the need to touch her.

Violet crawled up until she was kneeling between Liz's legs. She leaned forward, her blond hair mussed. She hooked her fingers around Liz's underwear. "Can I?"

Liz nodded, shifting her weight.

Slowly, so very slowly, Violet eased Liz's underwear off until Liz lay bare on the bed.

Violet nudged Liz's thighs apart and gazed between her legs, her expression reverential. "Oh wow," she breathed. "You're perfect."

Ordinarily, Liz would feel shy, a little too hairy, a little too exposed. But all those insecurities and doubts were gone. She didn't feel timid. She felt powerful.

Violet's voice was husky, her eyes low-lidded. "Can I go down on you?"

Liz felt like a volcano ready to go off. "Yes."

Violet wiggled down between Liz's legs. Liz's muscles tensed and untensed in anticipation. She held her breath. Closed her eyes. And then Violet's warm mouth was on her, touching her in the place she needed to be touched.

Liz let out a gasp, then a groan, then another gasp. "Oh *fuck.*" The feeling of Violet's strong, hot tongue teasing and stroking her swollen clit was the most intense pleasure she'd ever felt. Shock waves of pure sensation were racing up her back, down her legs, building in intensity. "Oh *god.*" She was no longer a person. She was pure feeling.

Panting hard, Liz managed to crack an eye. The visual of Violet, still in the T-shirt and the white thong, head bobbing as she ran her tongue back and forth, almost sent Liz over the edge. She was no longer conscious of the words and cries tumbling out of her mouth. She was approaching the peak, a tight, hot pinnacle of pleasure. Her stomach muscles tensed. Her vision went black.

Liz came against Violet's mouth. Against her tongue and her teeth and her breath, the peak not fading but somehow intensifying. It was almost too much. Liz was sweating and writhing and gasping and yelling, again and again and again. "Oh god! Oh god! Oh *god!*"

Finally the feeling began to subside. Aftershocks jerked her limbs like a puppet on a string as Liz settled back into herself, piece by piece.

The candlelit room. The cozy bed. The beautiful girl lying next to her, wiping her mouth and grinning.

Liz felt like she'd jumped out of a plane to land splat on the mattress. She rubbed her face in a daze. It took her several long moments to remember how to talk. "Wh-What just happened?"

Violet giggled, dropping a salty-sweet kiss on her mouth.

The feeling of Vi, still in the T-shirt and thong, helped reality firm up. Liz gazed at her, amazed. "That was—I didn't even know—like, I *literally* didn't even know—" She heard herself and laughed. "I'm a writer and I can't string a sentence together."

"Take your time."

Liz propped herself onto her side to face Violet. "That was the most incredible thing that has ever and will ever happen to me. You are a wizard. A maestro. Someone needs to make a statue of you."

Violet laughed in delight. "Well, it certainly sounded like you enjoyed it."

Sounded? Oh: she'd been loud. She'd been loud in her mother's house. She'd been loud in her mother's house *with all her family*. Liz had never lost control like that. Liz had been *yelling*. A *lot*. "Oh, boy." Everyone was home. Everyone would've heard. "I am never gonna live that down."

"We can try to be more quiet," Vi suggested, skimming her fingers over Liz's breasts.

"No." Liz's response was certain. She could handle being teased. A part of her was looking forward to it. But that wasn't important right now. "It's your turn."

Reenergized, Liz scrambled to kneel on the bed, picking up Violet's legs to place them over her own shoulders, admiring the shape of Vi's calves. The possibilities were endless. "What do you like? I take direction very well."

Violet smiled, eyes bright. "I'd always hoped we'd have this conversation one day."

Liz wiggled forward until she was lying on top of Vi. She couldn't wait to take the T-shirt off, but there was something undeniably hot about being bare naked while Vi was still partially clothed. "Tell me everything."

Violet explained what she liked. Fingers. G-spot. The palm-sized vibrator, already on the bedside table. Liz had never talked this openly with a bedmate. In the past, it had struck her as awkward or clinical. But now it seemed practical, and everything Violet was describing sounded unbelievably sexy. Just hearing about it made Liz certain she could come again, and soon.

When Violet finished speaking, she flipped Liz onto her

back to straddle her. Violet leaned down to kiss her, their tongues brushing, playing. Then Violet grasped the bottom of her *Turtles* tee. With a degree of theatricality, she pulled it up, over her head.

Violet had shot plenty of scenes and photographs in lingerie, but Liz had never seen Violet's breasts. They were milky curves, soft flesh. Her nipples were the color of apricots. She was a painting. A symphony. Liz shifted up until they were both sitting, legs wrapped around each other. She kissed Violet's mouth, then her breasts, taking her time, enjoying every scrape of teeth against nipple, every tiny whimper, every moan. Then she pushed Violet back until she was lying on the bed. Liz hooked her thumbs around the sides of the white thong. The beautiful piece of snow-white lace she fell asleep thinking about every night. Carefully, Liz peeled the underwear off. Over the curve of Violet's hips. Past her thighs. Around her ankles.

For a long, breathless moment, Liz gazed at the naked woman lying on the bed, her curves lit only by candlelight, her smile an invitation. Liz was a storyteller by trade—had written countless scripts, created entire worlds. They all paled in comparison to this. Violet was true art.

Liz started in the way Violet had instructed: kissing Vi's breasts, sucking her erect nipples.

"Oh, *Liz.*" Violet spoke her name on an exhale, hands fisting Liz's hair. "*Liz.*"

The sound of her name falling out of Violet's mouth as a pant, a plea, drove Liz even more crazy. She slipped her fingers down between Violet's legs, inhaling with pleasure. "You're so wet."

Violet moaned in response, whimpering as Liz started to circle her sensitive clit. In this moment, Liz was the maestro, able to pay attention to the tempo and adjust accordingly. Being pleasured was wonderful, but giving pleasure was just as good. It made Liz feel like a god. Expansive and powerful. And like a goddess, in touch with some sort of mysterious female divine.

"Fingers," Violet begged. "Please."

It was a pleasure to obey. Still teasing Violet's nipple with her tongue, Liz slipped two then three fingers inside Violet. She was so slick. So warm and tight. Liz could barely get the words out as she started fucking Violet with her hand. "God, you feel so good."

Violet groaned, reaching for the vibrator to press it against her clit. "Faster. Yes. *Yes.*" She started to buck and writhe, and Liz pumped and curved her fingers, pushing against her G-spot. "Yes. Yes. *Yes.*"

Liz didn't just hear and see Violet's pleasure. She felt it, in the pulsing tightness enveloping her fingers.

Liz had never seen anything so mesmerizing as Violet coming apart, face flushed, hair splayed, eyes wild. Liz had to press the vibrator against herself for only a moment to summon a second orgasm, just as powerful as the first. Her cries mixed with Violet's as they climaxed together, their shouts peaking then slowly starting to quiet.

Violet opened her eyes and smiled. The real one, the one that wrinkled the bridge of her nose. Liz felt impossibly happy. She was locked into Violet's orbit, circling her like a moon. She never wanted to stop. *I'm a goner,* Liz thought, as Violet pulled their mouths together into a sweaty, laughing kiss.

37.

One day till Christmas

LIZ AWOKE TO THE SOUND OF THE RAIN, A LIGHT, PERSISTENT patter. The bedspread wasn't Tiffany blue, it was Marilyn white. Violet was beside her, still asleep. Memories from last night rushed back, as if they'd been eagerly waiting all morning to relive the play-by-play.

Her nipple in Violet's mouth. Her fingers between Violet's legs. An arched back, a scream, a laugh. A kiss. So many kisses. Feeling *sexy*, in her own skin. Liz couldn't remember the last time she'd felt sexy—confident, alluring, her body a meal to be enjoyed. If only she could *Groundhog Day* it all, do it again and again and again.

Liz checked her breath. Not great. With the skill of a cat burglar she slid noiselessly out of bed, tiptoeing to the bathroom. There, she washed her mouth out with Vi's toothpaste. Her hair was a mess, but the face in the mirror looked flushed and bright-eyed.

Wow, Liz thought in surprise. *I look pretty.*

Slipping back into bed, she snaked an arm around Vi's waist, snuggling close. Vi shimmied back into her. The sensation sang in Liz's body, her heart hitting the sort of high C that'd shatter glass.

Vi's voice was smudgy with sleep. "So, you're the big spoon?"

"I'm whatever piece of cutlery you want." Liz kissed her bare shoulder. "Spoon. Fork. Spork."

Violet giggled. She rolled onto her back so they were face-to-face. Even first thing, she was a Renaissance level of beautiful, hair splashing liquid gold across the pillow, eyes the color of uncut amethyst. "Hi."

"Hi." Liz bent down, pressing her lips to Violet's. Vi's breath tasted clean and minty. Toothpaste.

They broke apart, laughing. "Great minds," said Violet with a smile, rolling on top of Liz and nudging her legs apart.

Rain beetled down the windows. It was one day until Christmas and all they had to do was shop for gifts and send off the pitch, in order to meet Liz's goal of crossing everything off her to-do list by December 25.

After another, quieter, climax each, they lay tangled together, wordsmithing the final line.

"Take a bite out of the second season?" Liz tried.

"Sink your teeth into Sweet Valley," Vi riffed. "Two's better than one." Then, in a stage whisper: "Because twins."

"Perfect." Liz made the change. "We are done." She sent it off to her agent, a few trusted friends, and Cat, underlining that she didn't expect feedback until after the holidays. Now they just had to cross their fingers and wait. "Do you want to get up?" Liz asked, putting her laptop on the bedside table.

Violet's smile was coquettish as she shook her head.

Liz didn't believe in magic, but each time Violet's lips

touched her own, she felt something like it. Burning herbs, refracted light. The orphic energy all around that our brains evolved to ignore. Being kissed by Violet was like downing the bottle marked DRINK ME. An invitation into another world.

Liz was drowning in emotion, willingly so. Her desire was as uncaged as the wind, in the air, beyond her control.

HOURS LATER, LIZ DROVE them both into town to shop for presents, parking in the small lot behind the store. Before they got out, Violet caught Liz's gaze cautiously. "We should . . . play it safe. Inside."

It took a moment for Liz to understand what Violet meant. No affection. No coupledom. "Of course!" Liz rushed to reply. "Totally. Operation Safe." Liz gave Violet a reassuring smile, ignoring a silly pang of disappointment.

They huddled under an umbrella, hurrying around the side of the building and into Woodstock's nicest general store.

Last-minute holiday shoppers thumbed through cookbooks, examined linen napkins, and sniffed hand-poured soy candles. Twinkling fairy lights hung from above, and garlands of holly and pine made the whole store smell like Christmas.

Liz picked up the gifts she'd had her eye on for weeks. A neon-yellow beanie for Birdie, a photography book on the male nude that'd absorbed Rafi when they'd last popped in. Oversized sunglasses for her mom. Shearling-lined slippers for Ash.

Violet was tucked into a quiet corner, examining a tray of tiny, beautiful things. "This is pretty." She fingered a gold ring set with one tiny sunstone and one crescent-shaped sapphire, Vi's birthstone. "Reminds me of the phases of the moon. How everything is cyclic but some things are stable. The moon is always there. I find that comforting."

Liz remembered thinking something similar at Lover's Lake. It was so appealing, Vi's soulful depth. It made Liz want to sit at her feet like a disciple. "I want to buy it for you," Liz said. "For Christmas."

Violet smiled up at her. "You don't have to do that." She checked the price tag. "It's kind of expensive."

Money had never meant less. Liz wanted to give Violet the actual moon and all the stars. "If you like something, I want you to have it."

Liz brushed Violet's cheek with her fingertips, letting her gaze linger, happily lovestruck. This feeling wasn't just a post-sex glow. It was a soul-deep connection. It was peace. Liz leaned in for a kiss.

Caution crossed Vi's face like a change in the weather. She backed up, darting an almost imperceptible glance around the busy store, and said she'd meet Liz outside.

AFTER MAKING HER PURCHASES, Liz returned to the car where Violet was waiting, under the umbrella. Liz didn't say much until they were out of town and on the road back to Belvedere Inn. "I'm sorry about before. I . . . forgot."

"You don't need to be sorry." Violet flicked Liz a complicated smile before returning her gaze to the passing trees. "I just never forget."

"That must be exhausting. To always be on guard like that. Constantly aware of yourself."

Violet shrugged, no trace of self-pity in her voice. "It's what I signed up for."

Which sounded practical, even humble, but also sad. The atmosphere in the car wasn't strained, but the cozy warmth of the morning had cooled. Liz wasn't sure what her next line was supposed to be. "So . . . we're a secret?"

"I think it's the best option." Violet shifted in her seat to face Liz. "But not wanting to kiss you in public has nothing to do with how I feel about you. It's about me protecting you, and myself, and *us*."

Liz understood. But it bugged her. Beyond Violet's lack of privacy, how long would this secrecy last? "I'm just trying to imagine, like, still being under wraps while we're in pro-duction. Sneaking around? Lying to everyone we work with?" The idea seemed emotionally unsafe. Not how two adults should conduct a commitment that'd last. "If we get green-lit," she added, responsibly. "And if this continues." Liz forgot that wasn't a given.

A pause. Violet spoke slowly. "Well, I like to hear you're thinking that way. But attention will just ruin what we have. I see it all the time."

This was true. Two of the other cast members, Xiao and Cashmere, had casually dated for a few weeks, but interest from fans and the press took the relationship to a boil before it had a chance to simmer, and it quickly fell apart. But this was different from a casual romance. Wasn't it?

"I really need to keep things private," Violet said. "For us, and for me."

"Makes sense." Liz kept her tone even, but she couldn't help feeling worried.

Violet seemed to sense it, glancing over. "Maybe, after a few months, we just tell a few people. A need-to-know basis. If, y'know . . . we're still doing this."

Liz couldn't imagine ever not doing this. "I really hope we are."

They traded a smile.

Violet squeezed Liz's thigh, the sensation melting her bones like butter. "Me too."

Liz let out a breath of relief. For just one moment, she let herself imagine arriving hand in hand to set with Violet or, even more impossibly, attending an industry event as a couple. The image was as bright as a spotlight, and Liz couldn't look at it directly. For now, they'd made it through this slightly awkward conversation to end on a hopeful note. All things considered, it seemed like a huge step.

Liz eased up on the gas. There was no rush to get home. They could just enjoy the ride.

BACK AT THE INN, Liz was eager to escape to Vi's bedroom and pick up where they'd left off that morning. But halfway up the staircase, she was stopped by Jin-soo. "Liz. I'm leaving in a few hours to spend Christmas Eve with my family."

"Oh, cool." Liz's focus was on Violet, who'd paused in the second floor hallway, frowning at her phone. "Merry Christmas Jin-soo. Safe travels back."

Jin-soo tried to catch Liz's gaze. "Keep an eye on Babs. Make sure she takes her meds."

Violet darted a confused look at Liz then continued toward her bedroom.

"Sure, will do. Sorry, I have to . . ." Liz hustled after Violet, following her into Vi's bedroom and shutting the door behind them. "Everything okay?"

Violet was chewing a thumbnail, eyes on her phone. "Cat asked me to call."

"Cat—Hunter?" Their publicist. "Why?"

Violet had already dialed.

Cat picked up, her voice direct. "Are you with Liz?"

Liz stared at Violet. "Um—yes?"

"Someone just posted a story of you two. I'm sending it now."

A ping. A link to someone's social media. A video. Taken inside the general store. In the smartphone-filmed footage, Violet admired the sunstone-and-sapphire ring. Liz's stomach dropped as she watched their flirtation play out, intimate and kittenish, until Liz touched Violet's face, leaning forward for a kiss, prompting Violet to coyly, *guiltily*, glance around the shop. Zero room for misinterpretation.

Cat was speaking. ". . . would've appreciated a heads-up. Do you want to make a statement?"

"A statement?" Liz was lightheaded. The video had herself and Violet tagged. Comments were flooding in faster than she could scroll. OMG IS SHE GAY? and who's the fugmo tryna kiss her? and that's her BOSS @lizbelvedere 😬.

Everyone would find out. The execs, the crew, the rest of the cast. *It was already gossip.* Panic surged into Liz's system. She couldn't speak, couldn't think, couldn't move.

"A statement," Cat repeated testily. "About your relationship."

Liz stared at Violet. Violet stared back, her face a darker version of Liz's unease—eyes angry and scared, lips pressed tight.

"Guys?" Cat prompted.

For one unhinged moment, Liz imagined Violet announcing, *Screw it. We're dating!*, Liz co-signing, and just like that, they were *together* together, laughing about being U-Haul lesbians because why wait? They were meant to be.

Violet looked away from Liz, addressing the phone. "No statement. We're just friends. We're not together."

An arrow, right in her heart.

Cat said, "Liz?"

"What Violet said," Liz said, trying to mask her disappointment.

"Okay." Cat sounded thoroughly unconvinced. "Company policy says all workplace relationships have to go through HR. But more important—in the court of public opinion, *secrets* can very quickly become *scandal*. And *scandal* is what we all want to avoid. Right?"

Liz didn't know if this was a tactic to get them to confess or a genuine warning. The idea of being a scandal was terrifying.

"There won't be a scandal because there's no secret," Violet snapped, and hung up. "*Fuck.*" She sank to the ground, continuing to scroll. "God, it's *everywhere.*"

The video had already been reposted fifty, sixty times. As Liz scrolled, it kept appearing, populating like a virus. She was having trouble breathing.

Liz tapped open her work email. Her treasured inbox zero was obliterated by an entire screen of new messages. When were you two going to tell me??? and Wow, congrats, you are viral and UGLY BITCH HANDS OFF from an address she didn't know. Liz's pulse spiked, a seasick terror. "Jesus *Christ.*" She tried to laugh but it came out more like a gasp.

"What?" Violet's face was as gray as the clouds outside.

"Nothing. Nothing. This is—nothing." A lie and they

both knew it. "I'm so sorry, Vi. I never should've—I should've known better."

"Yeah, you should've." Violet's sharp response cut through Liz's shock.

Liz's phone was radioactive in her hand. Messages flooded in, emails and texts and notifications. So happy for you! and 🏳️‍🌈🏳️‍🌈🏳️‍🌈🏳️‍⚧️🏳️‍⚧️🏳️‍⚧️ and You guys are cute.

Liz looked up from her texts. "A lot of people are being supportive."

Vi was scrolling through the comments on the video. "A lot of people are really homophobic." She sounded like she was already regretting everything. "This is exactly what I didn't want. Now everyone knows, and not on our terms." She read one of the comments aloud. "*Okay, now I understand Violet Grace. Another dumb blonde who fucked her way to the top.*" Her voice was strained. "Already has a hundred likes. It'll be a thousand in three minutes. Tomorrow, gossip. Next week, fact."

Liz's heart thumped in surprise. "That's not true."

Violet's response was bitter. "You have no idea how this goes."

"No, I mean, it's not true you slept your way to the top."

"That *doesn't* matter." Violet looked at Liz as if she were completely stupid. "I told you how important privacy is. I told you how much this stuff can get to me."

Liz felt herself getting defensive. "But this isn't my fault."

"You were pressuring me!" Violet's eyes were filling with tears.

"No, I wasn't." Was she? Liz was aware they were in the logic-free zone of a fight, adrenaline and emotion messing with their minds. "Why can't we just own it? Tell Cat we're together?"

"Together?" Violet barked an incredulous laugh. "We only *just* slept together. Last night!"

Vi's phone started bleating. Cat was calling back. Violet tapped accept. "What?"

"Looks like one of the caterers got a photo of you two at Liz's mom's holiday party, so this thing is snowballing. Autostraddle is picking it up, and I've missed calls from *The Cut*, *them*, *New York Post*—"

Violet threw her phone across the room. "*Fuck!*"

The caterers. Liz had a slippery memory of being asked to have them sign an NDA. She hadn't.

"I can't do this." Violet paced, panting, hands raking her hair. "I can't handle it, I'm sorry."

Liz scrambled for the right thing to say. "But we said we'd tell people in a few months, right? We're just ahead of schedule—"

"No, I can't do *this*." Violet sawed the air between them with a frantic hand. "A public *thing*. I can't. I just can't."

Liz's blood turned to ice. "You don't mean that."

"Don't tell me what I mean!" Vi yelled. Tears were slipping down her cheeks. "I *can't* handle this. I *don't* want this."

Liz sucked in a breath. This was her nightmare. Exactly what she knew would happen. She'd opened her heart to Violet and now Violet was running away, taking all the broken pieces of it with her.

"So, that's it?" Liz's voice was harsher than she meant it to be. "One hiccup and you're out?"

"This isn't a hiccup!" Vi shouted back, eyes furious. "This is my *life*. God, you don't get it. You don't get *me*."

A sick kick to the gut. How could this be happening? "What can I do?"

Violet turned away, sobs rising up her throat. "You can go."

Liz's heart split down the middle. The unfamiliar feeling of tears almost stabbed at her eyes. "Vivi—"

"*Go.*"

Liz went back to her room in a daze. Her bedroom didn't look familiar—the bedspread, her clothes: all foreign. Only when Liz became aware of the carols playing over the house speakers did she remember. It was Christmas Eve.

38.

*B*IRDIE WAS NOT ESPECIALLY PLEASED HER SISTER WAS having a sexual awakening. The "screamathon" from Violet's bedroom kept Birdie up until 3:00 A.M., meaning she'd overslept and was now running late to meet Jecka for their afternoon date. She also hadn't figured out presents for tomorrow—things had been busy!—but hoped Rafi wanted to go in on something for their mom.

"Raf Attack?" Birdie didn't bother knocking, hurrying into her brother's Swiss chalet nightmare of a bedroom. "Have you gotten anything for—oh my GOD. WHAT?!"

Rafi and Ash were both scrambling for clothes, sheets, anything to cover up the fact that they were extremely naked. And not in a we're-just-getting-changed way. In a we're-just-getting-railed way.

Birdie shrieked, stumbling back, batting away the sight as if being attacked by Hitchcock's birds. "Argh! Away!"

"Haven't you heard of knocking?" Rafi yelled.

"No, but clearly you've heard of banging." Birdie peeked through her fingers. Ash was under the covers and Rafi was wearing a plaid blanket as a toga. Birdie dropped her hands, not sure whether to laugh or scream. "What in the name of *Christmas?*"

Ash and Rafi glanced at each other, fighting back smiles. "Do you need us to lay it out?" Ash asked.

"No." Birdie sighed. "I did actually read *Flowers in the Attic.*"

Rafi threw a cushion at her, which she ducked, grinning.

Birdie glanced at the time on her phone. "Well, I'd love to stay and make this even more awkward, but I'm late to meet Jecka." Ash and Rafi? Rafi and Ash? She shrugged. "Stranger things." She headed for the door, pointing back at them. "Guy from that, also gay."

Ten seconds later, Birdie was in her station wagon, revving the engine. All of *that* would have to wait. Birdie suspected she had her work cut out for her with Jecka.

Birdie still couldn't think about Saturday's meet-the-parents dinner without cringing. That was three days ago, and she and Jecka hadn't spoken since. Birdie was so nervous, she let herself spike the apple cider in her thermos. Not for a repeat of Saturday night, obviously. Just something to even her out. After she parked her car, a few slugs of the hot, sweet liquid fuzzed out the razor side of her anxiety.

Jecka was already waiting by the picturesque little waterfall on the grounds of her parents' hotel.

Apologizing for being late, Birdie felt buoyed that Jecka accepted her kiss hello. A briefer kiss than Birdie would've liked, but they'd get back on track, right?

Jecka frowned as she pulled back, nose wrinkling. She glanced darkly at the thermos in Birdie's hand before dropping her gaze to the toes of her boots. "So, I've been thinking . . ."

Birdie took another fortifying sip of cider. "About?"

"Well, I'm going to Boston for the holidays, and when I get back, you'll be back home in Brooklyn, right?"

Birdie blinked, thrown. "I—I guess. I don't know. I usually head back to the city for New Year's."

Jecka nodded. Her gaze darted like a frightened bird before landing, tentatively, on Birdie. "So, maybe we should just end things now?"

Birdie's stomach fell out of her bottom and onto the ground between them. "But . . . why?"

"I'm just being practical." It sounded half like a plea and half like a decision already made. "We live hours apart," Jecka went on, "and I have to put work first, to have any shot of reaching my dreams. I want to experiment with stuff that's 'adventurous and personal,' but I've been so distracted, I haven't made any progress at all."

"Is this about the dinner?" Birdie asked. "I'm sorry about that. I know it wasn't my best look, and I'm honestly so embarrassed. The grocery store was packed, I had no idea Ma wouldn't be there—"

"Look," Jecka cut in. "I'm thirty. I want to build a life with someone. Someone who wants to be in a committed relationship. Is that what you want?"

"Sure," Birdie replied reflexively, but as she heard herself speak, she realized it felt true. "Yes. I think I do want that." She went on, nodding. "I want a partner. I want to build a life with someone."

Jecka made a helpless sound. "I don't know if I believe that. Someone who wants to build a life with me doesn't get obliterated around my parents, *the very first time* they meet." She ran her hand over her head in distress. "I spent the whole drive back defending you, but by the end, even I wasn't buying it. Birdie, I think you've drank, or planned on drinking, practically every time we've hung out. Do you realize that?"

Birdie couldn't speak. She knew she drank a bit more than most people. That Liz or Rafi could go days without drinking without realizing it, and she never had, never could. But no one had ever challenged her over it.

Jecka went on, her face full of desperate feeling. "You've really thrown me. I like you, Birdie. You're a good person. You make me laugh, you're kind. I care about you. You're very good at sex. But do you really want something monogamous and long-term?"

Of course smart, together Jecka Jacob was breaking up with her. *Of course* this was never going to be anything: Who was she kidding? She was a fuckup. Just like her father. She always had been a fuckup, and she always would be a fuckup, and who in their right mind would want to build a life with that?

Hot tears rushed her eyes. Birdie swung her gaze to the tumbling waterfall so Jecka wouldn't see. "Guess not."

Jecka went on, her voice soft and unshakable. "I just think it's gonna hurt way less if we end it now, and not in six months when we're more attached."

Birdie kicked at the ground, unable to meet Jecka's eye for fear she'd start sobbing. "Cool. Whatever."

"I'm sorry." Jecka took another step away, wiping at her nose. "I really am."

"Don't sweat it." Birdie made herself shrug. "Have a nice life."

Jecka pressed her lips together. Giving Birdie one final, sorrowful look, she turned and walked away.

BACK IN THE CAR, driving too fast, Birdie could barely focus on the road. She glanced in the rearview mirror, hating what she saw.

She was supposed to have followed in her mother's footsteps, not her father's. Liz was the family achiever. Rafi was having a self-growth moment. She was getting drunk at an important dinner in between scribbling her stupid ideas in her stupid notebook for a show everyone knew she'd never perform. Her best days were behind her, and they weren't even that great.

Her sobs became a howl. The road in front of her blurred.

A hard crunch of gravel. The sudden blare of a car horn, a sharp screech of tires. The world around her swerved, trees streaking in front of her. The heartbeat between life and death, *this* moment. Adrenaline slapped her into focus. Birdie wrestled the steering wheel into submission.

Panicked, she pulled over to the shoulder and flipped on her hazards. It took several long moments to still her racing heart.

She couldn't stomach going back to the house. Too-wonderful Belvedere Inn, the glorious success story she wasn't.

Birdie needed to escape everything.

39.

AS SOON AS BIRDIE LEFT RAFI'S BEDROOM, RAFI DROPPED his plaid blanket toga and headed over to lock the damn door. "Guess the word is out."

Ash arched a brow. "Guess so."

Rafi climbed back into bed, next to Ash. "That cool with you?"

Ash shrugged, smiling. "Yeah. Cool with you?"

"Yeah." Rafi pointed between them. "Should we get back to it?"

"Yep," Ash agreed, and they did.

IT WAS EARLY EVENING by the time they emerged from Rafi's bedroom.

Jin-soo was in the foyer, zipping up their winter coat. They were getting the Amtrak back to Queens.

"Merry Christmas." Rafi gave them a hug. "Hope you avoid any neighborhood carolers."

"Thanks Raf." Jin-soo wagged a finger between the two men. "Also this is cute."

Rafi blushed, knowing he was grinning like a goofball and not caring one bit.

"Goodbye, my treasure." Babs swept in, dressed in a candy-pink 1930s-style robe with a floaty, feathered trim, nabbed from a period film early in her career. "See you in a week."

The hug between his mother and her assistant was longer than Rafi was expecting.

The trio followed Jin-soo outside, into the twilight. Standing on the steps of Belvedere Inn, Rafi, Ash, and Babs waved at Jin-soo's taxi until the taillights vanished.

Ash draped himself around Rafi like the world's best wearable blanket. He leaned back into Ash, cozying into his heat.

His mother faced them. "So. What's going on here?"

Rafi glanced up at Ash, who smiled back, a permissive glint in his eye. "I guess Ash and I are . . ."

Babs planted a hand on her hip. "Gayer than Christmas?"

Ash let out a puff of amusement.

Rafi felt his cheeks redden, unable to stop smiling. "Guess so."

Babs nodded, looking impressed, as if she didn't think Rafi had it in him. "Since?"

Since always wasn't right, even if it sort of felt that way. "The holiday party?"

"Ah." Babs nodded, unsurprised. "It *is* the most wonderful time of the year." She tipped her head to one side. "And something's going on with Liz and Violet, isn't it? So that means . . . How did all my kids end up gay?"

Rafi gestured at the dressing gown. The diamond earrings and half dozen rings. "Mom, look at you. How could we not?"

Babs let out a loud honk of a laugh, which turned into a rolling, lustrous guffaw. She drew them close. "Come here."

Rafi hugged his mother back. His face was buried in her

gown's feathered trim as she leaned her full weight into him. This really was shaping up to be the best Christmas of all time.

Babs pulled back first, steadying herself with her cane. "I think I need to rest my eyes before dinner."

"Okay." Rafi put his arms around Ash's waist, his head fitting neatly under Ash's chin.

Babs went back inside, the dogs dutifully trotting after her. The early evening was smoke blue and as quiet as a shrine. Pearl-gray clouds feathered the waning moon. An owl gave an experimental hoot. They stood there for a long time, holding each other, watching the growing night. An evening star blinked awake in the night sky, and Rafi made a wish.

INSIDE, IN THE FOYER, Rafi proposed that they exchange their gifts before dinner, which was always simple and preprepared—Siouxsie spent Christmas Eve with her own family.

"My gift is sort of personal," Rafi explained. "I'd rather give it to you when it's just us."

Ash gave Rafi's butt a squeeze, turning his spine to silly string. "Give me two minutes to wrap."

The two men didn't usually go overboard with Christmas gifts, tending to choose one thoughtful or, more often, funny present. But this wasn't a typical Christmas. Rafi's idea had come to him a few days ago. He'd pulled the trigger last night. It was an assurance. A heartfelt declaration.

Ash entered Rafi's bedroom holding a box with a bright red bow. He sat cross-legged across from Rafi on the bed, looking cozy in his gray cashmere sweatsuit.

Rafi handed Ash a flat envelope. "Although it's been said many times, many ways . . ."

"Merry Christmas." Ash handed Rafi his gift. "To you."

Rafi ripped off the wrapping paper, excited to see what Ash had come up with. Rafi assumed his first in-person gift in two years *after* they'd started making out in the kitchen pantry would demonstrate the seriousness of Ash's inten-tion, the depth of his heart. A stunning piece of jewelry or a watch engraved with the day they met. Rafi wasn't quite ex-pecting: "A mug."

An ordinary white mug with a picture printed on its side. A sepia-toned candid of him and Ash: Rafi recognized it from their first Halloween together, both dressed as pirates, smil-ing big. Which made it not just adorable but also a nod to how long the two boys had been in each other's lives, side by side. But even as Rafi felt touched by the sweet idea, he started to regret his own choice.

"Cute, right?" Ash smiled at him, slipping one finger under the envelope's lip to tear it open. "I went through a thousand of your mom's old photo albums to find it."

"It's fantastic." Rafi's words were enthusiastic, but he was watching Ash open the envelope with slight alarm. "My present's a bit different. . . . Actually, maybe I should—" He tried to pluck the piece of paper Ash was unfolding, but Ash was too quick, pulling it away.

"No backsies, Belvedere," he teased. "What do we have here?" He scanned the printed words. "A flight receipt! For . . . you." Ash frowned, continuing to read. "A one-way flight from New York to London. Leaving next week. Same day I do. And, wow—that was not a cheap flight." He looked up at Rafi with a confused expression. "Sorry—is this my gift?"

Rafi's gaze dropped to the mug in his hand. The understated but charming kind of present he should've gotten. His cheeks heated. "I—I wanted to show you how serious I am. . . . But I should've gone with new underwear." He tried to take the printout back.

Ash didn't let him. "You bought a flight to London? To . . . visit me?"

With every passing second, Rafi regretted his "gift" more. It no longer seemed romantic. It seemed over-the-top and crazy. Hadn't he promised himself not to jump into things? To take things slow, so he could see things clearly?

"Raf?" Ash prompted, his face a study in confusion.

Rafi steeled himself. "You already know I want to quit my job. London sounds like such a vibrant city. I think I might really love it there."

Ash's eyes became saucers. "You're *moving* to London? Next week?" He stared at the flight receipt, then back at Rafi. "Doing what? Living where?"

Shame and dismay crowded Rafi's throat. He tried to smile through it. "That is the last time that I Christmas shop on eggnog. I was obviously blitzed." He snatched the paper back, balling it in his fist. "Forget you saw this and please act surprised when you open new underwear tomorrow morning." He aimed at the fire.

"No, wait!"

Rafi threw the crumpled paper into the flames, resolving to cancel the stupid flight as soon as he could get online.

"Raf!" Ash released a stunned laugh, which blossomed into a look of amazement. At the situation or at Rafi's nerve, Rafi couldn't tell. Ash's gaze fell to the mug. Ash's words were soft, as if to himself. "And I got you a *cup*. Fuck."

"I should check on my mom." Rafi scrambled off the bed.

"Raf, wait." Ash was off the bed and in front of the door, blocking his exit.

"You're obviously freaked out!" Rafi accused, half knowing he was angry only at himself.

"I'm surprised," Ash corrected. "You moving to London isn't something we've discussed." A smile twisted his frustratingly kissable lips. "Weirdly relating to Sunita right now."

Rafi knew Ash was kidding, but it landed like an insult. His mouth fell open. *"What?"*

"Babe, I'm joking."

Rafi's first *babe*, a pleasure overpowered by the reminder of his highly embarrassing breakup. "Proposing to Sunita was a huge mistake." Rafi flashed back on his ex-girlfriend's look of horror. "Are you saying this is a mistake too?"

"No," Ash said. "I'm saying you move fast. Faster than me and most rays of light." Ash tugged Rafi toward him, looping his hands behind Rafi's head, pressing their hips together. "I want you to come to London, Raf. I do. How about you come for a week or two in January, get a handle on the city, see what you think?"

Even though that sounded perfectly reasonable, Rafi couldn't help but feel disappointed. He was expecting tears of joy. Not a gentle compromise as if he were a child. "Totally. It's a refundable flight." It wasn't. He untangled himself from Ash's arms. "I'm going to check on Mom."

But that was just an excuse.

Hurrying out of his bedroom, Rafi headed for Babs's room. Why didn't he ask her, or his sisters, about the move to London before making such a rash decision?

The three Poms were whining outside Babs's bedroom door. Rafi nudged them aside and knocked. "Mom?" He knocked again. "Mom? You in there?" Nothing. Rafi opened the door.

His mother was lying face down on the carpet, still in her robe with the feathered trim. Her head was turned to one side. She wasn't moving.

The dogs ran to her, barking in distress.

For a moment, Rafi thought it was a joke. That his actress mother was playing dead.

"Mom?" Time stopped, suspending Rafi and everyone in the house. His voice was tiny. Not even a mouse. "Mom?"

Babs continued to lie there. No giveaway grin, no *gotcha!* Babs. Wasn't. Moving.

"Mom!"

40.

LIZ PAUSED AT THE FRONT DOOR TO BELVEDERE INN, IN-
haling a steadying breath. She'd gone for a drive to give Violet space. Now Liz prayed Violet hadn't meant all the things
she'd said and was ready to talk. But as soon as Liz stepped
through the front door, she was bowled over by Ash, bolting
from the direction of her mother's suite. "Liz!" Ash was wide-
eyed and frantic. "Come, now!"

"What's going—"

"Now!" He dragged her into her mom's suite.

An impossible sight. Her mother, unresponsive on the
carpet, surrounded by three manic dogs.

Her brother was on his knees next to their mother's body,
babbling about finding her like this, just now: "I don't know
how long she's been like this. Mom!"

The unreality of the moment threatened to cut Liz adrift.
Her sanity wobbled. Was her mother dead? "Is she—is she
breathing?"

"I don't know, I don't know." Rafi was panicking. "Mom!
Wake up!"

Liz hadn't seen her mom all day. Monster waves of guilt
and fear reared up, but she had to focus. Do the next right
thing. "Nine-one-one."

"I'm on with them." Ash had the phone pressed to one ear,
face set in concentration. "They need to know if she's breathing."

"She's breathing." Violet was kneeling by Babs's body. Liz hadn't even seen her enter the room. Vi held up a fogged hand mirror. "Her airway is clear."

The dogs were yapping, circling the room. "Can we get them out of here?" Liz snapped.

"—taking any medication?" Ash switched the 911 call to speaker, a woman's curt voice cutting through the noise.

"We need an ambulance." Liz grabbed the phone. "Now, right now."

"I've dispatched an ambulance to your address." The operator sounded efficient, unshakable. "Does she take any medication?"

Hadn't Jin-soo mentioned something about medication before they left? "Yes, I . . . yes," Liz said.

"What kind?" the 911 operator asked.

Liz whipped her gaze around the room. Violet came out of Babs's bathroom with a pink-and-white box, pushing it into Liz's shaking hands.

"It looks like she's taking Gilenya," Liz read the label aloud. Liz was expecting pain medication for her mother's ankle—Advil, maybe Percocet. This name was frighteningly foreign.

"Gilenya?" the operator repeated. "Are you sure?"

"Yes, what is that?" Liz's gaze rocketed from Violet to Ash to Rafi. Everyone stared back, shaking their heads.

Tell me. The instruction Liz gave her mother the night of the holiday party. *Even if you don't tell Raf and Birds: tell me the truth.*

But she hadn't. Liz was panting from the adrenaline, staring at her mother's inert body. "Oh, Mom," she whispered. "What is going on?"

Violet came into the room. Liz hadn't realized she'd left. "I think there's paparazzi on the street out front."

"Paparazzi?" Rafi gripped one of Babs's limp hands. "How could they already know?"

Liz knew the photographers weren't there for their mother, they were there for Violet. But what a scoop—Babs Belvedere carted away in an ambulance on Christmas Eve. Her mother would hate that. Whatever health issue she'd likely been covering up would be front-page news.

"I'll go." Violet addressed the group. "I'll take my car, make sure they follow me."

"Where?" Liz tried to understand. "You can't go alone."

"I'll be fine," Violet said, "trust me."

She smiled reassuringly at Ash and Rafi, knelt to touch Babs's arm, then ran out of the room.

The front door slammed. Ten seconds later, Violet took off down the drive, followed by the sound of engines revving, then receding into the night.

Time folded itself in thick, messy layers. Ash was talking about following the ambulance to the hospital, asking questions about health insurance Liz couldn't answer. A siren sounded, growing in intensity. Red-and-white lights streaked over the bedroom walls, so different from gentle holiday lights. Two EMTs, both young men, were moving Babs onto a stretcher, speaking in medicalese. They didn't take their shoes off. No one ever kept their shoes on in Babs's bedroom. And it was this silly detail that misted sadness up Liz's throat, threatening tears. She forced them away and somehow she was outside, getting into the ambulance with her mother on a stretcher.

Then she was in the back of the ambulance, the house

gone, Ash and Rafi gone, just her mother lying prostrate and the EMTs saying things she didn't understand while putting an oxygen mask over Babs's face. Liz tried to ask them about the medication, but she couldn't remember the name on the pink-and-white box. Gily-something?

Her mother's eyes fluttered.

"Mom!" Liz pitched forward, her heart thrown into her throat. "She's awake!"

The EMTs flashed a pin light in her eyes, asking questions.

Babs's head lolled as the ambulance zoomed over a bump. Her voice was croaky, gaze unfocused. "Jin-soo? I need . . . Jin-soo."

"Jin-soo's gone home, Mom." Liz took her mother's hand. "It's me, it's Lizzie. You're in an ambulance. You were unconscious." Liz was shaking with adrenaline, with the effort of not breaking down. "Mom? Tell me what's wrong."

Babs's gaze sharpened up. She took in the details—the interior of the moving ambulance, the wail of the siren, the two EMTs. Her gaze rested on Liz, lucid. Her voice was faint, but audible enough. "MS. I have MS."

IN HER MID-FIFTIES, BABS had played a character with breast cancer in a forgettable weepie. The character, a selfless and chatty librarian, told everyone who'd listen about her cancer diagnosis. *If it was me*, Babs had muttered to Liz on the way home from an under-attended premiere, *I'd keep my mouth shut.*

Liz had been in her early twenties, more focused on her new boyfriend and NYU than on an offhand comment in the back of a cab. Still, she filed it away as not only her mother's strategy, but one available to her. In order to protect herself, it might be wise to hide the truth.

Liz told her brother when he arrived in the hospital waiting room. They clung to each other, Liz in speechless shock, her brother heaving sobs, while Ash conferred with the admitting staff. The hospital was small and quiet, hung with sad holiday decorations. A fake tree strung with fake candy canes.

"It doesn't feel real," Rafi whispered, looking dazed and devastated. "She has *MS*?"

Liz knew nothing about multiple sclerosis except broad basics: A disease of the nervous system. Difficult to diagnose. No cure. Googling it, she was quickly overwhelmed by a language she didn't speak: *clinically isolated, relapsing-remitting, brain stem lesions, axonal loss.*

How long had her mother been hiding this?

Birdie wasn't picking up, every call going to voicemail, every text unanswered. Liz's hand tightened around her phone. *Of course* her careless little sister was MIA.

"I'll never forgive myself." Rafi slumped forward, head in his hands. "For not paying more attention. So caught up in . . . everything else."

Ash rubbed his back, murmuring words of comfort.

Liz wasn't in the mood to console her brother. Part of what he was saying was true. "I'm sure everything will be fine."

But she wasn't sure. Would their mother be okay?

The waiting room door flung open with a bang.

"*Guys!*" Birdie stumbled in, puffer coat flapping, hair a crazed mess.

Her shout was so loud, it woke a sleeping baby in a young woman's arms on the other side of the room. Startled, the child began to wail.

Birdie didn't notice, bolting over to the trio. "Guys, guys, guys! What the hell?"

She stunk of liquor. Her eyes were bloodshot and red-rimmed. "Jesus," Liz hissed, "of course you're wasted."

Birdie squinted, trying hard to focus. "What happened to Ma?"

The child's crying became louder, despite the woman's fussing.

"She has MS—multiple sclerosis." Rafi was sobbing.

"*Shhh.*" Liz glanced around the waiting room at the half dozen strangers bearing witness to all this.

Birdie's face went slack. "What?"

"She passed out," Rafi went on, gulping air. "In her bedroom—there was paparazzi—I found her." He whispered the diagnosis tearfully. "*MS.*"

Birdie stared at Liz. "Is that true?"

Anger was spewing into Liz's stomach. She couldn't yell at her mother's illness, but she could yell at her sister. "Of course you show up drunk. Of course you weren't there. Did you *drive* here? That's *so* irresponsible. You could've killed someone!"

Birdie flinched like she'd been slapped, swaying back and almost tripping. "Does Ma really have MS?"

"Yes!" Rafi wailed.

"Shut *up*," Liz ordered.

Her brother was as loud as the child howling on the other side of the waiting room. Why did he get to sit there and bawl? Why did Birdie get to miss the horrible drama of the ambulance and EMTs? Liz snapped. "Birdie, sit down. Rafi, stop crying." Her instructions were as sharp as a knife. "Both of you, grow up."

"Hey! I'm an emotional person!" Rafi shot back, wounded and wiping at his nose. .

"And there's nothing wrong with crying because something bad is happening." Ash's tone was a warning. "We all have different ways of coping, Liz."

Liz whipped on him. "*Don't*. You're not a part of this family."

Rafi sucked in a stunned breath.

"Liz." Birdie sounded shocked. "Defang."

"But he's not," Liz cried, her self-control starting to fall apart. "*We are*. We're her *children*, she's our *mother*, and we weren't there. Why didn't she tell me the truth?"

"Why are you the only one she'd wanna tell?" Birdie asked, then belched. Her hand flew to her mouth.

"Because that's my role!" Liz flung back. "And I'm fucking sick of it!"

Birdie had gone pale. "Actually, I'm gonna be sick." She stumbled toward the waiting room's Christmas tree, falling to her knees and vomiting into the pot. Once. Twice. Three times. The acrid smell of puke filled the waiting room.

Rafi was by his sister's side, rubbing her back. Ash got her a cup of water, helping Birdie rinse out her mouth.

Liz closed her eyes, willing this nightmare to smash cut to black.

"Belvedere?"

Liz jerked her head in the direction of the authoritative voice. A short, dark-skinned woman in a white doctor's coat entered the waiting room holding a clipboard. The doctor. News. Ash and Rafi helped Birdie up. Her skin was the color of oat milk, and her sweatshirt was stained with sick. Rafi's eyes were panicked. Ash's mouth was a hard line. The sorry quartet assembled in front of the doctor.

"How is she?" asked Liz at the same time Rafi asked, "Is she okay?"

"I'm Dr. Sampath." The doctor's manner was direct but not without kindness. "Your mother is going to be fine."

They all sagged, exhaling relief.

"She experienced a short loss of consciousness related to her MS."

Liz shook her head, hands bunching into fists. "What type does she have? How long has she had it? How is she treating it?"

"She can share those details when she's ready," Dr. Sampath said. "For now, I've administered a mild sedative so she can get a good night's sleep. Why don't you go home, and we'll call you when she wakes up."

"No." The siblings spoke as one.

Liz felt a primal need to be as close as possible to her parent. "We'll wait here."

The doctor shrugged, glancing around the not-very-comfortable room. "Suit yourself. There's a coffee machine downstairs," she added, glancing at Birdie. "If you need it."

Outside, snow fell in earnest. An orderly removed the puke-filled Christmas tree. Birdie mumbled something about getting caffeine. Liz, Rafi, and Ash returned to their seats, avoiding one another's eyes.

Liz messaged Siouxsie, canceling the drop-off of their decadent Christmas Day lunch and Venmoing her the balance.

Violet had texted, saying she'd gotten a hotel. Liz updated her, suggesting now would be a good time to pick up her pajamas and meds. Violet texted she would, adding Do you need anything?

Liz needed for her mom to be okay.

She messaged her mother's longtime publicist, Marty. He called, telling Liz that HIPAA, the Health Insurance Portability and Accountability Act, prevented hospital staff from privacy violation, but to make sure no one in the waiting room was taking pictures. Liz assured him she knew the drill, thinking, *Do I?* She hadn't earlier, a move that blew up everything with Violet before it even started. At least Violet was still in communication with her. Something to be grateful for.

Birdie returned with a paper tray of coffees. Liz couldn't stomach hers.

The lights were too bright. The syrupy holiday classics playing in the waiting room sounded grating. Enough with the fucking silver bells. This was a world away from how things should be on Christmas Eve.

Regret over her earlier outburst polluted her bloodstream. Liz felt strung out and tense, her chest tight with anxiety. She inhaled for a count of five and then let it out, recalling the lunch she and Violet had with Babs last week. Her mother had been so generous, so open: her best self. Babs Belvedere had not been a perfect mother—she could be vain, obsessed with success, not always honest. But she lived a life driven by passion and family. She was a workhorse and a raconteur. A funny, opinionated, ballsy mother. Liz loved her with all of her heart, discovering its depth anew in this terrible moment.

At least she was in it with her brother and sister and Ash. Liz finally met their eyes, and they all exchanged some wobbly smiles.

"Do you remember that Christmas," Rafi said, "when Mom sang 'Santa Baby' at the holiday party?"

Birdie exhaled a tentative laugh.

Liz let out a quick smile, recalling the very skimpy outfit their younger mother had poured herself into. "Didn't she practically give someone a lap dance?"

"Her accountant, wasn't it?" Ash recalled.

"His sexiest Christmas ever," Birdie said.

They all chuckled. Birdie put her head on Liz's shoulder. Rafi snuggled into Ash. The four lapsed into silence, exhaustion taking hold. Liz was the last to fall asleep.

IN LIZ'S DREAM, VIOLET was a journalist on the set of *Sweet*. Glasses, a blazer, holding a tape recorder. She kept asking Liz, "When are you going to announce it? When are you going to tell everyone?"

"Liz?" Dr. Sampath's voice broke into Liz's dreams. "Your mother's awake."

She blinked her eyes open. Rafi was asleep, his head in Ash's lap. A milky-pale dawn. Christmas Day.

"Squeak," Liz croaked, pulling herself upright. "Mom's awake."

"Ten more minutes." Birdie snuggled back into Liz, still reeking of booze.

Liz nudged her. "No, Birds, wake up."

Birdie cracked an eye, wincing at the waiting room's bright lights with a groan. "Oh *shit*." She slumped forward, cradling her head. "I am *never* drinking again."

"That would actually be a wonderful choice," Liz said. She shook Ash, then Rafi, directing her questions at Dr. Sampath. "How is she? How's she feeling?"

"She's in good spirits," the doctor said with a smile. "You can see her now. Family only."

They all glanced at Ash.

Rafi looked unsure. "What does that mean to you?" he asked Dr. Sampath.

"Whatever it means to you," she replied, turning back the way she came.

The siblings looked at Ash, who was looking only at Rafi.

An awkward beat passed before Ash spoke. "You guys go. I'll get a cab back to the house."

"No, you're family." Rafi drew himself taller, glaring at Liz. "Right, Liz?"

"Right." Liz's face flushed with shame. She regretted saying the opposite. "I'm sorry, Ash. I was upset and—"

"It's okay." Ash's warm brown eyes were compassionate. "We've all had a crazy night. Let's not overwhelm your mom now." Ash took Rafi's face with both hands. "I'll see you later." He firmly but tenderly kissed Rafi on the mouth. Not a kiss of passion. A kiss of support. Of care. Of love.

Liz stared at them in shock, then at Birdie, who pointed between the two guys, mouthing *gay* with a shrug.

Liz squinted, tucking her bangs behind her ears as she absorbed this surprising new information. The initial strangeness melted into undeniable rightness.

Ash murmured something into Rafi's ear that made him smile, easing his worry.

A wallop of affection caught Liz's breath in her throat. How desperately she wanted to love like that—open and unafraid. No caveats. No secrets. Birdie looked similarly moved. Similarly rueful. Rafi had always been the baby brother they had taught things: riding a bike, multiplication tables, dressing nice for a dinner out. But Liz was starting to glimpse a larger truth. Maybe, if they all relaxed their age-old understanding of themselves and one another, growth and change could occur. She could learn a lot from the way Rafi Belvedere loved.

Ash gave Liz and Birdie a reassuring nod and left.

"Ready?" Dr. Sampath indicated for the trio to follow her.

Birdie was drained of color and clearly struggling. Liz brushed her sister's hair out of her eyes. "How are you feeling?"

"Like I'm sick of discovering new versions of rock bottom," Birdie muttered.

Liz gave her sister's hand a squeeze. They paused outside a hospital room. Rafi took Liz's other hand so all three Belvederes were connected. It'd been years since Liz had held her siblings' hands.

Dr. Sampath opened the door.

Their mother's room was small but private, fitting not much more than the bed and a few chairs. Liz was prepared for the sight of her mother in a hospital gown, out of makeup, hair limp. She wasn't prepared for the sight of Babs, pale but animated, holding court with three nurses in scrubs. She appeared to be midway through an anecdote. "—So I said to him, 'Gimme twenty bucks and find out.'"

The nurses broke into laughter.

At the sight of them all filing in, Babs gasped theatrically, her face lighting up with a performer's precision. "My children!"

Rafi was the first to her side. "Mom! I was so scared. How are you?"

Birdie put on a braver face, pretending to sock her mother on the shoulder. "Y'know, Ma, there are easier ways to avoid my cooking."

Babs cackled, some color returning to her cheeks.

Liz was the last to approach her mother's bedside. She

readied herself to say something practical and sensible, but a knot formed in her throat before she could get the words out. The tears Liz had been working so hard to keep at bay for so many years finally filled her eyes, spilling down both cheeks.

Babs reached for Liz's hand. Liz was overcome with relief in feeling her mother's fingers, calloused and knobbly with age, fold into her own. Liz broke down, curling into her mother like a child, salty tears streaming hot and fast. "I thought you were dead," Liz choked out between sobs. "I thought you were gone."

Liz could barely imagine the end of her mother. Never again seeing her coming through the Inn's front door, the dogs dancing at her feet. Never again hearing her loud laugh across the dining room table or at the kitchen island. Never again feeling the warmth of her hug, the press of her lips to a forehead or cheek. Never again seeing the exact blue of her eyes. She'd never said it enough. "I love you, Mom. I love you so much."

Babs stroked the back of her head, abandoning all theatrics. "I love you, too," she said, her own cheeks wet with tears. "I know I have some explaining to do, but for now, just be with me."

They gathered close. It wasn't how Liz had imagined spending Christmas Day. She very much hoped to never spend another Christmas Day like this again. But as her mother's hand rested cool on her fevered face, Liz closed her eyes and gave thanks for this Christmas. Exactly as it was.

PART
THREE

*Jiminy
Christmas.
I'm in love.*

41.

Christmas Day

＊

ABS BELVEDERE HAD BEEN DIAGNOSED WITH RELAPSING-remitting multiple sclerosis when she was fifty-one years old. Eighteen years ago. Three years before Babs moved from New York City to the Catskills. Eighteen birthdays, eighteen Christmases. Each one celebrated with their mother keeping this colossal secret. How? Why?

Only a handful of people in her current orbit knew, including her specialist, whose Connecticut office Babs had been at the day Liz and Birdie first arrived at Belvedere Inn. And most recently, Jin-soo, who, in addition to being an assistant, was certified as a private nurse: Babs hired them once her symptoms started to worsen.

Between talking at length with the hospital's admitting doctor and some additional Googling, Liz was on her way to understanding MS by the time they drove their mother home in the afternoon on Christmas Day. Multiple sclerosis was a chronic, typically progressive autoimmune disorder in which a person's own antibodies start destroying their nerve cells. Many people could live for years, even decades, without visible symptoms, often recovering completely after an "attack," which could range from tingling or numbness to a complete loss of consciousness. As the disease progressed over time, the effects of each attack became more pronounced. Symptoms included impairment of speech and muscular coordination, blurred vision, and severe fatigue.

Almost falling in the foyer while dealing with the electrician. Her slurred speech at the holiday party. Their mother hadn't been clumsy or tipsy. She wasn't tired from another banner year. She'd never been thrown off a goddamn horse. Looking back, Liz felt like a fool for not connecting the dots sooner. Sooner, at least, than *eighteen years* after the initial diagnosis. She'd spent most of her adult life in the dark. Part of the reason why she didn't notice the disease's effects.

Even though MS didn't affect life expectancy, the recommended course of action for someone Babs's age was to eat well, exercise regularly, and get plenty of rest. Not star in a major television show with fourteen-hour production days. The future of Babs's ability to perform, however, hung in the balance. Her medical team needed to review her test results after the holidays. Relapsing-remitting MS was the most common initial diagnosis. As Babs's career had proved, it could be relatively benign and highly manageable. But most people developed secondary progressive MS over time, characterized by a worsening of symptoms. Irreversible disability could occur.

The house was oddly quiet when they all arrived home. Ash had left to spend a few days in New York City, to give the family some space. Liz, Birdie, and Rafi gathered around Babs's silk-sheeted bed to open a few presents. While everyone made an effort to be upbeat, the atmosphere was strained. Rafi's gaze kept straying to the spot on the carpet where he'd found his mother unconscious. Birdie made a lot of dark jokes about being the world's worst daughter. Liz was consumed with questions, each one its own difficult mountain to summit: How should they best care for her? What came next? And, of course: "Why didn't you tell us?" Liz glanced at her siblings for their support before addressing her mother. "Why did you keep it a secret?"

Babs let out a long breath. "Well, of course I was devastated when I found out. Rafi, you were still a boy, and you two"—she indicated Liz and Birdie—"were about to start your own lives. No one needed to know. Years passed, and it just became something I managed. The illness and the secret. I was protecting you. I suppose I didn't want you to see me any differently."

But that was the problem, wasn't it? "Maybe," Liz said slowly, "we all need to see each other a little differently. We can't stay the same forever. Change is inevitable. I know I'm not the same person I was." As if to prove the point, tears welled in Liz's eyes. They didn't feel bad. They felt like a release. "And that's a good thing. I think we're all changing. I think we need to."

AS THE WINTER-PALE LIGHT faded to night, Babs's eyes drifted shut. Her three children tucked her in and tiptoed to the kitchen.

"Thrown off a horse?" Birdie sounded bewildered. "How'd we believe that?"

"Because that's what she told us." Liz uncorked a bottle of wine and started pouring.

Birdie pushed her empty glass back across the kitchen island, reddening. "None for me."

Liz was taken aback. "I don't think I've ever seen you say no to a drink. Not even when you had the flu."

"Dark." Her sister looked embarrassed. Birdie retrieved a tote bag from the far end of the island. "Merry Christmas." She handed two presents out to Liz and Rafi, both wrapped in holiday mailers.

Liz unwrapped hers, holding it up with a quizzical frown. "A Wayne Gretzky bobblehead?"

"I've got LeBron!" Rafi held his bobblehead up happily.

"Might've been drinking at a sports bar last night, before I saw the texts about Ma," Birdie confessed. "Might've won a bet."

"What sort of bet?" Liz asked.

Rafi put LeBron down in alarm. "Or do we not want to know?"

"If I can put fifty chopsticks in my mouth," Birdie replied, opening the fridge to get a Diet Coke. "I can."

Surprising herself as well as her siblings, Liz laughed. God, it felt good to laugh. She examined her bobblehead with affection. "I love it."

"I'm starving." Birdie popped the can of soda. "I'll cook."

Over a plate of Birdie's Sunday Eggs, the siblings talked out their mother's diagnosis and secrecy. The signs they had missed when they'd been wrapped up in their own problems. Their powerful desire to do better. Be present. Help, in every way they could.

By the time Liz was crawling into bed, a smidgen of her pain had been relieved. Whatever came next, she had her brother and sister, ready to face it with her. And Ash, of course.

What about Violet? Emotions had run high—too high. Liz wanted to spend the rest of her life trying to figure out

Violet and what their future together held. Soon. But not now.

Her bedside lamp was the only light on at the Inn as Liz typed out a text. I'd like to talk. I just need some time to help my mom.

Vi's reply came the next morning, when the sky was the frozen pastel blue of dawn.

I need some time, too.

42.

One day after Christmas

*

WHEN BIRDIE AWOKE THE DAY AFTER CHRISTMAS IN THE Humphrey Bogart suite, the light streaming through her window seemed hopeful. Instead of crawling out of bed with a hangover the size of her mother's piano, Birdie felt well rested. On the nightstand was an empty teacup instead of her usual whiskey glass. It was the first night she hadn't drank in a very long time.

Facing herself in the bathroom mirror, Birdie didn't feel the usual spritz of shame or regret.

"Birdie 2.0." She spoke to her reflection. "We got this." A pause. "Somehow."

Birdie had long regarded therapy with suspicion. She had a roof over her head and food in the fridge (most days): What could she possibly complain about? But then again, Jecka Jacob had dumped her ass. Maybe it was time to ask for help.

A Google search led to a tele-therapist who operated year-round and took her extremely crap insurance. After filling in her details, Birdie was prompted to select an intake appointment. Plenty of options in the coming months. But there was one slot, just one, for the end of the day. She booked it.

As her appointment grew closer, Birdie's mind came up with a thousand excuses to postpone. It was midafternoon. Not too early for a cheeky mulled wine.

It was surprising how often her mind suggested a drink, like a boozy friend always up for another. But Birdie was starting to suspect that her mind wasn't always such a good friend.

By the time the appointment rolled around, the morning's hopefulness had been superseded by crushing anxiety and cravings for wine. She couldn't find a comfortable way to sit on her bed. Evidence of Christmas still populated her room—a half-eaten piece of fudge, some stray tinsel, a card. The holiday trappings seemed incongruous with this upcoming excruciating conversation, which was sure to focus on what a shit person she was, deep down.

Her therapist, Tamara, wore red lipstick and had curly bangs. She was younger than Birdie was expecting. "Birdie." Tamara smiled. "What brings you here?"

The question was so terrifyingly broad, Birdie had no idea how to answer. She channeled a spotlight, the place she felt at ease. "Well, I'm a New Yorker. Legally, I have to have a therapist."

She waited for the tick of a smile, the puff of a chuckle. Nothing.

"So, I broke up with my girlfriend," Birdie began again. "Technically, she broke up with me. Technically, we weren't girlfriends. Okay, *technically* she was a figment of my imagination, but a break-up's a break-up."

Tamara scribbled something down. "Do you do this a lot: deflect with humor?"

"I'm a stand-up," Birdie said, only mildly put off. "Sort of my default. Tough crowd, though," she added, playfully rolling her eyes.

Another uneasy pause. Tamara shifted forward, speaking directly to the phone's camera. "You don't need to entertain me, Birdie. You don't need to manage my emotions or reactions. I'm here to listen and help you understand yourself. So, let's try again: What brings you here?"

Freed from the need to make Tamara laugh, Birdie started talking.

Over the next hour, it all came flooding out. Her mom's collapse, and being so drunk on Christmas Eve she'd barfed in the hospital waiting room. Jecka breaking up with her, specifically calling out her drinking. Her father's death and her stalled career and her suspicion things might be better if she laid off the booze and hookups, but how embarrassingly hard that was. At first, it felt unbearably awkward to divulge such personal details with a stranger without the usual back-and-forth of laughter or mutual sharing. But Tamara's nonjudgmental acceptance was a release.

Birdie teared up when she tried to explain that her life was being lived on her terms, but it wasn't making her happy. Sometimes she felt like a car without brakes, careening from one merry disaster to the next. "I don't know what my problem is," she added, blowing her nose into some toilet paper. "I'm a middle-class cisgender white person doing what I love. Maybe I'm just having a bad week."

"Birdie." Tamara gave her a look of compassion. "You're not *having a bad week*. Your life and your choices and the stories you tell yourself are not working for you. It's possible you've adopted a cycle of casual sex and alcohol to numb the pain and unhappiness you're feeling."

Hearing this theory laid out so simply was both devastating and liberating. Birdie had always believed her personality and habits were set, and if some of those things made her life difficult, she just had to figure out ways to live with them. The idea of challenging or changing them felt new. And hard. When she expressed this to Tamara, her therapist smiled. "Were you expecting this to be easy?"

"I don't know what I was expecting."

"Therapy is an exploration of the self. We meet and we talk. About things that happened yesterday and one year ago and ten years ago. We connect the dots on who you are. And then we figure out coping strategies so you feel like you're behind the wheel of a car with brakes. A car that can take you anywhere you like."

Tears rushed up Birdie's throat. She let out a sob.

"What?" Tamara asked gently.

"I never thought I could change. The idea that I can direct my life where I want to go—god, I just want that so badly."

They agreed Birdie should extend her sobriety by taking it one day at a time and asking her family to help her stay accountable. Tamara listed potential withdrawal symptoms. "Depression, irritability, night sweats." She shared information about twenty-four-hour helplines, twelve-step meetings, and online resources. "Remember why you're doing it. And do something else instead of drinking."

Birdie nodded, writing all this down. "Well, I really want to finish my new show. I've actually made good progress. I was sort of workshopping it with . . ."

Tamara glanced at her notes. "Jecka?"

Sour-sweet nostalgia misted into Birdie's chest. "She was the first person I could, like, really see myself with," Birdie admitted. "Things were different with her."

"Sounds like you had an intimate relationship," Tamara said. "Not just an intense or casual one."

366 • GEORGIA CLARK

Birdie nodded. "I think that's why it felt like such a rejection when she dumped me."

"But if we accept that the self can grow and change," Tamara commented, "maybe it was a rejection of someone you're already moving away from."

THE EVENING WAS ARDUOUS. Tamara was right—Birdie felt like garbage. But the struggle was more mental than physical. Every two minutes, her brain kept suggesting a drink. Then encouraging. Then demanding, fist on the bar, screaming in her ear. Birdie locked herself in her bedroom with a Diet Coke and a pot of tea and, using the Pomodoro Technique, busted out a night of work. The hardest night of her life. And, in a different way, the best. Because she didn't break.

43.

Four days till New Year's Eve

*New York Post: "Love is Sweet! Showrunner
Liz Belvedere canoodles with rising star Violet Grace—
WATCH THE VIDEO."*
*The Cut: "Absolutely Everything We Know About
Violet Grace and Liz Belvedere."*
*BuzzFeed: "The Look of Love: A body expert breaks
down every #Violez red carpet moment."*

LIZ SLAMMED HER LAPTOP SHUT, BREATHLESS, DESPITE still being in bed.

When Liz had typed Violet's name into Google, it autocorrected to add Liz Belvedere, kiss, sex, and girlfriend.

Girlfriend.

Liz couldn't think about how that made her feel—equal parts panicked and ecstatic.

Cat told Liz it would all pass if they didn't "feed the beast." Their publicist's instruction was clear: "Don't give them anything to talk about."

Liz wasn't planning on it. The last text Violet had sent

drew a decisive boundary. I need some time, too. Liz would respect that.

It was the morning of Friday, December 27, and her mother had MS. That was the only reality Liz could focus on. Starting with a sibling call to Jin-soo, scheduled first thing.

WHEN LIZ CAME DOWNSTAIRS, Birdie was already on the sofa in the family room, nursing a coffee. Liz double-took at her sister's dark circles. "Hungover?"

Birdie sighed. "I wish. Withdrawal is rough, dude."

Night two of her sister not drinking. Liz was surprised and impressed. "How are you handling it?"

"Minute by minute. A lot of Diet Coke. And work, apparently," Birdie said, adding that she'd spent the evening slogging through her new show. "Maybe you're not the only workaholic in the family."

"Welcome to the dark side," Liz said, as Rafi joined them. Liz addressed them both. "Okay, Black Hearts. Let's face the music."

Even over FaceTime, Jin-soo's disapproving glare was excruciating. "I told you to keep an eye on her."

"I am sorry," Liz said, "but I'm not the only one responsible for my mother."

"We all are," Rafi said, and Birdie nodded in enthusiastic agreement, giving a thumbs-up.

"I'll be back at the Inn for New Year's Eve," Jin-soo said. "Your mom invited me for roast chicken and Champagne, so I'll be there to portion control. In the meantime, make sure she gets plenty of water, plenty of rest. And try to avoid trips to the ER."

The trio exchanged guilty *sheesh* faces.

Babs was instantly on the receiving end of Birdie's brand-new extra-healthy breakfast in bed, delivered with plenty of wisecracks that had their mother chuckling. This was followed by a "stretching and sharing session" led by Rafi, heavy on the sharing.

The siblings organized for Babs's doctor to make a house call that afternoon. They were all gathered around their mother's bed when he gave his diagnosis. Given the severity of her attack, and the test results he'd received from their local hospital, it was clear her MS had worsened to secondary progressive. It was his strong recommendation that Babs retire.

Babs's expression was a mix of horror, offense, and sheer disbelief. "I can talk to my team about scaling back. . . ."

Her physician shook his head. Not scaling back. Rest. Deep rest. "You've been incredibly fortunate not to have received this diagnosis sooner," he said. "Most people with relapsing-remitting MS develop secondary progressive within ten years. That you've made it to almost twenty is honestly astounding."

As always, Babs Belvedere was an anomaly.

But her face remained closed at the recommendation, lips pressing into the hard, familiar line that simply said *no*.

"What do you think?" Rafi asked gently, after the doctor left.

Babs fussed for a minute, listing obstacles—the signed contracts, the already written scripts. The paycheck. The fans. One by one, they worked through her concerns—they were impediments, but they didn't make it impossible. Finally, she was out of excuses.

"You've had a killer career, Ma," Birdie said. "You're gonna be remembered as a star."

370 • GEORGIA CLARK

"I don't want to be *remembered*." Babs mocked the term. "I want to be known. Now. Here. Who am I if I'm not a performer?" Babs's question was plaintive. "Who am I if I'm not *Babs Belvedere*?"

For Liz, the answer had never been simpler. "You're our mother."

44.

Three days till
New Year's Eve

*

AT BRUNCH AROUND THE KITCHEN ISLAND ON SATURDAY, there was once again soda in Birdie's glass, met with encouraging smiles from her family.

"Another night working on your show?" Liz forked a mouthful of gooey huevos rancheros as she nodded at Birdie's notebook, full of pages of scribbled ideas. "Can't wait to see some of it."

Birdie flushed with pride and inhaled a tentative breath. "Well, you won't have to wait long. I'm actually doing a work in progress, um, tonight."

"*Tonight?*" Rafi and Liz spoke as one.

"So soon?" Babs added.

"I was just in touch with Sydney." The booker for Fox & Fawn. The 9:00 P.M. slot had still been open—late December was the quietest time of year. "It's just a first draft, super rough." Birdie explained she'd spent the last few days stitching together all the work she'd done before Christmas. "It won't even be a full hour yet, probably half that. But I'd love it if you could all be there."

She met her mother's gaze. In the past, Birdie had mixed

feelings about Babs's attendance. It could distract the audience. It could distract her. She'd always wanted to be recognized independently of her mother. But now that seemed ridiculous. Who cared what other people thought? Birdie *wanted* her mom in the audience tonight. She reached across the table to pat her mom's hand. "Especially you, Ma."

"Of course I'll be there." Babs nodded decisively. "We all will."

BIRDIE ARRIVED AT FOX & FAWN well ahead of showtime. The stage was in the back, a postage stamp–sized area with a stool and mic, facing rows of empty chairs. To most people, less than ordinary. To Birdie, Mecca.

It was hard to walk past the bar. To consider that bars, in general, might not offer the comfort they always had.

Birdie put this out of her mind, sequestering herself in the green room to go over her notes. Usually, she was late to her slots and unprepared, with most of her success coming from winging it. But tonight, a cool certainty filled her, a seriousness of intent. She'd worked for this. She wanted this.

The room started to fill. About thirty people, sitting or standing in the back. In the front row, Liz and Rafi flanked their mother, who was dressed simply in her pink velour tracksuit.

Birdie had wondered if Jecka might've seen her sole social media post or a last-minute local listing, but she wasn't in the crowd. Birdie shook it off, trying to quell her nerves as Sydney introduced her. She walked on to a swell of applause, waving hello with a pounding heart and sweaty palms. Birdie had been in front of countless audiences before, but this one felt different. This one was important.

Birdie took the mic off the stand, moved it aside. Took a moment to let the attention settle on her. Her voice sounded over the speakers, clear and honest. "So, I've been thinking a lot about my dad."

Birdie started her show with a joke-heavy sketch of Stanley, for those unfamiliar with him as a public figure. A director of nineties rom-coms—"the ones where every meet-cute involved spilled coffee, taxi snafus, and everyone is aggressively white?" She made fun of his less successful films, including the box office stinker *Kisses on Cloud Nine*—"it was so bad, Cupid actually sued us."

Then she widened the lens to roast Stanley as a father: "the man who made Darth Vader look like a great dad." The show painted a portrait of a talented but troubled man who was "stitched together from red flags." Self-centered, arrogant, notoriously forgetful. "I remember when he called to wish me a happy seventh birthday. I was eleven." She told her wildest anecdotes of his worst parenting. The gasps of shock from the audience cemented her relationship with them. Their surprise and empathy assured Birdie they were with her, bolstering her confidence. She wasn't alone.

Out of respect for her mom, Birdie didn't discuss her parents' relationship. "Let's just say after their conscious uncoupling, Dad proceeded to do a lot of unconscious coupling with half the actresses in L.A." She paused. "And the fact that my own dance card has always been pretty full? Obviously unrelated."

She pointed out more similarities between herself and her father: how they were both born entertainers, good at winning people over, bad at commitment and at parking.

The jokes gave way to deeper introspection. This was uncharted territory. Birdie's grip on the mic tightened. "Just like his films, my memories of Dad are a mix of the good and the truly terrible. But I'm not here to spit on his grave. I'm here because I realized something recently. Something that took my little snow-globe world and gave it a good shake."

She paused to take a steadying breath.

"I'm not my father. I'm not his flaws, or his triumphs, his best self or his worst. I'm not destined to follow in his foot-steps." Her voice cracked with emotion. "I don't need to push people away for fear of hurting them like he hurt me, or pull them in to distract me from my own troubles. And if that's what I've done in the past, that's okay. Because every rom-com makeover montage will show you, people can change. I can change. I'm seeing a therapist, actually. I'm giving sobri-ety a go. Me? Can you—" She was cut off by unexpected ap-plause. The sound almost had her tearing up. "Guys, I'm just doing it to win back my ex," she riffed. "Just kidding, just kidding: I'm doing it for me. But seriously, can someone please tell my ex?"

The audience laughed, and it sounded different. Gener-ous, understanding. Her fingers relaxed their grip on the mic.

"This past month, I learned that success isn't about some-thing out there. It's something in here." Birdie tapped her chest. "Something I get to decide."

The room was completely quiet. Birdie recalled the si-lence at Jecka's art opening at the beginning of the month, after her mulled wine mistake. The bad sort of silence. Now, two days away from the end of the year, this silence was the good kind.

"I'm up here tonight to remind myself that I'm just me, and I'm still a work in progress. And if you haven't seen

Kisses on Cloud Nine, please don't: we are still in an active lawsuit with Cupid. Thank you."

Birdie had never felt a greater sense of accomplishment than when she placed the microphone back in its stand. She had the bones of a new hour, something she could continue fleshing out over the coming year. More than that, she had a new version of her story. A new version of herself. From now on things were going to be different for her. She was going to make sure of that.

The small audience erupted into applause. Even Babs got to her feet with her cane, hooting and cheering loudest of all.

Birdie just stood there, tears glistening in her eyes, her heart flung open.

Then she left the stage, trotting down its few steps to greet her people, their smiling faces flushed from laughter and emotion.

"Squeak, it was *brilliant!*" Liz said, bursting with admiration. "So funny and so *deep*. You really nailed Stanley, but I actually thought it was very generous. I can't believe he abandoned you at Disneyland to hook up with Minnie Mouse? I've never heard that story! That whole bit about if his bow ties could talk—I was *crying*. God, it was *so* good. Your best yet!"

Ash was still in New York, so it was just Rafi who threw his arm around her shoulder, beaming with pride. "You made the Black Hearts Club proud, sis."

Babs approached, and Birdie suddenly felt nervous. "I hope it wasn't too personal," Birdie said, earnestly. "If you want me to cut anything, I will."

"Absolutely not. No." Babs grasped Birdie's arm. Her gaze was full of wonder. "What a gift you've given us all tonight. Especially me. Oh, sweetheart: I had no idea how much he hurt you. *Thank you* for telling me. You are so clever . . . and so brave."

Birdie hugged her mother, feeling the weight of their shared experience. It wasn't just about the show. It was everything that had brought them to this moment. It was the fact that she still had a mother.

"Thanks for being here." Birdie pulled back, bashing away a tear. "Love ya, Ma."

"I love you, too, sweetheart." Babs smiled, the laugh lines around her eyes deepening. "I will never miss your opening night."

The reference to Stanley's absence all those years ago almost choked Birdie up, but she kept it together to greet the next audience member, a smiling guy in a plaid shirt who introduced himself as Josh.

Josh was effusive about her performance. "Very funny stuff. You crushed it." He handed her an embossed business card. "If you're in the market for a manager, I'd love to talk."

Josh Salzburg was a manager at UTA. U-T-fucking-A. "Holy shit. Okay. How'd you hear about the show?" Birdie asked, glancing over at her mom, assuming it had something to do with Babs.

"Instagram," Josh replied. "Your post."

"Oh." She'd landed this fish all by herself. Birdie rocked back on her heels, a happy blush rising in her cheeks. "Sweet."

BABS FADED EARLY, so Rafi took her home. Birdie said hi to everyone she knew, then sat at the bar with Liz, chatting until almost midnight.

Liz yawned, sliding off her stool. "Ready to go, Squeakie?"

MOST WONDERFUL • 377

"Yep." Birdie drained her third Diet Coke and gazed around the empty back room, a smile on her lips.

"How do you feel?" Liz asked, slipping on her coat.

"Amazing." Light. Free. Seen. Heard. "I had fun. I know this is going to sound extremely tragic, but I didn't actually think I could have fun without being blitzed or caught up in sexy gay chaos. But I had a blast tonight, stone-cold sober, with zero chaos. That's huge."

Liz wrapped her arms around Birdie, squeezing her tight. Her sister had gotten a *lot* more touchy-feely these holidays. Birdie wasn't mad about it. "I am so proud of you, Birds." Liz's expression was tender and protective. "I'm sorry Jecka wasn't here."

Pain bloomed in Birdie's chest. In the past, that was a sign to order a double. Now she let the uncomfortable feeling spread, then settle. She could handle it. "Me too." Birdie zipped up her neon-orange puffy. "But if it's meant to be, we'll cross paths again."

45.

Two days till
New Year's Eve

*

O N THE SECOND-TO-LAST DAY OF THE YEAR, RAFI BELVEDERE woke up in his childhood bedroom, alone. Again. The other side of the bed yawned, one thousand miles wide. Ash had been in New York City since Christmas Day, visiting college friends to give the Belvederes space. Yesterday on the phone, Rafi had told him that they didn't need any more time together as a family. "Come back tonight?" he'd asked, hopefully.

But Ash had equivocated, sounding vague and unwilling to commit to his return. After they hung up, Rafi's worries got a good grip.

Maybe his spontaneous ticket to London had spooked Ash, and this extended stay in New York had become time to reconsider everything—time to decide they were better off as friends. The glow of holiday magic was being replaced by the cold light of day, and soon Ash would be back in his regular life in London, a life that might not have room for Rafi. Even if it hadn't initially been Ash's intention, maybe it really wasn't the holidays without a holiday fling, and now Ash felt

it best if that fling was over. The thought turned Rafi's blood
to ice.

THE MORNING WAS CLOUDLESS, the winter sky an indigo
blue. Sunlight splashed through the windows with cheerful
insistence. Rafi dragged himself into the kitchen, needing
breakfast, caffeine, a foolproof map for his love life.

Babs was sitting at the kitchen island, sipping a green tea
smoothie as she pecked at her computer with her pointer fingers.

"Morning." Rafi poured himself the much-needed coffee.
"What are you up to?"

"Working on a statement about all this." Babs gestured to
her cane, hooked over the kitchen island. "For social media."

"What've you got so far?"

"Something like, *Hello, world, big news: I'm switching from
soy milk to oat, and also, I have MS. Any questions about the
milk?*"

Affection ballooned in his chest. "Funny." He plopped
down next to her with a sigh.

Babs removed her glasses, her gaze turning soft. "Everything okay, baby boy?"

Rafi groaned. "Mom, I'm not a baby."

"Oh, honey, of course you aren't. You're a grown man. I
know that." Babs put her hand over his, her expression sincere. "But you'll always be my baby. No matter how old you
are. You might not understand that until you're a parent
yourself. But, of course, I respect you as an adult, too."

Her words were a welcome surprise. "Well, thanks. I appreciate that. But honestly, I'm not doing a great job at adult-

ing right now." He explained his worries over Ash's absence and their upcoming time apart. "What if he gets back to London and everything changes?"

His mother's expression turned sage. "Can I tell you something I've learned about love?"

Rafi hazarded a guess. "Divorce is always an option?"

Babs gave him a look, but the twinkle in her blue eyes gave away her amusement. "Guess again, wise guy."

Rafi sipped his coffee, recalling some of his mother's better zingers. *"Men are like encores: it's always more fun the second time.* Or, *I love getting married. Staying married, that's my weakness."*

Babs permitted a chuckle. "Love," she began, "isn't out there waiting to hit you like a bolt of lightning. It's not something you capture or keep or make follow your rules. It's something you create, with another person. It's an act of will, and imagination, fueled by trust and perseverance. It's a practice. And it's possible for anyone." She leaned closer, her words impassioned. "That boy loves you, my sweet. He always has. Give him time. Give him your trust. You have a wonderful path ahead of you. Don't dash off ahead and get worried when he isn't catching up. Walk together, side by side. At a pace you both set."

RAFI DECIDED TO TAKE his mother's advice to heart by setting a slow, steady pace on his first solo hike of the season.

Snow clung to the branches of the pine and fir trees, bowing them close to the earth. Reverential forest. Few sounds but for his boots crunching through the woods and the occasional forest thrush calling for its mate.

The trail opened up to a lookout over the Hudson, a majestic swath of restless water spangled with the winter sun.

Rafi sank onto a jut of rock. Nothing but thick trees dotted with snow on either side of the waterway that flowed south, toward New York City. Toward Ash Sebastian Campbell. Someone he belonged with. If he worked at it. If he followed his mother's advice and walked together, side by side.

Rafi thought of the hard work Birdie was doing. Her radical, productive changes were inspiring. And Liz, who he'd always seen as his stoic, responsible older sister. In a way, he was grateful things had blown up in the hospital waiting room. Even Liz had big, messy feelings.

Maybe no human felt like they belonged all the time. Maybe belonging wasn't a constant state of satisfaction but something subtle and underlying that was felt most strongly in special moments. Gatherings like these, like Christmas. When his family, however imperfect, could offer the quietly wonderful space of true acceptance. Maybe he needed only to belong to a few people. With a few people. He belonged to and with Ash. However they figured out the logistics would be the right way.

Rafi let his worry go, imagining it being swept away on the river's current. Then he paid attention to the sound of the birds. The whisper of the wind through the trees. The feeling of the fresh air on his skin, filling his lungs. The sun goldened, sinking into the west. In his meditative state, grounded by the natural world, Rafi finally found peace.

46.

One day till New Year's Eve

※

ON MONDAY MORNING, BABS SCHEDULED A ZOOM TO INFORM her team and the show. Liz could tell her mom was desperate to postpone the meeting, but given the sheer number of people on it—Babs's showrunner on *Palace People*, her agents, manager, and publicist, even Richard Rollo, aka Dickie, head of her network—she was too much of a professional to flake.

Liz, Birdie, and Rafi gathered to support her, sitting off camera.

In a face full of makeup and her very best robe, Babs verbally tap-danced for a few minutes before catching Liz's eye.

Liz gave her a nod and a reassuring smile.

Babs let out a defeated sigh, then addressed the onscreen grid of faces. "The thing is, folks . . . I have MS. My dancing days are coming to a close."

A wave of shock. A round of questions. Which quickly unearthed how long Babs had known this diagnosis, which provoked more shock, more questions. It was a master class in showbiz to watch her mother work the virtual room, equally charming and steely, never giving an inch, always in control. And yet, as the team absorbed the revelation and began brainstorming how to orchestrate her departure from the series, the full razzle-dazzle was missing. It wasn't yet time for her swan song, even if the truth made it impossible to go on.

Or did it? Liz paused, thinking hard. Maybe her mother's team just needed to do what she and Violet had done when they were brainstorming—take a wild swing. Make the impossible possible.

The tips of Liz's fingers tingled. All at once, she had an idea. A good one. Maybe a really *really* good one. But it paused in her throat. This was her mother's business meeting. Liz was there to troubleshoot any technical difficulties and offer emotional support. She wasn't even onscreen. And yet, she had an idea.

Before she could lose her nerve, Liz cleared her throat. "I have a suggestion."

Her mother shot Liz a surprised look.

"My kids are sitting in." Babs swiveled the screen so her firstborn was in view. "Most of you know Liz, I think?"

Liz addressed the grid of faces. "What if you write it into the show? Crystal Palace has MS."

For a long moment, no one spoke. Next to her, Liz felt her mom stiffen. But even as the moment extended into true awkwardness, Liz couldn't regret speaking up.

Marty, Babs's publicist, cleared his throat. "It would actually be good publicity, assuming you want to go public, Babs. Authentic."

"I love it!" One of her agents leaped in—more work for Babs meant more money for everyone. "We don't hide it: we lean in."

"I'm not sure I've ever seen an actor with MS play a character with MS," mused the showrunner. "We could play against type."

"Crystal could join an Upper East Side support group just to find new clients," Birdie suggested. "But then, get overly involved in the politics of the group. End up running the whole thing, *her* way."

Everyone chuckled.

"One more season," Dickie boomed, in a way that indicated it was as good as decided. "Your last hurrah."

"Your swan song," Liz said, looking at her mother. Seeing her in all her complex glory. "You deserve it."

Babs Belvedere had been in show business for fifty years. She wasn't done yet.

Babs addressed her team. "Most of you have been with me through so many different times in my life. I cherish those times. I cherish the adventurous, stubborn girl I was in my twenties. The mother I became in my thirties. The comeback kid in my forties. The Catskills queen in my fifties, when no one wanted to hire me. And now, at the end of my sixties, I finally know myself, completely. And I've never felt less afraid." A smile curled her lips. "Let's give 'em hell. I'm almost seventy, I have MS, and I'm gonna blow your fucking socks off."

47.

*L*ATER THAT DAY, BIRDIE ROAMED THE AISLES OF THE supermarket in town, a sobriety podcast in her earbuds. Compared to the last time she was here—frantically shopping for the wine-soaked dinner with Jecka's parents—the store was deserted. Even though it'd been only a week or so ago, that night felt much further away.

In the meat section, Birdie was reaching for the very last packet of bacon when someone's hand brushed hers, going for the same thing.

Jecka Jacob. Her dark brown eyes widened in surprise. "Birdie!"

"Jecka." Birdie stepped back, her heart tapping a nervous beat. She fumbled to pause her podcast. "I wasn't stalking you."

"Good to know." Jecka's smile flitted between forgiving and cautious. "Shopping for your favorite breakfast food?"

"As are you." Birdie gallantly indicated for Jecka to take the package. "Please, m'lady. I insist."

After a moment's hesitation, Jecka picked up the bacon. Her gaze skimmed the contents of Birdie's basket: mostly Mr. Paws's too-expensive cat food. "You haven't changed."

"Actually, I have." Birdie shifted her basket from one arm to the other. "I'm, um, six days sober."

Jecka's mouth fell all the way open. "*Really?*"

Birdie hadn't ever seen anyone quite so surprised. She nodded, feeling an odd mix of pride and embarrassment.

"How do you feel?" Jecka asked.

Birdie wasn't going to answer that in a grocery store. "Like I just lost my best and worst friend."

"Are you going to go to, like, meetings, or . . . ?"

"Maybe." Birdie hadn't gotten that far yet. One day at a time. "When I'm back in the city."

Jecka nodded, her gaze supportive and serious.

Birdie was struck by the difference in their interaction. No flirting, no banter. Just honesty and a dash of care.

"Well, congratulations," Jecka said. "That can't be easy. Hope you stick with it."

"Me too."

They both let out a breath, which morphed into a chuckle. Birdie had come up to the Catskills to avoid run-ins with exes. But now that it was happening, it wasn't that bad.

"It was nice seeing you." Birdie meant it. "Happy New Year." It was almost the last day of the year, after all. Birdie gave Jecka a farewell smile and turned for the registers.

"I'm doing a pop-up." Jecka spoke in a rush. "Next month, in my home studio." She smiled shyly, eyes bright. This was important to her. "Portraits. I've started doing portraits. Deconstructed: weird."

Birdie connected the dots. "Personal and adventurous."

"Exactly! No idea what I'm doing, but who does, right? Maybe, if you're around, come check it out?"

The offering gave Birdie a familiar tingle. The old Birdie would say, *Yeah, hell yeah, let's throw in a sleepover to boot.* But the new Birdie sensed she had work to do before becoming the person Jecka deserved. The person she was committed to being. It wasn't something she could rush.

"Maybe," Birdie said. "Or, do you still have those tickets I got us? To the Chelsea art expo in February?"

Jecka nodded. "Still on my fridge."

"Check with me before you invite someone else? If you'd still feel like going together?"

"I will." A smile settled on Jecka's face. "I'd like that."

IN THE PARKING LOT, Birdie put her groceries in her station wagon's back seat, making a mental note she needed to book an oil change.

The streets were quiet. No one at the crosswalks.

It'd been overcast on the drive in but now the sun was breaking through. Rays of light illuminated the road home.

48.

✳

RAFI SPENT THE AFTERNOON HELPING HIS MOM PACK away most of the Christmas decorations, then, with his sisters, carrying the tree to the curb for collection. When Babs realized she still hadn't sent out her holiday cards, her gaze instinctively slid to Liz. Rafi saw his sister's shoulders sag.

He jumped in. "I can handle that."

The smile Liz gave him was worth the three hours of printing and envelope stuffing that followed. He drove into town to get the small mountain of cards into a mailbox, making sure to admire the last of the merry and bright shop windows he passed.

It was dark by the time he returned. Opening the Inn's cherry-red door, Rafi heard a peal of laughter from the kitchen. He followed the noise to find Liz opening a bottle of Pellegrino, Birdie slicing a loaf of bread, his mother putting the finishing touches on a cheese board, and, rising from a kitchen stool: Ash, in a soft apricot sweater and dark-wash jeans. His jaw was brushed with gold stubble, his eyes the color of butterscotch ice cream.

Rafi's heart rocketed into his throat. "You're back!"

"Hi." Ash stepped forward to catch Rafi's face with both hands and kiss him flush on the mouth. Stubble and warm lips. Security and heat.

"Get a room," groaned Birdie. "Not within earshot, please."

Rafi managed to kick her without breaking the kiss.

His mother and sisters resumed dinner prep, leaving Rafi and Ash to talk.

Rafi wrapped his arms around Ash's waist, feeling the softness of his sweater and the drumming of his heart, just as fast as Rafi's own. "God, I missed you."

"Missed you, Raf Attack." Ash held him tight, speaking into Rafi's hair, his voice deliciously deep. "And I have something to ask you." Shifting back, he addressed everyone else. "Fam? Hey, fam?"

Liz, Birdie, and Babs paused their movement, looking over.

Ash cleared his throat. "Last week, Raf took me to visit Dad's grave for the first time." His voice was calm, his expression a look of acceptance. "And while it was very hard, it also showed me what real love looks like. What real care feels like." Ash smiled at Rafi, his gaze tender and grateful. "Because you were there. By my side. And that made me realize something."

Ash's face flickered with something odd. Nerves? He reached into his back pocket.

For one surreal moment, Rafi thought Ash was about to pull out a ring. But to his surprise, Rafi realized that wasn't what he wanted right now. Marriage was what Rafi had wanted, desperately, for years. But not now. Not yet. His mother's words from yesterday echoed in his mind. *Walk together, side by side.*

To Rafi's relief, it wasn't a ring in Ash's hand. It was a key.

Rafi looked up at Ash quizzically.

"This is just the key to the greenhouse," Ash qualified. "But it's a symbol. I just signed a lease on a townhouse in North London, starting in March. That's why I stayed in the city the extra few days, to get it all sorted." He paused, taking in everyone's excited expressions before continuing. "Everything that's happened over the past few weeks has shown me not to take anything, or anyone, for granted. That life is precious, and love is what makes all the tough parts worthwhile." He stepped closer to graze Rafi's cheek, his touch summoning goosebumps. "I'm ready for the next phase of my life, Raf. And when you come visit, I want you to see that. For my home to feel like a place that could be your home someday, too."

"Really?" Rafi searched Ash's face. "That's not too fast?"

Ash shook his head slowly, his gaze not leaving Rafi's own as he drew Rafi close. "No." Ash's voice was certain. "I love you with every chamber of my heart."

Birdie slapped the kitchen island. "Put it on a T-shirt!"

"I love you too." Finally, Rafi could say it back.

"Crying!" Liz declared, fanning her face.

"I feel like the luckiest guy alive." Rafi gazed up at the man in his arms. "You've been here all along. Is that going to drive me nuts for the rest of our lives?"

Babs shook her head vigorously, stamping her cane. "This was your story, and it's perfect. No notes."

"No notes!" Birdie hoisted her Diet Coke. "To the gays!"

"To the gays!" everyone chorused, grabbing a glass to clink.

The two men kissed once more before being enveloped in a raucous Belvedere family hug, a multiarmed monster of arms and chins and laughter, squeezing tight.

He and Ash didn't have all the answers to life's big questions. But in this moment, surrounded by the loved ones he belonged to and with, it didn't matter. They'd figure it out together.

49.

New Year's Eve

WHEN LIZ AWOKE IN THE AUDREY HEPBURN SUITE THE morning of New Year's Eve, the first thing she did was reach for her phone.

Vi still hadn't texted. The last message in their thread remained the same. Liz dropped her device back onto the bedside table, heavy with disappointment and worry. How was Violet? Had the invasive online feeding frenzy after their public almost-kiss triggered her depression? Was she in one of her darker places, one absent of hope and joy and belief in good things? Liz would understand if Violet was already back in L.A., wordsmithing a message that called everything off, for good. As each day passed without an update, that seemed more and more likely.

So when Liz's phone lit up, midafternoon, she instinctively braced herself. But it wasn't Violet.

"Vampires!" Cat gushed into the phone. "I love it. So gothic-teen sexy."

"You like the pitch?" Liz hadn't yet heard from anyone else in her brain trust, so this first piece of positive feedback was significant. "I'm so relieved. Violet was a huge part of it. You were right—having her here was invaluable."

"Is she still there?" Cat's tone was light, but Liz could tell the publicist was fishing.

"No." An ax in her heart. Liz rubbed her chest as she attempted to keep her voice noncommittal. "I think she's back in L.A."

"Oh. Sure." Cat sounded vaguely disappointed before perking up again. "Well, this might cheer you up. A little birdie tells me *you* are about to get a second season order!"

Liz's entire being screeched to a stop. "*What?*"

"Don't be mad, but I *may* have slipped the pitch to Programming and everyone is *obsessed*! I hear the execs have notes, and there are some budget issues, but, overall, they're in. Congratulations!"

Joy skipped through Liz's body. She'd done it. *They'd* done it. It wasn't just fantastic news. It was, definitively, a reason to call Vi. And yet, Liz couldn't. Violet wanted space.

Possibly permanently.

DOWNSTAIRS IN THE FAMILY ROOM, Birdie, Rafi, and Ash were on their phones, scrolling in companionable silence, while Babs read a script in the armchair closest to the crackling fire.

Liz cleared her throat. "So, we got the second season order."

All four clicked their heads over, eyes popping wide.

"For your show?" Rafi and Ash spoke as one.

"Your *brilliant* show," Babs added, reaching for her cane.

Liz nodded, and then everyone was hugging and high-fiving her, celebrating.

"Congratulations, Lizzie." Babs gave her a big squeeze. "I'm *so* proud of you. My talented daughter."

Liz forced a smile. "Thanks, guys." This should be a victory lap. Getting a second season was her ultimate goal, what she'd been working toward for ages.

Rafi was the first to notice. "What is it?"

Birdie narrowed her eyes. "Yeah, why are you not, like, getting a tattoo of your own face?"

Liz let out a heavy exhale.

"Ooh." Birdie nodded. "Methinks this is about Grace Face. Or, as the kids are calling you: Violez."

Liz dropped her head into her hands. "The kids don't know shit."

Babs stroked Liz's back, pointing back at the sectional. "Sit," her mom instructed. "Spill."

"Start at the beginning," Rafi said. "And don't skip anything, except the sex stuff."

"Seconded," Birdie said. "I think we've all heard enough of the sex stuff."

And so, Liz spilled. She told them about meeting this girl, this woman, this muse, this best friend. The year's wild ride into the most insane corners of her creative mind, and the actor who made it all happen. Their early days eating green olives in the courtyard of Violet's Airbnb. Their karaoke night at Palms. Their first kiss in Rome. Liz's words flowed with increasing speed as she pieced together everything that had happened, ending on the past few weeks. "When we're together, everything just feels *right*. I love her mind and who she is. Who she makes me. Who we are together." A bubble of emotion burst in Liz's chest. In its place: clarity. The truth. Her words were stunned. "Jiminy Christmas. I'm in love."

It was as clear as a cloudless sky. As obvious as the sun in it.

"I'm in love with Violet," Liz said. "I *love* her."

Birdie clapped a hand on Liz's shoulder. "I think I speak for all of us when I say: duh."

Liz stared back at her family, feeling like a newborn lamb unsteady on its feet. "What do I do now?"

"Tell her!" Birdie exploded, thumping a couch cushion. "Make it canon!"

"But she said she needed more time!" Liz exclaimed.

"Then be patient," Ash said.

"She'll reach out when she's ready," Babs added, sounding convinced.

Rafi leaned back into Ash, lacing their fingers together. "In the meantime, make a Christmas wish."

"It's New Year's, bro." Birdie settled back into the couch cushions, unlocking her phone. "Christmas is ov-ah."

"A New Year's Christmas wish," Rafi amended. "Make one about Violet."

"A New Year's Christmas wish?" Liz repeated. If nothing else, these holidays had encouraged her to think outside her box, one that typically didn't allow for woo-woo wishes. It felt like an indulgence to imagine a wish in full. With extra Christmas cheer and a dollop of New Year's magic.

In the hearth, the fire popped, logs shifting.

Birdie peered at her phone. "Huh." She looked up, brow furrowed. "So, Violet just went live on Insta."

The words were like a bucket of water over Liz's head. "What?"

Outside of meticulously curated sponsorship or press commitments, Violet had never gone live on any social platform. Ever.

"Now." Birdie handed Liz her phone. "She's on now."

In the small screen, Violet sat cross-legged on a partially made bed. The room was instantly familiar: a suite at the Woodstock Way Hotel.

Violet. Was still. In Woodstock.

No makeup. Hair in a topknot. Dressed in sweats and her light pink hoodie. Her cheeks were flushed, eyes overbright. Vi looked—happy?

"—never really done one of these before. Oh, wow." Her gaze moved to the flood of messages pouring in, visible to everyone watching. She read some aloud. "Hi from Brazil. G'day from Australia."

"Is this a video?" Babs examined it.

Birdie rolled her eyes, explaining the basic concept of live streaming.

Liz's stomach was on spin cycle. Was Violet confirming she and Liz were just friends? That #Violez didn't exist?

Or was this something else?

"Hi, everyone." Violet waved at the camera. The phone slipped, swooping to end on the room's unmoving ceiling fan. "Whoops." Violet giggled, righting the device. The bottom edge of the T-shirt she was wearing under her hoodie came into frame. A soft gray T-shirt. *The* shirt.

"The holidays are almost over." Violet addressed her online audience. "And till now, I've never been that into Christmas."

Thirty thousand people were watching. Liz was peripherally aware of the endless flow of comments and hearts. She couldn't take her eyes off Violet.

"My parents died when I was young," Vi went on. "So I didn't have a proper Christmas, for years." She paused to inhale, a smile lifting her lips. "But this year, I was lucky enough to spend the past few weeks with the most wonderful people, and y'know what? I got it."

Liz could barely hear her family squawking, she was so focused on Violet.

"Sometimes, the holidays can be tricky." Violet's expression was knowing. "Sometimes things don't go as planned." And it almost felt like she was looking directly at Liz. Speaking directly to Liz. "Maybe we say things we regret. Or maybe we don't say enough."

Next to her, Rafi gasped.

"I couldn't wait any longer." Violet's eyes were planets, asteroids, the moon. "To tell the people closest to me how much I care about them. Or really, *person*. One in particular."

Birdie made a strangled sound of excitement.

Liz's heart was smashing against her ribs. She couldn't breathe, couldn't talk, couldn't move.

"So. In case there's any confusion." Violet smiled directly into the camera. "I love you, Liz Belvedere."

Liz's heart exploded out of her chest and set itself on fire.

"Oh my *god*!" Birdie screeched, shoving Liz. "She just said *I love you*! To *everyone*!"

"How romantic!" Babs gasped, a hand pressed to her chest. "When did she record this?"

Rafi gaped at Liz, eyes agog. "Was that your New Year's Christmas wish? *Was it?*"

Ash was fist-pumping and yelling about love winning. Liz could barely hear Violet over their hysteria.

Violet was waving at the camera, the look on her face untethered and joyful. "Jolly Christmas, y'all."

The live stream ended. And Liz was just . . . staring. In shock.

I love you, Liz Belvedere.

I love you.

Birdie, Rafi, and Ash were jumping around the room, hurling throw cushions in the air. "Liz loves Violet!" Birdie bellowed. "And Violet loves Liz!"

Hot, mad joy. It wasn't a secret. It was real and true and happening, right now. Liz rocketed to her feet. "I have to go!"

"*Go!*" everyone urged her.

The drive to Vi's hotel took thirty minutes. It was torture not to floor it.

When she arrived, she zoomed into the hotel parking lot and bolted out.

The check-in area at Woodstock Way was all leather sofas, funky artwork, plants. Liz was so wound up it took a moment to locate the front desk. She sprinted for it, the order racing from her lips: "Violet Grace, I need to see Violet Grace! She's a guest, I'm a friend."

The cheerful young concierge appeared unperturbed by Liz's frantic arrival. "Violet Grace, Violet Grace . . ." He tapped his keyboard, not at all in a rush. "Sorry: computer's running a little slow . . . So, New Year's Eve. Any big plans?"

Liz's heart was thrashing in her chest. "No plans, sorry, I really need to—"

"Violet Grace just checked out," the young man read from his computer before giving Liz another frustratingly chipper smile.

Panic spiked Liz's bloodstream. "Checked out? When? Where? Is she?"

"Guests tend to enjoy the local area for its quaint holiday charm and—"

"I know!" Liz was a just-popped can of soda, shaken for a full ten seconds. "I have to go!"

"Happy New Year's!" came the peppy call after her.

Liz ran back outside, whipping in a circle—no one. Where next? The town? Belvedere Inn? Her instinct to get to Violet was the most powerful urge she'd ever experienced, transcending desire into desperate need. Liz whirled in a circle, searching, searching—

"Liz."

She was there. Ten feet in front of Liz, duffel bag slipping off one shoulder.

All at once, Liz was swept back in time to the first day they met at the audition in L.A., before being buoyed forward on a choppy current of memories: the first time Vi hugged her, quick and excited, after Liz called *it's a wrap* on the pilot; the time Liz had a cold and Vi arrived on her doorstep with a Le Creuset of chicken noodle soup; that one day on set when everyone had the giggles, even the grip, and they had to shoot a family dinner scene eleven times; being stuck in L.A. traffic, singing along to "Islands in the Stream" (*That is what we are*); the time when Liz asked Vi how her first same-sex kiss scene went (Lila Fowler and Jessica Wakefield, seven minutes in heaven at a party) and Violet had replied, *Fun,* holding her eye contact three beats too long. And all the smiles and touches and intimate moments that kept building and Liz kept denying until Violet kissed her wrist—her wrist!—in Rome and everything changed and now they were here, in upstate New York, at the end of the craziest year on record, and nothing mattered except this.

Liz ran to Violet, cupping her face with both hands. "I love you. I've fallen in love with you, Vivi, and it's the most beautiful feeling in the whole world." Liz's eyes were filling with tears. She didn't need to protect herself anymore, she didn't need to fight it. It was so simple. It was so true. "I love you. I love how I feel when I'm with you. I love that you're smart and kind and funny and soulful and I feel like I'm learning from you, all the time." The words were free-flowing, a glorious rush. "You have depression and I love you. I'm an earnest dork and I love you. So much, I love you *so much*. And I'm going to tell you that every day, wherever we are, for as long as you'll let me."

Violet's hands were over Liz's, pressing into them. She was smiling so big, so joyful, the bridge of her nose crinkled. "I love you too, Lizzie. *So much*."

Their lips touched and Liz heard angels break into song. Even though it wasn't their first kiss, it felt like it was. Because it was the first kiss now, here, in this new space. A space out in the open, flooded with daylight.

50.

*O*N THE WAY BACK TO THE CAR, LIZ TOLD VIOLET ABOUT the second season order, celebrating with another heart-stopping kiss. Then Liz drove them back to Belvedere Inn, at a considerably slower pace. The final sunset of the year painted the sky in scarlet and orange and a feathered, delicate pink. Across the console, Violet took her hand, folding their fingers together.

The fire in the family room of Belvedere Inn was still crackling when they returned to an embarrassing and thrilling round of applause from Birdie, Rafi, Ash, Babs, and even Jin-soo, whose suitcase was in the foyer. Then it was time for roast chicken and mashed potatoes, eaten balanced on their laps on the sofa or sprawled out on the carpet, everyone talking and laughing at once, hyped up on love.

When she was done with dinner, Liz pushed her plate aside and wrapped her arms around Violet, putting her mouth close to Violet's ear. "I love you, Vivi. Merry Christmas." From her pocket, the tiniest gift.

The delicate sunstone-and-sapphire ring slid easily onto Violet's middle finger. "It's beautiful. Just like you." Violet snuggled close. "I love you, too."

From her queenly position in the armchair, Babs smiled down at them, addressing Violet. "I thought what you said this afternoon was very courageous, sweetheart."

"Thank you." Violet smiled back, resting her head on Liz's shoulder. "I thought we deserved a better beginning."

"Our whole lives are a rewrite," Babs exclaimed. "That's the great thing about them! Never accept a first draft."

Liz chuckled, tightening her arms around her girlfriend. She was content for this rewrite, this ending, to be her final draft.

"What Are You Doing New Year's Eve?" crooned over the speakers as the celebration in Times Square played silently on a television beside the fireplace. The hands of the Kit-Cat Clock were closing in on midnight.

Liz joined her brother and sister in the kitchen to pour six glasses of Champagne into elegant crystal flutes, and sparkling apple cider for Birdie. "Calling to order," Liz said, "the final meeting of the Black Hearts Club."

Rafi slipped a smile in Ash's direction, who returned it with a wink. "End of an era," he said.

"It is." Birdie topped up her cider. "Lizzie's going back to La La Land with Vi to become a queer supercouple, and Raf, you're going to power-bottom all over London."

Rafi choked out a cough. "Just with my boyfriend, I think."

Birdie flipped her newly acquired business card through her fingers. "And hopefully my next, and last, manager will help get my show on the road. Maybe Jecka will even be at a few."

Beginnings and endings, woven together like the red-and-white twine already back in the gift-wrapping drawer awaiting next year. Liz held up her flute. "Cheers Belvederes."

The trio clinked glasses, the holiday lights dancing in the golden fizz.

The final moments of the year drifted around them like snowflakes, settling at their feet. The three siblings gathered up the glasses, the flutes cold against their warm skin, and headed into the family room, and the new year that lay ahead.

THE END

Acknowledgments

WRITING THE ACKNOWLEDGMENTS IS ALWAYS BITTERSWEET because it means this book is really over and I don't get to write it anymore. Boo! More than ever, this story shows you the contours of my heart and the things that make life meaningful for me, such as queer joy, true love, and cauliflower gratin. I am indebted to the following people for helping me write the queer Christmas rom-com of my dreams.

Thank you to my most wonderful literary agent, Allison Hunter, as well as Natalie Edwards, and everyone at Trellis Literary Management. Thank you for believing in me. I can't do any of this without you.

To my incredible editors, Emma Caruso and Katy Nishimoto: Thank you for inspiring me to take this book to the next level. I am so grateful for our partnership, and for your passion and commitment. Thank you to Whitney Frick, Avideh Bashirrad, Debbie Aroff, Ada Yonenaka, Laura Dragonette, J. P. Woodham, Talia Cielinski, and everyone at The Dial Press for your vision, tenacity, and heart.

Thank you to freelance editor Sarah Cypher for invaluable early guidance. Thanks to authenticity readers Anvita Patwari, Alexis Reliford, and Kiran Josen.

Wow, who didn't read an early draft of this novel?! Those who did include Adam Waring, Andrew Maguire, Casey Elsass, Clare Mao, Dan Fox, Erin Fishman, Jenna Becker, Jessica Pascale, Julie Farley, Katy Stankevitz, Meg Hemmelgarn, Rachel Grate, Shannon Whitney, Stephanie Spear, and Taylor Hugo.

Thank you to Natasha Vaynblat, Danielle DiPaolo, Neil Collier, and Cherie Finns for generously sharing your specialist knowledge related to stand-up comedy, Hollywood, and MS, respectively.

Thank you to my dedicated book-to-film agents at UTA, Jason Richman and Addison Duffy. Thanks to The Writers Room in New York City.

I'm indebted to my brilliant writer friends for all the blurbs/support/drinks over the years: Alison Cochrun, Amy Poeppel, Becca Freeman, Christina Lauren, Courtney Kae, Elin Hilderbrand, Fiona Davis, Grant Ginder, Hannah Orenstein, Hannah Sloane, Jo Piazza, Kate Goldbeck, Kate Spencer, Melanie Cantor, Nora McInery, Stephanie Danler, and Suzanne Rindell.

Thank you to my gorgeous readers and everyone who shares their love of reading online and IRL, especially #bookstagram, BookTok, booksellers, and librarians.

Thank you to my talented Writers' Group students and the inspiring Generation Women community. Hugs for all my friends and a kiss on the forehead for the Gang.

Thanks to my family, the Clarks: Jayne, Ken, William, Louise, and Evie. I love you more than you love Bunnings and being on time.

Thanks to my in-laws, especially Chris and Craig, who always make Christmas extra festive.

Lindsay, my love. Thank you for loving me and giving me the time and space to dream up my books (even when it sometimes looks like I'm watching TV while drinking wine). Since my last novel, we've welcomed my littlest reader, Rozella, which has been the greatest adventure of all. My entire world has recalibrated and become wonderfully, blessedly simple and sweet. My greatest joy is being the trio that our baby girl loves to list: "Mama, Mummy, Rozie." How lucky am I? Truly, all I want for Christmas is you two.

MOST WONDERFUL

GEORGIA CLARK

DIAL DELIGHTS

*Love Stories for
the Open-hearted*

*T*HESE CONTAIN SPOILERS! YOU HAVE BEEN WARNED.

In the early days of dreaming this book into being, Rafi was straight, and the childhood friend he realized he had feelings for was a woman. Intellectually, I felt this would make the story more accessible to both queer and straight readers. But it never worked: Both Liz and Birdie's stories were starting to unfold, coming to me in a way that felt easy and intuitive. Try as I might, I could not *see* Rafi's friend or *feel* their story. Then, my aha moment—what if Rafi's friend was a *guy* and this whole book was capital G-Gay? Instantly, it clicked. Ash arrived all but fully formed and things started to flow. *Oh,* I realized, *this is meant to be a* queer *Christmas rom-com, not just a Christmas rom-com.*

I was an obsessive *Sweet Valley High* fan as a young (maybe too young?) reader. We didn't have TV when I was a kid, and the paperbacks felt risqué, soapy, and deliciously American. After I moved out of my TV-less home, I quickly discovered the same shows Liz grew up watching: *Veronica Mars, Freaks and Geeks, The O.C.* When I was writing this book, I'd gotten into *Riverdale* (still love a risqué soap), often having it on in the background as I edited. *Riverdale* is the key inspiration for *Sweet*, and being the showrunner of a show like *Sweet* is my (other) dream job. For everyone who's shared they wish *Sweet* was a real series—me too, friends. Me too. I would watch the fuck out of that show.

Fans of *It Had to Be You* (my 2021 rom-com) will spy Babs's flower delivery from Flower Power, Honey!, the florist owned by Henry and Gorman in that book. Hello, boys! Hope you're enjoying married life.

Babs meets her second husband while performing in the quirky off-Broadway play, *Pickles & Hargraves and the Curse of the Tanzanian Glimmerfish* . . . and that is a real play that I co-wrote! I and then-roommate/improv team member, Ryan Williams, wrote a totally bonkers locked-room comic murder mystery that was centered around an invisible talking mouse detective. We got a run at the 2014 New York International Fringe Festival (there are photos on my website). I played femme fatale Clara Owens alongside an all-star cast including Ryan and our dear friend, Aaron Jackson, who just co-wrote and starred in the hilarious gay film, *Dicks: the Musical.*

Pour one out for the characters cut from this book: We lost Ben, a trans writer on *Sweet* who traveled with Liz to spend the holidays with the Belvederes. Gerry (British, eccentric) and Carmen (woo-woo, sympathetic), Babs's oldest friends, who helped raise the kids and did all the cooking over the holiday season. Petra, a canny network executive who worked with Liz. And Devon, Babs's humorously stoic personal trainer. It's normal to see nonessential cast reduced through the revision process, but it's always brutal to type their name into a search bar and begin erasing their existence. Sorry, y'all. Hugs.

When I was growing up in Australia, Christmas was pretty much the opposite of how the Belvederes celebrate. First, it's high summer in December down under, so you're more likely to go for a swim at the beach than a snowy romp through the woods. Sauvignon blanc instead of hot cocoa, etc. Second, the Clarks are much more, er, casual. My mum, Jayne, a diehard environmentalist, refused to buy (i.e., kill) a tree and would instead drape a few bits of tinsel around a potted palm. I used to feel embarrassed by this, but now I just laugh at the memory. Classic Jayne!

This moment hit the cutting room floor, but I missed it too much not to find a way to shoehorn it in:

> Liz addressed her mother. "Ready to take on Christmas?"
>
> "Honey, I am Christmas!" Babs declared. "I played the manger. Tiny venue. Paid me in myrrh."

I always enjoy knowing what parts of an author's real life spill onto the page. In this book, Birdie's experience with tele-therapy was inspired by my (very successful!) year-long experience with tele-therapy. In fact, I ran that part by my actual therapist as I was writing it. Like Rafi, I had a quarter-life crisis at twenty-nine, which prompted me to leave my hometown of Sydney for New York City. Like Ash, I love jazz (Oscar Peterson's "Cakewalk" is our shared fave). Violet is a dream girl for me, too (and we are both readers). Jecka and I share deep thoughts on what it means to be a successful artist. And, like Liz, I am obsessively committed to inbox zero.

This book went through six drafts, with significant revisions happening at every step. I started in spring of 2021, and performed a Completion Ceremony with my editor Katy to mark the end of the project (it's on my Insta—yes, I am woo-woo!) in December of 2023. The final word count is around 98,000 and there is definitely another 98K, or more, that I cut and/or rewrote along the way.

I do, occasionally, have existing performers in my imagination playing the characters. If you're someone who prefers not to hear about an author's casting as it messes with your own, skip this paragraph. Ask me in person about the celebrity crush who inspired Violet (honestly, you can probably guess), but I'll share that there was an adorable *Great British Bake-off* contestant from 2015, Tamal, who was *a tiny bit* in my head for Rafi. Interestingly enough, I discovered Tamal is actually gay after I wrote the book! Maybe my gaydar is getting better?!

The story that Babs tells about the horse (IYKYK) was the same cover story a friend told me, months before he came clean with the same truth as Babs. (I'm being coy as this is the biggest spoiler in the book.) That was over twenty years ago . . . it's funny what ends up in the pages of a novel. I really did believe he'd been thrown off a horse . . .

There's a blink-and-you'll-miss-it reference to characters who "become vampires and start robbing blood banks," as part of a *Sweet* brainstorm. Reader, I made it: a short film, that is, about vampires, with that very premise. It was called *The Heist*, and it starred hot Aussie actors Emma Lung and Toby Schmitz. I was in my mid-twenties and one-hundred-percent convinced that it was my masterpiece and would catapult me into being the next Baz Luhrmann. It did not.

Like Rafi and Ash, I also love *Young Royals* and I also love alt-Christmas movies. The year I moved to New York, I was too broke to fly back home to Australia, and so I spent the yuletide cozied up in my Greenpoint basement apartment, watching *Die Hard* and *Gremlins* on my laptop with a big bag of weed. Good times!

I love hearing from readers (who have nice things to say)! Come at me: @georgialouclark on Insta. I have a free monthly author newsletter called *Heartbeat* (theheartbeat.substack .com). I host a monthly intergenerational storytelling night in New York City, often at Joe's Pub, called Generation Women.

Thank you so much for reading this book (or if you haven't yet, I hope that you do) I truly hope you love this story because I wrote it for you. I really tried and I really hope you like it. If you did, well, we have something in common—we both love the Belvederes. Cheers!

GEORGIA CLARK is a novelist, performer, and, in addition to *Most Wonderful*, the author of *Island Time, It Had to Be You, The Bucket List, The Regulars,* and two YA books. Clark is the host and founder of the internationally popular storytelling night, Generation Women, which is performed monthly at Joe's Pub in New York. A native Australian, she lives in Brooklyn with her hot wife and sweet toddler.

Stay connected to Georgia through
her free monthly author newsletter, *Heartbeat.*

Instagram: @georgialouclark

GeorgiaClark.com

This book was set in a Monotype face called Bell. The Englishman John Bell (1745–1831) was responsible for the original cutting of this design. The vocations of Bell were many—bookseller, printer, publisher, typefounder, and journalist, among others. His types were considerably influenced by the delicacy and beauty of the French copperplate engravers. Monotype Bell might also be classified as a delicate and refined rendering of Scotch Roman.

Books Driven by the Heart

Sign up for our newsletter
and find more you'll love:

thedialpress.com

⊙ @THEDIALPRESS

▶ @THEDIALPRESS